The purchase of this book
was made possible
by a generous grant from
The Auen Foundation.

BEYOND JUSTICE

Center Point
Large Print

**This Large Print Book carries the
Seal of Approval of N.A.V.H.**

BEYOND JUSTICE

Cara Putman

CENTER POINT LARGE PRINT
THORNDIKE, MAINE

This Center Point Large Print edition is published
in the year 2017 by arrangement with Thomas Nelson.

The text of this Large Print edition is unabridged.
In other aspects, this book may vary
from the original edition.
Printed in the United States of America
on permanent paper.
Set in 16-point Times New Roman type.

ISBN: 978-1-68324-409-7

Library of Congress Cataloging-in-Publication Data

Names: Putman, Cara, author.
Title: Beyond justice / Cara Putman.
Description: Center Point Large Print edition. | Thorndike, Maine :
Center Point Large Print, 2017.
Identifiers: LCCN 2017008791 | ISBN 9781683244097
      (hardcover : alk. paper)
Subjects: LCSH: Women lawyers—Fiction. | Large type books. |
GSAFD: Christian fiction. | Mystery fiction. | Legal stories.
Classification: LCC PS3616.U85 B49 2017b | DDC 813/.6—dc23
LC record available at https://lccn.loc.gov/2017008791

To Eric for always believing in me
through the crazy journey of
becoming a published author.
You've lived every step of this process
with me and been my greatest cheerleader.

And to the Grove girls for making
the journey so much more fun.

BEYOND JUSTICE

JANUARY

If he didn't find that flash drive now, he would have to disappear. Immediately. Some place *el jefe* couldn't find him. It was that or die.

"Where is it, Miguel? What have you done with the information you stole?"

The young man shuddered as he choked on a breath. Blood poured from his nose, broken in the first punch, the horror of it fresh. Blood dribbled out his mouth. Blood dripped off his chin. Still he refused to speak.

Rafael drew back his fist, ready to strike again, then held his arm back as if against a powerful force. This was not who he was. It was not who Miguel was. All of this was so broken. Somehow he had landed on the wrong side of the great family his own had served for three generations. How was he now opposing the young man he loved like a brother? He scanned the bare room. Four bunk beds lined a wall. A urinal in the corner. A barren sink with a square mirror. A single light bulb hanging well above his head. Where could Miguel have hidden anything in this desolate place?

The stench of urine and sweat, of bodies crammed into a space designed for half as many, mixed with the coppery aroma of fresh blood. Limp sunlight pushed back the shadows from a barred window high on the wall. Sunlight that reminded him of the times Miguel had tagged along when Rafael did odd chores at the estate. Sunlight that reminded him how wrong it was for Miguel to be here. He was the son of a lord, not someone who should be locked up.

"Where is it, Miguel? I can't ask again." He flipped open the blade of the knife he held and slid it under Miguel's chin. "Give it to me, or I have no choice but to kill you."

Miguel flinched. "We always have a choice." The youth lifted his chin and met Rafael's gaze with pain-filled eyes. "We are brothers, Rafael."

"We were. If you don't give me that flash drive, we are both dead."

"I don't know what you're talking about."

"Liar! *El jefe* knows you were in his computer. He told me himself. He sent me."

"You kill me, and my father will hunt you like a rabid mongrel." False bravado flashed in Miguel's eyes.

"Your father told me to kill you, amigo."

The spoken words resounded in the narrow space between them.

He looked at señor's precious son. His heir.

Could he somehow take Miguel with him and disappear? No.

Would Miguel give him the list?

The boy raised dark eyes to meet his gaze, defiance hardening them.

Somehow Rafael had imagined he could avoid killing while serving the family even as he'd crept up its structure. But now he had no choice.

Retrieve the information for *el jefe* before it falls into the wrong hands or be killed.

Heat flooded him and red clouded his vision.

"I'm sorry, Miguel . . ." He stepped forward, knife clasped in his fist.

Chapter 1

The euphoria of winning a hard case vied in her thoughts with wondering what came next as Hayden McCarthy left the Alexandria courthouse. A colorful dance of tulips lined a flower box of the town house across the street, and the faint aroma of some hidden blossom scented the air. It was over.

Her client had needed her absolute best.

Hayden had delivered it and obtained justice.

She shifted her purse and readjusted her briefcase as she started down the street. Continue straight on King Street, and in a block she'd be at the office. Turn, and in four blocks she'd be home. Her town house's proximity both to work and the heart of Old Town Alexandria was why she loved the space she shared with a friend from law school.

So . . . which way to go? The thought of going back to her office and confronting the waiting pile of work held no appeal. She would spend one night savoring success . . . and recovering from the adrenaline pace of a roller-coaster trial and jury.

She'd make a salad and cup of tea, maybe pick

12

up a novel. If that didn't hold her attention, she'd dig into her trial notes. Analyze what had worked and how the risk of requesting a new foreman after deliberations had begun had paid off.

Each step closer to home, her conservative navy pumps tapped the refrain. She. Had. Won. She let a smile spread across her face.

She left King Street and headed north on St. Asaph. Some of the buildings she passed housed businesses, but with each block the area became more residential. In one condo a senator lived. In another a congressman, next to him a chief of staff and other people with powerful political positions. When Hayden first moved to the city from small-town Nebraska, her head had turned at how easy it was to rub elbows with those who controlled destinies. Now it was only scandals or surprise retirements that caught her attention.

The evening was so pleasant she detoured and walked the couple blocks to Christ Church. The wrought iron fence around the church grounds beckoned her to settle in the shade of the stately trees. She opened the gate, then walked until she reached a bench. Settling on it, she breathed deeply and closed her eyes.

Father, thank You. It went well today.

She pushed against her eyes, daring relieved tears to fall.

There was no one else around, and Hayden sat

quietly, waiting . . . for something. Here within the shelter of a church more than two hundred years old, shouldn't she feel God's presence?

Yet there was . . . nothing.

Not even a rustle of a breeze through the leaves that she could pretend was the Spirit moving.

I need You.

Still nothing. Then slowly she sensed His smile as warmth spread through her.

A couple came around the corner then, strolling along the garden path arm in arm, smiling at one another. They looked at ease and in tune as their strides matched.

What would it feel like to be that comfortable and safe with someone? To know you could trust another person with your most hidden parts? Hayden shook her head. Her life was full to the brim—no room for a relationship. She stood and walked the rest of the way home at a brisk pace.

When she reached her town house, she crossed the courtyard and dug her keys loose from the pit of her purse. The Wonder Woman key ring, a gift from a grateful client after she won what he called the unwinnable case, jiggled as she unlocked the door.

The moment she walked inside, Hayden kicked off her heels and set her bag on the chair next to the glass table by the door. Soft classical music flowed from the kitchen, and the aroma of something spicy filled the small space.

"Emilie?" Hayden leaned down to rub one of her arches, then straightened and moved toward the kitchen.

"Down here." Emilie Wesley's bubbly voice came from the stairway leading to the basement. "Can you check the oven for me?"

"Sure. What are you making?" Hayden moved around the granite countertop and turned on the oven light. Emilie was a wonderful cook, but she often got distracted. "Mmm, lasagna. Looks great. It's bubbling around the edges, and the cheese looks perfect. You expecting company?"

Hayden opened the fridge and pulled out salad ingredients. A salad plus a glass of sweet tea and she could disappear into her room . . . though the pasta looked wonderful. If she was lucky, Emilie would save her some for lunch tomorrow.

Hayden was dicing a red pepper when two sets of footsteps echoed up the stairs.

"Look who stopped by, Hayden."

"Hmm?" Hayden looked up and into clear blue eyes that matched the Potomac as it moved into the bay. His pressed khakis and Oxford with pullover sweater portrayed an understated GQ elegance that screamed old money and matched the clean haircut and polite smile that revealed teeth so perfect they might be caps. Andrew Wesley, her roommate's cousin. She hadn't seen him in years.

The knife slipped, and she felt a sharp pain in

15

her finger. She turned on the tap and stuck her finger beneath the flow of cold water.

"Andrew, do you remember my roommate, Hayden McCarthy? Hayden, this is my cousin Andrew. It's been a while, but I'm pretty sure y'all have met before." Emilie's eyes danced as she tugged the man into the room. His mouth curved into a relaxed grin, the look as familiar and practiced as Hayden's in court.

The years had been good to Andrew Wesley. He'd been handsome when they'd first met, but now he was something more. He had the build of someone who worked out and took care of himself. Compact, muscular, and distractingly good-looking. Hayden pasted a smile into place.

"Hayden?" The deep voice was thick as the richest chocolate. "It's nice to officially meet you—again." He gave her a devastating smile. "Emilie is always talking about you."

"Good things, I hope." She grabbed a paper towel and turned off the water.

"What else would I say?" Emilie's eyes widened as she saw blood seeping through the paper towel. "Ooh, do you need a Band-Aid?"

"I'll be all right." Hayden took a deep breath and met Andrew's gaze. "Any friend—or cousin —of Emilie's is welcome here." With her good hand she scooped up the diced pepper and sprinkled it on top of the salad. "I'll leave you two to enjoy your dinner. It looks good, Em."

"You don't need to leave, Hayden." Emilie leaned closer, not hard to do in the galley space that felt even smaller with Andrew's presence, and handed Hayden a fresh paper towel. "We're working on plans for a spring festival. Think inflatables, fair food, and fun. It's a community event for his non-profit." She grabbed a purple grape from a bowl next to the sink and popped it into her mouth. "You can help us."

His cousin's roommate wrapped the paper towel tighter around her finger, then turned to the refrigerator, shielding her face from his view. Had they really met before? He had a vague recollection of an awkward girl visiting his cousin during a law school break, but his memory didn't match this attractive woman with the black hair and . . . stocking feet.

As Hayden put away the vegetables she'd used for her salad, Andrew looked for something to break the uncomfortable silence.

"I like the idea of a festival, Em, but I'm not sure we can pull it off."

"Oh? You already have the location." Emilie claimed the pot holders and opened the oven. "We can do this because we're the dynamic duo. Besides, you've got a staff and board of directors to help. We'll create the framework, and they can do the rest."

Andrew shook his head. "You haven't worked

much with a board. And don't forget, I'm not the senior guy in the office."

Emilie slid the pan from the oven and set it on top of the stove. "You're a Wesley. Everyone takes one look at you and snaps to attention. Your dad is too powerful to tick off." She softened the words with a smile. "You might as well embrace it."

That was something that hadn't happened yet in his thirty years. Being Scott Wesley's son was like wearing a coat made for someone else.

He leaned against the counter and redirected the conversation—a skill he'd picked up from his father. "I've heard about Emilie's day, Hayden. Tell me about yours."

Hayden paused, salad dressing in hand. "I won a case today."

"Oh?" He studied her face, but she didn't give anything away. Not much of a talker?

She shrugged. "I kept an innocent man out of jail. So it was a great day for my client and his wife."

"For you too." Emilie stepped next to Hayden and squeezed her shoulder. "This woman worked a lot of late nights on that case and is on the fast track to becoming a partner." Hayden started to protest, but Emilie kept on. "She'll never brag about herself, but she's good. Nobody will be surprised when she becomes the youngest partner in Elliott & Johnson history."

Soft color tinted the woman's cheeks, and she glanced at Andrew. "I'm not any better than a hundred other attorneys in town."

Only a hundred, huh? In a city overwhelmed with attorneys, she'd ranked herself fairly high. Well, the last thing he wanted to do was spend free time with an attorney. He'd spent too much time in their presence growing up to be wowed by their brilliance or awed by their stories.

She held up her salad bowl and fork. "I know y'all have plans to make, so I'll slip upstairs and not interrupt. It was nice to see you again, Andrew."

Andrew put a hand on her arm before she could disappear. "You really want to walk away from Emilie's lasagna for that?" He crinkled his nose and pointed at the bowl of greens.

Emilie grabbed an extra plate. "There's plenty, Hayden."

Andrew grinned. "Always is. She forgets there's only two of us."

He said it as though these evenings were frequent, but they weren't. Emilie was as busy as anyone in town, so he'd pounced on her invitation. When they all sat down at the island a few minutes later, he watched Hayden. She looked tired. A good trial would do that, his dad always said. He and Emilie kept a quiet conversation going, with Hayden interjecting now and then.

She'd made it through law school, and he

admired anyone who did that. He'd quit after a semester—but that had more to do with wanting to become his own man rather than an ever-lengthening part of his father's shadow.

A phone beeped, and Hayden glanced at hers and frowned.

"Sorry, but I need to prepare for a meeting in the morning. Nice to see you, Andrew." She stood and brushed past him with a small smile.

He watched her cross the living space and head toward the stairs. As she climbed from view he reminded himself that he didn't have time to feel attracted to anyone right now. Not when Congressman Wesley was gunning for a title change. Anyone he was seen with would end up plastered across the social pages of the *Post* the next day. Who would willingly sign up for that?

He turned back to the kitchen and found Emilie smirking at him.

"I'm not sure you're her type, Andrew." Her smile widened until her dimples showed.

He made a face at her. "Don't think I don't see right through you. I know why you had me meet you here." He was just surprised it had taken this long. "It doesn't matter. I'm too busy to get involved right now."

JANUARY

His cell phone rang.

The noise blared in the silence of the flea-bitten, no-name motel room. He was safe here. He couldn't go back to Mexico without that flash drive.

The phone rang again and his hands shook.

He had to answer it, but then he would have to confirm Miguel's death.

He hadn't wanted Miguel to die.

Even now adrenaline shocked his body when he thought of it.

He had killed a young man.

A man who had been as close as a brother.

The phone rang again.

Hours had faded into days as Rafael tried to find a way to stay alive.

El jefe must know what he had done by now. Rafael had followed his orders, but without the prize, his days were still numbered. How could he hope to stay ahead of the family leader?

He must become as ruthless as the man two steps behind him.

Hesitate one moment, one second, one breath, and the man would be on him with the full power of the family.

The cell phone fell silent, the quiet almost as shocking as the former noise.

He would destroy this phone, get a new one. He should have done that the moment he escaped the detention center where he had found Miguel. It had taken all his skill to work his way out as the alarm rose behind him. *El jefe* didn't care . . . not without the precious information on that flash drive.

Time was what he needed most. Time to formulate a plan. Time to find what Miguel had taken. Time to redeem himself so he could live.

The phone resumed its incessant ringing.

Rafael took a deep breath and picked it up.

Chapter 2

Early morning found Hayden in her office at Elliott & Johnson. It was little more than a closet, but it was better than the spaces new associates shared.

A light knock pulled her gaze from the spreadsheet on her desk to the doorway. Gerard Campbell, a partner and her boss, stood there without his usual suit coat and tie. Must be too early to present the perfect corporate image to the mainly empty halls. "Got a minute?"

As if she could tell him no. "Sure."

"I've got a case I'm kicking your way this morning." His eyes bored into her as if gauging her mettle.

Hadn't she already proven it?

"Okay." Her cases were routinely assigned unless she brought in the client herself.

"This one has potential. The kind that can make your reputation. Or destroy it." His stare held her captive. "Do you have the time?"

And guts was the unspoken rest of the sentence.

She swallowed at the implied warning. "As much as you ever give me." She softened the words with a small smile.

23

Hayden was bone-weary after the trial and had anticipated spending the rest of the week managing discovery for a couple cases. Leigh, her paralegal, had updated her schedule and brought in the spreadsheet of deadlines for her review just moments before. Three pending cases, none urgent.

"We'll meet immediately after the others agree it's yours."

So much for catching her breath.

Gerard took a step out before turning back. "Good job yesterday. The Commonwealth's office told me about your daring call. Pretty risky."

"It worked."

"This time." He studied her. "Your gut is good, but don't get cocky. Instincts have taken down many bright attorneys."

Hayden rocked back in her chair as he left. He'd followed her case? The partners barely tolerated her court-appointed cases, and some claimed they stole from her billable hours—even though everyone knew she worked them after hours.

But "tolerated" didn't mean they monitored her trials. As long as it didn't cost them anything, they'd let her run them as she liked.

So why had Gerard called the Commonwealth attorney's office?

An hour later she shifted against a chair in the large conference room and sipped her English breakfast tea as the meeting of partners and select associates droned on. She'd have gladly avoided it if Gerard hadn't told her to attend.

Donald Elliott chaired the regular meeting with his typical firm hand that matched the meticulous cut of his suit and perfectly coiffed white hair. The man was a legend, a founding partner of the firm, and though he regularly threatened to spend more time on the golf course, he hadn't slowed down yet. "Next up, *Rodriguez v. United States*. This one's yours, Campbell."

Gerard leaned forward until his elbows rested on the table. His tablet device rested next to him, but he ignored it. His gaze flicked toward Hayden, then back to the partners and senior associates sitting around the gleaming walnut table. "I filed the Rodriguez complaint last week. Now it's time to kick the investigation into focus. This is the perfect case for an associate, and yesterday McCarthy confirmed she's the one to run it."

This was the first time Gerard had championed her and not Angela Thrasher, his usual pick.

Hayden straightened as she listened to the partners discuss his suggestion.

"Her criminal experience is different. How does this one match?" Reed Johnson leaned back and crossed his arms. He was known for his bulldog tenacity, but he focused on the rare appeals the firm filed when clients pushed for a second try, so his opinion carried weight.

"Her court appointed cases gave her experience in a place she was expected to fail. You should have seen her at this week's trial."

Elliott raised an eyebrow at Gerard. "I didn't realize you were at court."

"I wasn't, but I heard the reviews. The Commonwealth thought they had her client on all counts. He walked. All because she took a daring risk."

"Our daring risk was letting you take this client." Johnson's frown deepened as he studied Campbell. "It's an unnecessary risk."

"Remember, Jason Randolph brought the client. I agreed to litigate the case."

Elliott shook his head. "Randolph was ambitious to take the case."

Gerard shrugged. "We disagree on the risk. We took the client, and she requires our best efforts. All of us at this table are too busy. This is one for Hayden—she's ready."

Johnson snorted and shook his head. "You don't want this quagmire."

Hayden silently watched the exchange, questions piling up in her mind, noting Randolph's silence. Sounded like Randolph had scored the client and handed Gerard the case, which he now wanted to shunt to Hayden. That wasn't his usual style.

Seth Jamison, another associate, elbowed her and leaned close, his stringy hair falling into his eyes. "Told you they were grooming you."

She gave a small nod.

Elliott shook his head. "You do like to toss them in the deep end." He glanced around the table. "Everyone okay with it?" He must have seen whatever he looked for. "Fine, she can have it, but you'll manage her, Gerard. Get her up to speed."

Seth gave Hayden a sideways fist bump below the table. "Here's your chance, McCarthy."

She let a smile escape even as her heart whispered a warning. The cases the firm worked often lacked the cry for justice that motivated Hayden, and she wondered if this one would be different. But in the end, it didn't really matter. She'd still give it her best efforts.

A few minutes later the meeting wrapped up with a flurry of noise and paper shuffling. Gerard barely looked at her as he nodded toward the door. "Come with me, McCarthy."

"Yes sir." She deposited her mug on the waiting tray and followed him into the hallway. Gerard's cell phone rang, and she paused a couple steps behind him, giving him the illusion of privacy.

"Good luck." Angela sidled closer, accordion folders stacked in her arms. The gilded associate always looked like she had somewhere important to be and urgent matters to resolve—most likely because she usually did. "I've heard this case is a loser, so if you turn it around you'll be a hero."

Hayden considered her comment. "The partners don't accept losers."

"Sometimes they have to."

Hayden could think of a case or two the firm had taken solely to keep important clients happy. Was this one? "Guess I'll find out."

Gerard stuck his phone back in his pocket and continued toward his office.

Angela stalled Hayden with a perfectly manicured hand and looked down the hall before lowering her voice. "Just be careful. There's something about this case."

"What do you mean?"

"I'm not sure. But I've heard rumblings."

"Thanks for the heads-up." Hayden took a deep breath and squared her shoulders. Angela had been in law school with her and graduated summa cum laude. If something about the case bothered her, Hayden would take note. At the same time, this opportunity would let her demonstrate what she could accomplish.

"Coming, McCarthy?" Gerard's voice pulled her attention.

"Right behind you."

Gerard had a large office with a bank of windows overlooking King Street, currently offering a view of busy traffic and a tour guide trying to corral a collection of schoolchildren. The windows bathed his office in a rich light the burgundy drapes couldn't restrain.

He hung his suit coat on a hook behind his door, then settled in his chair and tugged his shirt cuffs into place. Hayden lingered in the doorway, wondering if she should sit or stand.

"Come in, Hayden. This will take a minute." He gestured toward the leather chairs in front of his desk and pushed a fat expandable folder toward her. "Here's your new case."

"Thank you." She picked up the file and felt its heft. "Why are you handing it off?"

He studied her, gaze intense and focused. "The client is a woman, Hispanic, whose son was killed in Texas while detained by an alphabet soup of federal agencies. She passionately sold me on the evil done to her son. Now she's stopped communicating. We can't win without her cooperation." He rubbed a hand across his chin and shifted in his chair. "At the same time, any delay has negative implications."

The words settled around Hayden, lacing the air with the weight of caution. She flipped through the file, reading the section labels. "You filed last week?"

"Yes."

Interesting. "What makes it urgent?"

He steepled his fingers. "This isn't a case the feds want in the press—and it's not one we want before a Texas jury."

"Why was he detained?" Hayden pulled a legal pad out of the file and jotted notes.

"Entering the country illegally. He was under eighteen when Border Patrol nabbed him, so the government placed him in a juvenile facility. The partners accepted the case, but they want it settled or killed, so get discovery started. Yesterday would be fast enough."

"Okay." She cleared her rapidly closing throat as she rifled through the stack of files.

Gerard swiveled toward the mahogany credenza behind his desk. Lifting a single folder, he turned around and opened it on top of his desk. "One other thing. The case is in the wrong court."

"You filed last week, and it's in the wrong court?"

"After the boy was killed in custody, the mom was in my office within a month. She got referred to us through Randolph. The partners see the potential for more cases like this if we win. I filed the Federal Tort Claims Act claim with the ICE, Border Patrol, basically every agency I could think of. All were quickly denied. In some cases, the paperwork couldn't have even left the desk of the person who opened the mail. What that did is give us access to court, and my client wanted it filed. That lined up with the collective brain here, but as I said, a Texas jury will kill us." He studied her a moment, giving space for his words to sink in. "I'm too close, and it's time to bring you in. I want an unbiased opinion Monday morning."

"You said wrongful death?" Had to be, if he'd worried about tort claims.

"Yes." He watched her carefully.

"If it's wrongful death, your options are a federal district court or state court. Either one comes with a jury." The government would be crazy not to request one, with immigration as hot a topic as it was.

"Yes."

"You need a court like the Court of Claims." She tapped the top of the expandable folder as her thoughts raced through options. "No, that won't work." That court heard contract, tax, takings, and employment disputes against the federal government. Negligence didn't fit the court's limited jurisdiction.

"Don't be too quick to dismiss the idea." He looked past her shoulder as if formulating an idea. "Use some of that fancy legal know-how you earned in your clerkship. This kid deserves justice, but without us he won't get it. We have to find a way to get our day in court *here*. Maybe get your judge's opinion."

"I can't—" It pushed too close to the ethical line.

He waved her words away as if they were inconsequential gnats. "Of course. Forget I said that."

He paused, and Hayden rushed in. "What if instead of wrongful death we style it as a breach of contract since he was in ICE custody? An

31

implied contract of sorts. You detain these kids, you must provide a safe space."

Gerard considered her words, his fingers steepled beneath his chin, and a slow smile grew. "It could work brilliantly, or it could implode—this is why I wanted you on the case. Your clerkship means the judges know you." He rattled off a few more details, while Hayden took careful notes. "We've requested the kid's belongings. I'm hoping we'll find something worth the expense. Speaking of which, this case is burning through the retainer. Once that's gone, the partners want the case gone."

"The client won't provide more?"

"Nope." He closed the file in front of him and handed it to her. "This has the mom's contact information. Find a way to connect with her." He clasped his hands on top of the blotter. "If we win, this theory could open a floodgate of cases. So do your job well." He studied her, and Hayden held his gaze. His phone rang and he grabbed it while waving her toward the door.

Hayden collected the accordion file with the contact file on top and left, shutting the door behind her. The files felt heavy, light, awkward, but right . . . all at the same time.

Angela was waiting, perched on Hayden's desk, when she got back to her office. "So?"

Hayden sank onto her chair, setting the files on the desk. "I don't know."

"A partner calls you into his office for a big case and you 'don't know'?"

"He wants discovery started yesterday and the case moved to a new court. And this is what I have." She waved at the file.

Angela snorted. "That sounds right. The case involves wrongful death?"

"Yes, but a jury will kill us in Texas, so I need to move it."

"Federal government as defendant?"

"Yes. So move it to DC, but a jury here won't be much more sympathetic." Maybe the Court of Federal Claims *was* the best option. She'd have to refresh her memory, but it would be a stretch to get a wrongful death case there. Still, she could develop the breach of contract angle. All she knew for certain was that it was critical to move it from Texas. "I assumed it would be a small case, something too little for Gerard to bother with. But he claims it could open a new area of litigation for the firm."

"I'll leave you to it." Angela pushed to her feet. "Let me know if I can help."

When the cleaning crew came through the office hours later, Hayden packed the accordion file into her bag. She'd managed to read through it, but had been interrupted to put out fires on other cases. Now her stomach insisted she grab dinner. She'd take the file and leave another message for

33

the client, since her earlier call hadn't been returned.

Might as well try one more time.

As it had before, the phone rang repeatedly. About the time Hayden expected to leave a voice mail, she heard a soft voice. "*Hola?*"

"Mrs. Rodriguez?"

"*Hola?*"

Hayden frowned as she scrambled to resurrect her high school Spanish. "*Señora Rodriguez?*"

"*Sí?*"

"*Me llamo Hayden McCarthy. ¿Hablas inglés?*"

"*Sí.*"

Thank heavens. Hayden leaned against the chair. "I'm with Elliott & Johnson and Mr. McCarthy gave me your case. Could you come into the office tomorrow, so we can meet?"

"No, no, no." The woman's voice became increasingly frantic.

Hayden could hear a man's angry voice shouting in Spanish in the background.

"Mrs. Rodriguez? I know tomorrow's Saturday, but it's important we meet."

The male voice got louder, and then she heard a rustling like the phone was being yanked away, followed by a loud bang.

Hayden winced and pulled the phone from her ear. "Hello?"

A dial tone was the only reply.

Chapter 3

Traffic on I-395 barely moved as Andrew shifted lanes. One more mile and he could slip from the rush hour morass. He'd spent time today with Jorge, a new kid who'd arrived from Mexico a couple months earlier. The boy's steps were unsure and his grin unsteady, but Andrew had successfully coaxed him to talk. As Jorge shared about an older brother who had died, his pain showed. Yet as he kept talking, he showed a curiosity and intelligence that would serve him well. All he needed was a community to help him acclimate, and that's what New Beginnings provided.

Andrew signaled to take the exit ramp, then wound his way up a steep hill into Fairlington Village's back entrance. His condo, formerly Pentagon officers' housing, kept him close to work and available for the command performances his congressman father demanded.

Andrew parked in front of the brick condo and grabbed his messenger bag. He waved at Elaine Bedford, the retired schoolteacher who kept a close watch on the comings and goings in their cul-de-sac. If anything were ever amiss, she'd tell him.

What the spry seventy-year-old didn't know was that he counted on her to tell him if his dad's staff appeared. So far no one knew he'd turned his condo's attic into an art studio. He had done most of the work himself, with a little help from a handyman friend, to avoid a paper trail or other evidence of work being done.

An excited scratch at his front door built in intensity as he turned his key in the lock. The moment the door opened, Zeus, his large black Lab, launched himself at Andrew, who dropped his bag on the black leather couch and bent down to return the welcome. The couch was the selection of his mom's decorator. He'd wanted a basic sofa, but it was easier to acquiesce than fight his mother, the Virginia tornado.

Andrew snapped a leash on Zeus and took the excited dog outside for a quick stroll before returning inside to reheat a slice of pizza. Then he grabbed an Honest Tea and climbed the stairs to his attic.

He flipped the light switch, and his drawing desk was illuminated in such a way it tricked him into believing it was natural light. While he munched the last bite of pizza, Andrew studied the quick sketches he'd outlined the night before.

This week the politicians weren't cooperating to provide inspiration for his cartoons. He needed a good old fight in the capital. Something he could satirize with a few swipes of his pen.

Instead he had scrawls a five-year-old could improve.

He wiped his hands on a Lysol wipe yanked from the container on the desk, then spun around on his metal stool.

His thoughts ticked through the headlines he'd scanned on his phone throughout the day. Terrorist threats. Military challenges. Budget woes. Pork barrel squabbles. All old news. He needed something different. The twist that poked an issue in a sarcastic way while shedding light on something people understood but couldn't articulate. That was what the best political cartoonists did, and he wanted to join them.

Andrew straightened the pencils in their orderly rows, then swiveled toward the laptop sitting on the table next to his drawing desk. With a couple clicks he opened his browser and popped across various editorial pages, looking for inspiration.

As he picked up a pencil, his thoughts turned to Jorge and his journey to New Beginnings. Andrew's pencil started flowing across the page as he sketched the thirteen-year-old's thin face. Then his angular body. Jorge's mother insisted she provided four squares a day for him. Andrew could help the family access resources at local churches and nonprofits if she would let him, but she'd resisted, assuring him she had plenty.

In another box he sketched the ragged image of a Turkish policeman standing at the edge of the ocean cradling the shell of a toddler who hadn't completed the journey from his homeland to a new land. The photographic image had shocked the world a couple years earlier. It still sucker-punched Andrew. What horrors had chased the toddler's family and caused them to risk the lives of their small children on such a harrowing journey?

Was this the cartoon for this week? Contrasting the experience of two boys, both of whom had parents who wanted to live free from fear and tyranny. One made it. The other didn't.

His cell phone rang, and Andrew pulled the phone from his pocket. A glance at the screen showed his father's number. He sighed. Scott Wesley wasn't a man who called just to chat.

Andrew stared at the screen a moment longer, then took the call. "Dad."

"Andrew." The congressman took a breath. "Did you see the news?"

"I've scanned it."

"Senator Potter just resigned, effective immediately. No explanation, but plenty of speculation."

The capital ran on speculation. Interesting that the senator would quit with two years left in his term. Had the rancor gotten to him, as it had Representative Boehner, or was he forced to leave? Andrew grabbed a clean sheet of paper and jotted some notes.

"You with me, son?"

"Yeah, just thinking."

"I'm running for his seat and talking the governor

into appointing me to the vacant slot meanwhile. It's a fine dance, but I'm on his short list."

"Really?" His father had ambitions, but this appointment could be intense, with candidates appearing from nowhere, eager for a shot.

"The time's right. Keep your calendar clear."

Andrew sighed. Guess he'd never outgrow photo ops. "Just give me a heads-up."

"I'll have Washburn do what he can. This will ramp up slowly unless I get the nod."

"Okay." That was as good as he was going to get. Dan Washburn, his dad's chief of staff, would assign a minion to keep Andrew in the loop. "Let me know what I can do."

"There will be fund-raisers and campaign appearances. You know the routine. It'll be like the congressional races, only—"

"Bigger."

"Yes." His dad's voice deepened to the well-modulated tones he'd perfected as a successful Commonwealth's attorney. "This is it, Andrew. The perfect time to move to the bigger stage of the Senate. There's so much good I can do there."

"Sure." With only a hundred members, each senator wielded more individual influence than any individual representative to the House. And influence was what his dad craved.

Andrew's phone beeped, and a number he didn't recognize came up. "Dad, keep me posted. And congrats."

"Thank you." His father ended the call before Andrew could.

The Rodriguez file rested in front of Hayden on the dining room table, but her eyes were on her roommate. Quiet elegance, she decided. That was the right term for Emilie's loose chignon, khakis, and cardigan set. She looked ready to go out on five minutes' notice.

Emilie pulled something from the fridge and popped it into the microwave. "Are you working all night, Hayden?"

"I have a new client the partners want taken care of yesterday." Hayden glanced at the legal pad she'd slowly filled with notes. Legal theories were flooding her mind, but the core question troubled her: Why had the partners accepted the case and pushed to file already? The stack of papers she'd been handed might be thick, but it was short on key information. Like who killed the client's son, Miguel.

Prison officials owed a duty of reasonable care to inmates, but wrongful death was the wrong theory to get the case out of district court. Litigation 101 said to go for the deepest pockets, and a Bivens action alone, which assumed she knew which individual employees to blame for Miguel's death and could argue negligence, wouldn't bring justice to his family.

A jury would kill that case.

That's why filing the complaint as Gerard had done felt forced, unlike his typical meticulous planning. What unseen pressure was at play?

"While you're doing your workaholic thing, can I use your phone?"

Hayden glanced up and saw Emilie's phone resting next to hers on the counter. "What's wrong with yours?"

"Andrew will recognize the number, so he won't take my call."

"What? Why would he do that?"

"Because Andrew is busy Friday nights, and he knows I know that. So he'll ignore me."

Hayden rolled her eyes. "Go ahead." Her mind flashed across the photos she'd seen of Andrew when she'd Googled him that morning—an act she'd deny if anyone asked. Each photo showed a different model look-alike hanging on his arm—DC's best-of-the-best. No matter how long she lived in the pulsating city, she'd never belong in those circles. She could only imagine where and with whom Emilie's cousin was hobnobbing on this Friday night.

Emilie's phone vibrated, and she quickly shoved Hayden's phone back at her friend. "Here, I have to take this call. It's a domestic violence client. If Andrew answers, stall." She ducked down the stairs to her basement suite while Hayden looked at the phone in her hand.

"Hello?" a deep voice answered.

"Andrew?" She scrambled to hold it to her ear. "This is Hayden. Emilie grabbed my phone, dialed you, then handed it to me and disappeared."

He chuckled. "Sounds like Emilie. Any idea what she wanted?"

"It's Emilie . . . hard to know." Hayden walked to the stairway and called down.

"I'll call him back in a minute!" Emilie yelled.

Andrew chuckled again. "I heard that. Tell her I'm at my folks' place tonight."

"I will."

"Thanks." There was an awkward pause. *Just say good-bye and hang up.*

"So, has Emilie talked you into helping with the fair?" His voice was warm, friendly.

What had he asked? Oh, the fair. "Not yet."

"Give her a little time. Emilie thinks her enthusiasm for everything is contagious. Feel free to tell her you're too busy." Andrew knew his cousin well.

"I'll do that. Good night."

"Night, Hayden."

After she ended the call, Hayden held on to her phone. There was something steady and calm about Andrew. She bet little rattled him, a helpful characteristic for someone who worked with young people at risk.

She turned back to her notepad, wishing *her* Friday night consisted of more than working.

Chapter 4

SATURDAY, APRIL 1

Saturday's headlines proclaimed the resignation of Virginia's sitting senator. The election would occur at the expiration of the original term, Hayden read, and the governor had several individuals he was considering to fill the interim position for the intervening eighteen months. Hayden paused when she saw Congressman Wesley's name on the very short list. That would make Andrew's life interesting. The election commission didn't state a specific date by which the position would be filled, but it would be soon.

Hayden thought, not for the first time, how glad she was that her life did not revolve around politics. It might seem strange to those outside the Beltway, but when you lived inside it, you realized there was more to the city than Capitol Hill.

Instead of being subject to the whims of powermongers, her life was subject to the courts.

After a quick walk to one of Old Town's coffee shops, she headed to the office. While she didn't spend every Saturday there, this was far from the first case requiring her to book time on the weekend.

Several offices had light leaking under the doors, but overall, quiet and calm filtered through the hallways and conference space. Hayden opened the door to her office and put her bag on the desk, then set down her tea and pastry bag. As she waited for her computer to boot up, she sank onto her desk chair and pulled out a cranberry-orange scone. She took a bite, savoring the mixture of tart and sweet.

Today she must connect with her client.

Someone tapped on her doorframe, and Hayden glanced up. Seth stood there, looking more like a skateboarder than an attorney with his curly hair flopping in his eyes, wearing a T-shirt and hole-y jeans.

"What are you doing here?" She'd rarely seen Seth in the office on a Saturday, and definitely never this early.

He sagged against the door and crossed his arms. "Working on a project for Johnson. He's on a rampage about a pile of research he needs Monday."

"Sounds fun."

"Sure." He gestured toward a chair, and she nodded. "How's the case?" He pointed to the file. "Ready to be the hero?"

"Not quite. I've got a few ideas though."

"Be careful. Campbell would have kept it if it had any chance of success."

Hayden bit back a retort. Where was the friend

who'd been all encouragement yesterday? "It sounds interesting."

"So does my mom's grocery list." Seth scrubbed his face with his hands. "Sorry. Guess I was out too late last night. Should probably head home. If only I didn't need this job to pay my loans."

"Some days are like that." Any job was "just work" if you lost sight of why you did it. "Need help?"

"Nope. Just wanted sympathy." He pushed to his feet and unfolded like a gangly scarecrow. He picked up the file and flipped through it before returning it to her desk. "I'll let you get back at it, but let me know if you need help. Later."

Hayden watched him leave. What had that been about? There was an unwritten code that weekend warriors were left alone unless you needed help. And few attorneys would admit *that,* even when brainstorming might save hours of work. The law could be crazy competitive, even among members of the same team.

She turned back to the file. She needed to talk to her client. Until she heard Maricel Rodriguez's story, she wouldn't know how best to proceed. There was little beyond conjecture inside the file, and the complaint held the barest facts— not uncommon with the notice pleading allowed in federal court—a format that allowed bare allegations to be made in the initial court filing. Hayden liked to know more before she alerted

the defendant—in this case the US government—
to her case. If she moved courts, that sent negative
signals to the defendant, not the least of which
was that the plaintiff's attorney had made a
fundamental error.

She'd need to focus on non-parties for information or run afoul of the discovery rules. If she
could get some information without the laborious
interference of opposing counsel, she would. The
detention center management had to understand
there was a problem, but if by some miracle they
didn't, keeping them lulled to sleep was a priority.

She blew across the top of her Earl Grey and
tipped back in her chair. What she knew was basic.

Seventeen-year-old Miguel Rodriguez had
almost made it successfully into the United States
from Mexico. Another mile or two and he could
have disappeared into the masses of a Texas city
and remained undetected.

Instead, two miles into the United States,
Border Patrol intercepted him and about twenty
other kids. Thanks to the overwhelming flood of
unaccompanied children, it had taken a couple
days to place him in a detention center. After that
the details got fuzzy. A key question: If Miguel's
mother legally entered the country, why hadn't he
accompanied her? If she could immigrate through
legal channels, couldn't he?

Maybe.

All Hayden knew was he hadn't.

Instead, he'd journeyed with a bad coyote and landed in a detention center. Three weeks later, while his case lingered in the backlog of juvenile matters in an overwhelmed system, he died.

According to the notes, Maricel Rodriguez insisted her son was murdered, but the government denied it.

Never admit anything you didn't have to, and the center didn't have to.

Hayden closed her eyes and tried to imagine what had chased Miguel to the United States. What did he hope to achieve here? She needed to understand the human side of the story so the judge could grasp it.

Most people understood the basics: immigration was horribly broken. People on both sides had strong emotions about it. Those would be especially tense and dividing in a state as affected as Texas. A Texas jury would be loaded with members who hated the issue so much they wouldn't see the bereaved mother and dead son. Hayden had to humanize the story . . . and to do that she needed to understand Miguel and why he died. Had he really been murdered, or was his death an accident?

She broke off another corner of the scone and popped it into her mouth.

With a jury pool potentially set against her client, how could she move venue in a way that wouldn't immediately get Rule 12(b) motioned out of court? The motion was a quick, effective way for defendants to kill a case at the beginning. To pursue a wrongful death theory, Texas was the best option. The government would request a jury if the case made it to trial—a long shot in a state with a clear interest in the issue.

The Court of Federal Claims?

That Court was so obscure many attorneys didn't know it existed. Created as a court where the United States government is always the defendant, it had limited jurisdiction to hear cases. But if she could force this case to fit . . . the idea had real possibilities.

She might not know all the facts yet, but she could compile a list of those she needed to have a fighting chance in Court of Claims jurisdiction.

If that happened . . . then maybe she could get answers and closure for her client.

But first she needed more facts. After locating the phone number in the file, she dialed and waited.

"*Hola*?" A boy's voice came across the phone.

"Is Señora Rodriguez home?"

"No. She at work."

"Can I leave a message?"

There was silence, but she waited.

"Can you call? Leave message?"

She smiled at his charming tone. "Yes, I can. *Gracias*."

A minute later she called again, and this time left her work and cell phone numbers along with a short message. Now if the woman agreed to meet, she'd have progress to report to Gerard Monday.

She pulled up a legal search engine and confirmed that the basic jurisdictional restrictions of the Tucker Act hadn't changed. Despite a search for fresher cases that might have changed the status of the law, the Tucker Act excluded wrongful death cases from the Court of Federal Claims. The venue statutes indicated that when the federal government was the defendant she could file where the plaintiff resided.

That meant she needed a novel theory. One she believed in when telling a judge he should let the case proceed.

Her cell phone rang, and she glanced at it. A number her phone didn't recognize showed on the screen. "Hello?"

"Miss McCarthy? This is Señora Rodriguez."

"Thank you for calling. We talked briefly yesterday. I'm the attorney working your son's case and need to meet with you. Would today work? I can come to you."

"My son meets a friend for ice cream in Alexandria. He will be occupied and safe."

"Perfect."

Occupied and safe? What an odd way to phrase it. They arranged details, and a minute later Hayden hung up with an hour before she'd meet Mrs. Rodriguez. On the other side of the meeting, she'd have a better idea what was next.

Chapter 5

SATURDAY, APRIL 1

Andrew dug his hands into his sweatshirt pouch to protect them from the bite of wind sweeping off the Potomac. When Maricel Rodriguez asked him to spend time with Jorge, he willingly agreed. His Saturday was miraculously free of appointments, a fact that doubtless would change as his father's campaign swung into action.

Jorge had requested ice cream.

Andrew smiled. He used to be that teenage boy, wanting all the junk food he could nab. He stopped in front of the red brick and green creamery.

Jorge probably needed the comfort food as he and his mom adjusted to the United States. Then maybe he would stop looking over his shoulder all the time. What would a kid so new to the area—to the country—have to be afraid of . . . other than settling in to his new home?

Tourists strolled along the streets of Old Town, enjoying the deceptive sunshine. Less than a block away, the park that edged the Potomac waited, and the blocks up King Street led to all kinds of shopping and eating options.

Andrew people watched as he waited. About the

time he decided to grab a cup of coffee for a hand warmer, Jorge strolled up, with his mom a few paces behind.

Jorge lifted his hand in a small wave. "My mama comes. Must meet her attorney."

Andrew frowned. "Why? What's up?"

"Something she won't talk about." Jorge glanced at the display window at the front of the shop. "Is this where we eat?"

"Yep." Andrew clapped the boy on the back. "Be sure to get a waffle cone."

"*Sí, señor.*" Jorge grinned at him. "I need *tres* scoops."

"Three scoops it is." Good thing he'd stopped at an ATM.

Jorge's mother quickstepped toward them. A short woman with brown curls and warm brown eyes, she seemed to hold herself tightly together, as if a strong wind would toss her into the river. She was dressed impeccably, though. Andrew knew she could walk into any of the shops his mother favored and find herself at home. The image didn't quite fit that of recent immigrants, and yet the Rodriguezes faced many of the same challenges and heartaches as those who arrived with fewer resources.

"I see you found your *amigo*." A smile touched her lips but not her eyes. She reached into her jacket pocket. "Here is money to buy your treat, Jorge. I wait here for my appointment."

Andrew lightly pushed her hand away. "This one is on me."

"On you?" Her brows drew together, and she tilted her head.

"Today I'll pay. Next time Jorge can, but today is my treat."

Her shoulders relaxed a fraction of an inch. "*Gracias.* I will return as quickly as I can."

"Come on, Jorge, let's get you that ice cream." After he had his blueberry yogurt in a waffle cone and Jorge his scoops of chocolate, chocolate chip cookie dough, and cappuccino, they headed toward seats by the front window.

"That must be the *abogoda.*" Jorge took a bite, leaving a trail of brown ice cream on his nose and cheek.

Maricel was still waiting on the sidewalk in front of the shop, and walking toward her—Hayden McCarthy.

Andrew watched the interaction between the two women. Hayden smiled, yet held herself rigidly, and Maricel responded with newly stiffened posture. "Have they met before?"

Jorge shrugged. "Mama doesn't tell me about the *abrogados.* Says I focus other places."

She had a point. But Andrew wanted to know what was going on. He hadn't known the Rodriguezes long, but he wasn't about to let an attorney take advantage of them—not even his cousin's best friend. In his experience, attorneys wanted one thing: power.

And that had nothing to do with the best interests of their clients.

The trill of mingling birdsong wrapped around Hayden as she stood in front of Mrs. Rodriguez. When she was a child, she'd loved the way her dad identified each call, but all she knew was she liked the sound.

She observed the elegantly dressed woman. This was a struggling, out-of-place immigrant? If she had the resources her clothing indicated, why couldn't Miguel immigrate legally? This small woman in front of her might make Hayden look like a giant, but she radiated a confident core. Mrs. Rodriguez would make a success of her life in America . . . without her oldest son.

It didn't add up.

But it wasn't a conversation to have in the middle of a busy street.

"Mrs. Rodriguez, we're a couple blocks from my office. We can talk there in privacy."

The woman folded her arms across her chest and tipped her chin. "No."

"We must talk so I can understand your case. If we do it here, we lose important protections."

"Maybe I change my mind. Maybe I let my son rest in peace." Her posture was tense, and her gaze darted around the pedestrians walking past.

"Are you all right, Mrs. Rodriguez?"

The woman shook her head and frowned, then returned her focus to Hayden. "I see a ghost, but he is gone."

Hayden whipped around, but saw nothing unusual on the crowded streets. It was impossible to know if someone watched them.

"It will be quieter and private at my office." Hayden reached out to touch Mrs. Rodriguez's elbow, and the woman flinched. "Please, I want to help you."

The woman's chin trembled. "Miguel, he didn't deserve this."

"I know."

She squared her body toward Hayden like a boxer awaiting the next punch. Then she nodded as if she had come to a decision. "I will go with you, but I must tell Mr. Andrew first."

"Mr. Andrew?"

"My son's friend. They have ice cream inside."

Hayden nodded. "Of course. I promise not to keep you a moment longer than necessary."

"Jorge is all I have left. I must keep him safe." Mrs. Rodriguez opened the door and marched into the narrow storefront, Hayden following. "Mr. Andrew, I go with Miss McCarthy. You stay with Jorge?"

Hayden looked up, and her gaze collided with Andrew Wesley's. He was "Mr. Andrew," the Rodriguez boy's friend?

"Andrew. Nice to see you." She extended a hand.

"Hayden."

Jorge and his mother looked back and forth between them as they spoke, clearly surprised that they knew each other.

"Do you want me to come with you, Mrs. Rodriguez?" Concern flashed in Andrew's eyes, but hardened to something else when he turned to look at Hayden. "You don't need to do this alone."

"I must." Mrs. Rodriguez gestured toward the overflowing waffle cone in his hand. "You will be occupied with those."

Andrew nodded. "Where will you be? I can bring Jorge when we're done."

Mrs. Rodriguez looked at Hayden. "I do not know."

"Elliott & Johnson," Hayden said. "A couple blocks up King on this side of the street."

Andrew nodded. "I know where that is." He looked at her as though he thought she might hurt the older woman.

"Your ice cream is about to drip." Hayden pointed. Something in her couldn't resist pushing his buttons. "She'll be fine."

"Sure." He ground out the word between clenched teeth and pulled a card from his back pocket. "Here. Call my cell if you need anything, Maricel."

Hayden touched his arm, and he straightened

as if she'd shocked him. What had happened to the warm, approachable guy she'd met the other night? "We should only be an hour." She waited until his gaze collided with hers. "We're on the same side, Andrew."

"We'll see." His look said he doubted it.

"Maybe the ice cream will sweeten your disposition." Hayden winked at him and then waved her hand toward the door. "After you, Señora Rodriguez."

Did I just wink? As she and Mrs. Rodriguez walked away, Hayden wondered where on earth that had come from. Fortunately, Andrew didn't know her well enough to understand how out of character it was. She forced her thoughts from him. Men didn't affect her. Period. She didn't have time for them if she wanted to make partner at the firm that demanded her all and never thought she gave enough.

Andrew rubbed a hand across his head.

Well, that was one way to be a jerk.

He hadn't meant to take her head off, but something in him had risen at the thought that she'd take advantage of the Rodriguezes. Neither Jorge nor his mother had shared the reason they'd immigrated, and he hadn't pressed. He'd learned early at New Beginnings that sometimes the only thing his families retained was their story. It was something to be treasured and shared willingly, not coerced. Would Hayden twist and poke until Maricel told her things the older woman preferred to hold close?

That ignored the fundamental question: Why did Maricel need an attorney anyway?

Maricel Rodriguez was strong, but a fragile something hinted at hard times in the past. Hard times she had risen above.

Jorge was studying him with serious eyes.

"Let's finish our ice cream like we'd planned." Andrew smiled, but Jorge didn't return it.

Instead, the young man sank deeper into the small bistro chair and dutifully licked, eyes constantly on Andrew as if assessing the likelihood of another eruption. It was a look Andrew had seen in kids who had a reason to expect violence. It pained him to have caused it.

Andrew sighed and settled onto his chair. "Look, Jorge, I'm sorry. I don't often lose my temper unless I think someone is threatened. Lucky for you, I care about you. Not so lucky, I chose the wrong way to show it."

"Is all right."

"No, I know better, and I'm sorry." He took a bite of the blueberry ice cream, and then licked a few dribbles. It was too good to let any escape. "So how was school this week?"

As he listened to Jorge share about his week, Andrew prayed for a chance to apologize to Hayden as well.

A loud mariachi band ringtone resounded, and Jorge jumped. His gaze darted around and his complexion seemed to pale.

Andrew placed a hand on his shoulder. "Everything okay?"

Jorge set the remains of his cone on a napkin and then wiped his hands on another. He made an effort to look calm, but his trembling hands betrayed him. He tugged a small flip phone from his pocket and glanced at it before sliding it back.

"Jorge?"

"It is nothing. Just my *padre*." The boy tried to smile, but it was a pathetic effort.

Clearly he wanted to drop the subject, so Andrew let him, but not before he filed the incident away in his mind.

Chapter 6

SATURDAY, APRIL 1

Hayden led Mrs. Rodriguez through quiet hallways to a small conference room. It was perfect for the low-key meeting she wanted.

"Please have a seat." Hayden set a legal pad, the case file, and a pen at a seat on one side of the table and waited for her client to sit on the other. She'd been here before, with nervous clients who needed reassurance. "Can I get you some water? A Coke?"

"I'm fine." The woman perched on the edge of the leather chair.

Hayden grabbed two bottles of water from the microfridge tucked under a countertop and handed one to Mrs. Rodriguez before twisting off the cap on hers. She sank onto her seat and assessed her client, noting the fine lines around the woman's expressive eyes and lips. The clothes were better than any Hayden owned, and the ring on her right hand looked like a genuine two-carat diamond. What had led Maricel to the United States, and why now? Hayden needed a way to peel back the layers surrounding this woman to identify the heart of the matter.

"Mr. Campbell is my attorney."

"Yes, but he has many, many clients. He asked me to run this case, so it is pushed hard and fast in a way that serves you. He gave me your case yesterday, and I'll work closely with you to seek closure for your son."

"Are you good?" The question was clipped, hard, clear.

Hayden leaned forward and placed her elbows on the table. "Señora Rodriguez, I am very good. I won an unwinnable case Thursday. That's why I received your case Friday. I cannot guarantee an outcome, but I can guarantee my best efforts."

"You must understand. My husband . . . he is

a hard man. Brutal. We cannot fail." Maricel's dark eyes glistened with unshed tears.

"Your husband?" Hayden blew out a slow breath as she tried to interpret what the woman hadn't said. "Has your husband hurt you?"

"*Sí*. That is why I am here, with Jorge. It is why Miguel wanted to come. But it is not far enough." The woman looked away, and her words trailed off. "It is never far enough."

"We could get a restraining order against your husband. It will keep him away."

"Nothing will achieve that but winning." Mrs. Rodriguez cleared her throat and brought her gaze to Hayden's. "We must win."

How could she respond to the steel behind such an impossible demand? And why would winning a case make the man go away? "Do you believe your husband was involved in Miguel's death?"

"I don't know." Maricel looked at her with fear-filled eyes. "But we must win."

"I can't ethically promise that." Hayden slid the legal pad and pen in front of her. "But to win, I need to understand your story. All of it." She'd start with the heart of the case. "Who do you think killed Miguel?"

"Your government." But the woman didn't sound convinced, and her eyes didn't meet Hayden's.

"It's possible." But unlikely. It wasn't good policy to kill foreign nationals when they were in your protection. Hayden doodled as she considered how to proceed. "Who else might be involved?"

"I don't know. That's why I got an attorney. I need answers. I need to know what happened to my son and vindicate him." Maricel's voice cracked, and a tear slipped down her cheek. "You don't understand. Miguel was a good boy. He never was trouble. He always did what people asked and more. I cannot imagine him getting into trouble that killed him."

"How did you learn he was dead?"

"A call in the middle of the night from his *padre*." She shivered. "It was the last call I expected."

"His father does not live with you?"

"No."

"Are you divorced?"

Mrs. Rodriguez stiffened. "He paid a priest and had our marriage annulled." She wiped another tear away. "Two children. Five years. And annulled." She sniffed. "Bribes can accomplish any *injusticia*."

"*Lo siento.*"

"Me too." She squared her shoulders. "So Miguel is dead. In some *Americano* facility. It makes no sense, but that is all I am told. It is not enough."

"Do you know which facility?"

"In Texas." She waved a manicured hand in the air. "I gave the information to attorney."

Hayden let the silence linger a moment, hoping her client would fill in more information than resided in the file. "Texas is a big state."

"You work for a big firm."

"Not so big really." Hayden rubbed the base of her neck and considered her next question. "Why didn't Miguel emigrate with you?"

Mrs. Rodriguez sighed, a sound both desperate and empty. "He does not live with me."

"Was he with his father?"

She nodded. Hayden waited for Mrs. Rodriguez to expand on this violent husband who wasn't in the picture, but had one of the children. Finally Hayden tried again. "What is his name?"

"Miguel."

"No, his father."

"Daniel Rodriguez."

Hayden made a note to investigate Miguel's father, but with a name that common, she doubted she'd be successful. "Did Miguel want to come?"

"It was all he talked about. He wanted to see this free land that jailed him." She wiped her eyes. "My boy had dreams. Believed he could change the world. Now he never will."

"When did Miguel come to the US?"

"Weeks before he died. Not long."

"Do you know the day?"

"I'm not sure. I was not with him." Mrs. Rodriguez's voice rose with each word.

Hayden placed a hand on the woman's arm, a

gesture that had calmed her earlier. This time, Maricel barely noticed. "I ask so I can help. Who knows the answer?"

"I don't know. It's why I came. You get the answers."

It only took a few more minutes to determine that if Maricel knew anything more, she wasn't saying. The woman was here to gain answers and closure. As she listened to the mother's grief-soaked words, Hayden's heart broke. To have a son die before his time would be terrible, but to know he had been murdered . . . Hayden would use all the resources at her disposal to find answers.

"Tell me about your son, Maricel. What was he like?"

"Smart. Very smart. He could fix anything he touched. He programmed computers since he was just a boy. He wanted to study here."

"Why not come on a student visa?"

"He wanted to live here. Permanently."

"What did he like to do?"

"Tease people. All the time he had humor. Most of the time people loved it."

"Was he ever mean with his humor?"

"No." The response was immediate. "He was softhearted. Always helping others." The woman twisted the Kleenex in her hands until it lay shredded in a pile on the mahogany conference table.

Hayden made some notes, but this information wasn't what she needed. Maybe if she returned to key questions, she'd get more. "When did he die?"

"The paper tells me."

Hayden looked up. "What paper is that? Do you have it with you?"

"No. I do not know the kind of paper." She shrugged. "A letter. From an agency."

"ICE?"

"What is that?"

"Immigration and Customs."

"Yes, from them."

Hayden jotted a note. "Does it list a cause of death?"

"I do not know."

"Can you bring me the paper?"

"Later."

Hayden studied her firm jaw. Should she press? Probably not while she was trying to build rapport. "How do you know he was murdered?"

Maricel's gaze drifted past Hayden to the wall. "I received a picture."

"In the mail?"

"No. E-mail."

"Can you forward it to me?" Hayden pulled out a card from those she'd clipped to the front of the file. She circled the e-mail address before handing it to her. "At this address."

Maricel accepted the card, her hooded expression cautious. "I will try. Jorge will help."

"Thank you." Hayden sat back and considered her wary client. The woman looked like she might bolt any moment. "Who sent the e-mail?"

"My husband."

Again her husband. Was he the real force behind the lawsuit? What would he gain from it? "Why do you think he sent it?"

"To warn me." She shuddered, and her eyes filled with tears. "My baby . . . I cannot remove his image." She wiped a shaking hand across her forehead. "It is always here."

Hayden could feel her grief, a palpable presence in the room. She let silence settle while Maricel wiped the tears that slid from her eyes. "Why would your husband warn you?"

"Remind me of his power."

The answer settled on Hayden, unsatisfactory in its weight. It also reinforced her initial reaction that the man was controlling even across the border. "If your husband is powerful, why would he need to remind you?"

"He wants all to fear him. His reach is far, but he needs something. Something he thinks only I can get."

"Did you emigrate to escape him?"

The woman's shrug was eloquent in what she didn't say. "We have visas. We can stay two years, possibly longer."

"When did you arrive?"

"Three months ago."

And on the questions continued, yet the more she asked, the less Hayden learned. It was almost as if Maricel wanted to appear cooperative without really helping Hayden solve the puzzle.

Finally the woman asked her own question. "Can you help me get his backpack?"

"Backpack?"

"Miguel traveled with it." She wiped under her eyes. "I have nothing of his. I asked Campbell for it." She hesitated. "I need something from it."

"Yes, he has requested it. I will let you know as soon as we receive it." Hayden made a note to follow up with the prison. "What outcome are you hoping for with this lawsuit, Señora Rodriguez?"

"I want my son's killer."

The only way to do that was to identify him, and that could be extremely hard—especially if there had been any kind of cover-up at the detention facility. "I will do all I can."

As she said the words, Hayden meant them to the core of her soul. This mother was exactly the kind of client she wanted to help. One who couldn't make progress without a skilled advocate. This was why Hayden had worked so hard in law school—so that when people came for help, she could give it to them. "Get me that e-mail, and I'll work on the backpack."

She'd do much more, too, because if the United States hadn't detained him, Miguel Rodriguez would be alive today, and with his mother and brother.

Chapter 7

SATURDAY, APRIL 1

Maricel's story was a burden Hayden couldn't shake when she arrived home Saturday night. She kicked off her shoes and trudged upstairs to her sanctuary, which consisted of her bedroom, the landing/home office, and a bathroom. Hayden craved the sunlight the windows let in.

Emilie had the basement level, all the better to cocoon in for her late hours writing. She was a freelancer for one of the Beltway's online investigative sites and seemed to prefer it to the full-time practice of law. However, she still found fulfillment in working with domestic violence clients at a local shelter—working with women who needed help reclaiming their lives and moving forward.

As Hayden stepped into yoga pants and a comfy long-sleeved T-shirt, she felt like she'd gone ten rounds with Maricel Rodriguez and was no closer to the truth than she'd been before meeting her. For one who wanted answers so badly, Miguel's mother was reluctant to share details about her murdered son.

What if it hadn't been murder?

What if her son had simply died?

It wasn't common, but it happened. A seemingly healthy youngster, cut down in the prime of life.

The photo would be a start.

Hayden walked to her desk and glanced around as she woke the computer. Something wasn't right. She felt as though someone was watching her, but that was ridiculous.

No one waited in the shadows. Her odd conversation with Maricel had put her on edge. She headed for the stairs. "Emilie?"

"Hey." Emilie bounced out from the kitchen. "I thought I heard you come in."

Hayden went downstairs and grabbed a carrot stick from the bowl Emilie held.

"You were gone all day."

"Met my new client." Hayden sank onto a barstool. "Hey, Em, did you go into my office today?"

"Yep. Grabbed the three-hole punch. It's always easy to find yours."

"You could find yours, too, if you kept it in its place."

"Sure, but it's easier to nab yours. I put it back."

At least Hayden knew why her office had felt invaded. She rubbed her forehead and told herself not to be crazy. "This case would make a great law school problem. It doesn't fit any clear area. And

I've got to move it out of the court it was filed in."

"Sounds like a real puzzle."

"It is." Hayden grabbed the last carrot stick. "Remember Professor Richards, who always warned us our clients would lie? I didn't want to believe him."

"What makes you think your client is lying?"

"All the things she isn't saying." Hayden brushed nonexistent crumbs from the counter. Her brain felt like everything had mushed together into a congealed mass. "Tell me about your day."

Emilie grinned and pointed at the notebook she'd set on the countertop. "I simply organized the community fair for Andrew."

For someone who couldn't keep her space clean enough to locate a three-hole punch, Emilie had a talent for event planning. "So what will the kids do?"

"You name it, they'll do it. I've found arcade games, a few rides. Even got someone to donate pony rides. It'll be great."

Hayden laughed as Emilie held up her hand for a high five. "If anyone can pull it off, you can."

"Yep. There's plenty of time for the event to fall apart or come together. But at least the outline is here for Andrew. With his dad gunning for that Senate seat, he'll have less time than he expects."

"I saw that on the news this morning."

"Didn't take the congressman's staff long to circulate the word. Makes me wonder if they anticipated the resignation and were prepared." She shrugged as she put the empty bowl in the sink. "I hope he leaves Andrew out of it. He hates campaigning. Always has. Which sort of put a damper on his father's plans for his life. Did you know Andrew started law school and dropped out after getting all A's his first semester?"

Hayden gulped. She hadn't had all A's any semester, no matter how hard she'd worked. "Why didn't he stay?"

"Convinced himself he'd never become his own person. I love my aunt and uncle, but their family dynamics are a little . . . different. I can't imagine Andrew bringing someone home from school without a full vetting first." Emilie grinned. "Not that I ever did that."

Hayden laughed. "And I'm glad." Those had been some of the best breaks of law school. She'd spent a few days with Emilie's family several times, when the breaks were too short to travel home to Nebraska. She'd needed the reminder that families could be loving and whole and that school wasn't her identity. Sometimes she still needed that reminder.

"I've got plenty of jobs for you at the fair, by the way. If all the New Beginnings kids come, it'll be nuts."

"I met one of Andrew's kids today."

Emilie straightened. "You did? I love working with them when I can."

"His name is Jorge. His mom is my client. Neither of us realized the connection till we were all there together in the ice cream shop. It was . . . awkward."

"Awkward. Not usually a word people use to describe interactions with Andrew. He has the Wesley charm in spades."

"Maybe with others. Clearly, he didn't like me meeting with the mom. End of story." Hayden sighed. "I wish she had been more open with me. I got the sense she doesn't trust me."

"Is this the wrongful death case?"

Hayden nodded. "Only it can't be wrongful death. Not if I'm going to move it to a court where I have a shot. To do that I need more facts, and right now she won't give them to me." Hayden looked at her friend. "Maybe you can help, with your journalism connections."

Emilie held up her hands and backed away. "Hey, you know those aren't for sale."

"I need help pinpointing which detention center he was in. The complaint left it vague."

"And she wouldn't tell you?"

"Wouldn't or couldn't. But I know you can find out."

Emilie's impish smile emerged. "You're right. I'm your girl for this."

Emilie had a network that extended throughout DC's layers. If anyone could track down the information, she could.

"Thanks."

"Don't thank me yet. You're definitely helping me with Andrew's street fair now."

"Wait a second . . ."

"You know you need this information. Spill the beans and I'll get to work."

Hayden chewed her lower lip and considered the wisdom of her impulsive request. She really needed Emilie's help. "Okay, here's what you need." She grabbed a pink Post-it from the junk drawer and jotted a note.

"I'll have your answer by Monday."

Hayden headed upstairs and found an e-mail from Maricel Rodriguez waiting. She opened the attachment and stared at the image of a young Hispanic man lying on a hard concrete floor, a puddle of blood under his head. No, this wasn't an injury he had inflicted on himself. Someone had taken a knife and jabbed it hard and deep across his throat.

Bright and early Monday morning Emilie handed Hayden a Post-it note. "Here's your facility, madam. There are only three taking juveniles right now. He was at the one in Texas, as you thought." As Hayden reached for the slip of paper, Emilie pulled it back. "I don't know what you're into, Hayden, but be careful. This is big."

"Big enough for you to chase?"

Emilie shrugged, but still held the slip. "I don't know, but you need to watch what you say. I'd treat this as top secret."

"All right." It wasn't like she wanted to alert the government before she was ready. "Find anything else?"

"Nope. It's frankly amazing I discovered this. It's like they wiped his file. I found someone who remembered his file or I wouldn't have learned this much. What did the kid do?"

Hayden ignored Emilie's question, studying the name and address on the little square of paper. "Thanks, Em. This should get me started."

When Hayden reached her office on King Street, she settled at the desk and fired up her computer. Maricel's e-mail with Miguel's photo was at the top of her inbox, and she quickly closed it. She didn't need the photo to remember every detail of his violent death. This young man needed justice —and the best vehicle was a lawsuit that held the government and whoever killed him accountable. She stuck the Post-it with the detention center info to the side of the screen and waited for her browser to load.

Emilie's warning had not deterred her. On the contrary, it made her more determined to learn what had happened. Not just who had committed the horrific crime, but who had an interest in covering it up.

Were they tied to one of the many government agencies with tentacles in immigration?

She needed the date Miguel died and cause of death. Without those all she had to prove his death was a photo.

Without proof of murder, it would just be a sad event.

With murder, she might have an argument that would stand in court.

FEBRUARY

The road stretched on forever, a ribbon of six-lane vastness. The sheer number of vehicles, trucks zipping past, motorcycles zinging in and out, cars trailing along, could overwhelm him if he let it.

In a country this vast, disappearing was the easy part. Giving *el jefe* no excuse to chase him was harder. Simply throwing away the cell phone and cutting up the credit cards wouldn't suffice.

He glanced at the two cell phones resting on the rental car's seat. One tied him to *el jefe*, the other did not.

He kept the car right at the speed limit. No matter how fast he drove, he could not out-run his guilt. His hands had taken a life. How could he ever make this right?

Each evening a text arrived. Rafael kept the phone off until the moment he turned it on to read the message. Then he powered it off again, retaining a cloak of invisibility.

The boss was intense. Determined. Lethal.

To stay alive, he must show he could do everything demanded in a way that bought him more hours.

Rafael had not had long, but he'd searched

every crevice. The cell-like room had been empty of all but the beds and one backpack.

Could the boss be mistaken?

Had he killed Miguel, who was like his brother, for no purpose?

Rafael shook his head. Miguel should have been honest. Told what he knew.

No, Rafael should demand the same honesty of himself. He had felt trapped, but he had known exactly what he was doing. Remorse would be his companion, and he was determined never again to place himself in a position where death or life were the only choices.

His breathing accelerated as a state patrol pickup came into his rearview mirror. He eased his foot from the gas, keeping an eye on the speedometer.

A yawn stretched his face, followed quickly by another. He needed a break, some sleep.

An exit appeared in front of him. A McDonald's, a gas station, a small motel. A Dumpster he could park behind. Perfect for hiding . . . for now.

Chapter 8

As she fought a yawn, Hayden decided it was time for some caffeinated power. It didn't take long to walk to Starbucks and then return with her venti flat white to her closet-sized office. Her desk and credenza filled two-thirds of the space, with one chair for a client in front of her desk. The desk didn't match the credenza, and the room was small and dingy, but it was hers. She'd covered the walls with Impressionist-inspired prints. The bright colors reflected the light and gave the area a wisp of personality.

She sank onto her desk chair, took a sip of her coffee, and considered her next steps on the Rodriguez case. She took another sip of coffee and jotted some notes on her to-do list.

1. Finish motion to change venue
2. Compile discovery requests

The motion had to be filed before the government gave its answer or motion to dismiss before the court. If she waited too long the odds of a successful move shrank. The parties were required by Rule 26 to hold a meeting to organize discovery, and before that meeting, discovery was very limited. Her orders were clear: get discovery moving so she could report something.

Litigation was a delicate balance between learning all the information you could as quickly as possible and teasing it out while keeping the opponent off balance as long as possible. The federal government was such a bureaucracy it could take months to get anything moving.

Hayden pulled up a copy of Trial Rule 26, hoping there was a loophole to waiting for the planning meeting. She didn't have time for the parties to develop an elaborate calendar for requests and information to be exchanged. Time mattered because precious information could be lost. Memories would be muddied. Children could be shipped across the border, and witness impressions lost.

She flipped forward, scanning the rules of civil procedure, slowing when she reached Rule 41. She read it again, then flipped to check the exceptions, none of which applied. A rush of excitement filled her as she read the rule a third time. Because the government hadn't filed an answer, she could file a notice of dismissal, which essentially dismissed the case with the opportunity to refile. Then she could do the pre-case depositions and file in the Court of Federal Claims. This . . . this might work. It would buy her the time she needed to get information that wouldn't be available later when memories shortened or documents were shredded, while also moving the case to a court that wouldn't require a jury fighting prejudice.

It was gutsy, but leaving the case where it was and letting justice take its time wouldn't serve her client's interests.

She tapped the call button on her phone. "Leigh, can you see if Gerard is available? Thank you."

As she waited, she gathered her thoughts in a quick outline. If he agreed with her analysis, then she'd justified his faith in her. This plan involved thinking way outside the typical legal boxes, but still fit squarely within the rules—but only if she filed the dismissal before the government answered. Timing was critical.

She jotted another note, and Gerard walked into her office without knocking. "You need to talk?"

Hayden looked up and quickly tried to cover her surprise at his appearance. His eyes were bloodshot and his usual GQ perfection missing.

"I've discovered a way to refile this case and start discovery."

Gerard studied her a moment, then nodded. "Glad to hear it. Let's take this outside."

"It won't take that long."

He nodded his head toward the doorway and then pivoted back to the hallway. "Fresh air will do you good, McCarthy."

Mystified, Hayden grabbed her suit jacket from the hook behind her door and followed him downstairs and out the front door. He led the way onto the sidewalk along King Street, not speaking. After they'd walked a block, he slowed his pace and glanced at her. "What have you got?"

She launched into her idea. "So if we voluntarily dismiss the case," she concluded, "we reserve the right to refile . . . and that allows us to change courts. At the same time I can file to take key depositions in anticipation of pending litigation."

Gerard kept moving as he considered her plan. While it looked as though he was ignoring her, Hayden knew his brain was chugging through the options she'd presented and running a decision tree of possible outcomes. If he liked her recommendation, she'd know it was solid.

He turned onto a side street and kept walking.

"Is everything all right, Gerard?"

He snorted. "Why would you think otherwise?"

"Because you've never taken me outside for a meeting no matter how beautiful the weather."

"There's a first time for everything." He stopped and turned to face her. "This case is different, Hayden. Something is at play I haven't figured out." His intense gaze bored through her. "Maybe I shouldn't have accepted it, but it seemed the right choice."

"Should we dismiss the case and stop?" She forced the tremor from her voice. "Is that what you want me to do? You can explain to Mrs. Rodriguez."

Gerard looked across the street, but she knew he didn't see the row of historic townhomes or the cars rattling down the brick roads.

His chin lifted and he balled his hands before turning to meet her gaze. "File the dismissal today. Take care of it before the government answers. Then take the deposition of the director of the facility. You can ask for a tour, too, but I doubt you'll get it. Style it as a request for entry of the premises for the purpose of photographing the location of the death. The government will object, but get it done."

"Yes sir."

He studied her a moment, and she fought the instinct to squirm like a child called to the principal's office. "All right."

"Is there anything else I need to know?"

"No."

As they walked back to the office, Hayden knew she couldn't believe Gerard. Something certainly worried him about this case. The problem was she had no idea what.

The moment she marched into her office, Hayden grabbed Leigh. "We've got a priority pleading to file in Texas tonight."

"We've only got hours until the courts close."

"Then we'd better get to work." Hayden filled

Leigh in on the plan, and as the paralegal searched for a Notice of Dismissal form, Hayden located the name of the director of the juvenile detention facility.

A couple clicks and she'd identified the man and his short bio.

Carlton Snowden had spent twenty years in the Marines before entering the police business. He'd risen steadily through the ranks in his home state of Texas, and eventually landed in charge of a facility that had been hastily opened to handle the flood of unaccompanied kids and teens at the border.

Hayden took a deep breath and dialed the facility's number.

On the second ring someone picked up. "Snowden."

Hayden gulped. He wasn't supposed to answer. "My name is Hayden McCarthy, and I represent the mother of a young man who died in your facility."

Stone-cold silence met her statement. She let it build until she wondered if he'd hung up.

"Says who?"

"A letter my client received from ICE."

"I can neither deny nor confirm anything she may or may not have learned from Immigration and Customs. Your inquiry should proceed with the legal department."

"I hoped you could confirm this young man

was indeed in your facility. If there's been a mistake, I don't want to waste your time." *Or mine.*

"His name." The man paused, and she heard the swish of a liquid. "If he isn't in our records, I can confirm that."

"Thank you." It was a start. "He was seventeen-year-old Miguel Rodriguez. A Mexican caught north of the border in your great state."

She heard the click of keys and remained quiet as she waited.

"He may have been here. Rodriguez is a common name. I recommend you proceed through the legal office."

Clearly she wasn't going to get anything more from Mr. Snowden. "Thank you for your time." She hung up as Leigh walked into her office.

"I've got the Notice of Dismissal." Leigh handed her a slim folder. "Do you want me to start the new complaint?"

Hayden shook her head as she opened the file and scanned the document. "We'll file this and get discovery moving first."

Fifteen minutes later she called the paralegal back. "This looks great. I noted a couple changes, and then it's ready for my signature. Thanks for handling this so quickly."

Leigh grinned. "That's why you pay me the big bucks. I'll have this back in a minute and file it electronically."

As Hayden glanced at her computer's clock, she

realized they'd made her self-imposed deadline. Now what? How could she convince the government to cooperate? Maybe her mentor could help her unravel the best way to proceed.

She picked up her phone and called Savannah Daniels. "Have time for coffee?"

Chapter 9

Thirty minutes later Hayden crossed King Street on her way to meet Savannah at Common Grounds. A lot of people were enjoying the sunny spring day, so why did she have this creepy sense someone followed her? As she passed a dress shop with a large window, she glanced back. Her step hitched as she squinted to see if someone was really there or her imagination was being overactive. Gerard's behavior was rubbing off on her. Finally she arrived at the coffee shop ready to grab a cup of tea and brainstorm.

A comfortably plump woman with a welcoming smile waved at her from a small table in the corner of the coffee shop. She held up a mug and plate of pie. "I've got your tea and sweet."

Hayden smiled as she headed toward her friend. The woman had mentored Hayden from her earliest days at George Mason and understood Hayden at a deep level. Savannah often provided the sound voice of wisdom and experience when Hayden couldn't find it on her own.

As she reached the table, Savannah stood and wrapped her in a quick hug. "What's it been? Two months?"

"Try three."

"Three months too long, considering we've scheduled coffee every two weeks. Tell me what's going on." Savannah propped her elbow on the table and her chin on her palm, giving Hayden her full attention.

Hayden settled into her chair and smiled at her friend. This was a woman with whom she wanted to be transparent, because she valued Savannah's carefully earned wisdom and insight. In addition to serving as adjunct faculty at George Mason Law School, Savannah had a thriving practice of her own making. She'd defined success on her own terms and wore it like a cloak, one that surrounded her without weighing her down.

Her warm eyes studied Hayden. "I'm waiting." She reached over and touched Hayden's hand where it rested on the table. "You've got something on your mind."

Hayden glanced around to make sure nobody was close. "I've got a new case."

"That's good."

"Yes, but . . . it's odd."

"Odd how?"

"The client is the mother of a young man killed

while in a US juvenile detention center. He was an illegal immigrant, but she isn't."

Savannah listened with an open and curious expression as Hayden filled her in.

"Gerard likes the strategy I developed." Hayden sighed, trying to identify what was bothering her. "There's something about his behavior today that has me feeling paranoid. He hinted at trouble with the other partners. I'm beginning to wonder what I've landed in."

"You've only had the case since Friday. Maybe his caution isn't about you—or maybe not even about the case. He can't be concerned about the job you'll do, since he advocated so strongly for you to have it."

That's what puzzled Hayden. "I guess we'll see. What do you think about the pre-complaint deposition?"

"It's always a risk, but in this case sounds warranted. Time is important. Remember the world isn't perfect and you won't get everything you want in one deposition. You can always do notice pleading with basic facts to get the case moving."

"I need to get to Texas quickly. But you know the government will delay."

Savannah nodded. "So ask the judge for expedited discovery. What can it hurt?"

"I don't have a judge." Hayden crossed her arms on the table and sighed. "I need to get into the facility first and learn what I can."

"Surely there's a congressional inquiry of some sort going on with the detention facilities. Get attached to that somehow. Then you have an official reason to visit."

Hayden toyed with the thought as she blew on her tea. "I don't know. If that came out during the suit, it wouldn't look good."

"Who could go for you to find the information?"

"Maybe Emilie. She could go as a journalist and put her investigative skills to work."

Savannah cocked her head. "That could work. Emilie would probably think it's fun."

"And if it leads to a good story, she'd learn all she could."

"She is persuasive. Remember that moot court competition . . ."

The women shared a chuckle. Emilie had always been more interested in looking the part and sounding good than arguing the law. In the one required competition she entered, she'd created a few facts and convinced the moot court judges she knew the case better than they did. It was only in the semifinal round that a judge called her bluff. To this day there was an Emilie Wesley Moot Court Award for Most Creative Argument. Most of the time Emilie smiled when she gave the award, though she'd been conveniently out of town during last fall's competition.

"I'll ask her if she can take a quick trip." The more Hayden thought about it, the more she could see Emilie sliding right into the role and having a great time with it. Then Hayden would know exactly what she needed to uncover.

She and Savannah chatted a few minutes longer, finished their tea, and said their good-byes.

Time to see if she could talk Emilie into wearing her investigative hat.

Laughter greeted Hayden as she opened the door to her townhome.

"No. That's too soon." The authoritative male voice didn't belong to her roommate.

"Hayden, come in and tell Andrew I'm right." That voice did.

Hayden found the cousins on either side of the kitchen counter, its surface covered with a calendar and legal pads. "What are you two doing?"

"I'm telling Andrew how to make his street fair a success, and he's not listening." Emilie crossed her arms and stared daggers at her cousin.

Andrew, looking crisp and unfazed in his button-down with sleeves rolled up, said, "There's more than one way to plan an event."

"Sure." Emilie pointed at him. "Just because he's attended his dad's fund-raisers, he's decided he's an expert."

Hayden laughed. "Maybe Andrew has some ideas too."

Andrew grinned at her and then waggled his

eyebrows at Emilie. "I told you I knew what I was doing."

"Hey, I didn't say that." Hayden held her hands up in front of her. "I'm Switzerland. And I just got here."

"I guarantee I know more than someone who's never even planned a birthday party." Emily tipped her nose up. "Besides, I've already done half the work."

"Hey, don't forget that surprise party I planned for you."

"That wasn't a surprise, and it was ten years ago."

"Aw, Emilie." Hayden shook her head at her roommate's intensity. "Andrew looks competent to handle an event planned for kids."

Andrew rolled his eyes, but his grin was genuine. "Thanks for the vote of confidence, Hayden. You don't do my job on a daily basis without learning how to corral kids."

Emilie tossed a legal pad toward Hayden. "I can't believe you're siding with him. Fine, I'll leave you two to make a go of it. I've got an article to write and a motion for a protective order to review before the morning."

Hayden's brow furrowed. "Emilie, we're just kidding. Are you okay?"

"Fine. Had a dandy afternoon keeping a client from being killed by her ex." She rubbed her forehead. "I'm sorry, I can't deal with this right now. My plans are on that pad if you care to use them."

Emilie headed downstairs to her suite, and Hayden turned on Andrew. "What did you do to her?"

"Nothing." He stacked the legal pads. "I'll call her after she's had a chance to cool down. There are many things I don't understand in the world, and one of them is how Emilie Wesley swings between strong emotions so quickly."

"It only happens when she cares deeply."

"She's right!" came a voice from downstairs.

Andrew grinned—that model-perfect, mega-watt grin Hayden had seen in magazines. She forced her thoughts back to the event. "So . . . tell me what you've got so far."

"Sure." Andrew leaned into the counter. "I have space in my neighborhood. I've talked to vendors and volunteer organizations. It just kills Emilie that I didn't need her to tell me every step."

The voice from below floated up again. "That's not true. You need my sparkling wit and attention to detail."

Andrew's gaze collided with Hayden's, and his spontaneous laughter had her breath catching in her chest. The laugh spread to all three, and Hayden wondered at the pull she felt to him despite who he was. The guy couldn't help it that he was handsome. Or rich. Or the son of a congressman. His affection for his cousin and his zeal for his work were genuine. Could she have misjudged him? As his lips tipped in a slow smile, she hoped she had.

Chapter 10

Something shifted in the air, and Andrew settled back, forcing his grin to stay in place. He had tolerated the playboy image propagated by the press because it kept his parents at bay. His dad wanted him married so campaign materials could showcase the perfect family. His mother insisted it was past time for a grandchild or three. But for the first time, in Hayden he'd met a woman who made him want to show her he was different from the society page coverage. But as he couldn't tear his gaze away, he realized she had the potential to affect his life deeply.

Did he want that?

Part of him screamed yes. He was ready to settle down with someone who wanted to share his life.

And yet, another voice inside his head argued . . . intriguing as the beautiful young attorney might be, it didn't change the fact that she was an attorney—which meant made from the same mold as his father. Not the type to settle down and build a family. If she did, would she be available to her family or would the law steal her away?

His phone vibrated in his pocket, jerking him from the odd connection zinging between them. He pulled out the phone and scanned the number. His father's chief of staff. He sighed, grabbed Emilie's notes, stuffed them in his bag. "I've gotta take this call. Tell Emilie I'll call her later."

"I heard." The voice from downstairs floated up.

Andrew grinned as he turned to the door. "Thanks, Emilie," he called. "See you later, Hayden."

His smile slid from his face the moment he stepped outside.

Dan Washburn had been his father's right-hand man for fifteen years. The man looked like Archie Bunker from the old TV show, with the ability to turn on charm one second and snarl the next. Woe to the man who got the snarl.

Andrew took the call. "Washburn."

"Actually, this is Lilith Cleaver." The congressman's legislative director, point person for policy. The impetus behind many of the man's votes he couldn't focus on when there were more pressing duties like kissing babies and glad-handing donors. She had an elegant Audrey Hepburn throw-back grace that didn't quite match the mood on Capitol Hill most days, a look only marred by the Marilyn Monroe red lips she favored. Perfect for a caricature.

"Sorry about that." He walked to where he'd

parked his red Jeep Cherokee. "What can I do for you?"

"Dan wants you to attend a fund-raiser a week from Sunday. You need to be there and help present the unified front voters expect."

"Lilith . . ."

"Hey, don't shoot the messenger." She chuckled in her low voice—the one that made him wonder if she flirted with every man between twenty-five and forty or if he was just the lucky one. "Your dad really wants this."

"You all really want it. Quite a coup to move up to a senator's legislative director without changing staff."

"Sure. But your dad has a vision. The congress-man has a lot he wants to do that will be easier from a senate office."

"That's what they all say."

"But he means it. You should ask him about his vision."

"And four hours later he'll come up for air."

"Because he's passionate."

"Because he likes to hear himself talk."

Her soft sigh reached him. "I challenge you to watch your dad work. Not everyone would meet with as many constituents. Or have focused discussions with thought leaders." She paused. "He can make a real difference. You know how fractured the House is. Herding 435 representatives is worse than herding cats."

"Who else is in the running?"

"There are rumbles of a couple contenders, but no one has officially jumped into the race."

Andrew leaned against his Jeep and pressed the bridge of his nose between his thumb and forefinger. Maybe if he made an appearance they'd leave him alone for a few weeks. He had no excuses waiting and ready. "Fine. Text me the details."

"Great. Your dad will be thrilled. Get your suit out and keep your Rolodex handy, because you'll need a date for this one." She hung up as he started to sputter.

For a Sunday fund-raiser on less than a couple weeks' notice? The campaign staff must be insane. That was all the prompting he needed to mentally make sure he stayed far away. His phone buzzed, but he ignored it as he climbed into the Jeep and headed home.

Fifteen minutes later he parked in front of his condo. End of May the swimming pool would open, but meanwhile the tennis courts beckoned. He'd bought the condo planning to use the court sandwiched between his condo and one behind it. He'd deceived himself. The closest he got was to eat a sandwich looking down on the court, or occasionally give Zeus fenced boundaries in which to expend energy chasing a ball.

The dog barked from behind the front door as

Andrew entered the building and started upstairs to his condo. Before he could climb more than a couple stairs, Mrs. Bedford opened the door to her first-floor unit. "Andrew? Just who I wanted to see."

She stepped into the entryway, and he came back downstairs.

"Anything I can do for you, Mrs. B?"

"I wanted you to know a man was poking around here today. He seemed very interested in you." She pushed her glasses to the bridge of her nose. "He wandered around the building awhile, but he was definitely focused on your unit."

Andrew frowned. "What was he selling?"

"He said he was a satellite TV installer." She let out a harrumph. "He left me his card. Said I could call his supervisor, but the number was out of service."

"Do you still have the card?"

"Sure do. Let me get it." She ducked into her condo and a minute later returned with a standard business card. Even the name was generic: Jake Smithfield.

"Let me check into it."

"Thanks. He made me uncomfortable, so I decided to play along like I didn't think there was a thing odd about his name." Her indignant gray eyes met his over her glasses. "There may be someone out there named Jake Smithfield, but I'd bet one of my lemon pound cakes it isn't him."

Andrew nodded, his gut confirming her suspicions. "I'll let you know what I learn."

Zeus erupted with a string of short barks.

Mrs. Bedford laughed and shooed him toward the stairs. "Sounds like Zeus is ready for you."

Andrew said good-bye, then turned the card over as he marched up the stairs. It was a white piece of cardstock with *Jake Smithfield* listed above a phone number and e-mail address. No other information. He'd call the number when he got inside, but he had a feeling the result would be a dead end.

He unlocked the condo door, and the Lab bounded toward him, acting as though it had been a decade since they'd been together.

"Come on, Zeus." Andrew snatched the leash from its hook and tried to clip it on the dog's collar while the beast pranced about his feet.

Andrew turned up his jacket collar as they walked down the street, Zeus pulling hard after each squirrel. The dog sometimes forgot he was supposed to be a staid seven-year-old, instead acting like a frisky puppy.

As Zeus finally slowed to a respectable walk, Andrew ran his mind over the preliminary sketches he'd drawn over the weekend. His best one for tomorrow's eight a.m. deadline was the one with the two juxtaposed children. He had to finish the cartoon and e-mail it to his editor.

Oh, yeah. And find a date for his father's fund-raiser. No small problem since he'd sworn off taking his mom's suggestions. No, he wanted someone with substance. Someone who saw the problems in the world and wanted to make a real difference. And if she knew her way around Washington and wasn't overwhelmed or enthralled by it, all the better.

He turned Zeus toward home. When he reentered his condo, he looked on the counter for the business card. It wasn't waiting on the counter where he'd left it. He frowned as he shuffled the stacks of mail that had accumulated there. He bent down to look on the floor and found the card. A minute later he'd confirmed what Mrs. Bedford had told him. The number was a dead end.

Why would someone come to the condo and pretend to be a serviceman, complete with a fake business card? What had the guy been looking for?

Chapter 11

TUESDAY, APRIL 4

Hayden hauled her attaché case downstairs and dropped it on the bistro table. The night had passed with her tossing and turning, the photo of her client's murdered son filling her dreams. The young man had made it to the States, fearful yet expectant. Through his mother's words Hayden had sensed his purpose, that in coming he would make a new life and rejoin his family.

As she brewed a mug of tea, she couldn't shake the feeling that she was missing a key piece of his story.

Why would a young man take the coyote-led route when his mom and brother had already entered legally? If she could figure that out, maybe she'd gain insight into why he'd been murdered. Could it be drugs? Something he carried in his backpack? Neither fit, but if she could solve the *why,* it could lead to the *who,* which could give her client more closure.

Would she ever uncover the whole story? If she couldn't get it from her client, she'd have to locate it another way. She needed a contact inside the State Department. Someone who could look into the right database and see if Miguel *had* tried to enter legally and, if so, why he'd been denied.

She dumped the remains of her tea in the sink and headed to work. When she entered the office lobby, Annette, the receptionist who was time-frozen in the fifties with Lucille Ball, handed her a slip of paper. "Mr. Randolph's called down for you five times already."

Hayden glanced at her watch. "It's only eight thirty."

"Sure, but Randolph wanted to see you at seven. I'd skedaddle."

Hayden hurried up the stairs and through the warren of halls to her office. After dropping her briefcase, she grabbed a legal pad and pen and hurried toward Mr. Randolph's office. She had entered his office maybe one other time in her four years at the firm, and that was when she'd served as a summer associate. The man lived in the world of research and appellate litigation. When a case reached his desk, he didn't use more than a hand-selected number of associates, so why would he suddenly need her—and so urgently?

She passed Angela, who mouthed *Everything okay?*

Hayden shrugged. Until she saw Randolph she wouldn't know.

She'd barely rapped on his door before he waved her in, one finger pointing at his phone. "Great. We'll get that to you tomorrow." He chuckled, but the look he sent Hayden was anything but humorous. "Thanks again." He slammed the phone in its handset and then turned his dark gaze to her. "Have you forgotten anything, McCarthy?"

Hayden stood in front of his desk, wondering if she should sit down or dive behind the chair for cover. She stepped closer to his massive desk and met his gaze. If he wanted to hide behind his desk, fine. She wouldn't let him know she was intimidated by his brusque behavior. "Not that I'm aware of."

"Discovery in the Martin matter was due this a.m. Carmen reminded me, and I just got off the phone with opposing counsel. We'll get it to them tomorrow by close of business and then cut them some slack at a future date."

"The Martin discovery?" Hayden's mind raced to catch up.

"Yes. The multimillion-dollar breach-of-contract case. Lucky for you opposing counsel likes to golf at Queens Harbor. This week he'll do it at my expense with a promised round to help matters along."

She heard his words, but they still meant nothing to her. "I didn't have that discovery."

"I run the occasional trial when I'm bored. Lucky for you, this is one of those." He waved a hand at her to sit. "You inherited the discovery the week before your trial. Promised you'd get it reviewed and ready. So get to it. Carmen has it set up."

Hayden's mouth opened and closed, but she didn't know what to say. He'd never believe this was the first time she'd heard about the case. Plus, she was still struggling to imagine the detached partner engaged in the combat of a trial. He seemed better suited to the cerebral tasks of appellate work.

"That's all." He turned to his computer, not waiting for her to leave.

As Hayden walked out of his office, Carmen

stood in the outer office and motioned to the door. The woman's normal smile had disappeared, replaced by drawn eyebrows and a frown. Her long peasant skirt swished as she led Hayden to a conference room. "I'm sorry about this. He's all worked up."

"More than usual?"

"You could say that. He really should stick with appeals, but every other year or so he decides he's a litigator. Drives him—and me—crazy." She sighed, then forced a smile that didn't match her usual easy grin. "I'm not sure why he's pulling you in, but he insisted it was yours to fix. Sometimes all I can do is jump. Let me show you what I've done."

Carmen swept into the large room. Chairs had been pushed away from the oval table and against the walls, and file boxes were stacked three deep over two-thirds of the table's surface. Carmen tugged on the bottom of her shirt as she led the way to one stack. "If you start here and work your way around the table, you'll be in good shape. The discovery request is in this folder." She tapped an accordion file. "I've drafted a start for you. One of the wet-behind-the-ears associates took a stab at it. He's so new, I wouldn't rely on anything he did."

Hayden nodded and rubbed the back of her neck where her muscles had tightened and tension radiated. "Can you give me the case in fifty words?"

"Even fewer. Classic breach of contract. The essence of this request is proof of damages."

"So lots of numbers."

"Yep. Have fun, and let me know what you want for lunch."

"Thanks, Carmen."

The woman left in a swish of fabric, and Hayden reached for the phone on a side table. "Angela, what are you doing?"

Hours later, Hayden felt like her eyes had permanently crossed and her hands had dried beyond saving, thanks to all the paper she'd touched and sorted.

Angela kicked back with her socked feet on the table, flipping through a stack of paper in her lap. "How did you suck me into this again?"

"Promise of a future favor in return."

"I'll make it a good one." Angela eased her head from side to side, stretching her neck. "I thought we were beyond this duty."

"So did I. I'm still not sure how I landed the final discovery review without being told."

Carmen stuck her head in the door cautiously, as if afraid if she stepped in she'd get sucked into work. "Anything else y'all need before I leave?"

"Is it that time?" Hayden tapped her phone. "I don't suppose you know where the discovery fairies disappeared to?"

"I'm looking at them."

Angela laughed. "This fairy is ready to call it a night."

"Don't blame you." Carmen turned her attention back to Hayden. "Randolph told me to have you put the responses on his desk for review first thing tomorrow morning."

Hayden stood and arched her back. "That's assuming I leave. I haven't pulled an all-nighter in a while, but this looks like one."

"If his door is shut, you can slide it underneath."

Hayden looked at the boxes and snorted. "Sure. Thanks for your help. The discovery was better organized than I'd hoped." If only it came with a CPA. Sometimes she wondered if she should have earned an MBA to go with her law degree just to decipher numbers.

Angela stood and stretched after Carmen left. "You should have made her order supper takeout."

"We can have something delivered." Hayden looked at the pile of boxes left from the Chinese food Carmen had brought them for lunch. Thanks to Angela's help, she'd gotten through a good chunk of the review. And thanks to Carmen's organizational skills it wasn't as chaotic as some discovery messes. "You don't have to stay."

"And miss the opportunity to get paper cuts? Not a chance." Her friend settled back into the chair she'd occupied all day. "We should have grabbed a couple others before they skipped the office."

"I noticed people sliding past the door as fast as they could. Can't blame them."

Elliott & Johnson was not the largest firm in DC, but it was a boutique that prided itself on being the best. And that required the same commitment as the big firms demanded. As Hayden looked at the stack of boxes, she knew she'd have to work a long night if she was going to get this assignment finished in time to keep Randolph happy. Otherwise, she'd be fighting to stay gainfully employed.

Chapter 12

WEDNESDAY, APRIL 5

The stinging hot shower did little to wake Hayden. Her brain felt like mush. She'd walked home around five in the morning, but the discovery response waited in the conference room—it had been way too fat to slide under his door. A runner would make the copies while Carmen finalized the response to e-mail to the client for a signature that could be run back to the office and then filed. Hayden had met the artificial deadline, and now her stomach rebelled from the extra four mugs of coffee and her head pounded from the lack of sleep. If she lay down now, she wouldn't get to work before afternoon. Maybe she'd earned a few bonus points, but not if Randolph wouldn't admit she'd never had the assignment in the first place.

Twenty minutes after her quick shower she was downstairs brewing a cup of peppermint tea and nibbling on Nutella-doctored toast.

Emilie studied her from her post against the granite countertop. Her blond hair was perfectly coiffed, and her cranberry-colored suit looked tailored for her. Hayden felt like a thrown-together wreck next to her, even though she'd spent extra time hiding the circles under her eyes.

"Was that you who straggled in this morning?"

"Sorry about that. I tried to tiptoe." Hayden stifled a yawn that felt like it would split her jaw.

Emilie handed her a mug of coffee and a bottle of mocha creamer. "This will help."

"Thanks, but I'll stick with tea today." Hayden tried to think what filled that day's calendar. She hoped it wouldn't be anything challenging, because her neurons were firing on the slow side. The tea and an extra block on her walk to work would help. "I got the project done."

"Good, I was just worried about you." Emilie returned to her post by the door. "Have you heard anything from the detention center?"

"Not anything helpful." Move that to the top of the list now that Randolph would ignore her. Knowing her luck, Gerard would demand an update on Rodriguez. "I've got to find someone in ICE who can tell me about Miguel, because Snowden at the detention center wouldn't even confirm he'd been there." The secret was finding the right helpful bureaucrat, one who didn't ask too many questions and provided lots of answers. The challenge was ICE was thick with the unhelpful sort. "Maybe a Texas agency would have the same information."

"I haven't found one. At least that will talk to me."

Hayden turned to her roommate. "Emilie!"

"You couldn't give me information on a case like this and not expect me to dig." She met Hayden's stare with a smile. "You knew I would."

Hayden did know. And knowing Emilie was digging shouldn't bother her, even if Miguel's story was hers to tell. It wasn't fodder for an investigative journalism piece. At least not before the complaint was filed. "Can you promise you won't turn in an article until after I've filed the complaint?"

"I'll try." Emilie grabbed the kitchen rag and wiped down the spotless counter. "But I may have mentioned the concept to my editor. You know how he pushes for my next brilliant idea. Only Andrew understands how hard it is to generate fresh ideas every couple weeks."

Hayden looked at her, totally confused. "What are you talking about?"

"Never mind. I didn't say that."

Hayden shrugged. "Whatever. But if you find out anything, let me know first, okay?"

"What I learn can help you. You know I'm good at digging." Emilie said it as if she needed to convince herself. "Well, I have to get into the office. Put in the rest of my time for the week helping women."

"You love it."

"Most days." A shadow darkened Emilie's face. "It's been one of those weeks with a particular client."

"This the same one from Monday? Does she want to go back?"

"It is and no, but her boyfriend is everywhere. He was not happy with me at the protective order hearing Monday." She shimmied her shoulders as if shaking off the thought. "He's not the first and won't be the last." An alarm beeped, and she tossed the rag back into the sink. "See you tonight. I'm meeting a client in half an hour."

"Good luck."

"Thanks." Emilie breezed out the door, looking ready to tackle the world in her red suit. No one could accuse the woman of disappearing into a crowd.

Hayden sank onto a bistro chair next to the table and nursed her tea. She rubbed the tight muscles at the base of her neck. If Emilie wrote an article too soon, there was a chance other news outlets would pick it up. Hayden needed to control the release—she needed to feed information to Emilie rather than the other way around. The information in the media at the right time could be exactly what she needed to force a settlement.

She ran upstairs and grabbed her laptop. While she finished waking up, she could track down the right Texas agency. Then when she got to the office, she'd make a few calls. By the end of the day she'd know what every agency knew about Miguel Rodriguez. Then she could search for his father and, she hoped, learn why Maricel was so scared of him.

The morning light streamed through his bedroom blinds, hitting Andrew in the eyes. He groaned and flipped over, but the damage was done. Zeus's wet nose nudged his elbow.

"All right, boy, I'm up." Andrew rose to his elbow and rubbed his eyes. Yesterday he'd e-mailed the cartoon to his editor just in time. The way it seemed to happen lately. In college, ideas had hit him everywhere he looked. Now the well was dry, and he needed to do something to get it recharged.

Zeus nudged him again, and Andrew stood. "Let's go."

A minute later the cold air hit him in the face as they entered the courtyard. Zeus sniffed around for a few minutes and then took care of business.

Andrew grabbed his paper from the lawn and opened it. Below the fold, there was a story on the Senate vacancy. Looked like there were rumbles of competition for his father.

That wouldn't sit well.

Congressman Wesley fully expected the open Senate seat to be his. He'd earned the right to occupy that office for the Commonwealth of Virginia. Maybe the governor would agree and appoint him to the vacancy, but there would be pressure opposing the selection.

Mrs. Bedford stepped onto her front stoop to grab her paper.

He waved to her. "Morning, ma'am. I tried calling that number on the card. You're right. It's a dead end."

"I was afraid you'd say that. Should I be worried?"

"Not unless you see him again. If you do, call me immediately."

"Yes sir." Her smile was tentative, but she straightened. "Do you have a minute to change a lightbulb?"

Andrew smiled. Whenever she asked for help, it meant she'd baked something fresh. She would never let him assist her without repayment of some kind. His stomach appreciated her efforts. "Come on, boy. Time to be neighborly."

Mrs. Bedford wrapped her robe tighter around her body and led the way into the small unit. "It's in the hallway. You know how I hate standing on a chair."

"And you know I wouldn't want you doing that." Who knew how long she'd lie there with a broken hip before someone realized something was wrong?

It didn't take long to change the bulb, and a minute later she handed him a foil-covered plate containing four of her delicious fresh blueberry muffins. His mouth was already watering as he walked upstairs to his condo.

When Andrew arrived at the New Beginnings office, he knew it would be a busy day. Once the afterschool crowd arrived, he wouldn't have time to focus on anything but the kids. Which was why he was there. Why he'd taken the job as a mentor in college and come back after he decided law school wasn't for him. New Beginnings and its clients had given him purpose and meaning. The first preteen he'd been paired with had impacted him more than he'd impacted the kid. Seeing how hard he tried to transition to the United States humbled Andrew.

Until the kids trickled in, he would spend the day working on the community fair, start knocking off Emilie's daunting lists. He worked at his desk for a couple hours, then yawned and stretched his back. When that didn't release the kink in his lower spine, he decided to take a quick break. A five-minute walk might help his lagging concentration. But first he left a quick message for his cousin, begging her to accept his mea culpa and help with the fair after all. Then he slid his phone into his pocket and headed for the door.

A few minutes later he stood in line at Common Grounds, determined an espresso would power him through the day—at least to lunch. He glanced at the line in front of him and noticed a soft profile, long dark hair pulled back in a messy bun. It looked as though Hayden McCarthy had either had a rough morning or a late night. She stifled a yawn that hurt to watch and then turned his way as if she sensed his attention. He grinned at her, feeling a bit like the awkward and unprepared adolescent he'd been in high school when he'd decided girls were cool.

She saw him and nodded, then shuffled forward in the line.

That didn't have the earmarks of a warm welcome. Andrew wasn't the most eligible bachelor in town for nothing. He squared his shoulders and slipped closer with his winning grin. "Good morning, Ms. McCarthy."

"I'm not sure there's anything good about it." She harrumphed, then yawned again. "Yesterday was one of those days they warn you about in law school."

"Understandable." The line moved forward

again, and the barista looked at them with bored interest. "What do you want, Hayden?"

She glanced at the board, then down at the cups. "Venti café latte, one sugar packet." She managed a smile as she added a please to the end.

"Wow, you are tired, Sunshine. I thought you were a tea gal."

She quirked a look his direction before pulling her wallet from her massive bag. "I am most days. Today calls for heavy-duty reinforcements."

He stilled her hand. "I've got this." He placed his order with the barista before she could sputter a protest, then inserted his card to pay for their overpriced caffeine. He led her to the side where they could wait for their drinks. "Anything I can help with?"

Hayden's clear eyes met his gaze with a spark of life in them. "Not unless you want to suddenly complete that law degree. Though after last night, I would urge you to reconsider. A partner 'forgot' to tell me he'd assigned something to me until after that something was due, so I had to pull an all-nighter to fix things."

Andrew grimaced in sympathy. "Yikes."

"Yeah, not the best twenty-four hours of my life, but it's over. Now back to the normal zaniness." She smiled her thanks to the man who handed her the massive cup of coffee, then inhaled the steam from her cup. When she looked back at Andrew, she already seemed more awake. "What are you doing today?"

"Other than deciding I'm a fool not to adopt wholesale Emilie's suggestions for the fair? Board meeting coming up in a couple weeks has me consumed. If they don't believe in what we're doing, nobody will." He took his drink, and then gestured to the door. "Can I walk you back to the office?"

She considered him a minute, her gaze searching his as if she wanted to weigh his soul. Then a smile warmed her face, fairly stealing his breath. "I'd like that."

Chapter 13

All afternoon Andrew's thoughts returned to that short walk with Hayden. She'd relaxed as they chatted about nothing important. He'd hated reaching her office and watching her disappear inside. Then he walked back to New Beginnings and the board report.

The heart of New Beginnings was working with recently immigrated children. At New Beginnings they could be tutored, learn English, and talk with kids or mentors who'd walked similar roads. Those expressions of interest and help could make a huge difference to their future success in the United States. Andrew made it a point to be in the community room when the kids arrived to talk with them in his version of Spanish and show a genuine interest. Because many parents worked multiple jobs to make ends meet, another adult who cared was critical to the kids' success.

It wasn't long before Andrew found the newest referral, a recent immigrant from Central America who had a good handle on English, and had him sitting with Jorge and a couple others from Mexico. They were building a Lego Mindstorm kit, a STEM activity that got them collaborating.

"What are you building today?"

"A trash compactor, Señor Andrew." Manny, a sixth grader, gave Andrew a toothy grin.

"Interesting." He had no clue where they found inspiration.

"It is good, no?" Jorge looked at him, a question in his eyes.

"Sure. You can build anything you like." These kids had limitless imaginations. Today a trash compactor, tomorrow a Mars rover. The only restriction was what they'd seen and their willingness to try.

His phone buzzed, and he nodded to an intern before stepping away. "Hello?"

"Hey, Andrew, this is Hayden."

It was crazy how great it was to hear her voice. "What's up?"

"Thanks for the coffee and walk. It really helped clear my tired brain."

He grinned even though she couldn't see it, strangely warmed by her thanks. "My pleasure. I have a feeling that's not why you called, though."

"Yeah." She puffed out a soft breath. "Could you help me with a project?"

"Maybe." He braced himself, some of the good feeling evaporating.

"Isn't the congressman interested in immigration?"

"It's one of his issues."

"Can you give me his legislative director's name? Emilie thought you could connect us and cut through red tape."

"Hayden . . ." She couldn't know how much he hated using his dad's position for private purposes. He'd heard too many stories of congressmen on US business trips who stopped off in a country so their kids could visit. He'd never been that kid and wouldn't start now.

"I wouldn't ask if I hadn't run out of sources."

He pinched the bridge of his nose and sighed. "Can you tell me anything about this?"

"You don't want to know." She paused, and he could almost see her gearing up for one more try. "Please, Andrew?"

"You can find her name with a Google search."

"Sure, but then I can't say you suggested I call."

Andrew laughed. In a world filled with politicians and their minions willing to say about anything to get in and keep their jobs, she was refreshingly straightforward. He rattled off the info.

"Thanks." Hayden paused, and Andrew searched for a reason to keep her on the phone.

He didn't have time to mess with a distraction, he reminded himself as he hung up. But Hayden McCarthy was certainly intriguing.

Hayden hung up the phone and slumped in her chair. She'd spent hours on the phone and Internet searching for someone in the federal or Texas state government who would acknowledge that Miguel Rodriguez had come into this country and been detained. One state employee at the agency that oversaw prisons had made it clear she'd need more information, and the other agencies wanted her to believe they didn't maintain a simple, searchable database. They acted as if the young man hadn't existed—and she'd believe it except for the horrific photo. She'd searched for Daniel Rodriguez, too, but without more information the searches led to hundreds of hits.

Calling Andrew had been a last-ditch effort to make progress, and one she could tell he didn't welcome. She placed a quick call to his dad's legislative director and left a message begging for help.

Her intercom buzzed, with her paralegal's line lit. "Ms. McCarthy?"

"Yes, Leigh?"

"Maricel Rodriguez is here to see you."

Hayden sat straighter and pushed the legal pads and file folders on her desk into orderly piles. "I'll be right out."

She pulled up her calendar and confirmed that the afternoon was blank, and this visit wasn't an appointment she'd overlooked. After the last meeting, Hayden thought the woman was the most reluctant plaintiff in history, but now here she was, without explanation. Hayden quickly swiped on fresh lipstick, then hurried to the reception area.

Maricel Rodriguez sat on the chair as if afraid to sink into its buttery softness. Her black slacks and cashmere sweater contrasted with the rich aubergine walls. She clutched a Coach bag in her lap and lurched to her feet when she saw Hayden.

"Señora Rodriguez. What can I do for you?" Hayden held her voice steady and kept her expression neutral. Mrs. Rodriguez would not have come to Elliott & Johnson unless she had something to say.

The woman's fingers toyed with the handle of her bag, a constant dance of agitation. "Can we go somewhere . . . *privado*?"

"My office should work."

A few minutes later, Hayden watched her client over a mug of English breakfast tea. She had taken a seat in the chair next to Maricel, rather than retreating behind her desk. Maricel's back was ramrod straight and her hands trembled around her coffee cup.

Hayden set her cup on a coaster on the desk and leaned forward. "How can I help you, Maricel?"

"You can't." Moisture pooled in the woman's dark eyes, and she set her mug on the desk.

"Then why are you here?" Hayden softened her words by placing a hand on Maricel's arm.

"Miguel's father wants progress. He says he pays too much for no information. Miguel was his heir. And he wants his son's possessions."

"That's interesting, because I can't find anything on his father. I need you to give me his address or other contact information. I'll personally update him."

"No. That will not work."

"But if he's paying for this, I need to communicate with him."

"No. Only through me and Mr. Campbell." Maricel's jaw firmed, echoing the stubbornness.

"Gerard?"

"*Sí*. What can I tell Daniel?"

"Why does he want to know?"

"It is his money."

Hayden filled her in on the procedural aspects of the case, but the dazed expression on Maricel's face communicated that she didn't understand.

Hayden sighed and tried again. "I'm working on learning information and interviewing witnesses before I refile."

"Here?"

"Because we will sue the federal government, we can sue where you live. This will make things much simpler. But I need official confirmation about where Miguel was detained and what happened." If only Snowden had been helpful.

"The death paper was not enough?"

Hayden straightened. "What do you mean? I don't have a death certificate."

"The paper I mentioned before. I gave it to Mr. Campbell with the ICE letter."

Hayden frowned as she grabbed the file. She'd allowed the photo to distract her from getting this information. A mistake she couldn't afford to make, especially when she was positive she'd never seen it. Leigh did an excellent job organizing case files and wouldn't misplace something as important as the death certificate. Neither would Gerard. A first-year associate would understand the document's importance.

Her senses went on high alert. "Do you have another copy?"

Maricel opened her bag and pulled a sheet of paper from a plastic sleeve. She held the sheet in her lap, her fingers caressing the edges. "It is all I have left."

"I'm glad you brought it." Hayden pressed

the intercom button and summoned the paralegal.

"Leigh, I need three copies right away, if you don't mind. We'll give the original back to Maricel." Eventually Hayden would obtain an original, but at this point it seemed safer in Maricel's control.

While they waited Maricel didn't say a word, but her hands never stilled. Hayden's every attempt to initiate small talk fell flat.

"How is Jorge? Is he well?"

"He tries." The woman shrugged, as if dislodging a weight. "It is hard."

"I'm sure there are many changes."

"*Sí*, and he misses Miguel."

"Were they close?"

The woman waved her hand in an *así-así* motion. One that suggested they weren't.

Hayden jotted a note to follow up when Maricel wasn't so anxious and uncomfortable. "Where are you working?"

The woman stiffened, raised her chin, and met Hayden's gaze for the first time. "I do not work."

But Jorge had told Hayden his mother was at work Saturday. Was it a language issue? Hayden made a note and continued. "How do you live?"

"I am sponsored." The sponsor must be wealthy, if Maricel's clothing was any indication. "I have time to establish before I work." She slumped against the seat as if the small speech had exhausted her.

Hayden watched the woman, mystified. There was much more to her than she understood. Leigh brought the death certificate back and Hayden scanned it, then looked at Maricel. "How can I help you? You're here, but I'm unsure why. I can't help if I don't know."

"Miguel's father, he wanted me to check on the progress." She sank back into the chair, her accent heavier, causing Hayden to lean in to catch the words.

"I'll gladly update him."

Maricel's eyes widened, and she shook her head. "No. You talk only to me. You do not want to talk to him."

"Okay." Hayden waited, but the woman remained silent. "I can use the information on the death certificate to ask better questions." It would fill in a few gaps in her knowledge of Miguel's story, but wasn't enough alone. "It's more than I had before. Thank you."

"You will tell me everything?"

"Yes ma'am. Everything."

Maricel's eyes glistened as she blinked rapidly. "*Gracias*." She sniffed, then stood. "I must leave." She started to the door, then paused and turned back. "Promise. Everything." Desperation filled her gaze, more than a grieving mother should have.

"As soon as I can."

Hayden followed Maricel out of her office and

stopped at Leigh's desk and asked her assistant to request a certified copy of the death certificate. A new commitment to the case rose within her, accompanied by the desire to do everything possible to heal a mother's broken heart. In her office doorway she paused, then headed to Gerard's office. She knocked on his door and heard his muffled "Come in."

He was on the phone, but motioned her to a chair with the look of a highly important partner who couldn't be bothered on anything less than a serious request. Maybe coming to him about the disappearing death certificate was a waste of time.

Hayden had about talked herself out of staying when he hung up and glanced at his watch. "I've got five minutes. Will that be long enough?"

"Yes sir." Hayden forged ahead. "This is about the Rodriguez case."

"Hard to call it a case when you haven't refiled the complaint yet."

"We'll get there. Mrs. Rodriguez just left my office."

"You don't have to meet with her if she hasn't called ahead. Manage your clients." A flash of impatience in his eyes warned her to hurry.

"She told me she brought you a death certificate when she first met with you."

"Sure. Should be in the file."

"It wasn't."

"Then it got lost. What's the problem, McCarthy?"

"Has anyone been in the file other than you and Leigh?"

He leaned back in his chair, putting extra distance between them. "What kind of question is that? This is a law firm. Any associate or paralegal has access to it."

Something was up. This wasn't typical Gerard. His gaze wandered to his phone and then his computer. Hayden wanted to pursue the matter, but every signal said to leave it alone. "Okay," she said. "We'll have a certified copy shortly."

"Then get the complaint ready to refile. This is a priority matter."

"I need to go to Texas first."

"Why would you do that when the client can't front expenses?"

"You're the one who told me to request an advance deposition of the center's director before he conveniently forgets everything he knows." She gritted her teeth against the terse words she wanted to say. "It's a valid strategy."

Gerard took off his glasses, rubbed his eyes, and then replaced the glasses before looking at her. "Hayden, you know I agree with you, but the others won't front the expenses. My hands are tied. You'll have to get the information another way. Understood?"

"No. I can't just tell my client I can't do what we need to win this case."

"We don't have a choice."

Hayden could tell she wasn't going to get anywhere so she stood, but as she left his office, she heard him pick up the phone. She slowed and then overheard him say, "We have a problem."

Chapter 14

Hayden hurried down King Street to Il Porto, her favorite Italian restaurant, set on a corner of the historic district. She was more than ready to shake the trying day and relax with friends.

She glanced at her watch. Twenty minutes late. When she reached the entryway, Emilie waved at her from their usual table in the back corner. Hayden walked through the stucco-and-brick room, past tables covered in red- or green-checked tablecloths, her heels echoing against the red tile floor.

Emilie, Jaime, and Caroline had already ordered drinks and appetizers, and all three women greeted Hayden with wide smiles. Caroline jumped to her four-inch heels with a squeal and gave Hayden a hug. "It's about time, girl. I thought you'd stood us up, but Emilie insisted you'd get here."

With help from Savannah Daniels, the four young women had roomed together as they waded through more textbooks, legal briefs, and moot court experiences than Hayden had believed possible. The best part? They'd all graduated and still liked each other. Their dinners at Il Porto convened as often as the four could match their calendars—something that happened less and less frequently as the professional demands on their time escalated.

"She was ready to march to the office to get you." Jaime grinned at Hayden as she swirled her straw through an iced tea. "Can't you see Caroline teetering down the street in those stilts?"

"Might break an ankle." Emilie grimaced.

"Nope, I am a pro at these. All those ridiculous pageants my mother put me through were good for balance." Caroline wrinkled her nose and squeezed Hayden again. "It has been way too long, girl. Dish."

Emilie laughed. "Let the lady order her drink." She pulled Hayden to the empty chair. "Oh, wait. I already did that for her."

Hayden could feel the tension melt as she laughed with her friends. These women were her lifeline. They had seen her through the hardest intellectual experience of her life, and they would be there when she needed it, just as she was for them.

Friendships like these were irreplaceable.

She looked up as Emilie suddenly waved frantically at someone, and Hayden turned to see Andrew Wesley waiting by the hostess stand. She began to smile until she noticed he had someone with him. Someone tall, with beautiful, perfect blond hair arranged in an elaborate messy bun and dressed like a Banana Republic model. Hayden slid lower in her seat, hoping he wouldn't come by their table to say hi. Not when he had someone as perfect as that woman with him.

Andrew nodded to her, smiling, before turning back to his gorgeous date. Hayden sighed and turned her attention to her friends. These women would never make her feel less than.

She reprimanded herself. Where had that thought come from? Andrew hadn't done anything more or less than meet her gaze. The man couldn't help that he moved in an orbit completely separate from hers. He came from a family of financial and political privilege. She . . . didn't.

The four friends were soon engrossed in catching up. Caroline was loving her life of research and writing, and was an adjunct instructor at George Mason.

Jaime, on the other hand, was restless. Hayden had wondered how her friend would handle providing a defense for clients who had probably done the crimes they were accused of committing. It was one thing to believe in a criminal justice system based upon "innocent until proven guilty," and quite another to actively engage in the fight day after brutal day.

Jaime swirled her straw through her Coke. "If I have one more client who battered his wife or significant other, I'm going to run screaming from the courtroom." She ran her fork through her food. "It's like the judges look at me and think, 'There's the gal to get these guys off.' Who are we kidding? I'm the last person to defend them."

Caroline reached across the table and squeezed Jaime's hand. "They can't know."

"That's what I tell myself, because if they did . . ." Her words trailed off and her eyes brightened with suspicious moisture. Then she took a deep breath. Few people knew about her family's tragedy.

"How can we help?" Hayden hated feeling helpless to aid her friend.

"Let me know if you hear of a job?" Jaime sniffed and then swiped a finger under each eye. "Some days are just too hard to stay there."

Hayden nodded. Most jobs had those up-and-down moments. Still, Jaime's carried more opportunities for challenging days than the average. "I'll pray for you."

"Don't waste your time. I'll be fine." Jaime held up a hand as if shielding herself from Hayden's offer. "But you can pray for my clients. They're the ones who need it."

Hayden nodded, even as she disagreed. But this wasn't the time to push. Jaime knew that Hayden believed in a Savior who could carry you on your hardest days and bring hope into the darkest corners. Hayden would keep praying that someday her friend would know that reality for herself.

An hour later the group hugged their good-byes on the sidewalk. The time had given Hayden a chance to connect with people who really knew her and liked her anyway. That was a precious gift in a world that existed on long-distance social media connections.

Caroline squeezed her an extra moment. "Don't disappear on me again, girl." Her southern accent warmed the words.

"Yes, Miss Caroline." Hayden tightened her end of the hug, then stepped back. "Don't let the judge take advantage of you. I guarantee the court will still run if you don't work eighty hours."

"Maybe."

Caroline turned with a squeal to Jaime and repeated the ritual. Saying good-bye to Caroline wasn't for those on a tight schedule.

Chapter 15

Andrew stared at the e-mail sitting in his in-box. All the lights turned on in his studio couldn't push back the darkness the one message had abruptly ushered into his world.

You think you're so clever, using a pseudonym. Surprise! It doesn't take a good researcher long to untangle the truth.

That was it. The entire message. The blinking cursor at the end of the last sentence mocked him.

He stared at the illuminated screen and ran his fingers through his hair.

This was the last thing his dad needed right now. The news that his son, the one who refused to follow the party line and join the march to ever greater things in politics, was political cartoonist Roger Walters.

As far as his parents knew, his cartooning days had ended after college. He'd tried to quit since all eyes were on the rising congressman and his family.

Now Dad was one governor's appointment away from the US Senate. From day one his mom had been an equal partner in the march to ever bigger and greater arenas. Ultimately, anything less than the White House would be falling short of the goal.

It was in the editorial cartoons that Andrew could say all the things he really felt about the crazy world of politics and its convoluted games. His audience had slowly expanded from the William and Mary student newspaper to the *Richmond Dispatch* and from there to syndication.

He had been so careful. From the very beginning he had worked under a pseudonym that couldn't be traced. Yet one e-mail was all it took to threaten his sarcastic stabs at the political world.

He clicked on it again. A Hotmail address.

Doubtless a bogus account.

He sent a reply to confirm his instincts.

Within moments a ding alerted him to a failed delivery message.

Only a handful of people knew Roger Walters's real identity. Maybe one of the guys thought it would be hilarious to give him a scare. Andrew grabbed his cell phone and called the most likely culprit, Luke Standish. A friend since prep school, Luke had an offbeat sense of humor and the technical skills to pull off this prank. And if he wasn't behind it, he had the know-how to find whoever sent the e-mail.

Of course his editor, Michael Turner, knew his true identity, but most of their communication was done through an e-mail address in Roger's name and a PO box Roger rented. He was even paid through a fake company. Before he alerted his editor to the problem, he'd have Luke check on the e-mail, using all his IT skills to track the sender.

"Andrew, what's up?"

"Hey Luke, quick question. You told anyone about the cartoons?" It was blunt, but needed to be.

"Course not. Who would I tell? No one I know pays attention to the editorial page."

"Ouch, I make my living there."

"Sorry, man, but you know it's truth."

"You didn't say anything somewhere someone could overhear?"

"Andrew . . ."

"I know." Andrew sighed and leaned his stool back on two legs. "I got an e-mail."

"I get five hundred a day."

"Yeah, but this one claims to know I'm the cartoonist."

"Man." Luke huffed out a breath. "Forward it, and I'll see what I can discover."

"I don't think there's much. The address bounced when I tried to reply."

"You're an amateur. Leave it to me."

After they hung up, Andrew felt marginally okay. He had to decide whether to warn his dad that syndicated Congress-hating cartoonist Roger Walters was his son.

That conversation would be an easy one.

Sure. And Greenland wasn't slowly melting away.

———————

Hayden and Emilie walked home, enjoying the balmy evening. In a few days the Cherry Blossom Festival would open, and the trees were doing their best to show off. The dogwoods and cherry blossoms were on full display.

"You've been quiet, Hayden. Bad news?" Emilie's words were soft, but Hayden knew her friend would probe until she answered.

"No. Not really." She put away her phone as

they went up the short walk to their front door. Hayden unlocked the door and tossed her jacket over the banister. "Just my mom checking on me. Always makes me nostalgic for how things were . . . before . . ."

Emilie leaned against the counter. "I'm sorry."

"Thanks." What more could she say? Emilie was one of the few who knew about her family history. Life was good, and she had moved on, but some days the if-onlys pricked more. "Good night."

Hayden needed to focus on something other than how she'd believed her dad was innocent. That he'd been framed by his financial manager for embezzlement that rocked the large Omaha-based company.

The prosecutor had considered it an open-and-shut case with no room for alternate theories and suspects. The jury had bought his presentation of the facts so wholeheartedly that deliberations had only lasted an hour.

And Hayden's heart shattered when her daddy was placed in handcuffs and led from the courtroom, while her mother sat there without a tear or any sign of emotion. She believed he was innocent until she'd reviewed the case file when she'd finally had time after law school. He was not.

Hayden paused at the top of the stairs. A wall of white shelves filled with books lined the landing.

The soft gray space usually filled her with peace. Tonight she just wanted to flee.

She grabbed a Colleen Coble novel from her stack of to-be-read books. Maybe she needed a simple escape into book world. She sank onto her desk chair, a white chair on wheels with a soft pillow to support her back, and opened the book, but an image of Miguel sprawled on the floor superimposed itself over the page. She tried to force the image from her mind, but couldn't.

His story had been entrusted to her, and she wasn't sure what to do with it.

Father, help me.

She believed God could hear and see her struggles from such a short request. At times she had deeply known that truth. Now she felt the loss of being pulled away by the rush and busyness of a full calendar. If she grabbed a devotional now, it would feel like a check-the-box motion, the exact opposite of what her faith should be.

Once her dad had seemed like such a good model for her heavenly Father. But if he could be accused of something so terrible, what did that mean about God? The God who had seemed closer than her daddy had seemed to move away across space. She had slowly made her way back to Him through the distractions of law school and starting a career, but it wasn't the same. She knew that in the deepest part of her heart.

Hayden rubbed her tired eyes, then shoved away

from her desk. Maybe a good night's sleep would help her focus. But as she climbed into bed, the strange comment of Gerard's that she had overheard came back to worry her. *We have a problem.* Was she the problem he referenced? What should she do about that?

APRIL 1

The cars multiplied as he neared the city. Frustration pooled in his veins as he slowed with the rest of traffic. He had always avoided large urban areas like Mexico City, preferring the family estate in the mountains. Clear air to smog. Trails traveled by the occasional donkey to packed highways.

He blew air slowly through his nose. Breathing in, then breathing out the anxiety building in him.

This American city might be big, but with the help of technology he would find the address. The question was what to do then. He had often overheard *el jefe*'s men talk about their missions and how they successfully eliminated problems. He had never thought he would find himself doing the same.

He couldn't afford to get noticed. Yet he had to locate that flash drive.

Apparently the information on the device Miguel stole could destroy the empire. Miguel had been smart enough to realize that. Could Rafael do the same? Could he use the information to save himself?

He no longer heard from *el jefe*, but someone lower in the organization. The instructions arrived with a credit card and address, and it seemed a dark sedan was always behind him now.

El jefe was making his presence known. Rafael expected to meet him at any moment.

Receive his next instructions from the man himself.

Had he somehow overlooked the device in his adrenaline-laced horror after he killed Miguel? His hands trembled on the wheel as he tried to push the memory of those frantic moments from his mind.

He shook his head to clear his vision and focused on the highway.

Now to find someplace to hole up while he did reconnaissance. Maybe tonight he'd stay at a classy hotel. One last stab at the man who had sent him on this journey.

If he was successful, then what? The thought of claiming a place in the family no longer brought hope and pride to his heart. Instead, it felt like an unbearable weight. But perhaps here in the *Estados Unidos* he could disappear. He had new documents.

He took an off-ramp and turned onto a road named King. Shops bled into a high school and then homes to a modern office area. He found a hotel just a mile from his destination. Now to shift from transit to reconnaissance.

Future plans would have to wait.

Chapter 16

The next morning Hayden arrived at the office and found a steaming mug of tea and fresh coffee cake on her desk. It didn't matter that it was seven thirty, somehow Leigh had beat her in, and with goodies.

The woman was a lifesaver.

As she settled her attaché case beneath her desk and shifted the tea so she could wake her computer, Hayden paused.

Something felt odd about her office.

As she scanned the surfaces and then quickly unlocked and opened her desk drawers, she decided she was overly tired. Nothing seemed out of place. Not that she was meticulous enough to know for sure, but she didn't see anything clearly wrong. Then she noticed the Rodriguez case file tucked in alphabetical order in her files. She'd left it in the front of the drawer, so she could easily grab it. She walked to her doorway.

"Leigh, did you move the Rodriguez file?"

"No ma'am. Just set down your tea and cake."

"Thanks." Maybe she remembered wrong.

The morning passed in a blur while she fielded questions about different cases. Most revolved around answering discovery in a couple of them. She spent lunch working on a summary judgment motion in a government contracts dispute in between bites of a slightly stale sandwich.

She stood and stretched her arms over her head and then twisted side to side trying to ease the feeling she'd melded to her chair. Midstretch she noticed Seth standing in the doorway, grinning. Heat climbed her neck.

"You've never needed to stretch?"

"Not with my door open." He pushed from the doorway and walked to a chair. "Got a minute to brainstorm?"

"Want me to get Angela?"

"Not this time. It's about one of her cases."

An even better reason to get Angela in the room. Hayden frowned and wondered what he was really up to. "Okay. You should probably explain."

"Remember the Barnes case from last winter?"

"Sure. Angela slaved on the summary judgment motion and hearing." A summary judgment motion was one way to kill a case or part of it before it went to trial. It was a key strategy and tool for narrowing a case's scope, and Angela excelled at building a solid foundation for them.

"The other side filed a motion to correct errors with the appellate court, alleging she falsified an affidavit. It's not signed by the attesting witness."

"A key witness?" Had to be.

He nodded. "Without the affidavit there's no

evidence to support the motion. The motion falls apart."

"You've confirmed the allegations with the affiant?"

"Yep. Claims he never heard from Angela, let alone gave her information for an affidavit. Swears it's not his signature."

Hayden leaned back in her chair. This was not good on any level. "You have to let Angela know."

"She does. Gave me the file today. Maybe she wanted to cover it up and then decided she needed help."

That didn't sound like her friend. "Then she came to the right person."

"But I have to tell Garrison." Paul Garrison was a straight-laced partner who sat on the Virginia ethics committee. He would be horrified that one of Elliott & Johnson's star associates would do something so underhanded.

"Can you wait until tomorrow?"

Seth leaned forward and placed his elbows on his knees, his gaze intent. "I'm not going down with her."

"I'm not asking you to." Then what was she doing? She glanced at her watch. Almost four. Seth really only needed to hold off an hour. Which must be what he really wanted to do, or he'd be in Garrison's office right now. "Give me a chance to talk to Angela. See what happened. There has to be an explanation."

Hayden refused to believe Angela had done something unethical. At the same time, part of her mind whispered she'd believed the same of her father. She needed to evaluate Seth's claim, see whether there could be any merit to it. "I need a little time."

"I won't contact him until morning, but if he asks, I'm not lying."

"Thank you."

Seth nodded, then pushed to his feet. Hayden's phone rang, and he left her office as silently as he'd arrived.

"Hayden McCarthy."

"Did I catch you at a bad time?"

She realized that her words had held a hard edge—not her usual warm welcome-to-the-best-firm-in-town tone. "Yes. No. What can I do for you, Andrew?"

That was the golden question. Andrew watched the group of young men playing a loose game of American touch football in the field along the George Washington Parkway, their Spanish mixing with English. A jet taking off from Reagan National roared overhead, and he cleared his throat.

"I haven't heard from Emilie in a couple days."

"Why don't you call her? She's talked about you this week." There was a hesitant note to her voice, as if she couldn't figure out his real purpose. Not a question he could answer.

"Here's a quick hypothetical. Is it a crime to send someone a threatening e-mail?"

"Depends."

"On what?"

"Intent. How did the sender expect it to be received? How did the recipient perceive the e-mail? The state sent from and received in could also impact the outcome."

Silence settled between them, broken by clicking on a keyboard and the kids' football game.

"Andrew . . . if you don't need anything else, I really need to get back to work."

Jorge broke past a larger boy and sprinted toward the picnic tables that represented the west end zone. Andrew grinned as he watched his kids embrace Jorge in the way of young men, acknowledging his touchdown with whooping, hollering, and high fives.

"Look, Emilie hasn't called me back, and I need to talk to her. When you see her tonight, let her know, okay?"

"Wait." There was a soft expulsion of air. "Has she really been ignoring your calls?"

"Yes." It wasn't like his cousin. Sure, she put on the act of being a ditzy blonde when it suited her purposes, but she wasn't rude or irresponsible. "Maybe she's getting everything ready for our Cherry Blossom seats."

Hayden laughed, a rich sound, one without a

hint of flirtation in it. "She's got plans for the parade with her latest guy."

"What if you came instead?" The words just slipped out, but why not? It could be enjoyable to spend a couple hours with Hayden, taking in the trees' showy display before watching the parade. It was pretty clear she didn't have an interest in him, so he should ask her to attend the fund-raiser too. That would keep his mom at bay and make the evening bearable.

"When do you need an answer?" Hayden's words yanked him from his thoughts.

"Tomorrow works. I need to let my dad's staff know how many tickets I'll use." He grimaced as he said the words, but without the stash in the congressman's office, he couldn't get access to the parade without fighting for a decent vantage point. "If you don't want to see the parade, you can let me know Saturday morning. It's easy to pick you up and head downtown."

"I've lived in northern Virginia seven years and never been."

"Seriously? That's practically un-American. You do know people travel from around the world to see these flowers."

"Never a tourist in your own backyard." She breathed out a laugh. "First it was law school keeping me preoccupied. Then there was the clerkship, and now it's the firm. Time got away from me."

"Then you definitely need to see them. The blossoms are on track to amazing."

"All right. Pick me up at ten?"

"Sounds good." He jotted an old-fashioned note. "We can stroll around the Tidal Basin and then grab coffee."

"I'll probably need to work in the afternoon." She sighed. "This case needs attention."

Sounded like she needed some serious time off, not just a couple hours. Like his parents, she was married to her job, unless he could help her break free. "Anything I can do to help?"

She chuckled. "Not unless you work at Elliott & Johnson."

"I avoided that fate by dropping out my first year. See you Saturday."

Andrew hung up and leaned back in his chair. The weekend was definitely looking up.

Chapter 17

FRIDAY, APRIL 7

"I didn't do anything wrong." Angela's face was pinched as she huddled in the chair in Hayden's office. "I don't know how the affidavit got changed. Or why the witness denies he talked to me."

Her friend's gaze never wavered from Hayden's.

"Do you have any proof?"

"I pulled up my digital time logs for the case. Every one mentioning I talked with Garrison is gone. It's like IT scrubbed the records."

"Why would they do that?"

"Your guess is as good as mine. All I know is it's gone. I'm still looking for my paper notes."

As digital as Elliott & Johnson had become, the digital as well as paper originals could be gone too. It would be easy for someone to slip over to a dedicated drive and delete unwanted files—especially if that person wanted to frame another attorney. You didn't have to be in IT to pull it off. "Any chance you took those home?"

"No. It's against firm policy." Angela scrubbed her face, then shrugged. "Why would someone do this? I'm a team player."

"Something strange is going on." Hayden filled Angela in on Gerard's odd comments and the feeling that someone had been in her office, though she hadn't found evidence. "It started with the Rodriguez case."

"I've got it." Leigh skidded into Hayden's office waving a Post-it note in her hand, her peasant skirt swaying around her legs. She abruptly stopped when she noticed Angela. "Sorry, ladies. I finally got through to the right person. Texas isn't so different after all. Find the right woman, and the rest falls into place."

Angela stood. "I'll keep looking for the files. Thanks, Hayden."

Hayden watched Angela leave, a tightness in her chest at the way her friend was being framed. The why eluded her. Then she turned to Leigh. "What are you talking about?"

"I found the person who can give you the information you need on Miguel's time in Texas. I tried to talk to her, but she insisted she'd talk to the family's representative after she collected the file." She handed the note to Hayden. "Here you go."

Hayden settled back in her chair, a smile tweaking her lips. "You seem certain."

"Oh, honey, I'm positive. This is the best thing to happen since Maricel Rodriguez walked through the firm's door. Call in fifteen minutes, and she'll have Miguel's information."

"Thanks, Leigh." Hayden snagged the paper her paralegal dangled in front of her. She needed this break in the case. The guts of the revised complaint were sketched out, but until she had more data—when he was detained, any notes the facility had—it was a rough sketch. If she didn't hear from Director Snowden or his attorney about the deposition she'd requested, she'd have to start calling a couple times a day. Without that information, the new complaint wouldn't make it past a Trial Rule 12(b)(6) failure to state a claim.

The fifteen minutes stretched as Hayden watched the clock and prayed, each tick of the clock feeling like an hour. Finally she dialed the number Leigh had scrawled on the note.

"This is Judy Foster."

After exchanging introductions and small talk slowed down by the Texas drawl, Hayden steered the woman toward Miguel.

"My assistant told me you could help piece together when he was detained and confirm where he was held."

"Sure enough."

Hayden waited, attempting to be patient, as computer keys clacked in the background.

"Border Patrol picked him up December 17. He was held in a general facility down near the border, the first place to work into the system."

A few more clicks while Hayden continued to wait.

"Here we go. Then he was sent to the JD facility. It only takes juveniles, and he barely fit that definition."

"JD?"

"Juvenile detention, near Waco. Actual address is some small town near there. Should be turning eighteen in a few weeks, so he still qualifies. Not sure where they'll move him next."

Hayden blinked. Did the woman not realize Miguel was dead?

"Anything else you can tell me?"

Judy paused. "Can you remind me why you need to know?"

"His family is trying to locate him." Well, trying to track down the details. She hoped God would forgive her that little stretch of the truth.

"There's nothing else here."

Hayden froze, her pen suspended above the legal pad. "What do you mean?"

"Just that. Nothing's been recorded since his transfer. If he had a medical issue or something else to note, it would be here. Since his file is blank, he must be keeping his nose clean and out of trouble."

Hayden tried to process this information. How did her client have a death certificate if the state of Texas believed this young man was alive and in the JD facility? Had her client been lied to? Or had Judy lied? Her mind conjured up the image of Miguel's very dead body. No, Miguel was very dead, which meant someone had purposely not entered that information in the state database—or had purged it.

Her pulse pounded in her temple.

"Anything else I can do for you?" A tinge of impatience colored Judy's voice as another phone rang in the background.

Hayden cleared her throat. "I appreciate your help. If you have time, this young man's family would appreciate learning anything else you have. They're concerned about him."

"Sure. I'll fax what I have."

How could Miguel have disappeared from the system? He'd died in custody! A cover-up suggested more than murder.

Hayden doodled circles on her legal pad while she tried to make sense of the information. Stewing at her desk wasn't helping her find answers, so she grabbed her jacket and purse and paused at Leigh's desk. "I'm stepping out to grab something for lunch. Need anything?"

"No thanks, I packed one today." Leigh held up a brown bag and then made a face at it. "Though if you wanted to grab a pastry from La Madeline, that would balance out the salad I brought." She rolled her eyes. "This is what I get for trying to be healthy."

Hayden laughed. "I'll see what I can do."

Rather than take the elevator to the lobby, Hayden charged down the stairs as fast as her heels allowed. When she exited the lobby, she took a moment to simply stand in the sunlight and inhale. Seagulls swooped around the marina, and she tasted moisture in the air. The warmth of the sun on her face felt delicious and infused her with energy. Much better than spending another unproductive hour at her desk.

She decided to join the seagulls and headed to the water. If she strolled along the Potomac she'd get the best of fresh air without the crowds around the restaurants. She could always grab a quick bite at a restaurant along King Street; what she couldn't always do was take time to move in the sunshine. She wished she'd brought her tennis shoes. When she'd moved to DC, she'd thought the women who wore tennis shoes with their hose and suits looked a little odd. Now she knew it was practical for moments like this.

As she moved along the sidewalk, Hayden pumped her arms and forced her mind to clear. If she focused on something else, maybe her subconscious could wrestle with Miguel's murder and disappearance.

She'd found a good rhythm and was looking for a water fountain when she spotted a group of kids playing in a field. It looked like an ad hoc game of soccer or rugby as one kid took off down the field kicking a ball. All around him, other kids—mostly boys, a couple of girls—chased the first. It looked like barely contained chaos. Two kids ricocheted off each other and onto the sidewalk.

One screamed something in Spanish, then pulled the smaller kid to his feet.

"Everyone all right over there?" A man jogged toward the boys, then slowed when he spotted her. "Hayden."

"Andrew?" He didn't have his GQ style going. Instead, in well-broken-in jeans and a sloppy Georgetown sweatshirt thrown over a collared shirt, he looked like an overgrown college student. "What are you doing?"

He grinned at the kids, who now jostled toward him. "The school some of my kids attend had electrical problems, so they showed up early." Some boys pushed another into Andrew, and he sent a mock glare over his shoulder. "What are you doing? Breaking free of the firm?"

"I guess." She squared her hands on her hips and met his gaze. "Actually, I'm working on a case."

He glanced around and made a sweeping motion with his arms. "Here?"

She tapped her forehead. "In here. It works." Well, she hoped it worked, but she didn't need to let him know how desperate she was.

"Next time you might try walking shoes. They're more practical for strategy marches."

"I'll keep that in mind." Her gaze swept the field. "Speaking of shoes, you might want to have these kids get their shoes on so you aren't overrun with pneumonia."

His grin widened. "I knew you cared, McCarthy." The kids started tugging his arms, pulling him toward the field.

"Señor, we play."

"*Por favor?*" A boy of about ten with the most adorable gap between his front teeth tugged harder.

Andrew laughed, then let them pull him back. "See you in the morning. Ten sharp."

Hayden nodded even as she considered backing

out. Maybe she didn't want to spend part of her Saturday with the man. She wasn't sure what to make of him.

But standing here watching Mr. GQ play football with a group of junior high students who adored and trusted him wouldn't help her decipher Miguel's situation. Nor would remembering how his blue eyes sparked with interest when he looked at her.

If she planned to take the morning off to attend the Cherry Blossom Festival with Mr. Wesley, she'd better stop staring at him and get back to work.

Chapter 18

When Hayden set a pastry bag on Leigh's desk, her paralegal grimaced. "Mr. Campbell is waiting for you."

"In my office?"

"Yep." Leigh slid the bag into a desk drawer. "He told me to call your cell, but you didn't answer. Seemed upset you took lunch."

"I must have muted it." Hayden puffed out a sigh as she checked the phone. "All right. Let's see what's up."

She stopped as soon as she entered, because instead of waiting in the cramped chair in front of her desk, the partner was plopped in her desk chair rifling through the files on her small credenza. "Can I help you?"

"Get this case refiled." He held up an accordion file that contained the Rodriguez investigation. "Our client is getting impatient and threatening to switch firms."

Hayden frowned, as her last interaction with Maricel hadn't indicated her client was unhappy about the case. "Maricel didn't say anything to me."

"She's not footing the bill, McCarthy."

"Then let me talk to her husband."

"No can do . . . I'll run interference. What I need from you is reportable movement."

Hayden let his words settle between them. "Gerard, is there anything I need to know? Does it involve Daniel Rodriguez?"

"Not anything to tell."

"All right."

His look telegraphed to stop pushing.

"I'm working on it. Had a conversation this morning with a woman in Texas who doesn't realize Miguel is dead, let alone died while detained."

Gerard spun his hand in a "get talking" motion.

"How can Texas not know? He died in its custody. The government has files on everything, so this smells like a cover-up." She took a deep breath and studied her boss. Would he consider her idea? The only way to know was to ask.

"Director Snowden received the notice of deposition. I want to press him for a date and head to Texas. I can poke around while there."

"No."

"Then I can't file the complaint."

"Then you don't have a job."

Hayden froze and her thoughts whirled. Hadn't he threatened her job when he'd told her to get to Texas earlier this week? "I don't understand."

"There are no firm funds for extra expenses. I've already told you this, McCarthy."

"But you also told me to get there."

He looked blankly at her.

She took another tack. "It's not extra if there's no case without it."

"Find another way." His jaw squared as his stare bored into her.

"If this client is so important, it's critical we do this case right."

"To the partners it's simple." He leaned forward and rose out of his chair to lean on the desk. "Get the complaint refiled and the case settled or you're done."

She nodded. "I've spent a week trying to find information. I've talked to our client and so many people in different agencies my head's spinning. I've scoured the file and used our resources. It's like Miguel ceased to exist when he crossed the border."

"Then work the death certificate angle. Someone issued it."

Hayden didn't bother telling him Leigh had called that agency a dozen times and heard nothing, not even a reply voice mail. "I'll keep trying."

He took a deep breath and met her gaze. "Hayden, I picked you for this case. Convinced the partners to go along with the assignment. You can do this. Don't get so caught up in having all the information that you don't refile."

"But we need essential information."

"That's what post-filing discovery is for." He pushed to his feet, knocking a file to the floor. "Get it done."

Hayden bit back words as he left. If she waited, she risked more evidence being scrubbed as squeaky-clean as the file Judy Foster had read. She sank into her chair and clutched her head. Gerard was usually an intense but easy partner to work with. He knew what he wanted, pointed you in the right direction, and then got out of the way. Not this time. She had a preferred way to handle this case, but he'd made it clear she'd have to file regardless of what she thought, or risk her job. The thought sank like a stone in her stomach. With trembling fingers she gathered the files Gerard had rummaged through and reordered them. Then she picked up the Rodriguez file he'd dropped.

"I'm sorry to interrupt." Leigh's face was a mask of apology. She set a package roughly the size of a file box on the corner of Hayden's desk. "A courier dropped this off while you were at lunch."

"Thanks."

"Is there anything I can get you?" Concern laced her voice.

Hayden shook her head as she gathered her scissors from her desk drawer. "I'm fine." If she said it with enough force maybe she'd convince herself.

Leigh nodded, then returned to her desk in the hallway. Hayden looked for a return address on the package, but there was only the name of a Texas town she'd never heard of. Maybe they could track the shipping account if needed. When she opened the box, she found an old issue of the *Waco Tribune Herald* smushed around a black backpack. The bag was nondescript, with wear and tear that indicated it had been through intense use.

Hayden tugged it free and examined the outside. There were no tags or identifying labels. Then she opened the front pocket and ran her fingers around the inside. Empty. She unzipped the top and saw a hodgepodge of belongings carelessly stuffed inside. She pulled each item out and inventoried two pairs of jeans, a couple T-shirts, a hoodie, some socks and underwear. All looked to be the right size for an average male teenager.

Hayden frowned and looked in the box. Underneath where the backpack had sat was an envelope. When she opened it, she found a short letter addressed to Maricel Rodriguez.

Señora Rodriguez,

Inside are the sole items your son brought into the United States at the time of his detention. Stop your search. This is all there ever was.

Carlton Snowden, Director

Hayden reread the letter. What a callous way to transmit the belongings of a dead child. She set the letter down and checked the pockets of the jeans and hoodie and then shook each item of clothing. Nothing had been tucked inside a pocket or crumpled with the mess of clothes. If this was truly all Miguel brought to the United States, it didn't provide a motive for murder.

She buzzed Leigh. "Could you let Mr. Campbell know we have Miguel's backpack? Then I'd like you to create a short inventory and put it in locked storage. We can let his mother know it's here if she'd like to claim it."

As she hung up, Hayden's gaze fell back on the backpack. It was a sad testimony to a life cut short for seemingly no reason.

Chapter 19

SATURDAY, APRIL 8

The forecast called for showers around noon. Showers that Andrew hoped never appeared, so he and Hayden could enjoy the Cherry Blossom Festival. He needed the distraction after receiving another e-mail from Anonymous. Guess this guy didn't operate on a work week time frame.

The message was equally short this time.

What would your dad think if he knew? What would the party and hotshot donors think? I'd like to find out.

Nothing like reading that over a mug of coffee first thing Saturday morning. Andrew considered the fallout that might loom with exposure. Some power brokers wouldn't mind. They had a good sense of humor. Others would demand his head.

Andrew studied his tablet screen, but the words didn't suddenly morph into a message about a pleasant surprise. As a kid he'd thought the Lone Ranger and other masked men had an aura of sophistication and mystery. He didn't want to learn what it was like to become unmasked, especially since that always caused trouble for his childhood heroes.

The next e-mail in his in-box revealed that Luke hadn't been able to track down the source of the first message. Andrew reread the anonymous e-mails and felt anger boil inside him.

He had planned to use the next hour finishing details on this week's cartoon. A vote on legalizing recreational marijuana use had seemed like the perfect subject when he'd started the week.

He ran his fingers through his hair and vigorously scrubbed his scalp.

He sat at the table another few minutes, tried to think and pray, felt nothing except the slightest urge to tell his editor. Where one e-mail had felt like a fluke, the second made it an ugly reality that had to be confronted. It might be Saturday, but Michael would either take his call or Andrew would leave a cryptic message.

"Turner."

"Hey, Michael." Andrew told the editor about the two e-mails. "Has anything surfaced about the true identity of Roger Walters?"

"We treat it like the Holy Grail around here. Only two or three of us know your name."

"No security breaches or anything like that?"

Michael harrumphed, his New York attitude breaking out a bit. "Nope. Holy Grail, man."

Andrew rubbed his damp palms on his jeans.

158

"All right. Let me know if anything comes up, okay?"

"Sure. And since we're talking . . . you have something coming by Tuesday?"

"It'll be ready. Just needs some finishing work."

"Perfect. Talk to ya then."

Andrew stared at the phone a moment before tossing it on the table. He headed up to his loft and studied the sketch on his drawing desk. The sketch needed spit and polish before it was ready to scan and send over, but it wasn't bad.

He pulled out a black Prismacolor pen and deepened the dark boundary of the White House. A few light strokes and he'd added a shadow.

A timer beeped from downstairs, and he capped the pen before replacing it in its position. Time to put the e-mails and cartoon out of his mind and instead focus on cherry blossoms and Hayden McCarthy.

"What am I supposed to wear?" Hayden stared in the mirror while Emilie lounged on her bed. Agreeing to go to the Cherry Blossom Festival with Andrew Wesley had been a terrible idea. "He'll take one look at me and know he's completely lost his mind."

Emilie flipped to a page in the magazine she'd brought upstairs with her and then handed the issue to her. "Take a look."

Hayden glanced at the cover and frowned. "The

Insider Washington Most Eligible Bachelor issue. Why would I want to see this?" Then she looked more closely at the pictures of the featured men and froze. "Emilie. . . ."

"I didn't want you blindsided."

"What? They've started selling copies of this at the Jefferson Memorial?" Hayden's voice rose with each word. She scanned the article. "Oh no, no, no. Tell me I am not spending time with the man who 'travels around the DC elite circuit with only the top.' "

"I might have phrased it more artfully, but it's not anything you didn't already know."

"Except now it's in black and white. In front of me." But Andrew's picture wasn't in black and white. It was an explosion of colored perfection, reminding her in minute detail why he was out of her league. "He grew up in country clubs. I was lucky to get invited to the bowling league."

"Don't be ridiculous." Emilie snagged the magazine from Hayden and swatted her with it. "You can't pretend you're not good enough because of your old zip code. Nebraska's lovely." She grimaced as if she'd stepped in a cow pie. "Sometimes. Anyway, I guarantee Andrew would have traded all of this to have a real family."

"His dad is a congressman." Hayden pointed in the direction of the capitol. "The man makes policy decisions that affect our lives every single day."

"That might be a slight exaggeration." Emilie held up two fingers in a pinching motion. "But you had a real family. Real laughs. Real love. Andrew didn't."

"And real tears." Hayden picked at a piece of lint on the sweater that topped her jeans. "Look at me. I look like I'm dressed to rake leaves." She'd spent time agonizing in front of her closet. She sank to the edge of the bed. "Maybe I should cancel."

"Or relax and have a good time with a great guy." Emilie slid closer until their shoulders touched. "Hayden, you couldn't spend time with a nicer man. You know I adore him."

"We don't have anything in common." Hayden sighed as she thought about his silver-spoon upbringing colliding with her small-town reality. "I'm no good at this, Em."

"Then don't force it. Just go and relax for a couple hours. I know you. If he hadn't invited you, another year would evaporate without your having a single date."

"But I have cases."

"And before you had classes." Emilie stood up. "Don't go away, I'll be right back." She disappeared down the stairs and a few moments later returned, holding out a simple flower-print dress and jean jacket.

"I'll look like a floral-shop explosion."

"No, you'll look ready for a relaxing stroll around the Tidal Basin."

"If it's so great, come with us. You could use the fresh air too."

As the doorbell rang, Emilie stood and blocked the door. "I'll buy you a few minutes. Andrew can never resist a mug of my coffee." Before Hayden could protest, her roommate disappeared downstairs, leaving her with the dress and a knot in her stomach.

Soon laughter filtered upstairs as she heard the clank of ceramic on the kitchen counter. She loved her roommate, but Emilie lived life at full volume. As another round of laughter filtered upstairs, Hayden glanced at the dress and then at her jeans. If she was going to do this, she might as well do it dressed as Emilie suggested. Maybe Andrew wouldn't see through her facade. After all, it was only an hour or two.

———

Andrew bit back a stab of disappointment when Emilie answered the door. He tried to hide the bouquet of daisies, the ones that looked so right in the grocery store and now looked underwhelming when he was headed to spend the next hours with millions of cherry blossoms.

Emilie's grin widened as she glanced from him to the bouquet. "Nice touch, Wesley. Women love flowers."

"So I've heard."

Emilie's laugh surely carried to wherever Hayden hid. "I'm sure your tab is overwhelming.

How many bouquets does that make this week?"

Not her too. "Em . . ."

She stepped back to make room for him. "Well, you are one of the ten most eligible bachelors."

He groaned and set the flowers on the tiny table. "Tell me you didn't say that."

"Of course I did. I wouldn't be your favorite cousin and surrogate sister if I didn't tease you. Want a cup of coffee?"

"Hayden not ready?"

"The magazine about scared her away."

Andrew leaned against the counter and nodded. "I think I'll have that coffee." He watched as she popped in a fresh pod and then hit brew. "I didn't ask for the article, you know."

"You never do, Andrew. These things come to you."

"I'd rather they didn't."

"The real question is whether you want the women that article will send. Or are you ready for someone real?"

He was still pondering her statement when Hayden came downstairs. She wore a bright dress that revealed shapely calves leading to painted toes peeking from comfortable sandals. She smiled, but didn't really meet his gaze. Was she nervous? Today would have been so much easier if that blasted list hadn't been published. Who came up with those things anyway?

As he escorted Hayden to his Jeep, he wondered

. . . was she more real than the women his mom thought he should entertain? She'd lived in DC long enough to lose the ability to reveal who she really was. Some days masks made life easier, but it would be refreshing to find someone without one.

As he looked at her, and fought the desire to brush a strand of hair behind her ear, he wanted Hayden McCarthy to be different. If she was who he hoped she might be, he wanted to know her. She would be worth the risk.

Chapter 20

As Andrew helped Hayden from his Jeep, the reality hit her in the chest. She lived in the nation's capital.

There was only one Mall. One White House. It was like walking in a post card. And she lived here, could see it every day if she wanted. It wasn't the first time she'd had a pinch-me moment in this incredible city, but it was the first time it had been under the canopy of white blossoms.

The sidewalk around the Tidal Basin was a crush of people, and a glorious mix of nationalities. Tourists had descended in full force to take in the beauty of the Japanese gift to the American people years before.

As they merged with the tourists enjoying the

delicate pink and white explosion of blossoms, Andrew strolled next to her, his hands shoved in his pockets. As she studied his strong profile she wondered, did he regret asking her? The invitation had sounded spontaneous, but he sat squarely on DC's A-list. She didn't. She brushed the thought away—the fact that a magazine had named him to some eligible bachelor list shouldn't shake her core belief in herself. He had invited her, had brought her daisies, and she would enjoy every minute of the escape. Maybe it was just the break she needed to come back to the Rodriguez case with fresh eyes.

Before she could yank her gaze from his chiseled jaw and hooded expression, Andrew gave her a sideways glance. "What?"

She slid her hands into her pockets, mirroring his stance. "Thanks for inviting me. This is more beautiful than any photo can convey."

He looked at her, a slow grin breaking through. "I'm glad. Forgive me for seeming distracted. I got an e-mail this morning I'm having a hard time shaking."

She sucked in a breath and stopped, the crowd flowing around them. "Is there any way I can help?"

He shook his head, then straightened. "I'd share if I could. But hey, we're here in this incredible moment, so let's enjoy."

Hayden searched his eyes and then nodded.

She did want to be here, in this exact place at this precise moment. And acknowledging that, even to herself, sent a shiver of fear and wonder through her.

Her gaze slid from Andrew to the crowd around them and landed on a swarthy man standing behind him, his eyes laser-focused on her. Her arms jerked protectively around her stomach as she watched him.

Andrew's eyebrows squished together and he blinked at her. "What?"

"Don't turn around, but there's a man watching me." Hayden scanned the area around and then back to the man. Yep, he was still locked on her.

Andrew looked around, even though she'd just told him not to. "Okay. You can't really be surprised."

"Excuse me?"

"Hayden, you're a beautiful woman. Any guy who isn't paying attention to you is half blind." He stuck out his hand, and she looked at it before accepting it. "Let's keep moving and see if he follows."

She felt heat flare up her neck under his intense gaze. Then she glanced back to where the other man watched her, too far away to notice many details other than his focus. A photo could help. "Do you have your phone?" Hers rested in her purse, and by the time she dug it out, the man could disappear.

"Sure." He tugged it from his back pocket, flicked a finger across the screen, and handed it to her.

Hayden quickly raised it and snapped a series of photos as the man's scowl deepened. A cold sweat broke across her body. "Can we walk to the Jefferson? Quickly?"

There would be National Park Service employees there, the kind that could call Capitol Police if needed.

Andrew nodded, then took her hand and tugged her close to his side protectively. When she looked back over her shoulder, the man had disappeared. She must have relaxed, because Andrew slowed his clip to a more reasonable stroll.

"What was that about?"

"He was staring at me. Blatant about it. It wasn't admiration." She tried to slow her breathing and take in the beauty around her, but she found herself looking for the man in each group they passed.

"Got any clients that don't like you?"

"None. I don't work with at-risk clients like Emilie." Or criminal defendants like Jaime. She shook her head to clear the last flash of adrenaline, then planted her feet. "Things have been odd at the firm, so maybe I'm transferring that here. I'm sorry." She blew out a breath and forced a smile. "Let's keep walking."

"We could go somewhere else."

The cherry blossoms didn't feel like a safe canopy of beautiful blooms anymore. And the crowd felt like a threat waiting to erupt. Even the clouds conspired against her, scuttling across the sun and cloaking her with shadows that caused her to shiver.

What had felt like the beginning of a fun morning had turned into a cauldron of roiling emotions. Hayden longed for the safety of her case files. There she knew what to do, and how to stay safe. And yet . . . she didn't want to lose this moment getting to know this man.

Andrew could sense Hayden withdrawing. He'd seen her do it in her home, and now, in what should have been a place of restful beauty, she retreated again.

He took one more look around, intently scanning those near them. Even though she'd told him not to look, he needed to know what had spooked her so he could protect her if he could. Reminded him of a horse he'd had as a teen, yet another gift to distract him from all the time his parents left him with an au pair. That horse had been beautiful, perfectly formed, but get it on a trail and the rustle of leaves could send it into a spooked gallop. As he scanned Hayden's eyes, the same skittish look met his gaze.

"Let's finish our stroll. You've really lived here

all these years and never made time for this?" He widened his arms in a gesture designed to take in the full sweep of the Tidal Basin. "After you've taken as many photos of cherry blossoms as your phone will hold, I know just the place to grab a quick bite and cup of coffee."

"Tea." Hayden visibly relaxed in front of him, and a decision flashed across her face. "That sounds wonderful."

She turned into a delighted tourist, one who stopped every fifteen feet to get another snap of the blossoms against a now perfect blue sky. The sun warmed them, with the perfect hint of spring. As they wound back around to the parking lot, he led her on a path to the George Mason Memorial, one of his favorite haunts. Emilie liked the statue of the man her law school university had been named after. Andrew liked the reminder that the man from Virginia had been a key advocate for the Bill of Rights. And if it was like most times of the year, the area around the memorial would be sparsely populated.

A cool breeze swirled through the trees, sending a flurry of petals to the ground like debris to be squished underfoot. One fluttered into Hayden's hair, and Andrew reached up to pluck it out. Her gaze collided with his, and he felt the shock of it. He took a step back, creating space between them even as everything urged him to move closer.

He bet she'd fit perfectly next to him when he tucked her under his arm, but now was the time for a safe distance. He had to be wary. He refused to build any thoughts of a future with a woman who would act as his parents had. He would not allow his children, if he ever had any, to be nice add-ons for the family Christmas card. At the same time, Hayden might be different. She seemed to want to make time for the things that mattered to her friends. If she actually followed through and helped with the fair for his kids, that would clearly illustrate her priorities.

"Andrew?" Hayden's voice was quiet, concerned.

"Sorry." He rubbed a hand across the top of his head. "Guess it was a longer week than I thought."

"For both of us." Her smile was reflected in her eyes. If she ever really smiled and let joy escape, he knew he was a goner. To his surprise, he heard himself say, "My father has a fund-raiser for his campaign next weekend."

She arched her eyebrows and waited. A lawyer who didn't have to fill every moment with commentaries and opinions. Interesting.

"I need to bring someone. I don't suppose . . ." The words died as his throat became as dry as the Sahara. What if she turned him down?

"I'd like to come?" She glanced down at the

ground, then back to his face with a shy smile. "I could be persuaded."

"By what?"

"By a promise you'll stay near me." Her eyes twinkled with mischief. "I'm not used to fancy shindigs."

Andrew held up three fingers in a Boy Scout's oath. "I promise. Well, if my mother and father don't insist on introducing me to everyone attending." He quirked a grin, the one the ladies usually stumbled all over, and then felt a rush of regret. He was playing to her the way his father played to crowds. "But no pressure, if you really don't want to."

Hayden thrust her hands on her hips. "Wait a minute. It's not every day I get invited to a froufrou fund-raiser."

"Did you just call it froufrou?"

"Sure did." Her chocolate eyes lit up. "I'd like to meet the new senator from the great Commonwealth of Virginia."

"He's not senator yet."

"But he will be. All the pundits say so."

"All right then. Let's give them something to talk about."

Especially if it didn't involve his cartoons.

Her smile mesmerized him, and he found himself drawn a step nearer, then another. She shifted, and he reluctantly stepped back. "Want to walk around the basin again?"

"I should really head to the office." She tilted her face toward the sky, letting the sun's rays highlight her skin. "A part of me really wants to play hooky, but a louder part knows I have to get this case moving." But she sank onto the bench next to the large George Mason statue as if she wanted him to talk her out of work.

He placed a foot on the bench. "Work will always be there. But this view, it only happens once a year." He opened his arms expansively. "By next weekend it won't look the same, and in two weeks the blossoms will disappear altogether."

"In two weeks my job might disappear." She pushed away the arm he waved in front of her and he fell to the bench next to her. "I can't believe I haven't made time to see this. It's like walking through Narnia when winter finally leaves."

Andrew nodded. "There's nothing quite like it." He shifted on the bench so he could look at Hayden rather than the Tidal Basin. "Is there anything I can help with?"

"Only if you share what had you so disturbed."

"That might require a cup of coffee." And he'd have to decide if he could trust her.

Chapter 21

The coffee shop crowd had thinned as Andrew and Hayden enjoyed a black coffee for him and a hot tea for her at one of the outside picnic tables. The conversation flowed easily between them, though Hayden sensed that something was bugging him on the edges. Maybe that e-mail he'd received. She wished he'd trust her with it, but she realized their friendship was new.

She relaxed in the spring sunshine, letting it lull her into a warmth-induced haze. This was a man she could thoroughly enjoy spending time with. Suddenly a *woof* shook her from her peaceful daze.

She looked up and laughed at the sight of Emilie being tugged down King Street by a large black Lab whose feet were big enough for shoes. The dog looked suspiciously like the one she'd seen playing with the kids along the Potomac.

Andrew groaned, though there was a playful light in his eyes. "Do you mind company? Emilie called me this morning and was adamant we needed to spend serious time on the fair plans. I was supposed to meet her here in fifteen minutes."

"I wonder what happened to her plans for the parade." Hayden grinned as the dog dragged her roommate to the next light pole. "As long as the sun's shining and you keep the tea coming, I'm good. Who's the beast walking her?"

"That would be my dog, Zeus." He held up his almost empty mug. "Don't ask. It was a crazy phase that may have had something to do with Percy Jackson."

Zeus pranced up to Hayden and promptly sat on her feet, looking at her with adoring eyes.

"Hey . . . Zeus . . ." Emilie's words were exasperated and slightly out of air.

Hayden laughed and leaned down to rub the dog's ears. "You're a sweet thing, aren't you, boy?"

"Something like that." Andrew grinned up at his cousin. "How's life, Emilie?"

"Other than the deadline this beast kept me from making and my date dumping me for the parade? Hunky-dory." She handed the leash to Andrew. "I gladly relinquish control of the monster to his rightful owner." She flopped down in a chair and took Andrew's mug. She sipped from it and then sputtered. "I insist on real coffee. A white chocolate mocha, please."

Andrew looked from her to the leash with a comical air. "I'd love to do your bidding, but . . ."

Hayden laughed. "I'll grab it, Em."

When she returned to the table with Emilie's drink and a refill for herself, Andrew and Emilie had their heads bent over a spreadsheet and calendar. Emilie accepted the drink with a smile of thanks, then launched right back into her explanation. As she gestured wildly, Hayden was tempted to reclaim the coffee before it sloshed all over the plans.

"Sure you have time to do all this, Em? I don't want you biting off too much."

"I'm not." Emilie mock-frowned at him, daring him to disagree.

Andrew met Hayden's gaze. "What do you think?"

"She hasn't, Andrew. Not this time."

Hayden smiled, and Andrew's mind froze. She was beautiful all of the time, but when she smiled the world slowed. She quirked an eyebrow at him, and time restarted.

Andrew swallowed. "I appreciate the help, because I've had something come up that is claiming time."

"Em's had fun planning the fair."

"That's what this is? Fun?" Emilie grinned with a carefree toss of her hair.

Andrew pulled one of her waves as she squirmed in her chair. "I already knew you were amazing, Em."

They spent the next thirty minutes fleshing out more details, though Hayden frequently twitched and looked at the time on her phone. She seemed determined to stay there and make sure he and Emilie got along. By the time they finished, he knew the fair would be a success. "This is awesome. I can't wait to show the kids the great time you've got planned. They'll be psyched." He looked at the map of the games and hot dog tent. "It better fit by the fire station, though. That's the only location in Fairlington for this."

"It will. I promise. You wouldn't believe how many people wanted to know what I was doing with a tape measure along that intersection."

Andrew's phone rang before he could reply. He glanced at the screen, and then frowned when it flashed up as the Alexandria City Police. "Sorry, gals, but I need to take this." He turned slightly away and swiped the phone. "Andrew Wesley."

"Mr. Wesley, we have a young man here named Jorge Rodriguez who asked us to call you."

"Yes?" Andrew stood and began to pace. Jorge was not a kid he expected to get into trouble.

"His mother has been attacked, and he needs a place to stay. We can't send him home, and he asked us to contact you rather than social services."

"Where should I meet you?"

"We can bring him to you."

"All right." Andrew relayed his information, then paused. "How is his mother?"

"She'll be kept at the hospital at least overnight,

maybe longer. She was beaten pretty badly. Looks like a burglary gone bad."

"Can they return to their apartment?"

"Likely, but not sure. We'll have Jorge to you in fifteen."

Andrew hung up, a knot in his gut. Had it really been a random burglary? But if not . . . why would someone target Maricel?

He turned back to the table, and Hayden stood. "What's wrong, Andrew?"

"The mother of one of my kids was attacked in a burglary. The police are bringing Jorge to me, to keep him out of the system." He didn't want to think what that would do to Jorge, who was doing so well.

Hayden's brow furrowed. "Jorge Rodriguez? The boy I saw with you at the ice cream shop?"

"That's the one." Then he realized . . . "That's right, his mother . . ."

". . . is my client."

Emilie looked from one to the other, then at Zeus, who had stood and now paced between Hayden and Andrew. "I'll take Zeus home with me. You guys do what you need to."

The minutes stretched as they waited for the police to arrive with Jorge. As she waited, Hayden pulled out her phone and tried to reach Maricel. Surely a mistake had been made. Yet as the phone continued to ring without an answer,

Hayden's heart sank. Something had happened.

Could it really be a burglary? Or was it somehow tied to Miguel's case?

The thought should strike Hayden as crazy, but in her two conversations with Maricel, the woman seemed to always have one eye focused behind her. Who was she so afraid of?

Hayden shivered and rubbed the gooseflesh that had erupted on her arms. Someone was chasing her client and had caught her. Unfortunately, her client hadn't trusted her enough to tell her who. And because of that, Hayden had nothing to tell the police.

An Alexandria City Police cruiser pulled up in front of the coffee shop. An officer stepped from the driver's seat and opened the passenger door, and a shaking young man slid into view. The boy looked like he'd bolt at the least provocation.

The officer glanced up and down the sidewalk, then walked toward them, his hand resting on his gun. "Andrew Wesley?"

Andrew stood. "Thank you for bringing Jorge."

The officer nodded, and Hayden wished she could see his eyes behind the reflective sunglasses.

"He's spooked, but I've assured him his mom looks worse than she is." He reached into his breast pocket and pulled out a card. "This is my number. If he thinks of anything or you have concerns, call."

"Yes sir." Andrew turned his attention to the young man. "Ready to go to my house, Jorge?"

The youth gave a quick downward jerk of his chin, but didn't meet Andrew's eye.

"All right." Andrew placed a hand on the boy's shoulder and waited until he looked up. "You are safe, Jorge. I promise."

Jorge's chin trembled, and Hayden expected him to disagree. Instead he searched Andrew's face before giving another quick nod.

"Looks like you've got everything under control." The officer walked back to his cruiser, then turned back before climbing in. "Call me if he remembers anything."

Andrew gave a curt nod. Hayden stepped closer to Jorge and led him to a chair. He eased down as if afraid he would break it.

"Jorge, did you grab anything at home? Clothes? A toothbrush?"

He shook his head.

She squeezed him around the shoulders, and he trembled beneath her arm. "It's a short walk to my condo." She pulled her keys from her purse. "I'll grab my car and go to Potomac Yards and grab essentials for Jorge while you get him settled. Then I'll check on his mom."

"I'll come with you."

"We'll see how Jorge's doing first." She nodded to his young charge, who stared into space somewhere across the street. "Let's get him to your place and feeling safe. I'll meet you in forty minutes."

Jorge seemed glued to Andrew's side as they walked down the street to his Jeep. She'd never seen a kid look quite that lost and shell-shocked. What condition must his mother be in?

Chapter 22

Mrs. Bradford waved from the side yard where she was watering her hyacinths and tulips, but Andrew kept Jorge moving. The kid acted like he was a zombie trapped in some horror flick.

Jorge stumbled up the steps to the second-floor condo, then waited as Andrew unlocked the door and spread his arms wide. "Welcome. *Mi casa es su casa.*"

"*Gracias.*" The boy headed to the couch and plopped down in a heap on one end.

Andrew watched him a moment as he weighed his best approach. The officer had made it clear they needed to know what Jorge had seen. Yet as he studied the kid, he knew it was too fresh. The boy was in a state of shock. Andrew entered his galley kitchen and returned a moment later with two glasses of ice water. He handed one to Jorge and then sat beside him.

Jorge gulped the water, then set the glass on the coffee table, his hands trembling. Andrew placed a hand on his shoulder and gripped it a moment. "I'm here, Jorge, and I'm not going anywhere."

A tear drizzled down the boy's face, one he angrily swiped away. "She did nothing wrong."

"Did you see the man who did it?" Andrew kept his hand on Jorge's arm in an effort to calm him.

"No. He threw me in a closet before I could see his face." Jorge's head slumped forward. "I couldn't protect my mother." He tugged a small cell phone from his pocket. "Mami bought this so I could call the police if ever I needed to."

Had his mother really given him a phone for protection? If so, she had known someone was coming. This wasn't a burglary gone wrong.

Hayden balanced several bags in each hand as she walked up the sidewalk to Andrew's condo. Emilie had texted her the address, and now Hayden realized she'd gone a little crazy buying clothes and toiletries for Jorge. Maybe she'd submit the receipt to the partners. They'd love that.

When she reached the front door of the building, Hayden shifted her armload to free a hand. A bag fell to the stoop, and two LEGO T-shirts and a baseball cap spilled out.

An older woman with a spry step that belied her gray hair hurried over. "Let me help you with that." She grabbed a bag and used the opportunity to scrutinize Hayden through her bifocals. "I haven't seen you before."

Hayden nodded. "I'm a friend of Andrew Wesley's."

The woman eyed her carefully, then apparently approved, because she reached into her oversized gardening apron and pulled out a wad of keys. "He got home a bit ago. I'm guessing these bags are for the boy with him?"

"Yes." Hayden eased through the now open door and set the bags on the floor. Then she turned around and scooped up the items that had fallen out. When she turned back, the woman stood almost nose to nose with her.

"Andrew is a good man. Do not do anything that will make me regret letting you in."

Hayden nodded. The woman reminded her of her second-grade Sunday school teacher. One look and Hayden would sit straighter and listen quietly. "Can you tell me which unit is his?"

The woman studied her another moment, then nodded. "Second floor unit, on the left." She handed the bag to Hayden. "Good luck."

The moment Hayden reached the top of the flight of stairs, Andrew appeared in his doorway. "Can I help with those bags?"

"Would have been great to have it a few minutes ago."

"I knew Mrs. Bradford would help. She likes to do that."

"You mean she likes to interrogate people."

"With a charming smile and gaze of steel." He

held the door for her. "I'm convinced she was a detective in an earlier career, but she won't admit it. Welcome to my humble abode."

Hayden quickly took in the space. A living area, where Jorge was huddled on the couch, a dining area, and kitchen formed the part of the first floor she could see. An iron staircase spiraled toward what looked like a small loft area. "I didn't realize there was a second floor."

"It's small, but a definite perk." He gave her a quick tour of the condo with its décor that was attractive, but had too much of a stale designer air to put her at ease. It looked like a spread she'd see in *Southern Living*, beautiful but unrealistic for mere mortals. Throughout the tour, Jorge didn't move from his position on the couch. As Andrew led her down a short hallway to point out the bedroom and guest bedroom, he asked quietly, "Any ideas how I can help Jorge?"

"Maybe we should take him to see his mother so he can see she'll be okay. I'm going to visit her, and I can take him with me."

Andrew studied his ward as if he wanted to reach inside Jorge's mind and get a clear understanding of the young man's thoughts. "We don't know what condition she's in."

"But he does. And I guarantee images of her the way he last saw her are stuck in his mind. Maybe seeing her alive and recovering will be the best thing we can do for him." She touched Andrew's arm, drawing his worried gaze from Jorge to her. "Which hospital was Maricel transported to?"

"Arlington." He nodded. "Okay, let's do this." He marched back into the living area and sank onto the leather coffee table in front of Jorge. "Hey. Let's go check on your mom. You'll feel better once you see her and know she's okay. Hayden's coming with us, okay?"

Jorge nodded like one still asleep and then slowly stood. Hayden followed them to the car and slid into the backseat of the Jeep. She met Andrew's gaze in the rearview mirror and knew his concern matched hers.

Twenty minutes later Andrew parked in the hospital garage. At the visitors' station they talked their way to Maricel's room number from a suspicious volunteer. Jorge clutched Andrew's hand as the elevator transported them to the correct floor.

"She should be down this hallway." Andrew led the way, but Hayden slowed when a large man bumped into her.

The man looked like a well-muscled running back. He was tall and had a multi-color snake tattoo curling around his neck. He didn't apologize for bumping her, or slow down, but Hayden's gaze followed him until he entered the elevator.

"Andrew, have you seen that man before?"

"What man?"

"The one who bumped into me."

"Nope, sorry. I wasn't paying attention, I was looking at room numbers. Jorge?" He turned, turned again, then looked at Hayden. "Where'd Jorge go?"

She shrugged and glanced around the hallway. She caught a movement in the shadows beside a vending machine, and pointed to it.

Andrew nodded. "Jorge? Come out, buddy."

As Andrew coaxed the kid from hiding beside the machine, Hayden watched with growing concern. Jorge looked like he was diving deeper into his shock. "Andrew, what's wrong?"

"I don't know."

Hayden looked back down the hall toward the elevator. The only person they had seen on the floor was the man who had bumped into her. Had he said something to Jorge in passing that had left the kid a scared shell?

Questions chased through her mind during their fifteen-minute visit in Maricel's room. Although Maricel was sleeping, the nurse who stepped in to check on them assured them that she would be awake later and would recover fully.

As Hayden studied the woman's battered face and the cast around her left wrist, she was more convinced than ever that this had been no bungled burglary. What had followed Maricel and Jorge from Mexico?

Chapter 23

The sunlight filtering through her curtain pulled Hayden from a dream of shadows chasing her. Men with snake tattoos and terrified teens circled around a woman in a hospital bed. A shower helped shake the images, but Hayden didn't truly banish them until she reached her church and entered into the worship service.

Home again, she changed into comfortable clothes and decided to call her mom. She knew she couldn't focus on anything work-related anyway.

Her mother picked up right away. "Hayden? Is everything okay?"

A pinch of guilt zinged Hayden. "I'm fine, Mom. Sorry I call so rarely you think something's wrong."

"Honey, I know you're busy."

A few minutes passed in small talk as Mom caught her up on what was happening with her older brother and his family. Seemed life was golden for them in Colorado. Who would have thought that would be the place where he found a wife and a life he loved? Maybe nobody there cared what their father had done.

Hayden ran a finger along her quilt's pattern and listened as her mom told her about the novel her book club was reading. When they hung up half an hour later, she felt centered and ready to tackle a project. The question was, what could she do on the Rodriguez case? She was at the mercy of the government, and it was not where she wanted this case positioned.

"Do you have a minute?" Emilie looked too serious for a Sunday afternoon as she stood in the doorway.

"Sure." Hayden patted the bed next to her. "Come on in."

The mattress squeaked a protest as Emilie sat. "I've been thinking about Miguel's case. There's a story there. Something fishy is happening."

"I know. And I don't believe the attack on Maricel was the random burglary the police want us to believe it was." She filled Emilie in on what had happened at the hospital.

"You need to get to Texas."

"I know, but I can't unless the partners approve and pay." Hayden's bank account was thin. She'd repaid the last of her student loans, but coupled with her car and the rent she paid Emilie, she lacked margin. People thought you made the big bucks in DC, but they didn't realize how crazy expensive housing was. She valued her ability to walk a few blocks to work, but it meant she couldn't fly halfway across the country on her own dime.

"I also have to wait for the director to agree to a

time for the deposition," she continued. "Should happen this week."

"I could fly out tomorrow. Poke around while you work out the permissions you need."

Hayden forced herself to pause and consider the offer. At coffee she and Savannah had decided it was a good idea. And now Emilie offered before Hayden had time to ask. "I really want to go, but with the partners refusing, you should go instead. I can't pay you though."

"It's okay. Something big is brewing. I'll put my investigative prowess to work. Nobody there knows me, and I'm not an attorney on the case, so I can dig without the restrictions you'll have." She grinned. "Maybe I'll land my big story while I'm there."

"You can't publish anything until I approve, Emilie."

"And you're stalled right now, thanks to the government and the partners. Let me help."

Hayden hated the harsh reality of those words. Until someone cooperated, sending Emilie was her best bet for getting the information she needed. She hated that she couldn't cover the costs. "Are you sure you'll know where to look?"

"Don't forget the pro bono work I do for Andrew's clients and my own. Those give me plenty of opportunities to work cases."

"This could be a multimillion-dollar case. It's not a landlord issue."

Emilie's cheeks colored, and Hayden knew she'd pushed too far. "Sorry, Em. That wasn't fair, and your offer could change this case. I just hate the feeling I can't do anything for the case myself right now."

Emilie's intense green eyes bored into Hayden. "It doesn't give you the right to minimize what I do. My investigative reporting gives me a good knowledge of what you need. The fact I don't spend every day on law doesn't mean I'll kill your investigation. In fact, I'll make it better because I don't sound like an attorney. You do."

"Are you sure you can afford it?" When she and Savannah had discussed Emilie going, Hayden had still held out hope the partners would change their position.

"Yes."

Hayden nodded. "Thank you. By the way, he thinks I'm an idiot."

Emilie looked at her like she had become one. "What are you talking about? Who thinks you're an idiot?"

"Andrew." Hayden put her hands over her face and hunched her shoulders forward. "We were having a good time at the Cherry Blossom Festival, until I lost my mind and thought someone was following us."

"Why'd you think that?"

"Some strange man made eye contact." She paused as her mind flashed from that man to the one at the hospital. Details stood out that she hadn't considered. Both had pronounced snake tattoos curled up their necks. Could they have been the same person?

She reached for her phone. "I need to find out exactly when Maricel was attacked." While Emilie stared at her as though she had indeed lost her mind, Hayden dialed Andrew.

"Hey, Andrew. How's Jorge today?" She listened to his comments about the young man loosening up, and then turned to the reason for her call. "Did the police tell you when Maricel was attacked?"

Andrew said it had been around noon. Then it probably wasn't the same man. It would be difficult to travel from the congested Tidal Basin to Maricel's apartment in that time. And why would someone who'd beaten her up then follow her to the hospital?

She said good-bye and set her phone down, then looked up to see Emilie staring at her. "What was that about?"

"Nothing. The man I saw at the Tidal Basin and the one at the hospital had similar tattoos. I was crazy to think it meant anything."

"Well, it was an impressive distraction in an attempt to get out of telling me about your date with Andrew."

"It wasn't a date." Hayden rubbed her face. "It was awkward. And wonderful. And then he was so quiet as we drove to the coffee shop. You know how I get when it's too silent."

"You couldn't stop talking." Emilie grinned, and Hayden sat straighter.

"Wait a minute. You're supposed to be supportive. You talked me into going."

"Of course I did." Emilie popped to her feet and disappeared down the stairs, returning a minute later with two frosty cans of Dr Pepper. "Don't you see?"

"No."

"You rattled him."

"I rattled the illustrious Andrew Wesley, most eligible bachelor in the nation's capital?"

"You sure did." Emilie took a swig of her drink, then grimaced. "How do you drink this stuff?"

"Nectar of the gods."

"Whatever. Anyway, Andrew knows how to play debonair with the women his mom throws his way. Don't get too close, keep small talk flowing—he's a marvel to watch. If he was tongue-tied, that means he's mystified by you."

"You say that as if it's a good thing."

"Sure it is."

Hayden rubbed her temples. "Then why'd you wait so long to introduce us?"

"You weren't ready."

"Oh, and my babbling proves I am now?"

"A year ago you'd have run screaming at the sight of that dress I loaned you. Now you were at least willing to try it. You're losing that chip on your shoulder." Emilie softened her words by reaching out and squeezing Hayden's hand.

Hayden tugged her hand free. Chip? On her shoulder? That wasn't fair. "I've never had a chip on my shoulder."

"Yes, you have." Emilie took another swig of her drink and shrugged. "You were so insecure when we first met. You couldn't get past the fact that I have more . . . stuff. Things that don't matter one whit in light of eternity. But to you, they got in the way."

Hayden forced herself to consider Emilie's words. She prided herself on being open to criticism, but it was hard. She wanted to defend herself, even if a kernel of truth existed in the words.

"I'm sorry if I came across that way. I didn't mean to."

"I know you didn't. And it's okay. Really. Just keep an open mind about Andrew. He's a good guy, Hayden. And I'm not saying that just because he's my cousin."

Hayden nodded, then held up her can of Dr Pepper. "I'm going to put in a little work. Sounds like you have an airplane ticket to buy."

Emilie's smile slipped. "Already did." She studied Hayden. "Truth in love, friend."

"I know." Hayden tried to smile. "It's one of the things I love about you." Funny how you could

192

love and hate the same quality in your best friend.

Emilie slipped out of the room, and Hayden went up to her office and sat, thinking about the way Emilie had described her. If that's how her best friend saw her, then how did others? Had she built walls around herself because of her shame over her dad?

Maybe the more she'd held her head high, the higher she'd built the barricade that separated her from everyone else.

Usually, she loved the stark calmness of the dove-gray walls lined with bookshelves. One shelf was filled with the fiction she let herself fall into until the characters became her friends. The other was filled with textbooks and non-fiction, though she'd slipped *The Killer Angels* and other Shaara war-inspired novels there. She pulled out a book, then slid it back in. So many of these books had been gifts from her father, purchased on his many trips.

His job as a CFO for a major company had built his frequent flier miles and her library.

He had always sought to broaden her perspective by exposing her to different heroes. Men and women who had transformed their generations and worlds. William Wilberforce and Hannah More and their quest to end slavery and bring manners back to turn-of-the-1800s England. Dietrich Bonhoeffer and his vocal stand against the Nazis—and Corrie ten Boom's quiet rebellion.

Queen Victoria. Florence Nightingale. It was a truly eclectic collection.

Each volume inspired her.

She believed that one life lived in abandon to God could have far-reaching consequences for the world around her.

Yet as she examined the books and then thought about what she spent her life on, she wondered. Did her efforts matter?

Did the typical corporate clients allow her to make a difference?

She knew that was why the Rodriguez matter was weaving its way around her heart. Miguel's story had moved past her mind and taken up residence in her soul.

She could close her eyes and imagine his journey to the States. She could imagine his first days in the detention center. And she could imagine his fear in the moments before his throat was slit.

God, I just want to be used.

To live a life that mattered, one that made a difference in the world.

FRIDAY, APRIL 7

The last light in the building finally went dark. The night had cooled considerably, and he shivered in his jacket. He sank against the seat. Ten more minutes. Then he would slip inside.

Over the last few nights, no one had reentered the floors of the law firm after the cleaning crews vacated. What if someone worked late tonight? That would break the system, and he must trust what he had witnessed.

He hunkered deeper into his jacket, his hands shoved inside his pockets. He continued to scan the rows of windows as his thoughts returned to Miguel. He had attended a mass, begged God for forgiveness, but all he saw was the blackness of his heart. How could he have turned on his brother?

The work *el jefe* sent made no sense. Now he had hurt a woman who had done no wrong other than leaving. Who would *el jefe* send after him when he broke free?

He checked the time on his cell.

He stilled as an officer on a bike rode past. Now he must move. He would have time to get to the building and inside before the officer came back on his predictable cycle. He grabbed his bag of tools and slid from the car.

It only took a minute to get his key card to communicate with the alarm system. Then he was in. The question was where to start. Almost fifty attorneys worked in the building. He just had to find the right offices.

El jefe had sent him on a hunt in which he couldn't succeed.

He straightened and took the stairs. It wouldn't matter if there were video cameras or surveillance. He was invisible in all the ways that mattered.

Chapter 24

Hayden waited for Emilie, listening to the sound of a suitcase thumping up the basement stairs. "Did I give you enough information?" Now that it was time to drive Emilie to Reagan National, Hayden wanted to call her off.

Emilie flipped her blond hair and shrugged. "I'm prepared, thanks to you. It's a simple matter of asking questions." She tugged her bag through the kitchen and to the door, and paused. "You coming or should I call a cab?"

Hayden grabbed her keys. "Come on."

After dropping Emilie off, she returned to their town house and then walked to the office.

Starbucks and Common Grounds were open, but the downtown streets were otherwise quiet. She reached the office before the receptionist, and flipped on lights as she headed down the hall. The shadows made odd shapes, and she quickened her steps even as she told herself to quit being ridiculous.

Hayden reached her office, opened her door, and froze. Papers and files were stacked in orderly piles on her desk, nothing like the chaos she had left Friday. It looked like some kind of cleaning

197

fairy had come and organized. Leigh knew better than to mess with her piles. It hadn't taken more than two of the paralegal's macro-organization bursts for Hayden to tell her it wouldn't work. Hayden was a piler.

She eased into her small office, setting her attaché bag and purse on the floor beside her desk.

If she called security, nobody would believe someone had been in her office. Yet she knew it was true. And whoever it was hadn't even tried to disguise it.

She eased onto her chair and tugged her cell phone from her jacket pocket. After she took several photos, Hayden gingerly reached for her computer and jiggled the mouse. Her computer spun to life. Could she determine if someone unauthorized had accessed her files?

Her log-on screen appeared as it should, but her password didn't work. She called the IT office, but before anyone answered, Gerard burst into her office.

She looked up. "What's wrong?"

"You tell me." His face was a mask of anger. "Look at this." He stormed from her office and Hayden hurried to follow.

Gerard led her to his office and stopped in the doorway. Papers were tossed across the entire floor. Files upended. It looked like a tornado had whirled through.

"What on earth—?"

"That's what I'd like to know." His nostrils flared and he thrust his hands on his hips. "You have some explaining to do."

Hayden tore her gaze from the mess to stare at him. The partner had lost his mind. "Me? Why would I do this?"

"Clearly you needed something." He waved a hand over the mess. "Did you find it? If you wanted the backpack back, why didn't you just ask?"

"Find what? And I didn't know you had the backpack." Hayden was more confused than ever. "Did Leigh bring it to you?"

"Yes." His curt word communicated more than an essay.

"Gerard, if I needed something, I'd ask. Send an e-mail. Knock on your door. There's no reason I'd do this. And by the way, someone searched my office too."

"Your office did not look like this." He crossed his arms and stared her down.

"Exactly. You know how mine usually looks. It's considerably neater than I left it Friday. Were any other offices searched?"

"Not that I've seen." His jaw worked as he studied her. "Who else would want the Rodriguez file?"

"You already gave it to me." The accordion file had been in her possession since he gave it to her more than a week earlier. Is that what whoever had searched her office had sought? Or was it the backpack? "I wasn't in the office this weekend, so I don't know. I helped get Maricel Rodriguez's son settled after she was attacked."

"What?"

"Somebody attacked her in her home, and she's still in the hospital." Hayden frowned. "Gerard, is there anything about her you aren't sharing?"

"No." His answer was too short, too prompt.

"How did she find us in the first place?"

"She was referred by Randolph's former client." Gerard didn't make eye contact as he said it.

"If you weren't here, can you explain what this is doing here?" He plucked a large letter opener from the desk. Plated in faux gold, it was shaped like a sword with Hayden's name engraved on the side. It had been a gag gift from her grandmother when she graduated from law school, to save her fingers from paper cuts when opening the million letters she'd receive.

"I have no idea." Hayden reached for the tool, but he held it out of reach. "It's a letter opener, Gerard. Maybe whoever searched my office grabbed it and left it here." Had the invader wanted to frame her?

Gerard ground his teeth together and surveyed the wreck. "He must have decided I needed a reminder." He gave a hard nod, then refocused on her. "Why were you helping Jorge, anyway?"

200

Hayden noted his use of the young man's name. "Maricel was attacked at home." She grimaced at the memory of the woman's battered condition. "Jorge is staying with a friend of mine while she recovers. He witnessed the attack and needs time to adjust and realize he's safe."

She took another glance at the floor. If someone had come in looking for something in a Rodriguez file she hadn't been told about, maybe she should help clean up the mess. And if there was another file he hadn't given her maybe she'd find it. "Would you like help?"

She crouched as far as her pencil skirt allowed, but Gerard stopped her.

"Get back to work. I'll have Carmen take care of this." She glanced up and met his hard gaze. "I'm taking a chance, McCarthy. Do not make me regret this decision. Stay away from my office unless I'm here."

She murmured, "Yes sir." Then she stood and fled his office. As she passed Leigh's desk, she paused. "Do you know where the Rodriguez backpack is?"

Leigh looked up from her computer screen, reading glasses still resting on her nose. "It's in the evidence storage room until Mrs. Rodriguez picks it up. She hasn't returned my call."

"Thank you." So whoever broke in hadn't gotten the backpack. Or had they? "Can you confirm it's there?"

Leigh's eyebrows knit together, but she nodded. "IT changed your password, by the way. Here's the new one." She handed Hayden a Post-it note.

"Thanks." Settled at her desk, Hayden stared at her computer screen, but all she could hear was Gerard accusing her of destroying his office. What a horrendous mess of paper—a snapshot of that scene would be a poster child for paperless offices.

Was Gerard right? Had someone broken into their offices to get access to information about Miguel's case? If so, she needed to reexpose the lawsuit to light. Then whoever had broken in would have no need to commit B&E, because they could learn everything Hayden knew through discovery.

She opened the complaint again and scanned it.

A young man arrives in the United States.

He's detained north of the border, and because he's a minor traveling without an adult, he's sent to the juvenile detention center.

Three weeks later he's murdered.

Surely he had planned to connect with his mother and brother. Or had he dreamed of starting completely on his own? Maybe he just needed to escape whatever had prevented him from coming legally.

She paused.

If he was as intelligent as Maricel thought, he should have journeyed on a student visa. What had kept him from applying for and receiving one? Immigration law was not her expertise. But she knew people who stayed up to date on the niche.

She picked up her phone and called Ciara Turner. Her friend had been a couple years ahead of her at George Mason and a mentor as Hayden navigated the troubled waters of the first year. Ciara could help her understand the immigration system.

"Hey, girl. This is Hayden." After a couple minutes of enthusiastic small talk, Hayden launched into her questions. "I've got a situation involving a client. I need to better understand visas and what could prevent a smart kid from getting one to study."

"That's a complicated issue. Do you want to grab a quick lunch? Say at 11:45? We should beat the crowds and find a quiet corner to talk."

Hayden double-checked her calendar, then agreed. "I'll meet you at La Madeline. Thanks."

As soon as she hung up she reread the legal section in the complaint. The Claims Court judge just needed enough to become curious about what she'd do with the case. She wanted the judge to understand this was a case about a young man whose American dream was cut short when he was murdered in US detention. She'd never make an argument about whether an informal contract existed between the government and the detainees if she couldn't convince the judge this young man's story mattered.

She didn't mind taking risky cases, but she liked believing she had a stronger than 50 percent chance of success at trial. Here she wasn't sure she could get past the answer stage. Not without the early deposition and a couple lucky breaks.

Hayden leaned back in her chair. She closed her eyes and searched for some kind of direction. *Lord, does this make sense?*

Some people might not believe God cared about one case for a young man who couldn't even be helped by the outcome. Hayden chose to believe it mattered. If the God of the universe couldn't be bothered by what happened to one young man who died an unseen death, how could she matter? Either everyone mattered or nobody did.

It was that cut and dried.

It was in the process of uncovering the heart of a person's story that a case came to life.

As she thought about the Rodriguez case, she understood a mother's heartbreak, but so many other pieces of Miguel's story remained missing. Why was he murdered? Who was behind it? Did Miguel have something the murderer wanted? Was that something still in his backpack?

It couldn't be a coincidence that the break-in occurred right after the backpack arrived.

Chapter 25

When Hayden reached La Madeline, Ciara was waiting at a quiet table in the corner with a bowl of soup and bottle of water in front of her. No one sat near enough to overhear their conversation, making it an ideal location. Ciara waved, her bright-pink suit barely concealing the bump rounding her stomach. Hayden ordered her food and then joined Ciara at the table.

Hayden couldn't hide her smile. "How many more weeks?"

"Seven." The sigh that accompanied the word made it sound like seven years.

"Really? You aren't as big as a barn." She grinned at her friend as color flooded Ciara's cheeks.

"I feel like I am." Ciara shifted uncomfortably and then rubbed her belly. "I'm glad the first five months are behind me. It's nice to actually like the smell of food again." She made a face and set a napkin over her stomach. "So what's the immigration issue that has you in knots? How can I help?"

Looked like most in the shop were grabbing their lunches to go. "A client's child was killed while detained in a government facility. His mother and younger brother immigrated on visas, but the older son travelled illegally. Why couldn't he get a visa too?"

"Did he live with his mom?"

"His father had the marriage annulled. In the settlement, Dad kept the older boy."

Ciara stirred her soup. "It happens, especially south of the border."

Hayden nodded. "He was from Mexico." She leaned forward. "Here's what bothers me. From everything his mom tells me, he's the kind of kid who could have come on an educational visa and possibly worked his way into a green card."

"Instead he walks across the border."

"As far as I can tell."

Ciara blew on a spoonful of soup and then ate it. "There are some automatic reasons the state department won't grant a visa. If he had a criminal background. If he or a member of his family was involved in drug trafficking. If he was supported by the proceeds of trafficking. Security reasons. The list is endless."

"He didn't have a criminal background."

"Have you filed the complaint?"

"Refiling it as soon as a pre-deposition occurs."

"Try a third party request to the Bureau of Consular Affairs to get his application and all accompanying documentation. If you get it, you should gain insight into why he was denied."

"Emilie's on her way to Texas now. Maybe she can track it down."

"Maybe."

Hayden's phone buzzed, and she checked it. A text from Emilie? She should be almost to Texas.

"Oh no. Emilie's flight was cancelled due to weather. Flights are grounded to Texas."

Ciara brushed a strand of hair out of her eyes and then tore off a piece of bread to dip in her soup. "Why were you sending her instead of going yourself?"

"She volunteered, and the partners aren't keen on me making the trip." Hayden took a sip of her sweet tea.

Ciara considered her. "Emilie would have more freedom—you'd have a government representative with you."

"That's why it made sense." Hayden glanced up. "There is something odd going on at the office, and I can't decide if it's tied to this case. Over the weekend someone came into my office and organized it. Someone trashed Campbell's office, and he thinks it was me."

"Why would he think that?"

Hayden shrugged. "Whoever it was left my letter opener in his mess. But it's hard to believe that Campbell would really think I was responsible." She speared a tomato with her fork. "He's convinced whoever did it was after the client file for this young man. The file he didn't give me."

Ciara frowned. "He was withholding a file? Why would he do that?"

207

"I don't know. Until this morning, I thought he'd given me everything. This case feels bigger than it should, with all kinds of artificial pressure to finish everything yesterday but not go to Texas." She closed up her to-go salad. "I'll take this back to the office. Thanks for your help."

Hayden gave Ciara a quick hug, and her friend stopped her with a hand on her arm.

"Be careful."

"I will."

"Don't let it rattle you. You're a great attorney, Hayden. Look how many people you've helped. You can find a way to get justice for this kid too."

Hayden swallowed back the feeling that she was only pretending to be an attorney and her recent success had been a happy fluke. If she was the great attorney people thought, she wouldn't struggle with indecision on what to do next. The path would be clear and she'd follow it as easily as Dorothy followed the Yellow Brick Road. Instead, the case was shrouded in a fog that left her wondering if she had the skill to win.

She battled the thoughts as she walked back to the office, barely noticing the way the sun warmed her face. Her cell phone rang, and rather than hurry to the office, Hayden took a seat on a bench in front of the city building. "Emilie?"

"Hey, sorry about Texas. It was going to take all day or a ton of money to get me rerouted.

Instead, I have a voucher for another flight. It's yours if you want it."

"Thanks, Em. Somehow I'll get the partners to cover it."

Hayden had barely ended the call when her phone rang again. The caller ID indicated that it was a call rerouted from the office.

"Hayden McCarthy."

"I'm Jacqueline Reynolds, attorney for Director Snowden with the juvenile detention facility in Texas. The director is a very busy man, but he can schedule the deposition for Wednesday at four. He'll have an hour for you at that time. Otherwise, I'm afraid he will be unavailable for the next four weeks."

Hayden bristled at the woman's pompous tone. It was clear as spring water that she expected Hayden to say no. Hayden wouldn't give her the satisfaction.

"I'll be there. Please e-mail me the directions, and my assistant will arrange a court reporter and videographer."

The woman on the other side of the call sputtered a moment, then quickly recovered and exchanged the information. She sputtered again when Hayden pressed for up to six hours of deposition time, but Hayden insisted. This was her one shot to get the information she needed. She'd never get the partners to agree to a second trip.

Her chest constricted. In fact, she still had to et them to agree to a first.

Chapter 26

Hayden rehearsed arguments as she climbed the stairs to the front door of Elliott & Johnson. A man in a sharp suit with a tattoo peeking from his collar stepped out of the way as she approached. He held the door for her, but seemed intent on something behind him. She breezed past him and said hello to the receptionist, then climbed the stairs to her office. She stopped long enough to drop her things, and then strode purposefully to Gerard's office.

Carmen sat behind her desk outside his door, typing on her computer. "Hey, Hayden."

"What kind of mood is he in?"

Carmen tilted her head. "He's still muttering about finding his office in disarray, but I've got everything back in order. How much time do you need? A key client arrives in five minutes."

"That'll do." Either he'd agree or kick her out. Hayden took a deep breath and went in.

Gerard looked up with a grunt.

She refused to look away as he scowled. The good of her client and case demanded she go to Texas. Should be easy since she made her living through communication, yet she couldn't swallow around the Sahara Desert that claimed her voice.

"Yes?" Gerard placed his hands on top of his

desk and leaned into them. "This hasn't been the best day, and I have a critical meeting in five minutes. If you need something, spit it out."

She nodded. "The deposition is scheduled for Wednesday in Texas."

He made a winding motion with his hand as if telling her to get on with it.

"The facility's attorney said the director could only cooperate with the pre-trial deposition Wednesday. Otherwise we have to wait a month." She leaned into her side of the desk, meeting him halfway. "We need that deposition and anything else I can learn."

Gerard sighed as he flopped in his chair. It rocked under his weight. "And what do you hope to learn?"

"Who was working that night? Have there been other acts of violence? I need to know if this is a pattern or a one-time event. What made Miguel the unlucky kid? I have to communicate that to the judge."

Gerard rubbed his hands over his face, then stared up at her. "I admire your passion, Hayden, but there are forces at work you don't understand."

"Then tell me about them." She felt her blood pressure building. "You've been keeping something from me this entire case. I need to know what you know, because it's beginning to feel dangerous to be kept in the dark."

"This is for your protection. You do not want to know all the details."

"Then we shouldn't have the client." Saying the words felt like a betrayal of Maricel, but she needed the games to end. "I can't do my job if I don't know everything. And it's already feeling dangerous. I noticed you didn't report the break-in to security."

"It wouldn't do any good. Look, this case is bigger than you and me."

"Then why assign me?"

"Because you're the attorney here smart enough to figure out a way to win an unwinnable case." He held up his hands. "I can't tell you any more, McCarthy. It's for your own good."

"What does that mean?"

His jaw jutted and he stared her down. "You have to trust me, Hayden. Keep your focus on Maricel and getting this case to trial."

"But . . ." The words died on her lips as color crept up his neck. "Fine. But I have to go to Texas."

"The retainer is about gone, and the partners won't authorize more funds."

Carmen's voice broke in over the intercom. "Your appointment is in the lobby."

"Tell him I will be there in a moment."

"He has another appointment in half an hour."

"On my way." Gerard collected a folder and legal pad from the side of his desk. "I'll talk to the partners, but that's all I can promise." He straightened. "We have a problem if we don't get this case moving and resolved. I want you to get the government to settle, without a trial, but now our client wants you to push."

"Why?"

"I'm not sure." Gerard shook his head. "He's got strong ideas."

"He? I'm working with Maricel. Are you talking about her husband? If he's here, I need to meet him."

"Never mind. Just do what you can to get this moving."

"I have a scheduled deposition, Gerard. I have to leave tomorrow."

"It might be a bill you pay." He brushed past her and slipped into the hallway as if a ghost were on his trail. "Win and that will change."

She followed him, mystified by his abrupt departure. Why hadn't Carmen brought the client to him? She slid into her office to grab her purse, so it would look like she was heading out on a mission, then went back into the hallway and toward the lobby. If Gerard saw her, she needed him to think she wasn't following him. She entered the lobby in time to see him striding toward a dark-complexioned man in an Armani suit. The man who had held the door for her was the epitome of relaxed, with his ankle over his other knee. At the same time, Hayden sensed that he didn't miss a thing.

She straightened her skirt, pushed back her shoulders, and pasted a smile on her face as she waved at the receptionist and breezed out the door.

Just one thing about the man seemed out of place with his expensive suit: the snake tattoo coiling around his neck.

Hayden walked around the block on her "mission," circling back after calling Leigh to make sure Gerard and the client were gone. She spent the next hour working on another project, then gave Carmen a buzz to see if Gerard had returned. She needed to try one more time to convince him the partners should pay for the trip. It was generous of Emilie to have offered her the voucher, but she couldn't accept.

"He didn't come back after his meeting. I'm guessing he went on a run over a late lunch."

"Thanks, Carmen. Let me know when he returns, okay?"

"Sure thing."

Hayden opened her browser to a travel web-page. She'd buy the ticket and beg for forgiveness later if they were angry with her.

A knock on her doorframe jolted her up. "Come in."

Angela's dark hair was cut in the perfect bob, and her suit didn't look the least bit rumpled. How did her friend manage to look like that every single day? But the shadows under her eyes couldn't be hidden even by her expertly applied makeup.

"Do you have a minute?"

"Sure. What's up?"

"I've been called to a meeting with the partners." Her shoulders slumped. "I'm going to be fired."

"You don't know that."

"Why else would someone go to the trouble of setting me up? That summary judgment motion was perfect when it left my hands."

"I know." Everything Angela did was excellent. She was simply incapable of less. "Close the door." After Angela did, Hayden leaned forward. "The question is why? Are you working on anything that ticked them off?"

"It's all I've thought about since Seth first came to me."

Hayden frowned. "He told me you came to him."

"No, I had no idea there was an issue until he appeared in my office Friday."

Add that to the list of odd things happening in the firm. "He talked to me on Thursday," Hayden said. "Why on earth would he even be involved?" Her phone rang and she answered it. "Hayden McCarthy."

"Hayden, I'll be back in the office in fifteen minutes." Gerard sounded breathless. "We need to meet as soon as I get back to discuss a development in the Rodriguez matter. If you see Angela, tell her we need to talk as well."

"She's here in my office."

"Good. I'll see you both there as soon as I return. It's time to bring you two into the loop. There's a lot going on at the firm and you need to know about it."

Hayden replaced the phone on the cradle. "Gerard is on his way back and wants to meet with both of us."

"Any idea why?"

"Something about the Rodriguez case with me. You? I have no idea."

"All right. Tell him I'll wait in my office. I might as well use the time to brush up my résumé."

"He wants you to wait here. No need to rush into a job hunt."

Angela looked like she wanted to disagree, but settled back in the chair instead. "Then give me something to work on."

"How someone breaking into Gerard's and my offices over the weekend is tied to your troubles."

"I don't see how they could be."

"Tell me more about your case."

Angela moved her hands in a helpless gesture. "It's one of a hundred summary judgment motions I've defended for a client. This one involved a man who was allegedly injured by our client's employee. Yet there was nothing I could find anywhere that indicated our client was at all involved. The alleged employee was no longer an employee. Had been fired the week before. The issue seemed simple: I had the paperwork to prove it, and the affidavit simply reiterated what the paperwork showed."

"Then why is the affidavit critical? Even if it was forged somehow, the paperwork still covers the defense."

"Exactly. That doesn't change the fact that I didn't fake it, but no one is listening to me."

"Who was the client?"

"A corporation buried under three or four shell corporations from Mexico. I never felt I got a good answer on who was calling the shots, but ultimately, a partner called mine." She sighed. "I wish he'd called someone else's."

"Mexico?"

"Yes."

Could it somehow be tied to Rodriguez? Mexico was a big place, but still . . . "Could you forward what you have on the company?"

"Why?"

"Call it a hunch. What if your case somehow tied back to Rodriguez?"

"That's a leap, but it's worth checking." Angela pulled out her phone and clicked some buttons. "It's on its way. What were you working on when I arrived?"

"Buying the plane ticket to Texas and

wondering if I'll have a job when I get back." Hayden turned to her computer and the open screen. The dollar sign taunted her. "Here goes." She closed her eyes and pressed the purchase button. "Guess I'm going to Waco Wednesday."

The women discussed Hayden's plan for the deposition and then Hayden reviewed the company information Angela had forwarded to her. There was no clear connection to the Rodriguez case, but then, she wasn't fluent in Spanish. When Hayden glanced at the clock on her computer, more than forty-five minutes had passed. "Gerard must have gotten detained."

The hallway outside her office began to buzz with commotion, and Hayden looked at Angela. Angela shrugged, but stood and opened the door. "Leigh, do you know what's happening?"

Hayden's paralegal came in, a stunned expression on her face. "The partners just sent an e-mail," she said. "Gerard was shot. He's dead."

Hayden sank back onto her chair. "I talked to him less than an hour ago."

Leigh nodded and stepped forward, reaching out to take Hayden's hand. "I'm so sorry."

Hayden looked at Angela, but her friend's face was as blank as she felt. "He was so alive . . . and frustrating. There must be a mistake."

Angela pulled out her phone to read the e-mail. "Police contacted the firm at 2:45 p.m. to confirm that Gerard Campbell was a partner in our firm and inform us that he intervened in a purse snatching and was shot. He died at the scene. Police have asked for our full cooperation in the investigation, and we expect each of you to do so."

"He was being a hero." Leigh grabbed a tissue from the box on Hayden's desk and wiped her eyes.

Hayden opened the e-mail on her computer and stared at the words. Seeing them didn't help the message feel less daunting and heartbreaking. "Has his family been told?"

"The firm was his family after the divorce." Leigh sniffed, then drew in a breath and squared her shoulders. "What a senseless tragedy. I'm leaving after I check on Carmen."

Hayden nodded, but part of her still refused to believe he had died. "When will the police be here?"

"The e-mail doesn't say." Angela put her phone down on the edge of the desk. "This doesn't make sense. Gerard didn't strike me as the kind of man who walks into trouble."

Hayden nodded as Leigh slipped from her office. "He might have been an attorney, but he was content to let us handle the courtroom conflicts."

"That was strange too. You know the war stories. He used to be a beast in the courtroom, then he moved up and away from cases." Angela propped her chin on her fist. "Hayden, I didn't fabricate that affidavit."

"I know."

"Gerard was helping me prove I didn't." Angela's face took on the fierce expression that always sort of scared Hayden. "What I don't understand is why the witness says I did. I watched him sign the affidavit. But I can't win a he said/she said argument."

"If you leave, they'll believe you fabricated it."

"But I can't prove a negative, so they'll fire me."

"The firm software keeps multiple backups. There must be something that supports you."

Angela laughed a bitter sound. "All of it's gone. For whatever reason, I'm a good target." She shook her head and then stood. "Let me know if you need anything while you're in Texas. I'll try to stay that long."

"Thanks." After Angela closed Hayden's office door, Hayden swiveled her chair and tried to absorb the reality that Gerard was gone. The police would want to know if any of his clients had a reason to kill him. Carmen would know all his cases and clients. All Hayden could say was he had acted erratically on the Rodriguez case. Pressure was coming from somewhere related to the case, and he had applied it to her. That didn't mean anyone would kill him. The law was filled with high pressure cases because each client's matter was the most important thing in their lives at that moment.

Unhappy clients abounded.

Most didn't take the final step of killing an attorney.

Chapter 27

Hayden couldn't let go of the idea that Gerard's death wasn't a simple tragic accident. All the odd ways he'd acted, the out-of-character things he'd said, coupled with the call he'd made in the hour before his death, created the impression it wasn't. But if his death was murder, did it mean she also was in danger?

She needed to see if there was anything in Gerard's office that would indicate what had happened. She'd start with finding the Rodriguez file he'd alluded to.

Carmen wasn't at her desk when Hayden walked by, so Hayden let herself in. Gerard's area was thoroughly cleaned, almost as if he'd never arrived that morning. Hayden frowned and glanced back at Carmen's desk. Had the paralegal come in and organized after getting the call? Hayden sank onto his chair and looked around his desk and credenza. Gerard should come bursting through his doorway any moment. Instead, he would never return.

She didn't want to disturb anything, but if there was any indication of who had Gerard on edge, she needed to know. She also needed that Rodriguez file. She slowly thumbed through the files set in an organizer on the credenza. Nothing there. Then she opened the file drawers and noted the alphabetical arrangement. As she moved past R to S, she didn't see Rodriguez. She closed the drawer. Where else would he put it?

Digging through his desk drawers felt invasive, but she took a breath and forced herself to open the first. It was a pile of folders and legal pads. No organization at all. It looked like a catchall for random paper. She pulled out the stack and flipped through it, pausing to slowly fan each legal pad. In the middle of the stack was a plain file labeled *Daniel Rodriguez*. Hayden frowned. Shouldn't it be Maricel or Miguel?

Then she recalled that Gerard had said Miguel's father was paying for the lawsuit. Maybe this file focused on that elusive man.

As she scanned the information, the blood drained from her face. Gerard had collected proof that Daniel Rodriguez was the leader of a powerful cartel in Mexico. What had made him uncomfortable enough to investigate his own client? The last three pages were handwritten notes . . . notes that contained a column of dates and then scrawled notes she could barely decipher. It looked like he'd intentionally altered his handwriting. One scrawl was her name. It was underlined three times and next to it was a word that started with D but made no sense after that.

Voices echoed down the hallway, so Hayden scooped the papers into the file. She'd photocopy them and bring the file back. Then she could decipher the contents of the file at her house.

She walked to the door and glanced out into the hallway. Randolph and another man were headed toward her. Randolph's voice neared. "His office is right here."

Hayden closed her eyes and took a quick breath.

Randolph's eyes narrowed. "What are you doing in here?"

Hayden lifted her chin and met his gaze. "I left a file in here this morning." She swallowed as tears clogged her throat. "I need it to prepare for a deposition. If you'll excuse me."

The man beside Randolph wore a basic suit, but he took in everything. She prayed he wouldn't challenge her. "You are?"

"This is Hayden McCarthy, an associate who worked closely with Campbell." Randolph's beady eyes locked on the file as if trying to discern what was in it.

She clutched it to her chest. "We discussed an important case this morning. I left this by mistake."

The man nodded. "Are you taking anything else?"

"No."

"We'll make her one of the first we interview."

"Certainly." Randolph turned to her. "Don't leave until Detective Grearson talks to you."

"Yes sir." Hayden slipped around them and hurried down the hall, heart pounding. She didn't stop until she entered her office and closed the door. Where could she stash the file so it wouldn't disappear? She couldn't stay locked in her office, and she couldn't take the file home.

Leigh knocked on her door, eyes red-rimmed and shoulders slumped. "Do you need anything before I leave?"

"Could you copy this file for me? But don't let anyone see what's in it." Should she risk Leigh getting pulled into some danger Hayden didn't understand? She rubbed her temples, ready to pull back the request, when Leigh nodded.

"It would be nice to do something normal. I'll have it back to you in a minute."

Maybe she didn't want it on one of the firm's copiers' hard drives. Until she better understood what the file contained, she couldn't know. "Would you mind doing it at Kinkos? I'll reimburse you."

"Okay . . ." Leigh looked skeptical, but took the file. "I'll be back in twenty minutes."

"Better yet, drop the copy in my mail slot at home."

Leigh looked at her with knitted brows. "Are you okay?"

"No, not with what happened to Gerard. But I know what I'm doing." Just concerned about something she couldn't explain, even when the lack of explanation made her look crazy. "Just bring the original file back when you've copied it."

"You'll tell me why when you can?" At Hayden's nod, Leigh took the file. "I'll drop the copy at your house."

An hour later Hayden left the original file in a locked drawer, and sat in a small conference room with Detective Grearson and his sidekick. The detective had the salt-and-pepper hair to go with the ring of doughnuts around his middle. Officer Nanci Tucker took a backseat role, noting every word on a pad of paper.

Detective Grearson shifted in the chair. "Did the file have what you needed?"

Hayden set her hands in her lap, determined not to use them. "Yes."

"All right. Tell us about Mr. Campbell."

Hayden filled them in on her working relationship with the partner, and then told them about seeing him before lunch. "He was focused as he pushed me on the case, but nothing unusual. Then he called an hour before he died. Told me he needed to see me when he returned."

The detective simply sat there watching her as the silence stretched between them. The officer kept her attention on the notepad. Hayden wondered what more they wanted her to say. She couldn't walk into her office, hand them a file, and say *here's the killer.* Even if she thought Gerard's death might be tied to the Rodriguez case, she had no proof.

"Gerard was in the wrong place at the wrong time, right?"

Detective Grearson tapped the table with his thumbs as if drumming a beat of music. "We're exploring all options."

"The partners' e-mail said he intervened in a robbery."

"Maybe, but usually the victim stays until police arrive."

"The victim left?"

"As soon as Mr. Campbell was shot, both the shooter and the victim took off. Different directions, according to witnesses, but both gone. Makes me wonder."

"He's a curious man." Officer Tucker looked up and met Hayden's eyes. "He likes to explore all the options."

"Often our first thought isn't right." Detective Grearson studied her intently, as if he could look directly into her mind. "If there's anything else you know or suspect, tell me."

Hayden closed her eyes, deciding how much to share. There was the man who'd come in to meet with Gerard about the Rodriguez case, and the argument when a couple partners urged him to kill the case. Hayden opened her eyes and met

Detective Grearson's skeptical gaze. "Gerard accused me of going through his office over the weekend. It was completely trashed, but I don't know why. Mine was rummaged through as well."

Detective Grearson sat forward as Officer Tucker made a note. "Did you trash it?"

"No! I didn't even come in this weekend." She shrugged. "I can't tell you it's related to a specific case. His paralegal, Carmen, would be the best person to ask about all of his cases. But we have worked together on one case that has unusual pressure on it."

"What kind of pressure?"

"It's a case involving a young immigrant murdered while detained. The partners have been back and forth about whether to keep or kill it. I think a drug boss may be the actual client, but I'm not sure."

"Interesting. Which one?"

"Gerard hadn't told me. The young man's name was Miguel Rodriguez. His mother, Maricel, was beaten severely Saturday."

"You think these events are linked?"

"I don't know." How she wished she did. "Miguel's father's name is Daniel Rodriguez."

Detective Grearson studied her a moment and then nodded. "All right. If you think of anything related, give me a call. I'd also like to see your file on Rodriguez." He slid a card across the table to her.

"I need permission from the partners first."

"Get it."

She stared at him. "The request would be better coming from you."

He smirked. "I'll get it. To get to the bottom of this, I need everything you have. Everything." He paused, his gaze intent. "Even if you think it's unimportant, call me."

Hayden took the card, then tipped her chin. "I will."

She pushed back from the table, stood, and walked from the conference room as calmly as she could while the thought that Gerard's death hadn't been an accident echoed in her head.

Chapter 28

The sun cut through the late afternoon clouds as Andrew watched his kids run around in a field along George Washington Parkway. Zeus chased the group as they played a pick-up game of flag football that looked more like rugby or soccer. What mattered to him was the laughter that surrounded the kids as they ran.

One of the larger kids tackled Jorge aggressively, more than was called for by the game. Andrew stood back, waiting to see how Jorge would respond. Would he erupt or let it go? The kid still seemed shell-shocked and didn't say anything unless he was asked a question directly. Andrew had taken him to visit his mom again the day before and again this morning, but while Maricel assured her son she was fine, the stitches running along her hairline and her obvious headache belied her words.

Where the other kids tended to feel safe and open up, the assault held Jorge in reserve. Manhood was around the corner, but he shouldn't stride into it today.

Jorge stared at the kid who had tackled him and started to say something, then glanced Andrew's direction. When he caught Andrew watching, he clamped his mouth shut and pushed to his feet. He didn't go far, just to the cluster of picnic tables, but far enough to remove himself from the game.

Andrew looked at his watch.

Four thirty.

A good time to return to New Beginnings and make sure the kids had a solid snack before they left.

"All right, everyone. Head to the van." Zeus seemed most disappointed as the kids collected the sweatshirts and backpacks they'd abandoned. The big dog danced from one to another, as if begging to play a few more minutes. With as much energy as he had expended, he'd sleep well tonight.

Andrew counted noses as the kids climbed aboard the van. When he was one short, he looked at the picnic tables. Jorge still sat, his back to the van, his face turned to the breeze blowing off the Potomac.

"Can we leave him, Andrew?" The kid who'd body-checked Jorge sneered. "It will help him man up."

"Not how we roll, Domingo, and you know it." Andrew looked around the rest of the eager faces in the van. "Everyone stay here."

The kids knew he'd take the time Jorge needed. Coming into a new country. Struggling to learn a new language. Trying to find a group who understood and accepted you. Each of the young men had experienced what Jorge was living right now. They all understood.

Andrew prayed as he approached the kid. Slouched over as he was on the bench, he looked even younger than his thirteen years. He looked like Atlas's burden rested on his back . . . a burden much too heavy for a young man.

As Andrew neared, he shuffled his feet through a pile of leaves. Jorge's head jerked up. "You okay?" Andrew plopped next to him and kept his face toward the river, mirroring Jorge's posture.

"*Sí.*" But the word conveyed something very different.

Andrew laced his fingers and placed his hands lightly on his knees, staying open and relaxed. "It's okay to admit things are hard."

Silence was the only reply.

"Is there anything you need?"

"Nothing you can give."

"Maybe not, but God can meet any need."

Jorge flinched, but still didn't turn toward him.

"I know it's true, Jorge. It's not just words." Andrew thought a moment, then decided that was enough for now. He'd learned the best exchanges came when the kids came to him rather than cramming it down their throats. "Ready to join the others?"

"Sure, Señor Andrew." Jorge stood, pushed his shoulders back, and grew an inch in the process.

There was so much potential in this young man, but one misstep could derail him. As he drove the kids back to the clubhouse and then corralled them through their peanut butter and jelly sandwiches and cleanup, Andrew said a prayer for Jorge.

It was close to seven when Andrew, Jorge, and Zeus made it back to the condo, a Chinese takeout bag in Andrew's hand. Zeus danced behind him, snuffling the bag and begging for a bite.

"When we get upstairs, boy." His words did nothing to calm the dog's exuberant display. Jorge laughed and rubbed Zeus's ears while Andrew got the door unlocked.

Andrew had been distracted over the weekend getting Jorge settled, but as soon as he entered his condo, the tension of the e-mails returned. He sighed as Zeus pressed against his leg.

"It's okay, boy."

Once Zeus and Jorge were eating sweet and sour chicken, and his plate was loaded with egg rolls and General Tso's, Andrew punched buttons and checked his voice mail. The first message was a telemarketer. Time to get back on the no-call list. The second recording sounded muffled and distorted. Andrew forked a round of spiciness into his mouth and chewed slowly as he listened.

"Wesley, you disappoint me. So much time, and you haven't found me. Your father's enemies would be interested to learn what the illustrious Congressman Wesley's son does at night."

The beep sounded the end of the message, and Andrew realized he was clutching his fork like a weapon.

What was he supposed to do with this crazy person and his allegations?

Appetite demolished, Andrew pushed the plate away and replayed the message. As with the e-mails, there was nothing to indicate who the person was. The voice was too distorted.

Jorge looked at him with wide eyes. "Everything okay, Señor Andrew?"

"Yeah. I'll be upstairs for a bit." He stalked upstairs to his studio.

As he studied the mock-up sketches he'd

worked on for this week's cartoon, he knew he couldn't work on them while angry.

He turned to his computer and moused over to his e-mail. He opened a message from his editor.

Strange woman here today asking for you. Wouldn't take no for an answer. Said you needed to talk. She was way too pushy and aggressive to know you—and of course, if she did, she wouldn't have to go through me. Anyway, here's a number to call her at. Don't forget I need that extra cartoon from you this week. Fitting for you to provide the illustration for the local profile on your dad. Wouldn't be surprised if it gets picked up for syndication.

Andrew clicked the e-mail shut with a groan. The last thing he wanted to do was a cartoon specifically of his dad. Sure, he could sketch his father's image, but for it to be true cartooning, it'd have to include the element of parody. He'd done hundreds of those sketches of his father over the years. Now his sketches mirrored those and made his dad look like a caricature.

If he didn't do it, someone else would. He could imagine the caricature they'd draw.

The more pressing problem was identifying the who behind the e-mails and phone call before he was exposed. Odd a woman had gone to the paper looking for him. Could it be this stalker? But why would she go to his office to see him when she already had his number?

Boxing shadows was exhausting and fruitless.

He picked up his cell and dialed the number. Might as well confront this shadow, but the call didn't go through. He frowned and redialed, but got the same message: the number was disconnected. Another dead end.

The next e-mail was from Emilie, with a checklist of things he needed to do before the community fair. The detailed agenda included who needed to be contacted each day, vendors to talk to, and a list of everyone she'd already contacted. He shook his head at his easygoing cousin's attention to detail. If the event was a success, it would be due to her efforts.

His phone rang and he hesitated to answer. What if it was another call about his alter identity?

He sighed and picked up the phone.

Chapter 29

Hayden paced her home office. The review of the file hadn't revealed anything. Gerard had left as much unsaid as he'd written down, and she'd need his help to decipher what he had written. She sank onto her chair and brushed a tear from her cheek.

Gerard had been a good man and mentor, one who pushed hard. Now he was gone.

Should she tell Andrew about his death and the questions surrounding it? Even if she was wrong about it being connected to the Rodriguez case, better to warn him and be wrong than omit important information he might need in helping Jorge. She reached for her cell phone, but nervous energy had her hands trembling.

She rubbed her neck where the muscles had tightened to rocks. First she needed to clear her head.

After throwing on a light jacket and tennis shoes, Hayden headed outside. She'd never been much of a runner, but when she needed to clear her mind nothing was better than getting outside and moving. As she walked she prayed for Gerard's family, whoever they were. Although she had worked with the man for several years, she didn't know much about his private life beyond the photo on his desk.

The burden she felt for them didn't ease, so she kept walking and praying. As she passed a store window, she noticed a man behind her in the reflection. A few stores later, he was still there. She crossed the street and continued, yet he remained behind her, always keeping a few people between them.

She broke into a jog and hurried toward the park. If he followed, there would be no doubt he was tailing her. Why hadn't she grabbed her cell phone?

Before she reached the park, she ducked into the Torpedo Factory. The former weapons facility had been transformed into a home for more than eighty artists' studios and seven galleries. Its multiple outside doors and nooks and crannies provided a place to hide.

As she hurried across the first floor, she glanced over her shoulder. The man had followed her, but she bet she knew the facility better than he did. She brushed past a mom and kids and hurried upstairs to the second floor. Then she raced along the walkway and down the stairs to a door on the opposite side of the building. She burst out the doors and raced across the patio toward DC. She hoped he would expect her to go toward Old Town. When her lungs were on fire from the sprint, she stopped and looked behind her, gasping for breath. No sign of him.

She tried to form a picture of the stalker in her mind, but nothing stuck. It was as if his image had disappeared along with him. Once she could breathe again, she rubbed the stitch in her side and started moving. She could run parallel to where she needed to go along the Potomac.

Twenty minutes later she crept back into the town house like a cat burglar and grabbed her phone.

Emilie stared at her from her position curled

in a chair with Denise Hunter's latest romance. "What on earth?"

"Don't ask." Hayden hurried to the kitchen and filled a glass with water. After she gulped it down, she plopped into one of the chairs at the small table. "Gerard Campbell is dead."

Emilie startled and uncurled. "Oh my goodness. Are you okay?"

"Yes. No." She huffed out a hysterical laugh. "I don't know. I think it could be tied to Rodriguez, and then as I went for a walk to clear my head, a man followed me. But maybe I imagined it. I couldn't tell you the first thing about him now other than he wore a ball cap and followed me through Old Town and the Torpedo Factory."

"You should call the police."

"And tell them what? That some man I can't describe was after me?" She thought of Detective Grearson's card, but shook her head. "They wouldn't believe me. Nor should they." She rubbed her fingers along the phone. "I need to warn Andrew, but he'll think I'm a kook."

"Hayden, no one says 'kook' anymore." Emilie's eyes were wide and she looked paler than usual.

"Are you okay?"

"Sure. Taking a break from my article. I've got good stuff brewing. My editor says it's my best yet."

"That's high praise."

"Yep." Emilie's lips curled in a stiff smile. "So are you going to warn Andrew?"

"Yeah." She needed to, especially after her race through Old Town. "I want him aware." It was the right thing to do, even if the man would think she'd lost her sense. "I'll call him from upstairs."

She needed to do it before she lost her nerve. When Andrew's phone went to voice mail she felt a pang of disappointment. She'd sound even odder leaving a message, but she needed to close this loop.

"Andrew, this is Hayden. Gerard Campbell was killed today. It might have something to do with the Rodriguez case. I'm not sure, but am trying to find out. I wanted you to be aware since Jorge is with you. Also, someone followed me around Old Town earlier this evening. Let me know if you have any questions."

She hung up with a sigh. That was definitely the last time she'd hear from Mr. Most Eligible Bachelor. She squared her shoulders and reminded herself it was okay. She had Gerard's notes to decipher and a deposition to prep for . . . not to mention a mentor to grieve.

Tuesday passed in a flurry of meetings as the partners divided Gerard's cases among them. Angela wasn't in any of the meetings, but Hayden couldn't check on her because Randolph somehow snagged Rodriguez.

"We'll discuss how to fire the client first thing Thursday morning."

"Sir, I won't be here."

"If you want your job you will be."

A twisted-up feeling settled in Hayden's gut, and she didn't bother telling him she'd be in Texas. Better to confront that later when she had everything she'd learned from the deposition. "What would you like me to pre-pare?"

"A letter firing the client."

As she left the conference room, she collided with Seth. "Have you seen Angela?"

"Not since yesterday afternoon." Seth shoved his hands in his pockets. "So you're working with Randolph now?"

"Doesn't make any sense, since he doesn't like litigation."

"Not much makes sense." He glanced over his shoulder, as if to confirm no one was near. "I think he got Angela canned."

"He didn't work with her either."

"No. But watch your back. He's on a rampage over everything and getting rid of anyone he doesn't like. I can't figure out why." He took a step closer. "That's what he was doing with that discovery mess."

Hayden nodded, even as she wondered why he was telling her this. "Let me know if you see Angela?"

"Sure, but I don't think we will." He turned and headed to his office.

Hayden detoured by Angela's small office, but it had been stripped bare of everything but the furniture. Nothing left, from books to framed diplomas. When she returned to her office she tried to reach Angela, but her calls went directly to voice mail. What was going on?

Over lunch she went to the hospital to check on Maricel. The woman had been improving, but now her doctors were concerned; a fever she was running suggested an infection. The bruises on her face looked worse, a kaleidoscope of yellow, green, and purple.

The afternoon flew with deposition prep that reinforced how much she would have to learn to have a prayer of keeping the Rodriguez case moving forward.

When she got home she was ready to put the terrible day behind her.

As she packed and readied to leave first thing in the morning, Hayden's stomach churned. She couldn't push aside the reality that Gerard Campbell was dead. In a city filled with political news, another anonymous murder didn't make the cut, so she had to scan online newspapers for information.

Emilie joined Hayden in her room, plopping onto the bed as Hayden packed.

Hayden rolled a pair of jeans and set them in the

suitcase. "Emilie, I can't make heads or tails of Gerard's notes, but I know the police are making a mistake. His death was no accident."

Emilie's eyes widened. "How can you know?"

"Detective Grearson didn't answer when I asked. He left the door open for it to be murder." Hayden sank onto the bed next to Emilie and leaned into her friend. "It's unreal that he argued with me about traveling to Texas, and now I'm packing my suitcase, knowing he'll never frustrate me again. Could I have done something?"

"Not if you weren't with him on his jog, and I've seen you run. You'd never keep up." Emilie tipped her head on Hayden's shoulder. "I am sorry."

"Me too." Hayden sank into Emilie's empathy for a moment. "Somehow going to Texas now feels wrong, yet making something of this case is the best way to honor him."

Emilie straightened, and Hayden watched her shift to reporter mode. "What was he like the last time you saw him? Was there anything odd about his behavior?"

"Not any more than the rest of this month." Hayden stood and grabbed a pair of navy heels. "I've told you how abrupt and unfocused some of our conversations were. The pressure he had me under on Rodriguez was unusually amped up. But that last call makes me wonder what he wanted to tell me." And that big client with the expensive suit and dead eyes. She needed to check the calendar to see who it was, but Carmen had been out all day.

Please tell me going to Texas tomorrow is the right decision, Lord.

"I'll keep digging too."

"Leave it to the police, Emilie, because after that chase last night I know someone is watching the house. I don't want you getting hurt."

"I can take care of myself." Emilie huffed out a breath, then brightened. "Let me tell you about the cutest five-year-old who came in today." She chattered on, a welcome distraction, as Hayden folded another pair of pants and placed them on top of the pile of clothes. Emilie paused and glanced at the suitcase. "You said you're gone two nights."

"Yep."

"Then why are you packing like you're going to Europe for two weeks?"

Hayden eyed the suitcase. She had two suits, two workout outfits, some kick-around clothes, and shoes to match each outfit. "Looks right to me."

Emilie rolled her eyes. "Diva."

"Yeah, I'm so diva-ish I'm taking a cab rather than make you drive me at oh-dark-hundred."

"We all have our kryptonite. Mine is early mornings after a deadline." Emilie glanced at her watch. "Speaking of which, I have one tonight.

Guess I'd better get at it." She stood but didn't leave. "Be careful, okay?"

"You sound concerned."

"Of course. I need my roommate back in one piece. Try to keep your job while you're at it."

"I don't know if I can, with Gerard gone. I can't tell if he was a buffer or the source of the threats. Randolph's already conveyed he wants the Rodriguez case gone." Hayden's heart roller-coastered at the thought that she might be out of a job because she was representing her client well. She shut the suitcase and rolled it to the doorway. "I'm flying down, getting my information, and coming straight back to file that complaint. I'll see you Thursday night."

"All right." Emilie gave her a quick hug that lasted a second longer than normal. "Wish me luck on this article. I've got the guts, but they ain't pretty." Emilie said something similar with each article, yet the end result sang with prose that led the reader so easily through a 2,000-word article they didn't realize how much time they'd invested.

"What's the topic this week?"

"Something." Emilie shrugged with a wink. "You'll have to find out with everyone else."

Hayden pulled out her phone and started entering a note.

Emilie crowded close, trying to read over her shoulder. "What are you doing?"

"Setting a reminder to look for the article Thursday."

"It'll wait until Friday." Emilie's laugh held a nervous edge. "See you then." She sashayed out of Hayden's bedroom and down the stairs.

Hayden flopped on her bed and sighed. The floral comforter embraced her as she tried to relax each vertebra into the softness. One of these days she'd start an exercise regimen— hence the clothes in the suitcase—but right now she just wished this trip was over.

Gerard's service was scheduled for Saturday, after she returned.

She wanted to win the case he'd given her and prove to the partners he hadn't made a mistake. That meant she had to stop thinking about his murder and focus on the deposition. She also needed to find the guards who'd worked the night Miguel died. See what they remembered before memories were tainted by witness preparation.

She'd jotted down the information she needed with accompanying questions, but she wasn't satisfied. It would take luck and divine guidance to find everyone in the few hours she'd have in Texas.

She fired up her laptop and did one last search. The International Juvenile Detention Center located outside Waco didn't have much published about it. In fact, she'd dug for more than an hour before she found a hint on anything other than a watch-dog website.

The lack of information meant she'd go in blind. Was this a homelike foster care facility? It could be that, or it could be an industrial facility a half step removed from jail.

As she closed her laptop and brushed her teeth, her thoughts turned to Miguel. Had he understood what was happening, or had his English skills limited comprehension?

Her alarm blared before Hayden realized she'd fallen asleep. She hit snooze and snuggled under the covers. It was much too early for her alarm. Seven minutes later, it blasted her again and she jolted.

Airplane. Texas. This morning.

In record time she was ready and placing her suitcase in a cab's trunk. After the cabbie dropped her at the main terminal at Reagan National Airport, she worked her way through security. She made it to her gate with time to spare, so she grabbed a hot tea and a chocolate croissant.

The gate area was busy, people crowding into each seat, tipping into each other's space as they stacked carry-ons in a precarious array. Hayden kept a close watch on hers to make sure no one grabbed her red Husker case by mistake. One flight deplaned and in minutes the bulk of the crowd jockeyed for a place in line. The faces were a mishmash of dejected, bored, intent, and honeymoon love. One man in a three-piece suit looked like he was about to have a heart attack as he yelled into his phone.

The public address system announced a gate change for her flight, and she collected her bag then worked her way to the new gate. When she reached it she glanced around, but all seats were taken. She pulled her bag to the wall and leaned against it.

As she settled in, Hayden noticed a man watching her. She straightened and met his gaze. He was roughly six feet tall, solid like a line-backer, and dressed in jeans and a pullover. He had a baseball cap pulled low on his face and grinned at her with a smarmy leer. He looked familiar in a vague way. Had he chased her through Old Town Monday or been at the Cherry Blossom Festival? She raised her eyebrows and tipped her chin in defiance. When he didn't waiver, she decided to grab a bottle of water and escape the unwanted attention.

She snagged her suitcase and, after she'd gone a few feet, she glanced back. The man had dis-appeared. She stopped and scanned the waiting area, then the crowd.

It was as though he'd disappeared with a snap of his fingers.

The hair on the back of her neck stood at atten-tion, and she scanned everyone as she walked to the bookstore and glanced at magazines. Time to rein in her overactive imagination. No one could follow her through security nor be here without a valid ticket.

She picked up a bottle of water and moved into the crowd around the cashier.

"Are you buying that?" The man behind her in line nodded at the water she held and the empty space between her and the counter.

The cashier looked at her with studied indifference, and Hayden felt heat climb her cheeks. "Yes, thank you."

Once they had boarded she pulled out the file of Gerard's notes and settled in to spend the flight deciphering his shorthand. Her phone rang, and she reached down to turn it to airplane mode but stopped when she saw Gerard's number on the screen. Reluctantly she swiped a finger across the screen to take the call. "Hello?"

"Hayden, you have to get off that plane post-haste." Carmen's voice sounded ragged.

"They just closed the door. I'll be back Friday by early afternoon. Can it wait until then?" Hayden leaned against the small window and watched the airline's employees on the ground chucking suitcases on the conveyor belt. A flight attendant came toward her and motioned to turn off the phone. "I've got to go. The plane's about to push back."

"I don't think this can wait. The partners are on the rampage, and you're next. Call me the minute you land."

"I'll try. Before I go, can you tell me who Gerard had an appointment with the day he died?"

"Rodriguez."

The flight attendant frowned at Hayden as the word settled in her mind. *Rodriguez.* That must have been Miguel's dad, the drug lord. "I have to go before the flight attendant grabs my phone. I'm sorry about Gerard." Hayden hung up and tucked her phone in her carry-on as a lump filled her throat. She looked at the attendant. "Sorry about that."

"Keep it off during the flight." She moved to the next row.

Hayden settled back and closed her eyes. The flight would take about two hours, and then she had a drive to reach the facility. Her thoughts were spinning like an unbalanced load of laundry. Why had Carmen called to warn her about her job? And why had Rodriguez met with Gerard?

Chapter 30

Andrew arrived at New Beginnings a couple hours before the kids. Zeus lumbered beside him, a content grin on his doggy face as he settled into the dog bed next to Andrew's desk.

His office was sparse, but nice. Andrew liked the way the kids scrawled their names across the desk's battered surface. As he read each name, he prayed God would watch over and protect them wherever they were now.

Andrew settled at his desk and kicked off his loafers. If he was lucky he'd find his anonymous tormenter before the kids arrived.

His cell phone buzzed, and he answered without glancing at the screen. "This is Andrew."

"Hey, handsome." Lilith's voice honeyed into his ear, and he wished the voice belonged to a dark-haired beauty named Hayden McCarthy instead. Lilith only talked like that when she needed something, especially since he'd made it clear he wasn't interested in a relationship.

He pinched the bridge of his nose and sank farther into his office chair. "What's up, Lilith?"

She huffed, then turned it into a giggle. "Your dad wants you to join an oversight."

"I don't go on trips at taxpayer expense."

"This isn't a junket. We're headed to a juvenile detention facility in Texas, and he wants you since you work with immigrants."

Andrew kept his eyes closed as he considered what his dad really wanted. "Is this another photo op for the congressman? He wouldn't go for any other reason during the campaign cycle."

"You haven't heard? The governor appointed him to the vacancy over lunch. He'll be a senator in days. And he has always been an advocate for refugees and legal immigrants. This is a trip to make sure Congress's rules for the kids who come alone are followed." She paused, and he could almost see her sweetness factor increase. "You could be a big help on this trip."

He didn't like the pressure. It felt forced, with another reason hidden behind the request. "When's the swearing-in?"

"Not scheduled yet, but soon. You'll need to be there."

Of course. "Will you still have the fund-raiser?" Part of him wanted the answer to be yes so he still had the excuse to see Hayden.

"We'll need more money to keep this seat, so that hasn't changed. I need an answer on the trip."

"When is it?"

"You know how these things go. Can you leave in the morning? Six o'clock?"

Andrew glanced down at his calendar. It was empty. "A standard one-day trip?"

"The congressman, I mean senator, plans to visit several facilities. You can come to Texas and catch a separate flight back. We've heard from a guard at one of the detention centers. If there's any truth to his allegations, heads will roll."

"Anything more?"

"Nope. Don't want to skew your perspective. You're the unbiased observer."

He snorted. Like anyone would consider him unbiased when he worked with kids similar to the detained. The crucial difference was the route they had taken to the US.

Not many had the opportunity to check the kids' welfare. See how they were treated while in US custody. He'd be a fool not to rearrange his schedule, when a couple calls was all it would take to locate volunteers to cover the day. "All right. I'll be there. Private hangar at Reagan?"

"Yes. Bring an overnight bag in case you extend the trip."

"Not a chance." Twenty-four hours of togetherness would be plenty, based on past trips. He and his dad could only handle so much, especially with staff. "See you tomorrow."

Andrew hung up and turned back to his original project of finding his stalker. He'd give it an hour, then make some calls so he could join tomorrow's trip. Lilith had succeeded in stoking his curiosity.

Whatever the guard had mentioned must be serious or his dad would stay in DC.

His thoughts returned to who could have revealed his real identity. The list was too small. His editor insisted the list at the paper hadn't grown. That left a couple college buddies who knew he doodled, and the small staff of the campus paper—he hadn't been too concerned about his privacy back then, when it had been a few cartoons for the college daily. Other than that, Andrew drew a blank. He groaned and ran his hands through his hair. *Someone* knew—and that someone was enjoying keeping him on edge.

Zeus nudged his knee as if sensing his stress. Andrew rubbed behind the dog's ears, but his thoughts stayed on the puzzle.

Maybe he should focus on his dad's enemies. Problem was, that list could be quite long. You couldn't build a meaningful career in Washington without ticking people off. He might not appreciate his parents' priorities, but he couldn't fault his dad's work ethic. If anything, the man was über committed to his constituents.

Andrew did a bit of online research and built a list of party hopefuls who might want to force his dad out. Then he added some serious detractors to the list. During the flight to Texas, he'd feel his dad out about anyone he might have missed—though how to do that without alerting Dad would be tricky.

The door to New Beginnings opened, and an intern be-bopped in.

"Hello, Mr. Wesley. I've got today's activity like you requested." The bubbly brunette patted her backpack. "It'll be a great way to get the kids talking."

Andrew followed her into the main room and pushed tables into the configuration she requested. "Remember, they might not share much. They tend to like active games." The kind that involved balls, mud, and a few bruises. Many didn't have the language skills, and those who did weren't apt to share them in a crowd.

"They'll love this one. My prof assured me it would work. And if not, we'll play Twister and work on colors and body parts."

She continued to talk, but Andrew's thoughts strayed.

Could getting out of town even for a day throw off whoever was threatening him?

Chapter 31

Hayden wrestled with her phone's GPS as she drove across the area outside Waco. If she didn't hurry, she'd be late for the deposition. Thanks to a flight delay, her extra time had evaporated, until she wondered if the trip would be a waste of money she didn't have. She rubbed the back of her neck and prayed for time to stand still as she pushed the car as fast as she dared. She should call Carmen back, too, but she couldn't spare the time or the distraction. She had to get her game face on for this deposition.

The Texas expanse could swallow her whole and no one would ever see her again. The pocket-sized car she had rented didn't help the feeling the world was eating her. A haze discolored the road where it met the horizon, the shimmer of heat distorting the scrub trees. The trench coat she'd brought would stay unneeded in the trunk.

After driving to the point at which she was sure she'd missed her turn, the GPS barked directions, taking her from the interstate to smaller highways to county roads until she came to a stop in front of an industrial government-issue building. It must have been constructed during the Cold War, a concrete building that rose from the dirt with nothing to distinguish it from a hundred other government buildings—but not here. This one stood alone, with only the Texas desert surrounding it as the county road ran like a ribbon into the distance.

Hayden pulled into the small parking lot and turned off the car.

She sat in the car a moment, glancing at the dashboard clock. The drive had eaten up every last second prior to the deposition. Calling Carmen would have to wait. She swallowed around an excessively dry throat and snagged her attaché case. The perfect world of having an hour to review her notes wasn't happening. Instead, she had to go in there and be brilliant on her prior preparation. If only her butterflies would fly in formation. Well, she'd come too far and spent too much to let the delays stop her from taking the best deposition of her life.

Lord, help me make the most of this time. Help me ask the right questions.

Hayden had long believed that if God placed her in a job, He would help her with the day-to-day issues. This was more than asking for guidance and insight as she wrote a brief or searched boxes of discovery. She pulled her attaché case from the backseat and slipped the car keys into an out-side pocket.

When she straightened, she pulled her shoulders back and tipped her chin a bit.

The double doors led into a facility with cracked white linoleum floors and old plastic chairs whose best days and color selection had been in the sixties. A woman in a security uniform sat behind a high counter, Plexiglas separated her from the lobby. A bank of monitors sat on a counter behind her, and a computer and multi-line phone rested on the desk. The woman's skin was the color of cinnamon, and a Hispanic lilt accented her voice when she spoke. "May I help you?"

"Hayden McCarthy. I have a deposition scheduled with the director."

The woman looked at her with an expression that Hayden wasn't sure how to read—half disbelief, half impressed. "May I see your ID?"

Hayden dug out her driver's license and bar card and slid them into the drawer the woman pushed out like a bank teller or gas station clerk. She studied the cards, then placed them on a scanner. After she returned them, she picked up the phone and mumbled.

She gestured toward a set of double doors. "Run your bag through the x-ray machine and pass through the metal detector. Someone will meet you on the other side and escort you." She slid a visitor badge into the drawer and shoved it to Hayden. "Wear this at all times. We close at five sharp."

"Thank you." Hayden pinned the badge on the lapel of her jacket, then walked through the doors.

On the other side she submitted to the screenings and was met by a stern-faced, uniformed man. He'd indulged in a few too many bagels, and the stench of his cologne surrounded and gagged her. His salt-and-pepper hair was greased back, and he strutted with one hand on his holster as if she posed a threat.

"The director's office is down this hall."

"Wait. We're supposed to have a deposition with a court reporter. In the conference room."

"I don't know nothing about that. You can ask him." He glanced over his shoulder. "He's got fifteen minutes tops. Busy man running this place."

"I'll remember that. Thank you." Hayden strained to hear anything that sounded like the voices of children. Instead she was met with an eerie silence, broken only by her heels clicking against the concrete floor. "Where are the residents?"

"We've got two wings for them. One for the girls, another for the boys. Never the two shall meet." He laughed, a harsh, grating sound.

"What do they do?"

"Do?" He stopped and studied her, his brows knit together and his legs apart. Definite power stance.

She squared her body to meet his. "Yes, do. You've got hundreds of kids. Surely they do something during the day."

He snorted and turned back toward the expanse of the hall. "Lady, this is a detention center, not a preschool. They eat, they sleep, they go outside. The rest of the time, they do whatever kids do to entertain themselves."

Hayden bit back a retort. Children were children, no matter their circumstances. Each had basic needs that included more than food and water. She'd wager he gave his pooch more affection than these kids received.

"Here we are." He stepped to one side and waved her through a doorway.

Hayden stepped into a suite of offices. A woman looked up and pasted a smile on her bright red lips. Her hair was Texas big, teased on the sides and high. She wore a bold floral dress, slashes of neon color against the gray walls.

"May I help you?" Her drawl honeyed her words, and her gaze was clear and direct.

"Hayden McCarthy. I'm here for a deposition with Mr. Snowden."

The secretary stood and knocked on a door behind her desk. She opened it and then stuck her head inside. Muffled words filtered out, and she turned around with a tense smile. "Can I get you anything to drink?"

"Water would be fine. Thank you."

"The director will see you now."

Hayden followed her into the office. Carlton Snowden didn't look much like his official bio photo. He had put on a few pounds and lost some hair, but had the same hard eyes and cutting gaze.

"Ms. McCarthy." He gestured to a man sitting to the side of the desk, his suit indicating he could be opposing counsel. "This is Jim Beauman with the Department of Justice."

The man stood and adjusted the gold frames of his glasses before offering her his hand. "I'm looking forward to our conversation today."

"It's a deposition. As I agreed to Monday with your pit bull of an attorney."

"Sure, sure. She's sick, so you get me. We're waiting on the court reporter." The attorney grinned at her and then at Director Snowden. "People get lost coming out here."

"It's true." The director nodded as if following a script. "The wide open spaces confuse folks."

"I'll call her." Hayden pulled out her phone and checked for messages. Seeing none, she placed the call. "Hi, this is Hayden McCarthy. We're expecting you at the juvenile detention center for the deposition."

"I'm on my way. Strangest thing, but I came out of lunch and had a flat tire." The woman huffed a frazzled breath. "I'm never late, but I didn't anticipate this."

Hayden stifled a sigh of her own. "When do you think you'll arrive?"

"I'll be there in an hour."

"See you then." Hayden hung up and turned to the men. "She'll be here in an hour." She kept the information about the flat to herself.

"Now wait a minute. I only have an hour."

"The agreement was for up to six hours of deposition. Maybe we could make use of the time by having a tour."

"Is this true?" Director Snowden looked at the government attorney.

Beauman shot his shirt cuffs, then pasted on a smile. "Yes, it is."

Snowden's assistant bustled in with a chilled

bottle of water, which Hayden accepted with quiet thanks.

"If we had anything on this young man, we'd be happy to provide it after the proper FOIA request was made." Mr. Beauman's smile got smarmier. "However, there isn't much to give."

Hayden shifted against the chair but kept her own smile in place. "I can't imagine any child in this facility doesn't have a file filled with information. Even that would put his mother at ease."

The need for justice burned through her, and she itched to serve the revised complaint here and now. Watch the smug expression slide from the man's face with the realization that she was very serious about pursuing Miguel's murder. She restrained herself because if she presented it now, the conversation was over. She had to bide her time, learn what she could, and then launch the official process.

"I'm sure you can spare time for a quick tour while we wait, Mr. Snowden, since opposing counsel is here."

Snowden steepled his fingers under his chin and studied her. She willed him to understand how determined she was. A flash of communication passed between the men and she waited for the result. Finally he nodded.

"A tour won't hurt anything and could prove you're on a ghost hunt." He stood and gestured for her to do the same. "Ladies first."

Chapter 32

Any time Hayden saw something to explore, Snowden physically pointed her in another direction. When he didn't, Beauman did. The places they showed her were corridors of narrow, cell-like rooms. Bunk beds were crammed into them, topped with navy comforters and basic pillows. In the hallways there were stations of bookcases, puzzles, and random toys, but no children.

Finally she couldn't hold her question in any longer. "Where are the children?"

"Here and there. A few groups are outside for fresh air and exercise. Another group is having medical checks. We keep them active and healthy for their stay. One illness can spread through a facility in no time."

That wasn't the impression the guard had given her, but she kept that to herself. Snowden led her down another sterile hallway and around a corner, down some stairs, and into a security center.

"This is where our guards monitor 24/7. The best defense is a good offense, so we stay alert for trouble and catch its inception rather than let it spread. Kids from rival gangs are here, so we keep a close eye on them."

Hayden's gaze roamed the bank of monitors. "Are these the only monitors?"

"Ma'am?" His sugary southern sweetness about made her gag.

"Do you have more cameras monitored elsewhere?"

One of the guards cleared his throat, and Mr. Snowden glared at him. "The only thing not visible here is the sleeping quarters."

"I see that. Are those monitored?"

"Not during a time like this when most are empty."

"But there are cameras in the rooms?"

"Sure."

"Are those records somewhere?"

"I'm not sure why you're asking." Yet his shifty gaze told her he'd figured it out.

"If Miguel Rodriguez was killed in his room, then video captured his murderer." Someone had seen the last page of the boy's life.

"Now look. Nobody was killed here. A few may have died, but from illness or an injury they arrived with."

Beauman stepped between them. "We should see if the court reporter is ready."

Hayden wanted to protest, but restrained herself. Snowden might not realize he'd opened a line of questioning for the deposition, but Beauman understood. She needed Snowden's answers captured by the court reporter while he was under oath. Then the answers could be used in court to prevent him from changing his testimony later.

The walk back to the office was quiet while Hayden took in everything and memorized what she saw. Snowden's assistant stood as soon as they entered her space.

"The woman set up in your office. I hope that's all right, sir."

"Fine." Snowden walked past her and opened the door to his office. "Please bring four bottles of water."

"Right away."

The stenographer's equipment was stationed on the edge of Snowden's desk. Ten years ago that would have been a machine to type on; now it was a digital recorder with an attached microphone.

The court reporter looked about fifty and wore bling-y jeans and a cardigan set. Her cat's eye glasses caused her eyes to look big and curious. "I'm ready whenever y'all are." She reached for a White Castle cup and slurped through the straw. "I'll run a test and get started."

"Thanks." Hayden slipped her attaché case from her shoulder, grateful to set it down. She sank onto the chair closest to the court reporter and pulled legal pads covered with notes from the bag. When she had arranged them in order on her lap, she glanced at the gentlemen. "Ready when you are."

Beauman considered her pile of legal pads. "Exactly how long do you expect this deposition to last?"

"That all depends on the director." She turned a sweet smile on him. "If he answers my questions it shouldn't take more than a couple hours." Neither needed to know there was only one question on each page with a couple blank pads on the bottom.

"We'll see." With that he settled against the chair and crossed one leg over a knee. While he might look relaxed and bored, Hayden knew he would pounce the moment he thought she'd gone too far. He waved to the court reporter. "Let's roll."

"Yes sir." The woman pressed a button on the impossibly small recorder. Then she looked at Snowden. "If you would say something." She watched a reading as he counted from one to five. Then she turned to Hayden. "It's your turn."

Hayden grimaced at the microphone. She never really knew what to say without sounding slightly ridiculous. A mic check at church could be a Bible verse, but here? "I can't wait to ask all my questions."

Snowden's skin paled, and she wondered what he was afraid she'd ask. She wanted to find that question and nail him.

"We're good." The court reporter turned to Snowden. "Sir, I need to swear you in. Please raise your right hand. Do you promise the testimony you are about to give is true, so help you God?"

He nodded with a sharp jerk of his chin.

"You need to speak your answer, sir."

"Yes."

"Your witness." The court reporter sat back, and Hayden leaned forward.

Hayden tried to tilt the notepads away from Beauman's line of sight. "Please state your name and address for the record."

She quickly led him through routine questions. The key was to be friendly and keep an open face so the witness slowly forgot he should be guarded. She wanted him in a rhythm so Beauman had nothing to object to and questions and answers would flow in a dance of words. As she ticked through his education and job history, the director's shoulders relaxed and his hand quit drumming the table. He leaned back in his chair and gazed at her as if wondering if this was the best she could do.

Then they reached his work history at the detention center.

"How long have you worked here?"

"Two years."

She made a notation. "Have you always worked as the director?"

"I started as the assistant and moved into the director role a year ago."

"What does your job consist of?"

"I am responsible for ensuring that the children in our custody are well cared for while here."

"What does 'well cared for' mean?"

"I don't understand." His back stiffened away from the chair.

"How do you define 'well cared for'?"

"Getting all my wards through the day success-fully."

"So no injuries?"

"Yes."

"No deaths?"

"Of course." He turned to Beauman, who stayed silent.

"Definitely no murders?"

"Yes."

She jotted a note, letting his answer linger. "Who is your boss?"

"Ultimately the governor."

"This is a state agency?"

"Operating under contract with Immigration and Customs."

"Whom do you report to? The governor of Texas? Or the director of ICE?"

"Both . . . I guess."

"Please don't guess. Simply answer to the best of your knowledge."

The director sputtered a moment and looked at Beauman. The government attorney didn't flinch as he straightened the cuff on his pant leg. "Answer the question."

The director huffed out a breath. "Both."

"Who funds this facility?"

"Both."

"In what ways?"

"We receive block grants from the federal government and a per diem from the state."

"Which is the larger source of income?"

"I'd have to check."

"All right." She made a notation, then turned to Beauman. "Please make a note to provide the documentation. A formal request will follow."

Beauman nodded, but didn't write anything down. This would be a good test of how he'd cooperate. Hayden paused and considered whether she had enough to establish that the federal government shared responsibility for the facility. From Snowden's testimony, it was at least partly culpable. She'd tug that string more, but direct him to another area first. Let him think he was off the hook.

She moved him through the process they used when checking in new detainees and checking them out. "What do you document in the children's files?"

"Anything of note."

"Give me some examples."

"Medical needs. If the guards have to intervene in a situation. Those situations."

"So if there was an assault, it would be documented?"

"Yes."

"An injury requiring medical care?"

"Yes."

"What if someone was stabbed with a knife?"

He hesitated a beat. "Yes, if it required medical intervention."

"But not if it didn't?"

"Not likely. We have too many residents to track every situation."

"So if a child in your care was stabbed by another resident, that might not be noted."

"Not if medical care wasn't needed."

"So if someone were killed, it wouldn't be documented?"

"I didn't say that."

Mr. Beauman leaned forward. "I think that's enough on this line of questioning."

She smiled sweetly at him. "I've only begun. Thank you." She noted how both men bristled when she poked here. They were trying to create the illusion that nothing was in Miguel's file. She could lay a foundation for how ridiculous that was. "So if a child died of natural causes and medical care wasn't provided, would anything be noted?"

"What the death certificate required."

"What happened to Miguel Rodriguez?"

"What do you mean?" Mr. Snowden's features hardened into a mask.

"When did he arrive here?"

"I can't tell you off the top of my head."

"Did you review his file in preparation for this deposition, as the summons requested?"

"No."

So this was how he wanted to play it. Fine. She pulled a copy of the request for deposition from a legal pad and handed it to the court reporter. "Would you mark this Exhibit A?"

The woman filled out the sticker and affixed it to the front of the document, then handed it back to Hayden, who handed the labeled copy to Snowden and a second to Beauman. "This is a copy of the request that was mailed to you."

"Okay."

"Did you read the request when received?"

"I forwarded it to our counsel."

"Mr. Beauman?"

"Yes."

"Did he read the document?"

"He told me how to prepare for today."

"How did he tell you to prepare?"

Beauman glared at Snowden, but the director kept talking. "He told me to leave the file to him."

"Objection. The answer is outside the scope of the deposition."

She stared at Beauman. "No it's not. It's why we're here."

He pointed at the court reporter. "Note my objection for the court."

"Already done." The woman looked at Hayden and rolled her eyes.

"Please answer the question."

Chapter 33

"There's nothing to tell." The director set his chin in a stubborn jut.

"I can get a judge involved."

Beauman grinned at her, a gotcha grin that set her teeth on edge. "Actually, you can't. There's no judge overseeing this deposition."

"I'm happy to get a magistrate involved. That's what they're appointed for."

"Not in this part of Texas. They like attorneys to work out differences without involving them. Much more important things demand their attention."

Hayden stared at him, but he didn't back down. Could she force the issue with a magistrate who wouldn't have jurisdiction? She did not want to tip this pompous attorney off to her legal theory. One call to the Court of Federal Claims was all it would take to lay out her strategy. What she wouldn't give to have Gerard a call away.

She turned back to Snowden. "Looking at the request I've handed you, doesn't it request a copy of Miguel's file?"

"Does it?"

She smiled around a clenched jaw and pointed out the page and line.

"Somehow I missed that." Snowden leaned

forward and pressed a button on his phone. "Eudelia, could you find Miguel Rodriguez's file and copy it for our guest?"

Her reply came over the speaker. "Sir, you know that file's—"

Snowden picked up the phone before his assistant finished. "Just get it." He hung up. "Anything else?"

"Yes." She glanced at her notes and forced herself to take several breaths before she restarted. "Who worked the night Miguel Rodriguez was killed?"

"Which night was that?" Snowden held his hands in front of him. "I don't have his file in here."

She'd bet money the file had conveniently disappeared. She pulled out a copy of the death certificate. "Please mark this as plaintiff's Exhibit B." The court reporter did so and returned it to her. Hayden then gave that to Snowden and an extra copy to Beauman. "This document is a copy of Miguel Rodriguez's death certificate. What date does it list as his date of death?"

"January 23, 2017."

"And what does it list as the location of death?"

"The juvenile detention facility."

"Which is?"

"This facility."

"And what does it list as the cause of death?"

"Murder."

"January 23 was less than three months ago. Do you want me to believe you don't remember that occurrence?"

"Objection." Beauman examined his manicure as if nothing interesting had happened. "Argumentative."

"So noted." The court reporter nodded at Hayden.

"Let me rephrase. Do you remember the events detailed on the death certificate?"

"No."

"Really?"

"Argumentative." Beauman grinned. "You'll have to try harder, counselor."

Hayden puffed out a breath. "You don't remember a young man detained in your facility being murdered?"

"No."

"Why?"

Snowden smiled, a tight-lipped gesture. "I was in the hospital recovering from gall bladder surgery." He gestured toward Beauman. "He has a copy of the relevant medical records."

Hayden continued the deposition, but her passion felt blunted. The director was still responsible for what happened on his watch, but the fact he wasn't on site for two weeks around the murder meant he might not have directed the cover-up. But someone had, and that someone reported to Snowden. As the saying went: the buck stopped here.

She moved him through a series of questions regarding who had access and how. "If it's as safe as you say, why not give me the video from Miguel's room the day he died?"

Mr. Snowden heaved a large sigh. "Complete the FOIA request, and I'll send what we have."

"How long does your video store?"

"Thirty days, give or take." He glared at her. "Even low resolution takes a massive amount of server space. Now if you're ready to continue."

Her mind raced as she realized that time had expired. The video she needed could be gone, but if she filed the complaint tonight and filed a discovery request with it, maybe she could locate what she needed. But a quick glance at her watch affirmed the court had already closed. There was nothing she could do tonight but finish the deposition.

An hour later, the deposition whined to a stop.

"I'll transcribe the deposition this week and send a copy to each of you. Mr. Snowden, you'll have thirty days to review and make any changes. Otherwise, it will stand as transcribed." The court reporter packed up her equipment and left after exchanging cards and a bill with Hayden.

Beauman watched her leave and then extended his hand. "Get what you need, counselor?"

"You'll know soon enough." She batted her eyelashes at him and extracted her hand from his. "Always a pleasure to meet the DOJ's finest."

He nodded an acknowledgment, then grabbed his briefcase and turned to Snowden. "I'll be in touch, Director."

Since his assistant had left for the night, Director Snowden escorted Hayden toward security, but not before one of the guards gestured for her to wait. She slowed her steps, and the guard came closer. "Wait for me outside when you leave."

As Mr. Snowden turned around to check on her, the guard returned his attention to his station.

"May we continue?"

Hayden nodded and hurried to catch up. What did the guard want to tell her that he couldn't say in front of Snowden?

Half an hour later, Hayden sat inside her car, her stomach growling. How long would she have to wait for the guard to arrive?

The kids might be cared for at a basic level, but Director Snowden hadn't let her see any. Someone knocked on her car window, and she startled before lowering it a crack.

The guard leaned toward the window, meeting her gaze through the crack. "You're still here."

Hayden nodded. "I'd have waited longer." Though not much.

The man was solid and looked like he'd spent serious time in the military or border patrol. His biceps bulged beneath the edges of his T-shirt. He glanced around, then nodded toward a beat-up

Dodge pickup. "Follow me to town, and we can talk."

"Okay." Was it smart to follow him? Surely as long as they stayed in public she'd be okay. She started the rental, pulled out, and followed him along the road. Only two people knew where she was, and no one would know where to look if she disappeared.

You've read too many thrillers, Hayden. Nothing will happen.

It took a few minutes of trusting him before her GPS finally synced up. She never wanted to live anywhere so remote that GPS struggled to find its satellite. As they entered town, she drove by the sole hotel, where she'd spend the night. Then he pulled into the parking lot of a place that looked more like a bar than a restaurant. An odd assortment of dusty pickup trucks, sedans, and one VW Bug filled the parking lot.

He waited for her and held the door like a gentleman, and Hayden felt her spine relax just a bit. Public was good. Very good. And acting like his momma raised him with manners? That helped more than a bit.

The inside of the tavern smelled musty, like decades of cigarette smoke had soaked into the walls before public smoking bans took effect. The smell of fried food sat on top of the smoke, coupled with the sound of an old jukebox playing country music and the crack of pool balls. The lighting was decent for a large room, with two windows at the front. Florescent bulbs lit the darker recesses.

The guard nodded at the waitress, then led Hayden to a corner booth. He claimed the side facing the door, so she eased opposite him, cracked vinyl catching her hose as she slid across.

"Why are you here?" His words were harder than his tone.

"I'm looking into Miguel Rodriguez's death."

His dark gaze bored into hers as if testing her words. He gave a slow nod. "Why?"

"His grieving mother needs to know what happened." This guard didn't need to know about the pending lawsuit.

The waitress sauntered up with her order pad held out and a ready smile for the guard. "Roy, what can I get you tonight?"

He ordered a beer and burger, and only then did the buxom waitress turn to Hayden. "And you?"

"A glass of water and a bowl of chicken noodle soup."

The woman made a note on her pad, then left, and Roy returned his focus to her.

"So your name is Roy. Care to give me your last name?"

"It's not important." His gaze hardened, and she felt a whisper of fear. This was a man who could hurt her in a moment, yet even as his gaze chilled her, she sensed he didn't intend to. "What's the real reason you're here?"

"Miguel Rodriguez." She refused to flinch under his scrutiny.

"Why care about one more Latin American kid entering the country illegally?"

"If you were his parent, you'd care."

"If I were his parent, I wouldn't send him the coyote way."

Hayden placed her hands on the table and met his gaze. "You're right. You and I wouldn't. But we've never been desperate enough to be willing to do anything to save our child." She took a deep breath as images of other refugee children filled her mind. "His mother didn't send him that way, and she deserves to know what happened."

"And the other kids?"

She stilled. "Other kids have died in detention?"

He shook his head. "The other kids there. Do they matter?"

"Absolutely."

"Do they matter to you?"

His question went deep. She wanted to insist they did, but something inside her prevented the lie. She hadn't cared about them until she learned about Miguel. Even then, her focus was defined. She hadn't considered other kids in his position.

"There are hundreds more kids in that facility, and nobody's doing anything to move them through. They linger for weeks and months. Some have lived there a year." He shook his head. "Five days a week, I watch these kids devolve. There's little school. Little medical care. And nothing the director can do about it. His best isn't much."

"Help me figure out what happened to Miguel, and I'll do what I can to help the others. I have to start somewhere. Miguel is someone I can focus on and make a difference."

"That's where you're wrong, lady." Roy's Texas twang deepened. "He's dead. There's nothing you can do that matters to him. It's the other kids who need your attention." He studied her but must not have found what he sought, because a look of defeat settled on his face. "I wasn't working the night Miguel died. One of my friends was. I'll see if he'll talk to you."

"I need a real tour of the facility too. One where I can examine where he lived and see the conditions up close."

"Even if I can do that, it's different from when Miguel was here."

"What's changed?"

"Little things. The kids had free access to each other's rooms. Now it's key card access, like a hotel. Doors kept closed all the time."

"That must have cost a pretty penny."

"It did. What else could he do?"

She considered his words, but knew it was important—not just for Miguel, but for the other kids—to see what it was really like. "I need to visualize it so I can create the scene for a jury."

He grinned, and Hayden realized her mistake. "That's what I wanted to hear. I knew this had to be bigger than one kid." He took a swig of his beer, then slapped a hand against the table, and Hayden jumped. "There's a congressional tour tomorrow. Maybe I can get you on that, and you can slip away to your own tour."

"That might work. Who's the congressman?"

"Some bigwig. Someone who listened to my calls." He pulled out his phone and typed a message.

The waitress delivered their food as he tucked his phone away. Hayden watched as he dove into his food, her bowl of soup looking small next to his half-pound burger.

"Why do you work there? If it bothers you to see the kids like that?"

He swallowed his bite and set down the burger. He rested his elbows on the table and looked past her. "My grandfather immigrated as a teen. He walked across the border to a new life. It was hard, but he had a community to help him." He shrugged. "These kids, there's nobody to help. So I try. It's not much, but maybe I can ease their fear and protect them while they wait."

His words soaked into her mind. "Do they need protecting?"

"The little ones do. There are gangs here. Anywhere there is a void, evil likes to take a foothold." He looked at her again. "I do my part to keep it at bay."

"But you couldn't for Miguel."

Roy shook his head. "No, but I don't want it to happen to anyone else."

"Did you know Miguel?"

"Not really. With so many detainees, I can only know twenty or thirty. He was quiet. Kept to himself. Always watching, like he expected something to happen."

"Was he friends with anyone?"

"He was a loner."

"Surely he had at least one friend. Someone he hung out with." She didn't want to imagine him so alone.

"He didn't." Roy's phone vibrated, and he tapped the screen. "My buddy will meet you for an early breakfast, then get you on the tour." He threw a twenty on the table and stood. "Be here at seven. The waffles are good."

"How will I know who he is?"

"He'll know you."

Hayden turned and watched Roy stride from the room. The slightest bit of swagger affected his walk. The waitress approached with the bill. "Need anything else?"

Hayden looked down at her half eaten bowl of soup, but her appetite had vanished in nerves for the morning. "I'm fine."

As she walked to her car, her gaze took in the

surrounding area. She slid behind the rental's wheel and used the rearview mirror to scan behind her. There were so many shadows she didn't see anything until she pulled out and the headlights swept the area. Then her pulse raced as her foot jerked on the gas pedal. Director Snowden stood by the Dumpster, watching.

Chapter 34

Hayden was still shaking when she pulled into the motel parking lot. The small Texas town didn't have options, so she'd booked the only room she could. Should she search somewhere else, somewhere Director Snowden couldn't easily find her? But with a seven a.m. meeting, driving the forty-five minutes to Waco wasn't appealing.

Even so, she drove around the small parking lot to diffuse the shadows before she parked. Then she pulled her rolling suitcase from the trunk and hurried inside.

As soon as she was in her room, which surely hadn't been updated since the early eighties, she pulled out her phone and called Emilie.

"Hey, girl. How's Texas treating you?"

"Fine. Just feeling off balance."

"Why?"

Hayden took a deep breath. If Emilie thought she was overthinking things, she'd know to relax.

"I met a guard at a restaurant after his shift. He didn't know much, but when I left I saw the director lurking in the parking lot."

"Maybe he was eating there."

"Then he wouldn't hide by the Dumpster."

"He could have just arrived."

"I don't think so. He was watching."

A soft whoosh of air filled the line. "Need me to keep you company?" There was light teasing in Emilie's voice, but Hayden also heard concern.

"No, I'm seeing a problem everywhere." She paused, then plunged ahead. "Emilie, there's only one hotel in town. What if I kicked a hornets' nest?"

"Stay out of the way."

Hayden smiled. "Gee, I didn't think of that. Any tips for doing it?"

"Come home."

"I can't . . . not yet."

Hayden quickly filled her in on what she'd seen and the deposition. "I didn't get much. The director was adept at dodging questions." She collapsed against the slim pillows. "Tell me about your day."

They chatted for a few minutes, but Emilie still wouldn't tell Hayden what her new story was about. "You'll have to wait for the finished product."

She'd always been that way, even in law school, refusing any help on her papers, even a proofreading. Her four A's in Legal Research and Writing backed up the efficacy of her process.

Hayden got ready for bed, then stuck a chair under the doorknob. She'd read that would keep an intruder out, or at least delay an invasion. There wasn't anything she could do about the big plate-glass window. She crawled into bed and closed her eyes, but sleep was a long time coming.

As the first traces of the sun slipped salmon and gold over the horizon and pushed up the darkness, the private plane waited on the runway. Zeus hadn't been thrilled to wake so early, only to be left behind. Andrew ducked at the top of the stairs and entered the small jet. Lilith and his father sat in leather chairs, coffee cups in hand; his dad's would be black while Lilith's would be some froufrou dessert in a cup.

"Morning, son." Congressman Wesley reached up to shake Andrew's hand. "Glad you can join us."

"Any particular reason?" His dad flinched, and Andrew wanted to resay the words, remove the bite from them. "Sorry. It was a short night, Senator."

"Not quite, but soon. I'm still the congressman." Dad's grin was as excited as he'd ever seen.

"For a bit longer." Lilith gestured to a chair. "Join us, and I'll brief you and the senator. It should be an interesting trip."

Andrew eased to the edge of a chair opposite the others. "Anyone else joining us?"

"Just the chief of staff."

Andrew whistled. "Must be important if you have the CoS and LD along."

"I wouldn't waste my time. Until we can get ahead of the stream of kids, we need a safe place to keep them while immigration courts process them. This facility needs to follow the rules Congress outlined." His dad frowned as his phone dinged. "I'd better check this. Could be about my swearing-in." He swiveled toward the window to answer the call, shielding his mouth with his hand.

Andrew watched his dad a minute. So much of his life had been like this. He'd learned before he was thirteen that his own job was to avoid trouble. It wasn't the family he'd imagined as a kid. More X-Men than Waltons. He could feel Lilith's gaze and knew she sensed the tension, but he didn't want to linger there.

His thoughts turned toward Hayden McCarthy. He'd bet she could mingle with the crowd at events without a problem. He could imagine her slipping from group to group with a smile. Did they teach that in the third year of law school, in some class he hadn't taken?

Hayden was intelligent and beautiful in a quiet way, yet he knew from Emilie she was a force to reckon with in the courtroom. He wanted to see that side of her. The side that didn't shyly admit she was good at what she did, but knew it with an intensity that won cases.

His phone vibrated in his pocket and he tugged it free. He turned away from Lilith as he read the screen.

Where are you?

Emilie texting him this early? That wasn't normal.

He texted back.

With the congressman. What's up?

Can you have coffee?

Nope. On a plane for Texas. Back some-
time tonight.

K. Call when you can.

He held the phone a moment, but the screen stayed blank. As he got ready to put it in airplane mode, it buzzed again.

Hayden's in Texas too.

Okay . . . He wasn't sure why she was telling him that.

Can I give her your number?

His brow furrowed as he read the question again. Emilie had to know they'd already exchanged numbers.

Y?

Just a feeling.

TX is big. But sure.

Thks. Check out today's article. TTYS.

K.

As he put his phone away, someone pounded up the steps. Chief of Staff Dan Washburn hauled his bulk up the last step, then stood in the doorway a moment. "Looks like we're all here, Senator."

Dad pulled the phone from his ear. "Nice of you to join us." Only a slight layer of sarcasm coated his words. "Tell the pilot we're ready to leave."

The CoS stuck his head in the cockpit. "Let's roll, boys."

The captain turned around, her delicate features highlighted by her arched eyebrows.

"Ma'am."

She nodded. "We can take off in five minutes." She turned around, effectively dismissing the chief. Andrew bit back a smile.

Washburn sidled down the aisle then flopped into a chair across from Lilith. "Ready to investigate?"

She waved a hand in the air. "Won't be much, but it will keep him happy."

The congressman closed his phone and leaned toward her. "He can hear you, you know. Don't discount how important this is. We've got a continuing crisis. The media may have lost focus, yet streams of unaccompanied minors still cross our borders. It's our duty to care for them, and I don't like what I've heard about these centers." His frown settled into his face. "Makes me think of last week's Walters cartoon."

Andrew froze.

"Which one?" Washburn waved his hand in a dismissive gesture. "His pen's as poisonous as other editorial cartoonists."

"I kind of like them." Lilith looked at the congressman with adoring eyes. "They have a way of making you think."

"The one where he alludes to the kids coming across our border being like the kids fleeing Syria and other points in the Middle East. Really made me think."

Andrew reminded his lungs to breathe as his heart hiccupped. His dad liked his cartoon?

The copilot slid from the cockpit. "We'll take off shortly. Please turn off your phones until we're in the air. We'd prefer they stay off, but"—he shrugged—"we know you won't do that. Do you need anything before I close the door?"

Andrew shook his head. "We're good, thanks."

The copilot looked at the senator. "Sir?"

Dad waved at him. "Fine."

The copilot slid back into his seat. Then he turned around and closed the door separating the cockpit from the rest of the plane. A moment later the latch clicked.

Hayden felt groggy as her alarm blared in her ear. The night had been too short, her dreams active. A young man murdered where he should be safe. Pools of blood leaking from his body, staining concrete beneath him. Alone in a flood of people.

She tried to slide from the bed, put distance between the lingering dream and the reality of the morning, but she was trapped. Tied down by eddies of fabric wrapped around her legs.

Her heartbeat quickened, and she glanced around frantically, then sucked in air. She was fine. In a hotel. In the middle of Nowhere, Texas.

But her heart continued to race.

She took a deep breath and forced herself to blow it out slowly. A prayer flitted through her mind.

Her meeting was in half an hour. She had to collect herself. Get ready and then see what this guard could tell her. Hopefully it was more than

Roy had. She struggled free from the comforter and sheets and lurched to her feet. She didn't have time to waste if she was meeting the guard for waffles at seven.

With only a minute to spare she arrived at the tavern. The alcohol signs didn't flicker their neon messages, but the door was unlocked and the sign turned to *Open*. A few battered trucks and dusty vehicles sat in parking spaces, a small crowd for breakfast and coffee hour.

Her phone dinged and she glanced at the screen, then frowned. Why was Emilie texting her Andrew's number?

She shook her head and sat in the car a moment, refocusing on what she hoped to learn. If this guard couldn't slip her onto the tour, she'd have to get back to DC and figure out what was next. It would be time to face Randolph, her new supervising partner, have Leigh file the complaint, and then get the discovery requests off to the govern-ment attorneys. She could kick this case into high gear and see what happened. And if Carmen was right and she didn't have a job?

She couldn't control that.

As she opened the rental's door and stepped out, she hoped she would find out enough to bring justice for Miguel and peace for his mother.

APRIL 10

El jefe had a network embedded inside the *Estados Unidos* that made Rafael a very nervous man.

He would never be free until he deciphered that puzzle. He needed to slow down and think. Stop reacting and start analyzing. He may not have much education, but he had the smarts to figure this out. He'd been trained by the best in the family, and what they hadn't taught him he'd learned through observation.

He parked the vehicle and climbed out. He'd walk Fort Ward's grounds and see what his subconscious revealed.

While he tried to maintain the look of a man enjoying light exercise over lunch, he stayed alert.

The device had information *el jefe* was desperate to reclaim and keep hidden. Why had Miguel taken it? What did he hope to accom-plish? The boy was smart, smarter than most of the men and even *el jefe* himself. He wouldn't have done it without a solid plan. And if Rafael could uncover that plan, then he might rebuy his life. Maybe he could complete what Miguel had planned. What he died to protect.

The key question: What would be so valuable to *el jefe* that its loss and the need to reclaim it was worth his son's life?

He had to locate the device. A device that he would use to purchase his freedom.

If not from *el jefe*, then from the man's enemies.

Chapter 35

THURSDAY, APRIL 13

The waitress, a younger, more harried version of last night's, hair pulled into a brunette ponytail and a dusting of makeup around her eyes, pointed to an open table. "Help yourself. I'll take your order in a minute." She grabbed a coffeepot and hurried to a table to refill cups.

Hayden glanced around the room, but no one paid attention to her. The only folks seated alone were either engrossed in old-fashioned newspapers or devices.

One large table was surrounded by men in battered baseball caps, jackets of every size and shape slung over their shoulders. One of them guffawed, and as she glanced back at the table she noticed Roy sitting with them. He didn't acknowledge her.

Hayden walked to a booth tucked against a window. The sunlight didn't seem to warm the location, even as she slid closer to the plate glass. Her glance traveled to Roy's table, and he nudged the guy next to him and jerked his chin in her general direction. The man stood, slapped a bill on the table, then grinned at the others before ambling her way.

His compact size made her think of an NFL running back. Stocky, but muscled rather than fat. He had an aura that emanated authority. The certainty he saw everything and processed it faster than the average person. Yet his grin didn't slide from his dusky features until he slid into the booth across from her.

"You must be Hayden McCarthy."

Her muscles refused to release their bunched tension as she reached out to shake his hand. "Thanks for meeting me."

"If you came all this way, seems I should spare a few minutes for a pretty lady like you." He relaxed against the seat back and studied her. "You're out of your element."

She couldn't dispute his words. He knew more than she did about this situation. "Then help me sort it out."

"It's not that simple."

"It could be." She met his gaze, and stilled her hands where they trembled beneath his line of sight. "Did you work the night Miguel died?"

One slow nod. "Sure you want to dive into this? Before I say anything, I need to know."

Hayden looked down for a moment, then brushed her hands along her black pants and placed them on the table. She leaned toward him and met his gaze. "I am absolutely committed to helping Miguel's mother discover answers." He opened his mouth, but she continued. "I might be chasing windmills, but I will do everything I can to help her. No mother should live with these questions."

"You're rattling big cages."

"Whose?"

"I'm not sure." He glanced her way, then looked toward the front doors. "You can't kill a kid in custody without high-level access."

"The facility doesn't seem that secure."

He nodded, his green eyes becoming catlike with laser focus. "Did you notice how isolated it is? Restricts access in and out. You must have a reason to be there. The cameras monitoring the parking lot help too."

The waitress wandered over and plopped coffee mugs in front of them, then left without a word, as if the guard had prearranged everything.

"Do you know who killed Miguel?"

He shook his head. "That night was nuts—more so than usual. Someone musta slipped something into the kids' drinks." He half chuckled. "Just kidding. But it was like Friday the Thirteenth, a blue moon, and Christmas Eve combined."

"Sounds like you have kids."

He nodded. "It's one reason I agreed to transfer. I figured the guards should understand kids. Otherwise it would be hard to handle them." He looked out the window, and his composure broke. "My family crossed the border. I was the lucky one. Born here. A citizen because of the location of the hospital. Thirty miles south, and I wouldn't have that gift." He pulled his attention back to the diner. "These kids are taking the hard road. We don't need to make it worse once they're here."

Hayden thought about his words. "Do you think the government should allow them to stay?"

"Not my call. My job is to keep them safe while detained. We failed Miguel."

She captured his phrase on her phone. "What happened?"

"I was in the cafeteria with five others. All good guards doing their best." He glanced down. "The kids were crazy, and our radios blared to life about the time the first group headed to their dormitory. They eat in a rotation. Usually keeps the chaos down."

"This night?"

"It's a good idea that doesn't work every time. Some of the kids were clowning around, others were crying for no reason, others yelling."

"Chaos."

"Only word for it." He rubbed his hands together on the table. "A female guard corralled her kids and headed toward the hall. That's when my radio went crazy. She saw someone slip out of a dorm room, and when she looked in she saw a young man on the floor and lots of blood. She kept her kids moving so they wouldn't see. I secured the scene. And that was it."

"Was a crime scene team called in?"

"No. The prison director said it wasn't necessary. He said somebody claimed the body. Someone else cleaned the room. Then everyone went back to their activities."

"Director Snowden said he wasn't there. Out with a surgery."

"He might not have been physically present, but he directed the response." He looked down at his hands. "I called a buddy with the state police, and he did some checking. State police didn't have jurisdiction. Nobody did. By the time my friend arrived it was all cleaned up anyway."

"A cover-up."

Hayden barely breathed the words, but the guard nodded. "Exactly."

"Did you know Miguel?"

"Not really. He was a quiet kid who kept to himself. Some seemed afraid of him, though I can't see why. He was respectful, athletic, alone."

"Most of the kids are alone."

"True." He studied his cup of coffee. "It felt different with him."

"Did he have friends?"

"Not that I noticed."

Hayden tried to paint the picture in her mind. A young man, almost an adult, decides to come to the United States, but instead of coming legally with his mom and brother, he takes the hard path guided by a coyote. "Miguel's mom and brother went through legal channels to immigrate. Why would Miguel come illegally?"

"There are a number of reasons. The main one being he doesn't fit an allowed group. Or maybe there weren't enough slots. Some lotteries are in high demand and fill in days." He tapped the side of the mug, then glanced at his watch. "We've got a VIP tour I have to get back for."

"Any chance I can join the tour?"

"I'll need to gauge the mood."

He slid from the booth without waiting for her to say anything. As she followed him, she realized she didn't have his name. "Wait a second. What's your name?"

"Not important."

"I might need to reach you later."

"If I learn anything new, I'll contact you. For now, follow me to the detention facility. I'll try to talk you onto the congressional tour. It'll be sanitized, but you'll see more than the director showed you."

"Shouldn't we pay?" The coffee hadn't been great, but still.

"Already did."

"Thank you."

"Don't. The coffee is terrible." He held the door of the restaurant as they exited, then climbed into a battered sedan. Funny, she'd imagined him as a pickup truck kind of guy. She trailed him through the twisting roads to the detention center. Was the director involved in the cover-up? If so, she'd add him to the complaint and nail him for lying in the deposition.

She stalled her musings as she pulled into a parking spot.

A black SUV was parked a few spots over, looking very out of place amid the dust-covered older model cars and trucks.

The promised briefing never arrived as the CoS, LD, and congressman huddled in a conversation that sounded a lot like campaign strategy. Andrew was happy to be excluded. He leaned against the headrest and hoped Jorge was doing okay at Mrs. Bradford's. Andrew hadn't liked leaving the boy when his mom's condition was still uncertain, though he knew his neighbor would do all she could to make him feel secure.

The next thing he knew, wheels bouncing against the tarmac jolted him awake. His closed eyes must have signaled his brain it was time to snooze. He rubbed a hand down his face, wiping away drool as he straightened in his seat.

"Welcome back, sleepyhead," Lilith's voice teased. "Ready for our tour?"

"Sure. After I get a gallon of coffee."

"Don't think this town has a Starbucks." She grabbed her bag and settled it in her lap, ready to spring from the jet the moment the door opened. "You'll have to make do."

"I'd settle for a Coke if it was cold." He stretched, then turned to his father. Dad was back on his phone scanning something on the over-sized screen. "Ready to tell me why we're here?"

The congressman looked up with a jolt and then slid his reading glasses down his nose. "Reports of unacceptable activities. The best way to find out the truth is a spot visit."

"One the administration has known about for a few days." Lilith spoke the words under her breath, but the congressman heard.

"True, but if there are serious problems, they couldn't cover them up."

"What kinds of problems?" It always helped to know what he was looking for. His phone buzzed in his pocket and he looked down to find a message from Mr. or Ms. Anonymous. As he read it, he felt sucker-punched.

Monday, I reveal your identity.

"Son, everything all right?"

Andrew scanned the message again. How had this person obtained his cell phone number? He swallowed, then answered his dad. "Nothing to worry about." He took a steadying breath. "What kind of problems?" he asked again.

His father studied him. "At least one detainee has died. Questionable circumstances."

"All right." Something about what his dad had

said niggled at his mind. Had he read about this death or one similar to it? What had happened to Jorge's brother?

The copilot opened the door, and a gush of warm air blew inside. "Welcome to Texas, folks."

Washburn stood and strutted toward the door. "There's the SUV we rented for today."

Andrew waited until the congressman and Lilith exited before stopping at the cockpit. "Thanks for a good flight."

The pilot turned and smiled. "My pleasure."

It took a while to get from the small airport to the detention center. Nothing much broke up the dry, brown landscape. A few head of cattle ignored them from the pasture, but eventually the institutional government building rose from the brown vista.

Dan pulled the vehicle into a slot. "We're a few minutes early."

"That never happens." The congressman didn't bother to look out.

Lilith slipped closer to Andrew. "Guess we get to wait here."

"Sure." Andrew slid as far away as he could from her.

A pout slipped on her face. "Come on, Andrew. Loosen up."

"Not today." Hayden slipped across his mind. She was so genuine compared to Lilith and others he routinely met.

A door slammed a few cars down, and he glanced that direction. As if he'd brought her here with his thoughts, Hayden adjusted an attaché case on her shoulder, looked across the SUV, and then smiled tightly as a stocky man in jeans and a hooded sweatshirt strode toward her.

Chapter 36

"Come on. I can't promise this will work, but let's try." He led her toward the main doors. "I'll introduce you to Joanna Osborne. She'll lead the tour and decide whether to add you."

Hayden nodded. "Thank you."

"You might want to put that case back in your car."

"I kept it yesterday."

He frowned at her words. "That was a breach of security. Someone could easily smuggle a weapon inside with a bag that size. No offense."

"I had a similar thought, but thought I got a pass because of the deposition."

He shook his head. "Things are worse than I thought."

She should request the visitor list from the day Miguel died. If she could bring in a bag like hers, another person could have easily smuggled in a knife. She jotted a note on her phone to ask during discovery.

A vehicle door closed behind them, and the guard hurried her into the lobby. "Let's get you settled." He looked uneasily over his shoulder and picked up his pace. He waved at the guard behind the reception center. "I'm taking her to Joanna."

"Matt, she has to sign in." The guard pointed at a clipboard as Hayden made a mental note of her companion's first name. She quickly scrawled her name on the pad, noting that one person had arrived after she left the center last night. The guard checked the information, then nodded. "Go on."

Matt scuttled her through the x-ray machine, ignoring its beeping insistence that she carried contraband, then shuttled her down a side corridor that led to the suite of empty offices. An industrial wall clock showed eight fifteen. She heard voices and clanking metal like silverware hitting plates, indicating that somewhere the children were eating breakfast. Her stomach growled in response. The promised waffles hadn't materialized, and the coffee hadn't exactly filled her up.

Matt opened a door and stepped inside. "Wait here while I talk to Joanna." He closed the door, leaving her in an office.

Hayden slowly turned, taking in the bare gray walls and the few accolades that hung on the wall. Whoever's office it was, it didn't belong to

Matt; at least none of the awards did. Instead, they listed Joanna Osborne and Carlton Snowden. She leaned closer to reread the names.

There was a photo of the director with Congressman Wesley and a short letter praising him for his work with the juvenile illegal immigrants.

She took another slow turn to note whether anything else felt out of place. A stack of newspapers sat on the only chair in front of the desk. If this was Joanna's office, she didn't often have company. The desk was bare, a work space ready for immediate use. The credenza behind it and the chair in front sagged with piles. A newspaper's headlines blared that a young man had been killed in the detention facility. She stepped forward to read the date. January 27, the week Miguel died. She pulled out her phone and snapped a photo of the article.

Why hadn't it appeared in her online searches? Had it somehow been scrubbed? She heard heels clicking down the hallway, and quickly refolded the newspaper and set it back on top of the stack.

Hayden picked up her bag and returned to the middle of the room and pasted on a smile as the doorknob twisted. A petite woman wearing three-inch stilettos walked in and startled. Her hand pressed against her chest as she stared at Hayden with wide green eyes. "Who are you, and why are you in my office?"

Hayden tried to relax into a non-threatening position. "Matt left me here. I'm Hayden McCarthy and hope to join today's tour."

The woman's eyes narrowed, and she placed her hands on her hips as if she were Wonder Woman getting ready to battle the enemy. "You were here yesterday."

"I had a deposition with the director and short tour before that."

"You got his panties in a wad. It's not a great idea for you to be here. Why'd you come back?"

"I have more questions, and Matt thought this was the best way to get them answered."

"He did, did he?" The woman crossed her arms and didn't lessen her stare or frown. "He didn't mention anything to me."

The door opened and Matt stepped into the room. "There you are, Joanna. What's the pulse?"

"Nuts. She's got the director in a tizzy." The woman tipped her head toward Hayden. Joanna wore her hair in a loose French twist, a colorful scarf around her neck in the pastel shades of spring. "I'm meeting the congressman in five minutes, so you have three to tell me what you are doing, James."

James? His last name?

"Calm down. Hayden's looking into Miguel Rodriguez's death."

"You mean murder." Joanna's expression hardened more.

"Yes. You are one of the few people here who agrees this whole situation was bungled."

"Botched."

Hayden bit back a grin. This woman could be exactly the internal advocate she needed to ensure Miguel's family learned the truth. Then Joanna turned and leveled her petite intensity at Hayden, an intensity her oh-so-sweet Texas drawl couldn't hide.

"So should I believe you mean to fix this mess?"

The question was valid. As far as this fireball was concerned, Hayden was snooping in a place she didn't belong. "Everyone's death should be fully investigated."

"Not good enough."

"It should be." Hayden took a deep breath. "Miguel didn't deserve to die. And he certainly should have expected safety while the United States detained him. My job is to help his mother discover what happened, peel back the layers of the government's bureaucracy, and ensure this doesn't happen to another child."

She tried to step back from the passion that filled her voice. She could feel the transformation to advocate, and though there wasn't a judge and jury, it felt like it. Joanna could end this investigation right now, and there was nothing Hayden could do about it unless she somehow persuaded the woman of her sincerity.

"The government essentially promised these

children would be safe while we detain them. We failed, and I don't want that to happen to another child. The only way to make the government change is to force it to acknowledge this failure."

Joanna didn't seem swayed by Hayden's passion. Instead, she glanced at Matt. "What do you think?"

"Roy believes she's the real deal. You claim she got to Snowden."

Joanna considered that. "Okay. But I can't put her on the tour. Before yesterday, I could have pretended she was just another shirt from DC. Now? Not a chance. We need another plan."

"I need to know who worked the night of Miguel's murder, and if there were visitors."

"The tour won't get you that information." Matt shifted toward the door as if listening for someone.

Joanna held up her hand. "Can you get copies of the logs?"

He paused. "If they still exist."

"Check on that while I lead the tour." She returned her laser-like focus to Hayden. "What did you hope to accomplish on the tour? The names aren't related to that."

"I want to meet any detainees who knew Miguel and ask what they know. Also, it would be helpful to get a sense of where the guards are and how they interact with the kids."

Joanna nodded. "I can help with that, but not through a VIP tour. Everyone will be on their best behavior." She turned back to Matt. "See if you can sneak her to the yard when the older kids get yard time. She can stay here until then." She turned her focus back to Hayden. "I'm trusting you to not poke any deeper than that pile of newspapers."

"Thank you. Anything is helpful." Her mind sparked with an idea. "I think I know someone who can help on the tour, but that means I'll need to follow you out before going to the yard."

Joanna frowned as she considered Hayden. "If you're sure, but I need you to be discrete and quick."

"I can do that." Hayden forced more confidence than she felt into her words.

Matt moved to the door. "I'll find you at your car."

Andrew resisted the temptation to slouch against the wall as the foursome waited in front of the reception area. Dan Washburn was going all DC on a woman behind a Plexiglas enclosure that made her seem either invincible or scared. His approach was having zero effect. She couldn't have been more disinterested if he'd been the pope or the president.

"You have to wait for someone to escort you," the woman snapped. She picked up her phone.

Andrew could almost see the steam rising from her ears. She gestured with broad strokes and set the phone down with a huff. She mouthed some words before turning to Dan with a pasted-on smile. "Someone will be with you shortly." She turned to the monitors, checked something, and then picked up a paperback. She deliberately swiveled away from them and started reading.

Interesting.

If she reflected employees' attitude, this place was a security sieve. It wouldn't take much to walk right past her and into the next room, unless she had eyes in the back of her head.

Lilith grimaced and turned to Dan with a snort. "What backwater town did she crawl from?"

"Probably this one." Dan checked his expensive watch and then shook his arm until his sleeve slid back into place beneath his suit coat. "Time to be all ears and take in everything we can."

The way Dan said it, Andrew wondered what he expected. Kids to jump out of the aisles and attack them with plastic spoons? A guard using a cattle prod to keep the tour in order?

"I'm curious about how they occupy the kids," he said. "Days can get long and kids restless if there isn't sufficient planning."

Lilith rolled her eyes. "This isn't a daycare, Andrew. These kids are lucky to get a meal and protection."

"Then what's really going on? You don't need me if it's simply a care facility."

She frowned then turned and walked away.

"Was that necessary, son?" Dad looked up rom his device long enough to scold Andrew. Message delivered, he went back to whatever important e-mail or report required his attention.

Andrew sighed and watched the second hand on the industrial clock hanging on the wall above the receptionist's head. With his parents, reality tended to differ from the image presented to others. Was an in-the-trenches, gut-level love relationship still possible? He wanted to find out.

The only woman who had enticed him to think along these lines was Hayden McCarthy. If his thoughts kept returning to her like a puppy to his owner, he'd need to do something. Something more than invite her to the Cherry Blossom Festival and snag a couple short phone calls.

There was much he didn't know. Her favorite movie. The song that made her weep. The joy that filled her heart until it nearly exploded. Her relationship with God. And what she was doing here.

The door opened, and the woman who'd just filled his thoughts filed in behind another woman. Andrew's hands turned clammy. And he wondered what he should do about it.

Chapter 37

The congressman was easy to identify. Salt-and-pepper hair, controlled, laser-focused attention. A famed prosecutor before he ran for congress, Congressman Wesley hadn't lost the edge he'd acquired as a courtroom opponent.

Then Hayden's attention shifted to the team around him. She'd seen photos of the chief of staff in articles and exchanged messages with the legislative director. Seemed like overkill to bring both.

"Congressman Wesley, I'm Hayden McCarthy."

The congressman put out his hand. "It's a pleasure to meet you."

Andrew stepped forward with an easy smile. "Hayden is Emilie's roommate and works with a firm in Old Town."

"Then you're a constituent. What brings you here? You're a bit far from home."

"I'm here at a mother's request." Hayden closed her mouth before she could say too much. Then she turned toward Andrew. "You're a long way from New Beginnings."

He shrugged. "Dad asked me to lend my perspective." He glanced around the sparse, sterile lobby. "This isn't as far from my kids as you might expect. Any of them could have landed here."

Hayden's phone vibrated with a ring. "Excuse me a moment." She glanced down at the screen, expecting to see a work number, but instead saw Emilie's. She frowned but hit the screen to decline the call, as Joanna began her introduction on what they could not take into the center. Then she turned back to Andrew and whispered, "Do you have a minute?"

"I want to listen to this first." He gestured to Joanna.

"All right."

Joanna gestured to the metal detector. "You will each pass through the detector. No weapons, knives, string. Really anything that could be used to harm yourself or someone else."

Andrew frowned. "Has anyone done something like that?"

"No, but we want to make sure no one does. Easier not to let anything potentially dangerous inside than chase it once it's here." And with that she deftly side-stepped the reality of Miguel's death. She turned with a warm smile to the congressman. "Sir, I think you'll be pleased with what you observe. We pride ourselves on stellar care for these children. If you'll follow me."

Hayden felt time evaporating and slid next to Andrew. "Do you have a second?"

"Sure."

Hayden's phone vibrated, alerting her to a voice mail. She shoved it deeper in her pocket.

Knowing Emilie, it could wait. In fact, knowing who the tour was with, Emilie would expect her to call later.

Lilith looked up from her red manicure. "How many children are here?"

"Frankly, too many. We need more staff and greater resources to handle the several hundred housed here. While their plight has fallen from the headlines, we receive children faster than they are released to family or sent home." Joanna gestured toward the glass door leading to security. "If you'll go through that door, you can deposit your bags and we'll get started."

Lilith grumbled as she set her Kate Spade bag in a dingy tray similar to those used by homeland security in airports.

Andrew hung back with Hayden. "What do you need?"

"Would you be my eyes on the tour? I can't participate, but I need to know what you think of the security and dormitories. Joanna will let you know when you are near a room where a few pictures would be helpful. By the time you're done with the tour, I should be waiting in my car."

"Coming, son?"

"Just a second." Andrew turned back to Hayden. "You'll tell me what's going on?"

She kept her face forward but shot him a sideways glance. "It's confidential."

"Ah. A case."

She gave a quick downward nod. "I can't talk about it."

"You forget, I dropped out of law school."

"Oh, I didn't forget."

Andrew caught the twinkle in Hayden's eye and knew he'd been had.

She turned to him, and a cloud settled over her face as if she'd remembered something. "Enjoy the tour."

Andrew half listened to the guide's spiel after walking them through security, while he wondered what Hayden was involved in. Why a tour of a facility without a visible problem? Of course, that didn't mean there wasn't a doozy beneath the perfect facade.

Andrew slowed his steps and drifted to the side, trailing the group. He glanced around. They'd reached the residential section, and cell-like rooms lined each side of the hall. Looked like a jail had been hurriedly adapted for kids, and not very well. The rooms were no more than five-by-eight, with dingy white-painted concrete blocks. The doors had small windows made of reinforced Plexiglas that gave a limited view into the narrow rooms. Two sets of bunk beds were shoved against each wall with a bland dresser at the foot of each. The dresser gave a modicum of privacy to whoever claimed the lower bunks, but not much.

There was nothing personal. Nothing childish that made the space a place for youth.

It was stark, spare, empty. A dreary place for kids to live.

He cleared his throat. "Where are the kids?"

Joanna looked at her watch and then at the folder she carried. "They're wrapping up breakfast and then they head to gym. A PE teacher comes each day to make sure they expend their energy in healthy ways."

"What are the unhealthy ways?"

She turned and met his gaze, a frown darkening her expression. "When you put this many children in one place, Mr. Wesley, they won't all get along. Add in cultural issues, clan and family challenges, and it creates a dynamic mix waiting to explode."

He shoved his hands in his pockets and tried to look casual when in reality he wanted to lean in and ask hard questions. "Do they have tutors?"

"Many of the children are too young for school, and almost none speak English, let alone speak it well enough for school."

"We're in Texas, aren't we? Doesn't someone who works here speak Spanish?"

"Son." His father's tone said back down, but he couldn't.

"These are kids. Shouldn't we give them a great impression of the United States so they want to return legally?" He clenched his fists inside his pockets. "Leaving them to fend for themselves isn't the way to make them friendly adults."

The woman stopped walking and gave him her full attention. She seemed to grow a couple inches as she faced him. "Mr. Wesley, I hear you, but the reality is we cannot. These kids are here anywhere from days to weeks or even months. It's a logistical nightmare to keep them fed, healthy, and safe."

His dad cleared his throat as he looked back at him. "The tour is this way."

Lilith rolled her eyes, muttering something about leaving the juveniles behind. Why did his dad keep her around?

Joanna led them through the cafeteria, where Andrew stopped. His feet refused to move as he took in row after row of children, toddlers up to surly teens, shoveling dry cereal into their mouths like they wondered where the next meal would come from. Adults skirted the room, watchful gazes locked on the children, but the little ones struggled to feed themselves. There were too many kids and too few adults to provide what the youngest needed.

The kids were clothed and had food, but he knew from working with kids similar to these that much more was required.

While the tour continued, Hayden moved from the lobby to her rental. She didn't want to risk running into Snowden. Since she had some time, she finally returned Carmen's call.

"Hayden, you've got to get back here immediately."

"What's happened?" The panic in Carmen's voice made Hayden wonder if another attorney had died.

"The partners have fired Leigh. She's gone—something about copying files outside the firm. A security officer walked her to her desk and watched her clear out her personal things. I didn't even know we had security. I'm also supposed to tell you you're gone the moment you get back." There was a muffling sound as if she put her hand around the phone's speaker. "It's got something to do with the Rodriguez case and Randolph being a coward."

"What do you mean?" Hayden was still caught on the part about Leigh being escorted from the building and confirmation her job was gone the moment she landed in DC.

"Something is very wrong. Randolph is getting orders from someone, and it ain't a partner." She took a breath and her next words were muffled. "I think Rodriguez is involved."

"Maricel?"

"No, her ex. He calls at least once a day. Let me tell you, I get off the phone as fast as I can." She paused. "Is there anything you need me to get from your office?"

Hayden shook her head, grateful she'd already copied her electronic files. "No, I'll be okay. Sounds like I don't need to come back in."

"Maybe not. Good luck."

"Thanks." Hayden's mind was spinning. Daniel Rodriguez called the firm every day? He'd also come to see Gerard . . . had he also ordered Gerard's death? She dialed Savannah, her hand shaking. She swallowed in a futile attempt to steady her voice.

"This is Savannah Daniels."

"Savannah, they're doing it."

"Hayden? Doing what?" There was a hard edge to Savannah's southern-tinged words.

"The partners have fired Leigh, and I'm next as soon as I get back. Angela's already gone."

"Did you get the deposition?"

"Yes. But not much more."

"It'll be enough." There was a pause. "Don't go to the office, come to mine instead. We'll figure this out."

"Okay." Someone was walking toward her car. Hayden squinted, then whispered into her phone, "I've got to go. I'll call you tonight."

Matt stood outside her car with an oversized envelope. She rolled down the window and took it from him.

"This has the logs from the couple nights before and the night Miguel died. I don't know if it will have what you need."

"Thank you."

"I also included the employee logs that show who was working." He glanced around. "Come with me."

She climbed from her car and followed him around the front of the building to a side entrance.

"I'm not sure the kids will talk, but your best bet is the yard. Older kids come out in five minutes." He gestured to a bench sheltered under a large tree. "Wait there, and the cameras shouldn't reveal your identity."

"And I leave . . ."

"When the first rush of kids is over. The younger detainees won't be much help."

"Thanks. Quick question. Daniel Rodriguez?"

He looked at her, expression as hard as stone. "A dangerous man. Stay away from him."

His hard words settled on her, confirming what she already knew in her gut. He stalked away, and Hayden settled on the bench and tried to relax. Matt had made it clear she wasn't welcome at the facility. The last thing she wanted was to kill her case by doing something harmful, but she had to talk to these kids. As the children filtered into the yard, a few discretely headed her direction. When they neared, she quietly asked if they knew Miguel. Many of them looked at her blankly.

She bit back frustration at the lack of help and the fruitlessness of the trip. If she didn't get some kind of clue, she'd have to seriously consider not refiling. The thought of suggesting that to Maricel left the remnants of her coffee souring her stomach.

Then the bench shifted as a teen collapsed next to her. He scowled at her, distrust and anger darkening his eyes.

"Why you ask for Miguel?"

"His mother sent me."

"Too late."

"*Sí.*" She couldn't deny it was too late for Miguel. "But I want to find out who killed him."

The kid shook his head, and his face tightened as his gaze skittered around the yard. "A man. Drawing on his . . ." He gestured to his neck.

"Tattoo?"

The kid nodded.

"What was the tattoo?"

"Serpent. Ugly. He didn't belong."

"He was here the day Miguel died?"

Again the young man nodded. He froze as the sound of feet and chatter approached. "He not here now."

"Have you seen him since Miguel died?"

"No." The kid thrust his hands in his jeans pockets and studied her. He seemed to reach a decision. "Miguel scared. Knew someone want him."

"Who?"

The young man shrugged. "Tall guy. Mexican. With snake. Miguel knew him."

Tall, Mexican guy with a snake tattoo. That didn't give her much to go on. But just knowing Miguel was concerned helped.

"*Gracias.*"

"You will find him?"

"I will try, but it would be helpful to know more. Is there anyone else I can talk to?"

The young man shrugged. "*Yo no sé.*"

Hayden nodded and then watched as a flood of younger kids gushed into the yard. The young man went to join them. She hadn't gotten his name, and when she turned back he had disappeared.

Surely someone could confirm what he had said. He couldn't be the only one who had seen the man or heard of Miguel's fear. Someone had to have let the man in. She returned to her car, the heat boiling up around her.

While she waited Hayden couldn't get her voice mail to open so called Emilie, but didn't bother to leave a message. She'd catch up with her when she got back to town. She'd learned what she could. Now she'd have to make the case work.

Chapter 38

The tour ended, and Andrew waited next to the door for his father to quit receiving fawning accolades from the center director and his staff. Where was Hayden? Oh, right. She'd said she'd probably be in her car. He'd check on their way out.

Time ticked until Lilith touched his dad's shoulder. "It's time to head back to the plane, sir." She turned toward Joanna. "Thank you for the enlightening tour. I think we've seen everything we needed."

Andrew's father raised his eyebrows. "I think the plane will wait for us."

"True, sir, but I don't think Eastman Klondike would be happy if we missed our appointment with him. He seems interested in supporting your campaign with a nice check and some from his wealthy friends as well."

His father hesitated, and Lilith leaned closer and whispered something in his ear.

So much for a tour for the sake of the children.

"All right." He turned to Joanna, and the woman blushed as he poured on his charm. "I add my thanks. It's helpful to see the excellent work you do here."

Andrew bit back a retort; the center staff probably did the best they could with the number of children assigned here.

Dan and Lilith exited, and Congressman Wesley paused, hand on the door. "Coming, son?"

"I need to check on something. I'll catch a ride with Hayden or grab a cab."

"That might be difficult out here."

"I'll catch up."

"Don't take too long. Lilith reminded me about

an important meeting. Guess that's why I keep her around . . . otherwise I'd miss half my appointments."

"I'll be quick as I can. If I get delayed I'll find another way back to DC." Hayden had disappeared, and Andrew needed to find her. He hurried up to Joanna and waited while she finished talking to the woman behind the Plexiglas divider.

She finally turned her attention to him. "Yes?"

"Did Hayden McCarthy sign out?"

Joanna turned to the guard. "Did she?"

"Yes." The woman swung the clipboard sign-in sheet to her, and Joanna ran a manicured nail down the list.

"She signed out about the time we started." Joanna frowned and pulled her phone out. "Matt, did you deliver the information I requested?" She listened a moment and then nodded. "Thanks." She turned back to Andrew. "Matt says she was killing time in her car after he got her the info. Try there."

Andrew nodded as he headed to the door. "Thanks."

"Be careful." Her words pulled his attention around.

"I will."

———

Someone pounded on her car window, and Hayden jumped as she shoved the small sheaf of logs onto the passenger seat.

Director Snowden leaned into her door. "What are you doing?" The words growled from between clenched teeth as a muscle pulsed along his jaw.

Hayden straightened, grateful for the door separating them, but wondering if he'd crawl through the cracked window and choke her. Was her presence alone enough to enrage him, or had she somehow gotten close to something important without realizing it? She hadn't done anything—other than sit and talk to one young man.

"You need to leave. Now." His intense gaze bored through her. "I'll have you arrested for trespassing on government property."

"I didn't trespass." Hayden hesitated. She probably shouldn't mention who had issued the invitation. She held up her hands in a placating motion. "I'm just sitting in my car."

"You think I don't know you were in the yard with the detainees?" He breathed in and out while watching her intently. It felt like he wanted to read her mind.

Hayden held her breath. She matched his gaze, even as she wanted to roll up the window and speed away. She hadn't done anything wrong and certainly hadn't disrupted any of the center's activities. But in the end she had only gained a vague description of a man who may have been involved in Miguel's death. No judge or jury would accept that as confirmation of an individual drawing the knife across his neck.

She stifled a shudder. Someone tapped Director Snowden's shoulder, but he didn't budge. Didn't say a word as his gaze bored through her.

His reaction seemed far beyond what was reasonable. What did he want to hide?

Miguel's killer or an inept cover-up?

That had to be it.

Her resolve to pursue the case deepened, despite losing her job.

Someone edged him to the side, and she looked into Andrew's concerned face. "There you are. I've been waiting for you." He nodded to the director. "Hayden was kind enough to wait for me, but we should leave now or I'll miss my flight home. Thank you again for the tour."

"Don't think I don't know what's going on." Snowden stepped away from the car.

Andrew climbed into the passenger seat, and Hayden turned the key in the ignition.

"We need to get out of here," Andrew warned. "That man was seriously miffed at you."

Soon they were on the highway headed toward Waco.

Andrew dialed a number on his phone, then waited. A moment later he tried again. "No answer. Let's head to the Waco airport."

"No problem, if you'll pull up directions on your phone." As Hayden tried to slow the car to take a curve, the brakes failed to respond. Instead, the car picked up speed down the short incline.

"What's wrong?" Andrew grabbed the door handle and braced his feet.

Hayden bit her lower lip as she concentrated on slowing the car. She wobbled the steering wheel from side to side, continued to stomp on the brakes, and prayed. The car slowed fractionally, but the curve arrived before she could control the turn.

She tried to relax as everything in her screamed that they were seconds from a crash.

Andrew reached an arm across her. "Hold on!"

The car flew over the shoulder and into the ditch.

Chapter 39

The car engine moaned, and the wheels spun almost as much as Andrew's head.

"Hayden, take your foot off the gas."

Andrew's voice seemed to cut through her panic. She looked down at the pedals. "It's not on it."

A bump already grew where her head had collided with the steering wheel, but fortunately the air bags hadn't deployed. He'd bounced off the dash, but the seat belt had restrained him from crashing into the windshield. He blew out a breath and slowly turned toward her as his muscles protested. "Try backing up the car."

Hayden's hands trembled on the steering wheel,

and she seemed dazed. He touched her arm and she startled. "Look at me, Hayden."

Slowly her head swiveled toward him. "Shift the car into reverse and see if it will back up. If it does we can drive to a gas station. If not, we'll call a tow truck."

"Okay." She took a shuddering breath, then shifted into reverse and pressed on the gas. The car didn't respond.

A pickup truck eased onto the shoulder behind them, and a guy in jeans and a flannel shirt climbed from the cab. "Looks like we've got help."

Hayden turned and looked. "That's Matt. He's a guard at the detention center. He got me records I need."

Matt crouched to knock on the window, and Hayden rolled it down.

"Everything okay?" Matt's voice held the appropriate tone of concern, but Hayden still seemed nervous.

"No. The brakes stopped working and we slid right off the curve."

"All right. Stay here, and I'll check under the hood." Before Andrew could stop him, the man was under the vehicle. Andrew stepped from the car and followed him. He hunkered down and watched the guard. The man grunted as he slid back out.

"Looks like someone cut the brakes. Who did she tick off?"

Andrew shrugged. "I don't know." But if someone cut the brakes, they didn't only want her out of town, they wanted her hurt. "This could have been a lot worse."

The man nodded, and Andrew sensed he was on their side.

"Why were you behind us? Shouldn't you be at the center?"

"Today was my day off. It would look odd if I spent too much time there." He stepped up and brushed his hands across his jeans. "I wanted to dig, but Snowden wouldn't leave."

"Maybe the congressional tour was too much." His dad could put people on edge even when they had nothing to hide. What did the director not want the world to know?

Hayden opened the door and leaned against it. "I'm calling AAA for a tow truck."

"Good plan." Andrew gave her a reassuring smile and turned back to the guard. "I'm Andrew Wesley."

"Matt James." He glanced at Hayden. "She's in over her head. Something bigger is at play." They chatted quietly while Hayden made the call.

"Tow truck is on the way." Hayden glanced between the two of them. "What do I need to know?"

Suddenly she froze and fear shadowed her face. Andrew turned back and stilled when he saw a gun in Matt's hand. He cautiously raised his hands in front of his body, then took a step to the side to better position himself between Hayden and Matt.

"Matt?" Hayden's voice was admirably still. "What are you doing?"

"They have my family." His eyes were wide, pupils dilated, and color flooded his face, a startling transformation from the man who had been so forthcoming earlier. "Somehow they know I helped you."

"Who's 'they'?"

"I don't know. They called thirty minutes ago. I have no choice."

Andrew's mind raced as he tried to catch up with the conversation between Hayden and Matt. He was caught in the middle without a playbook. The gun wavered momentarily in Matt's hand, but the man quickly steadied it.

"Hayden." Andrew gritted the word between his teeth. "You've got to catch me up. Now."

"I'm trying to figure out what happened to my client's son. He was murdered in that detention center. His mother needs to know why."

"There has to be more." Nobody took a man's family over an unrelated death.

His phone buzzed in his pocket, but he ignored Emilie's ringtone. She'd have to wait.

———

A droplet of sweat slid down the small of Hayden's back. "Who has your family, Matt?" She forced a steadiness into her voice she didn't feel. Nothing in law school had prepared her for a situation like this.

"I don't know." He groaned. "I have to protect them. Please understand."

The look on his face was agonized as Hayden reached below the car window and slid her phone from the door handle where she'd stashed it. One flick and she could alert 911, but she also needed what Matt knew. She flicked, never removing her gaze from him. "You have to have some idea."

The man swore, a broken sound.

"You wouldn't do this if you didn't believe the threats were serious." It was risky, but she had to learn everything before help arrived. The sun glinted off the gun's barrel, warning how real this was. Not some scene from a movie, but real-life threats with a bullet behind them.

He mumbled something in Spanish, and she glanced at Andrew. He just raised a shoulder while keeping his hands in front of him.

"Matt."

"Drugs. It's always about drugs along the border. Some of the kids, they are nothing more than mules. The stories I hear. It's heartbreaking. I just wanted to help." His words cracked on a sob. "Now they have *mi familia*."

The minutes dragged by. When would help arrive? They were less than thirty minutes from

Waco, and there had to be a sheriff's deputy or highway patrol closer than that.

Hayden cleared her throat as she tried to buy time. "Let us help you."

"How?" He looked at her with wild-eyed hope. "Tell me how you can help."

She took a moment to collect her thoughts. What would she ask if she were in court questioning a witness? She'd want to know the elusive how and why. "How do they know you helped me? You've given me nothing that exposes them." What had she learned in her time at the detention center? "Does a snake tattoo along the neck mean anything to you?"

"It's a symbol for one of the cartels."

"Which one?"

"The Rodriguez cartel." His voice steadied as he talked. "It's placed on its most trusted."

Rodriguez? Why would Miguel's own family come after him? "What does the cartel deal in?"

Matt shrugged, but the gun sank lower, pointing at her abdomen rather than her chest. "Drugs. Possibly heroin or a new one."

Why was Andrew stepping around her? She edged forward. She needed to keep Matt talking until help arrived. "What new drugs?"

"Meth. Ecstasy. Anything that can cross the border. The cartels change with the addictions."

Hayden frowned. When had it evolved from cocaine? "Why come after you?"

"They said someone saw you with me at the detention center."

"It has to be more than that, for them to grab your family. The timing is too tight."

"I only met you this morning." His eyes were wild, and the gun wavered in his hand. "You have no idea what it is like here."

"Help us understand." Andrew's voice was calm yet firm as he stepped toward Matt. "I work with kids and teens who made the trip legally. I understand their journey."

"But you haven't lived it. I wanted so much more for my family." His words broke Hayden's heart even as he cocked the hammer of his gun. "I must save them."

"Yes." Hayden nodded and edged toward him.

Sirens pulsed behind them, and Matt's gun jerked as he searched the road. Andrew took another step between them, and Hayden wanted to yank him back. Clearly Matt didn't want to hurt her, or she'd already be dead.

"Matt, help me help you. Who's behind this? You know."

He jerked toward her, then back to the road. Cars skidded behind them, and doors popped open. Matt's eyes widened even further.

"Put the gun down," a man bellowed.

Hayden didn't turn. "Matt, I know you don't want to do this." If she could get him to put the gun away, maybe she could defuse the situation and they could save his family. She twisted slightly toward the officer behind her. "He says someone has taken his family." Turning back to Matt, she asked, "Where are they?"

"The photo was our living room." He gulped, his eyes now fixed behind her. "My home." The words were louder, clearer. "My phone has the text. Front pocket of my jacket. The photo shows them at my house." He rattled off an address as Andrew slowly approached him.

Matt froze as Andrew retrieved the phone and then turned and walked it toward an officer.

"Slide the screen and it should pop up. I had it open as I came."

Hayden took a breath, and then asked another question. "Did you disable my vehicle?"

His brow furrowed as he frowned. "No. The text told me to follow you and use an opportunity to take you."

Andrew stood next to her as uniformed officers swarmed Matt. He was pushed to the ground but not as roughly as Hayden expected. The officers must know him as fellow law enforcement. "If he didn't mess with the car . . ."

"Someone else did." Hayden sagged as the adrenaline abandoned her. "We need to get out of here."

Chaos flowed around them as a tow truck labeled Ned's Recovery pulled alongside the rental. "Someone call for a tow?"

Hayden started to laugh, an uncontrollable burble.

"Talk to the officers." Andrew pointed toward one of them. "Maybe he can help." He leaned against the car next to her, and she sagged into him. As he slid an arm around her, it felt so right. She didn't have to be strong enough on her own.

Chapter 40

One car transported Matt, while an officer took Hayden's statement. Andrew watched her from his post ten feet away answering questions from another officer. The Ned's Recovery truck waited on the side of the road, ready to tow the rental as soon as the circus cleared. Andrew's phone kept buzzing, but the officer had made it clear he couldn't answer. He slid it out far enough to see it was Lilith . . . again . . . and then hit the prepared message that he couldn't take the call. Maybe she'd take the hint this time.

"What else can you tell me?"

"Nothing." Andrew sighed. "I just got here this morning, and I was supposed to be on a return plane two hours ago."

His phone buzzed again. What was going on? He slid it back out.

Time's up. Monday the world will know who you are.

Seriously? This message on top of all Lilith's calls? The number for the text showed as 0000000. A big blank of a clue.

"Sir? This would go faster if you answered my questions." The words were said with a polite air that made Andrew wonder if the deputy had listened to his previous answers. He reined in his frustration, then rifled his fingers through his hair.

"Sorry. There's nothing more I can tell you. I had never seen the guy with the gun before. And I don't know why Hayden is in Texas. She'll have to answer that." He shoved his hands in his pockets and tried to relax. "That's it."

The deputy's speaker squawked, and he clicked a button to talk into his radio. Then he jotted a couple more notes. "Stay put while I check on the lady."

Hayden looked up with a harried air as the officer approached, and all Andrew wanted to do was whisk her as far away from this mess as he could. Instead he pulled out his phone and started listening to messages.

The first, from Emilie, was a little odd: "Hey, Andrew. Call me as soon as you can, okay? I think Hayden needs help. I might have something on your leak too. Not sure yet."

Then there was a message from his dad asking where he was, and a couple after that from Washburn and Lilith asking the same question. Looked like they'd called about the same time the car drifted off the road. Then another from Emilie: "Your leak is closer than we thought. I've got to go."

Two more calls from Emilie followed but no voice mail. Then Lilith and the annoying text.

Andrew wanted to pound his frustration out on something. He'd have to settle for calling his editor. After a quick conversation with Michael's assistant he was patched through.

"Andrew."

"Any progress on leaks, Turner?"

"None. Everything seems clammed up like it should be."

"Well, someone's talked. I just got another text that the word will be out Monday." Andrew watched the officers grilling Hayden and felt his blood pressure build. "Listen, my cousin thinks she's got a lead, but I can't reach her right now."

"Give me her number, and I'll follow up."

"Thanks." Andrew gave Michael the number and hung up. He had to get back to DC and talk to Emilie.

Hayden walked toward him. "They say we can leave."

"Just like that?"

She shrugged. "I guess. I want to get out of here . . . The officer said Matt's wife was beat up and his kids forced to watch. I told the police I don't want to press charges against him. I don't believe he wanted to hurt us."

"I'm not so sure." The words slipped out, earning Andrew a glare from Hayden.

"Can someone give us a ride to the airport?" she asked.

"Sure," one of the officers said. "Grab your things from the car, and I'll take you."

Andrew got Hayden's things from the rental while she climbed into the cruiser. On the way to the airport she peppered the deputy with questions about the Mexican cartels and whether local law enforcement had noticed an upswing in drug activity. Seemed she was taking Matt's theory for a test spin.

"We are seeing more unaccompanied minors," the officer said. "It's another surge, and that strains the system. In turn that makes it easier to sneak in drugs."

"Do they use kids as mules?"

"I have heard of situations."

They passed the rest of the trip in silence, and soon the officer pulled the vehicle into a parking lot. Across the tarmac they could see several private planes.

"Wait a minute," said Hayden. "Is there a commercial airline here?"

The officer laughed and shook his head. "Not here. But this is where you asked me to take you."

Andrew met her gaze. "We flew in here this morning." He started walking toward a low hangar. "I'll get us a plane."

When he returned, Hayden was going through her e-mail and messages. She frowned at him. "Listen to this message from Emilie. She left it while I was at the tavern this morning."

She put the phone on speaker and Andrew leaned closer. "Hey, something's wrong. Give me a call as soon as you can. This story is bigger than we thought."

Hayden looked at him, concern shadowing her face. "I tried to call her but it rings and rings. It never kicks over to voice mail."

"We'll keep calling." Andrew rubbed a slow circle on Hayden's shoulder. Her muscles were tense as rocks. "You know Em. She probably walked away from her phone without realizing it was on, or turned it off and forgot."

Emilie could take care of herself . . . Andrew knew that. But the messages she'd left him added to his sense that something was wrong.

APRIL 13

He had a new target.

One that didn't match his earlier directives.

El jefe was losing focus.

What had distracted him from his earlier attention to the pursuit of the boy and the device?

Rafael sank against the uncomfortable hotel headboard and opened the Internet window on the tablet. A quick search of the woman's name revealed she was an attorney and sometimes journalist. Why focus on her?

A link to her articles appeared, and he clicked on the most recent.

It only took a moment to find the article. It took longer to translate the words into something he could understand. He frowned and tried again. Surely he had made a mistake.

But as he deciphered what he could, understanding dawned.

This woman had uncovered what had happened to Miguel.

Somehow she had unraveled the events at the detention center. And figured out why he had entered the *Estados Unidos* illegally.

He looked at the article again.

She did not have his name nor his image.

She did not understand what Miguel had carried with him.

But she knew enough.

He reread his instructions from *el jefe*. Make it look like an accident.

Much easier instructed than accomplished. He'd start by following her. See what he could learn. A tracking device on the woman's car and he could follow her anywhere. It was he stuff of TV shows and movies, but it worked.

First he'd find and take care of this woman. Then?

He had a new idea, one he wouldn't share with *el jefe* or anyone else.

Then he would find Miguel's brother.

Chapter 41

Hayden felt washed out while the small plane flew from Texas to the private airport in a DC suburb. The plane ride had experienced more turbulence than she was used to, and she couldn't shake her concern for Emilie or the fact that someone had cut her brake line and sent Matt to harm her. What would have happened if he'd succeeded? Was he going to shoot her, or take her to someone, and if so, to whom? Daniel Rodriguez? To distract herself, she read Emilie's article, then reread it, and her heart sank. The article was a blow-by-blow account of Miguel's trip to the United States.

Somehow Emilie had filled in the gaps in time during his coyote trip, confirmed when he'd been detained, and sketched out his murder. There were still holes, but she had written a roadmap of Hayden's case that pointed to the Rodriguez cartel.

Hayden rubbed her neck, feeling knots of tension at the base spilling into her shoulders. Warm hands slid hers to the side and worked the knots. Her muscles tightened against the pressure, and she glanced back at Andrew.

His eyes were intense as he continued the firm yet gentle pressure. "Let me do this."

She tried to break their locked gaze but couldn't. Instead, she read the desire in his eyes and wondered what to do with it. Did it match the intensity building inside her to know him? The day had been crazy and scary and she wanted to pretend this tension between them meant nothing, but his gaze narrowed on her lips.

Her heart rate hitched and she bit her lower lip.

His head tipped forward, and then the plane bounced through another pocket of turbulence, and she snapped to her senses.

"Thank you."

He nodded and kept up the smooth motion, but the moment was broken. Slowly her muscles eased and she relaxed until she almost started purring, but the spark of attraction was dimmed.

While she'd been reading Emilie's article, Andrew had blatantly ignored warnings to stay off phones as he clicked from website to website. When she'd asked what was wrong and if she could help, he'd ignored her, so she'd pulled out her laptop and put the finishing touches on the Rodriguez discovery requests. First thing in the morning, she'd serve those along with filing the complaint at the Court of Federal Claims and courier a copy to the Department of Justice. Then the excitement could begin, as she figured out where she was working.

For now she wanted to sit here and never have Andrew stop kneading her shoulders.

The plane bumped to a landing then glided to a stop on the runway. "Where are we?"

"A small airport outside Leesburg. Can I give you a ride home?"

"Thank you." The benefit of the private airport was it took only minutes from when they walked off the plane until they reached Andrew's Jeep. The downside was it was too far from public transportation to make it an affordable ride home. Andrew helped her into his Jeep, then stored her suitcase in the back. His silence as the ride began told her more was going on than he'd shared. "What's wrong?"

He sighed as he pulled out of the airport and onto the road. "Nothing you can help with."

"Are you sure?" Hayden studied the tense line of his jaw and the way he kept his gaze locked on the road. This was more than concern about Emilie. "I'd like to help if I can. I've been told I'm a pretty good listener."

"Thanks, but this is something I have to figure out. And unfortunately, no one can help me." He huffed out a sigh that matched the tapping of his fingers against the steering wheel. "I've tried, and it's one big blank." His gaze slid to the rearview mirror, then to his side mirror.

"Is everything okay?"

"I'm not sure." He glanced in the rearview

mirror again. "Someone might be following us." He turned on his blinker. "I'll take a circular path."

Hayden turned around, but all she could see in the dark was the silhouette of an SUV-type vehicle hidden in the shadows behind its headlights. She turned back around and kept her gaze glued to the side mirror as Andrew executed a series of turns. An on-ramp for I-66 appeared, and as he swerved onto the ramp at the last possible second, the SUV shot past them on the highway. Still Andrew floored the gas and zigzagged through traffic until he'd put space between them and the ramp.

"Looks like we lost them." He settled back against the seat, but Hayden noticed his gaze kept moving between the mirrors.

She tried to relax, but her neck had knotted again.

"Who would follow us?"

"I don't know. Could be whoever's harassing me."

Hayden nodded. "No one knew I was with you." How could they? She hadn't known until an hour before they boarded. Her phone beeped at her, and she pulled it out. A voice mail from work? Why call hours after the working day ended?

She rubbed her forehead and temples. It could wait until she was in the privacy of her town house. "Have you tried Emilie since we landed?"

"Still nothing."

"She must have let her phone die." She would believe that until she didn't have a choice. Then a thought crept over her. What if the article on Miguel's murder had caught the wrong person's attention? She started ticking through the times she'd felt like her home or work offices had been disrupted. Then there was Gerard's office destruction a week ago and Angela's termination. Add in Gerard's client visit and "accident," and Hayden felt the urgency building. His death was anything but an accident, and when you added in her rental's brake failure, it felt like a sinister force was out to keep her from this case. Some-thing bigger was happening, and she didn't know what, why—or if it had swept up Emilie as well.

"Ease up, Hayden."

She startled and looked at Andrew. "What?"

"You're about to push through the floor-board. This vehicle might not be much, but I like it."

Hayden glanced down at her feet. "Sorry." She pushed out a breath and forced her attention to him. "You asked about harassment earlier. I'd like to help if I can."

He shrugged while keeping his gaze locked away. Then he seemed to reach a decision. "Someone's threatening to reveal my other job, and people I care about will be hurt."

"Your other job?"

He ignored her question. "I've spent two weeks tracking them. I can't even tell you what part of the country they live in, but they must be good with a computer."

Hayden thought about that. Often her biggest worries involved the unknown, but maybe it could feel smaller if she helped him attack the problem. "What's the biggest harm that comes from this revelation?"

"My father might lose his appointment to the Senate."

The extremeness of the reaction got her attention. She studied the profile of the man she'd come to respect and considered what she knew about him. His actions earlier at the detention center had confirmed he fiercely defended those he knew. Their time at the Cherry Blossom Festival had revealed a different side, and his work on the kids' festival showed his desire to improve lives in even small ways. None of those seemed designed to create the extreme reaction of resigning. "The congressman should be fiercely proud of the work you do. What could you do that has those consequences?"

Andrew briefly glanced at her. "Do you read the op-ed page?"

"In the newspaper?" Hayden shook her head. "If it's not easily seen on my phone or computer, I don't pay much attention."

"Unfortunately, the people that matter aren't

like you. They start their days on the op-ed page and work around the paper from there." He thumped the steering wheel a couple times, then blew out a breath. "I'm political cartoonist Roger Walters."

Hayden stared at him blankly. "Sorry, who?"

"I draw a weekly political cartoon that's syndicated to papers around the country, including one of the big Washington papers." Andrew slowed as a light turned yellow. "I've used the pseudonym since college, but someone's figured it out and plans to reveal my identity Monday. They've e-mailed, texted, and called me for two weeks, and I can't ID them. My editor assures me no one at the paper said anything, and I've talked to the few friends who know my alter ego."

"I'm sorry." Hayden could see from Andrew's clenched jaw and tight stance that this was incredibly important to him. "Help me understand why this would be a terrible thing."

"These cartoons are my way of telling the world what I think about politics. The ridiculousness of it, the parts that are inane. This week I drew the caricature of my dad that accompanied a profile piece."

"In the *Washington Post*? I saw that cartoon, it was good."

"Sure, but do you think my dad liked it? He thinks I quit cartooning back in college. And he's never understood why drawing was important to me. In fact, he ordered me to give it up."

Hayden got it. It was hard when parents couldn't understand an important part of your life. "So why didn't you?"

"It gave me a voice and an outlet." He glanced at her as he took the King Street exit and headed toward Old Town.

"But why would this be catastrophic for your dad? It's not as though you've done something illegal or immoral."

"He'll be publicly humiliated." He groaned. "My parents keep up the image of the perfect family, but it's far from the reality. I was mostly raised by nannies, with the occasional parental appearance."

Silence settled over the car until Hayden pointed to the cloverleaf of grass on the off-ramp. "One time I saw a couple deer in that space. It scared me to death. What on earth were deer doing in the middle of an urban area two hundred feet from a major interstate?" She placed a hand on his arm and felt him stiffen.

"Not all of us fit the normal molds, Andrew. This is an important part of who you are. Your parents love you." He snorted, but she pressed on. "They might not show it well, but all parents love their kids. They just do. They'll understand—but you should tell your dad before he finds out from someone else."

Andrew's jaw clenched even tighter.

"Take the proactive stance. Beat whoever is threatening you to the announcement. If your cartoons are as popular as it sounds, a lot of people would be interested in knowing the man behind the pencil."

"Pen. I use a pen."

"Exactly." She smiled at him. "They will be fascinated by the process, and knowing who you are will make your cartoons more important. People will value your perspective and what you have to say."

He nodded, then slowed to a stop at a stoplight and glanced her way. "You might be right. It would be best if he heard it from me."

"Think about it. Pray about it. Don't they always say the best defense is a good offense? Take away the power of revealing you."

He turned back to the road and pushed out a breath. "I'll call my editor tonight. We could get the word out Saturday." He moved his head from side to side as if loosening the tension in his neck. "I've spent two weeks wondering when I'd get the next call or text. Not knowing who's behind this makes it hard to fight back."

"So don't fight. Just bring it all into the light."

Justice tended to work better when everything was out in the open.

Chapter 42

Andrew executed a couple turns, then pulled in front of her town house. The brick facade had never looked better. She turned to open the Jeep's door, only to see Andrew was already there and opening it. All looked quiet in the dark, but her stomach still clenched as she wondered if Emilie waited inside.

Hayden accepted Andrew's hand as she stepped out of the Jeep, warmth flooding her at his chivalrous gesture. She glanced around the street, but didn't see Emilie's car. That in itself didn't concern her; sometimes they parked a block or two away and walked to the house. She hurried up the sidewalk, her Wonder Woman key ring clutched in her hand. The soft scent of her neighbor's dogwood perfumed the air as she fit the key into the lock.

Before she could turn the key, the door eased open.

"Em?"

Only the echo of her voice responded as unease slithered up her spine.

Hayden slipped into the living area and set down her attaché case. Her heels tapped across the floor as she entered the kitchen. The marble countertops were clean, with none of the telltale piles of chaos Emilie usually left. Hayden poked her head out the back door to confirm that her roommate wasn't stargazing at the patio table.

Andrew took the stairs to Emilie's space and Hayden followed, her heart climbing her throat.

"Emilie, are you all right?"

Silence.

The stillness felt eerie. Unnatural. If Emilie were here, she'd have one of the Fab Four playing on her speakers, not loud enough to bother Hayden, but loud enough to fill her rooms. Hayden flipped on a light and called again. "Em? You're worrying me . . ."

Andrew muttered a soft curse as he stepped into the bedroom. "Someone's trashed the room."

Hayden glanced in. In addition to the piles of clothes on the floor, books had been tossed from bookshelves around the room.

"Oh, Em." Hayden wrapped her arms around her middle but couldn't stop the chill seeping through her. "I should check upstairs."

When she reached her office, the mess in Emilie's room seemed tidy by comparison. Every piece of paper had been pulled out and tossed on the floor, her books thrown on top. Her bedroom was in similar shape; even her mattress was flipped off the box spring and sitting cockeyed on the bedframe.

Andrew's arm snaked around her, and she sank

against him as he pulled out his phone. "911? I have a crime to report."

Hayden shivered on her front stoop as a police vehicle pulled up in front of the town house without sirens or blazing lights. Andrew paced in the small front yard.

He strode toward her and joined her as the officers stepped from the vehicle. The one on the passenger side had a hand on her service revolver and studied them cautiously. The one by the driver's door spoke first.

"We had a 911 call regarding a possible home invasion and missing person."

Andrew nodded. "I called it in. My cousin is missing and someone searched her rooms."

"I'm Hayden McCarthy, I live here. The front door was unlocked and open when I got home half an hour ago, and my roommate's car isn't here." Hayden rubbed her arms. "I'm really worried."

The officers moved from the car and stalked up the walk. The driver stuck his hand out. "I'm Officer John Stanfield. Have you checked the house?"

"Yes. We did a quick search."

Officer Stanfield kept a sharp eye on them, stance loose yet alert. "Explain again why you called us?" He wasn't rude, just efficient.

"We've been away all day, and my roommate

left us both lots of messages and texts. Now she's not here and the house is trashed." Hayden forced herself to stop, take a breath, and try to collect her thoughts. She had stood in front of juries, for goodness' sake, she could do this.

Andrew stepped toward her. "Her name is Emilie Wesley, and she's also my cousin. She's an investigative reporter and an attorney who works with domestic violence victims."

"Okay." The officer jotted a note.

Hayden unclasped her hands. "She was nervous about reactions to a story she wrote."

Andrew placed his arm around her shoulders. "The disaster in her room and Hayden's worries me. Add in the way the front door wasn't locked or shut, and something happened to my cousin."

"I've tried to reach her since we got back in town." Should Hayden mention they were followed from the airport? It only mattered if Emilie was somehow involved in something Andrew was working on. Her thoughts swirled in a muddied mix. How could Andrew be tied to Miguel's murder? Because that was the only way everything fit. Andrew had been at the detention center, but he didn't know about Miguel before the ride to the airport.

"Did you touch anything?"

Hayden shook her head. "We were careful to leave everything as we found it."

"All right. Wait here with Officer Thompson, and I'll do a sweep." Officer Stanfield squared his shoulders and, after exchanging a look with his partner, headed inside. His footsteps echoed as his partner pulled out a slim notebook.

Hayden sank onto the front stoop and buried her face in her hands. *Lord, help us find Emilie and have a good laugh over our worry.*

Officer Thompson opened her notebook to a blank page and looked at Hayden. "Mind repeating your concerns for me?"

A niggle of unease pricked Hayden as she retold what she'd said.

"Thompson, get in here." The abrupt bark seemed to startle the officer as much as it jolted Hayden.

"Stay here."

The minutes ticked by as Andrew and Hayden lingered outside the front door. Within fifteen minutes the original two police officers had been joined by four more, their squad cars filling the narrow brick street. None of them paid her any attention as they hurried downstairs, two carrying bags.

Every episode of *NCIS*, *CSI*, and *Law & Order* she'd ever watched filled her mind. What could the officers think they'd find?

Her phone rang, and she jumped. She scrambled to pull it out, and saw Emilie's name on the ID. "Hello?"

Nothing but silence reached her ear. "Emilie? Can you hear me?"

Andrew, standing next to her, grabbed the phone. "Em, where are you?"

A moment later he grunted. "She's not answering." He hurried toward the stairs, and Hayden followed in time to see Andrew grab the nearest officer. "Hayden just got a call from Emilie's phone, but Emilie couldn't talk to us. Can you trace the call?"

The officer brushed Andrew off, but took the phone. "I'll see what we can do."

A man in plain clothes stepped up to Hayden. "I'm Detective Peter Harlan, miss. Would you both come downstairs?" He turned and made his way toward the steps without waiting to see what she'd do.

Hayden glanced at Andrew, who motioned her to follow the detective as he led the way downstairs and into Emilie's bedroom.

Hayden had always loved the room, with its French country feel. A pale-blue loveseat sat against white walls and carpet. The bed was pushed against the far wall of the next room and covered with a creamy voile duvet. The faint scent of vanilla lingered in the air from the collection of half-burned candles that rested on a tray.

Two officers worked around the chaos of ``books, while another held a phone in a plastic bag.

The detective watched her closely. "When was the last time you saw Emilie?"

"Two nights ago." Hayden waited for him to take out a notebook, jot a notation of some sort, but he simply watched her as if weighing each word. "I left town early yesterday morning and got home just before we called 911."

"Was that the last time you talked to her?"

Hayden swallowed and tried to think. "We talked for a few minutes last night. She seemed fine, and then this morning she started leaving messages for me, but I was in meetings. I knew I'd see her tonight."

"She did the same with me." Andrew met the detective's gaze. "We ran into a delay in Texas, and by the time we got a plane and were headed back, Emilie wasn't answering my calls."

"What were you doing in Texas?"

Hayden bit her lower lip as she considered him. "I'm an attorney. I had a deposition related to a case."

"My father asked me to accompany him on business. Although Hayden and I were acquainted, neither of us knew that the other would show up at the same place the same day."

Hayden found it interesting that Andrew didn't mention who his father was in a situation where it might expedite matters.

"We put out a BOLO for your roommate," the detective said. "I just received word she's been found."

Hayden almost sagged with relief. "Where is she?"

"At George Washington University Hospital."

"The hospital?"

"She was in a car accident. I'll have an officer drive you there."

"What about the town house?" Should she leave while officers crawled all over the space? Could she stop them from looking wherever they wanted? She didn't have anything to hide, but what about Emilie? Did she have sensitive research stashed somewhere?

"A uniformed officer will be here until you return." He reached into his inside jacket pocket and pulled out a business card. "I'll be in touch, but if you think of anything I should be aware of . . ."

"Thank you." A minute later she and Andrew were in the back of a squad car crossing the river. He held her hand for the minutes it took to reach the hospital and she drew strength from him. No one was at the information desk, so she and Andrew followed the signs to the emergency room, an officer trailing behind.

The stale, antiseptic aroma assaulted her, and she closed her eyes. The receptionist in the emergency room looked harried as she talked with a young woman cradling a listless toddler. Several people sat scattered across the large waiting area. None was Emilie.

Chapter 43

Andrew approached the information desk in the ER, a cold knowing filling him. "I'm here to see my cousin, Emilie Wesley."

The elderly volunteer stared him up and down, an appraising look in his eye. "I'm guessing you don't have proof you're her cousin. HIPAA won't let me tell you anything without more information."

"I'm her only relative in town, because Congressman Wesley is traveling and Mom is at some function."

"I'm afraid I need more than your word."

"Sir, I'm her roommate." Hayden gave him a sweet smile, one that Andrew wished she would turn his direction. "A police officer drove us from the town house I share with Emilie, where they are investigating a break-in that could be tied to why she's here. Can you please let us see her and make sure she's okay?"

"Who did you say brought you?"

"Someone with the Alexandria City force." Hayden shot a worried look at Andrew.

Andrew's phone began beeping. "His name was Officer Lovelace." He stepped back and pulled out his phone. Mrs. Bradford? His pulse accelerated. Why would she be calling? Had something happened to Jorge? "Hello?"

"Andrew, you need to come home right away."

"What's wrong?"

"Jorge saw a man break into your condo when he went out to get my mail a few minutes ago. He hurried back inside to tell me and has retreated to my spare bedroom. Andrew, Jorge won't come out." Her words had picked up speed even as the volume dropped. "I don't know what to do."

"Have you called the police?"

"Did the moment Jorge told me about the intruder. They're on the way."

"We're keeping them busy." Andrew rubbed a hand up and down his face, fighting the waves of exhaustion from a long day. His car was at Hayden's, Emilie was here, and Jorge needed him. "I'll get there as soon as I can."

What he needed was a friend he could call to get there ahead of him. Instead, he'd grab a cab and reclaim his Jeep later.

"Everything all right?" Hayden touched his arm.

"I need to get home." He took a step toward the door, but the officer didn't budge. "Can you stay and find out how Emilie is?"

She stepped closer. "Is it Jorge?"

"Yes. He's okay, but my neighbor's concerned. Someone broke into my condo, police are on the

358

way, and Jorge is still shaking." He tugged her close and wrapped his arms around her. "I'll call as soon as I can."

"I will too." She stepped back and tipped her head until she could meet his eyes. "Be careful. This is big."

"Yeah." Bigger than they could understand. Could the two disjointed pieces be connected? The thought wouldn't leave him as he nodded at the policeman and then hurried to the main doors and the taxi stand. He prayed God would be with Jorge and Emilie, and that he would get home in time to help Jorge and find out who had broken into his home.

Hayden paced the floor in the emergency room waiting for someone who could tell her anything. The volunteer was only doing his job, but everything inside Hayden screamed to know Emilie was okay. While she waited she'd called Savannah, Caroline, and Jaime. The three had trickled in over the last half hour, and now it felt like the vigil wasn't hers alone. Andrew wasn't answering his cell, and she felt desperate for information from any front. Finally Savannah marched off, insisting she would learn something or heads would roll.

Caroline and Jaime huddled next to each other on a vinyl-covered couch, while Hayden couldn't stop moving.

"She's fine." Caroline looked up with a forced smile. "You'll see."

"If she was fine, we'd be back there." Jaime snapped, and Caroline shot her a dagger-filled look. "You know it's true."

"Maybe, but you don't have to be so quick with the glass half-empty."

"And you don't need to be so Pollyanna-ish."

"Ladies." Hayden sank between them on the narrow couch until it felt like they were back in law school beating their heads against some outdated tome. "Arguing won't help Emilie. Did y'all read her article?"

"Today's?" Caroline shook her head. "Not yet."

"It's a blueprint for my case. Somehow Emilie worked her magic and discovered things I hadn't."

Jaime smiled. "Sounds like our girl."

"Yep." Hayden filled them in on the crazy happenings in Texas. "When you add in the attack on Miguel's mom, it can't be coincidence. It's all related somehow."

Jaime arched a dark eyebrow at her. "When did you become a conspiracy theorist?"

"I'm not, but I got fired over this case, my home has been broken into, and now someone broke into Andrew's place? It can't be unrelated."

Caroline listed against the couch. "How would Andrew be connected to any of this?"

"Jorge, Miguel's brother, has stayed with him since Jorge's mom was attacked Saturday. Maybe whoever's behind all this figured that out." Hayden rubbed the heel of her hands against her eyes, the fatigue and stress crashing over her in a wave. "But there is a connection." She leaned back next to Caroline, and Jaime collapsed on her other side. "What if Miguel brought something to the US that someone else wants?"

"If he did, wouldn't you have it in his personal items?" Caroline looked like she wanted to help but wasn't sure whether Hayden had gone off her rocker.

"It wasn't. What if he sent it with his mom or Jorge and planned to reclaim it when he arrived? What if it was so valuable he didn't want to risk losing it traveling via coyote?"

"But whoever wanted it didn't know that?" Jaime's mouth dropped open. "And they killed him for something he didn't have?"

Hayden nodded. It all made terrible, perfect sense. "The question is, what did he have, and who wanted it?"

"And where is it now? Did you figure out what he was running from?"

Hayden shook her head softly. "I asked around in Texas. There's at least one man with a snake tattoo who seems to show up in a couple different places. It's a long shot, but if he's tied to all of this, the tattoo indicates he's part of a Mexican drug family . . . one dealing in new drugs like meth."

Caroline suddenly launched forward, knocking Hayden into Jaime. "What if that's the connection? You said Miguel's mom and brother came legally, but he couldn't. What if the reason was he's connected to drug money?" She scrambled to pull up her phone and did a quick Internet search. "See?" She pointed to the screen. "If your support comes from drugs or other illegal proceeds, you can't immigrate legally."

It fit. "Ciara said that could prohibit someone from obtaining a visa. So Miguel was stuck in the perfect storm. He wanted to leave, but couldn't unless he came illegally. So maybe he brought something with him—or sent it with his mother or brother—to barter for his freedom." She shook her head. "That's a stretch."

Jaime dislodged herself from the couch and took a seat across from them. "Not really. I've seen it with clients." She made a face. "They believe if they have something the government wants they'll go free. What if Miguel watched one too many movies where that worked—without the flip side that shows the real-life nightmares?"

"The cinematic legal system doesn't match the real one." Hayden felt a pulse of excitement. It all fit. "We have to find whatever it was he sent north."

"Because someone is still looking for it." Caroline rubbed her arms as if fighting a chill.

"I don't want anyone else caught in the crossfire." Hayden's phone rang just as Savannah reappeared.

"Hayden, this is Andrew. I'm almost home. Anything on Emilie?"

"Not yet."

"Listen. I wanted to tell you. My editor is announcing my identity in Saturday's paper. That means I've got to talk to Dad tomorrow."

"I'll be praying for that conversation."

"Thanks." There was a long pause. "Let me know as soon as you know about Emilie."

"Savannah went after information, and she's just back. I'll call after I hear what she learned."

"All right. Thanks, Hayden."

She nodded, even though he couldn't see it, and then clicked to end the call.

Savannah sank onto the seat next to Jaime.

"How is she?" Hayden pushed the words around the sudden lump in her throat.

"The doctors won't know for sure until she wakes up."

Chapter 44

Andrew scrambled upstairs to the condo.

He unlocked the door, and the flashing lights of the police vehicles strobed around him. The media hadn't arrived, but he imagined it wouldn't take long once word circulated that police had been called to Congressman Wesley's son's home. He could feel the last vestiges of his carefully constructed separation between his public persona and his second career collapsing. If the police were in his condo, then someone would figure out he was Roger Walters. And when they figured that out, there was nothing left to protect. It was a good thing it would be public Saturday.

"Slow down, mister." The voice held quiet authority, and Andrew lifted his frantic gaze. "You can't barrel up these stairs, not while my fellow officers are in the condo." The African American officer's gaze narrowed as he looked Andrew up and down. "You'd better start explaining who you are and why you're here."

"I own a condo on the second floor."

The man stared him down.

"I think mine's the one that was broken into."

"I'll need to see ID."

Andrew slowly reached for his billfold in his back pocket, as the door to Mrs. Bradford's unit opened.

"Thank goodness you're here, Andrew." Her face looked haggard and shadowed. "Jorge still won't talk. He's got me worried." She turned to the officer. "He lives here, Officer Williams. This is Andrew Wesley, Congressman Wesley's son."

Andrew tried not to grimace as she led with his identity.

"I still need ID."

Andrew nodded. He opened his billfold and slid his driver's license out. As the officer studied it, Andrew turned his attention to Mrs. Bradford. "Are you okay?"

"Yes, the police arrived quickly. But I'm worried about Jorge. Ever since we went to visit his mom this afternoon, he's been too quiet." Her eyes were wide yet her voice calm as if she didn't want Jorge to know how bothered she was. "Then the intruder arrived, and he panicked. I can't get him to believe he's safe. Even my chocolate chip cookies wouldn't coax him out."

Andrew grinned at her. "That is serious. Where is he now?"

"Still lying on my guest bed."

Andrew nodded and followed her to the room. A minute later he saw Jorge resting, eyes wide open. "Jorge? You okay?"

The boy muttered in Spanish, *"Mi Dios, mi Salvador."* Over and over he whispered the words from his clenched lips.

"Jorge." Andrew reached out and placed a hand on his shoulder. "You are safe."

Jorge shook his head and pulled into a tight ball.

"He is here." The broken words, spoken in English, cracked Andrew's heart.

"Who? Who is here?"

"El hombre."

Andrew sank onto the bed. "Who?"

Jorge looked at him with panic-filled brown eyes. "*El jefe*'s man. The man who hurt my mother."

Hayden scrubbed the grit from her eyes. The night in the emergency room and then outside Emilie's hospital room as her friend lay unconscious, tethered to a host of machines, had been long and yet too short. Savannah had told her to meet her in Old Town at eleven, and the short shower she'd allowed herself had done nothing to make her feel more human. Her thoughts spun in so many directions, it felt like her mind had hyped up on an overload of caffeine while her body begged for the sanctuary of her bed. Twenty-four hours earlier she'd been in Texas meeting with Matt, and now she was trying to figure out where she was.

Andrew had called and updated her on Jorge, but it all made so little sense. The pieces had to be connected. But what had Miguel sent and where was it? She knew Andrew needed to help Jorge, keeping him protected until the police could catch whoever had terrorized him, but she felt safer when Andrew was with her.

She had to be strong, but as she swiped a spider's web from the corner of her doorway, she felt trapped in her own web of events that had spiraled out of her control.

Her phone vibrated, and she swiped a finger

across the screen to read a message from Savannah.

Are you coming?

Guess Savannah didn't allow time to stand paralyzed. And her mentor was right. She had a case to move forward even if she didn't have a firm from which to do it.

Thirty minutes later she adjusted her attaché case strap and tried to breathe in strength the moment before she pushed open the door to Savannah's law firm in a prime location in Old Town.

"If it isn't Miz Hayden McCarthy." Savannah's warm-hearted secretary, Bella Stoller, greeted her with a big smile. Her black suit looked dignified and strangely comfortable as she stood to engulf Hayden in a big hug. "Savannah is paging me every fifteen minutes to see if you've arrived." She tapped a button on the headset as she retook her seat. "She's here." She nodded and then pointed Hayden toward the hallway. "She says to go on back. You know where."

"Thanks, Bella." Hayden stepped around the desk.

Several closed doors fed off the hallway. One led to a small conference room and library, the others to offices and a kitchenette. Hayden couldn't think of a time when all the offices had been filled, yet Savannah insisted she needed the space. Her lease would make firms like Elliott & Johnson weep with envy.

Savannah stepped from the office farthest down the hall. "Come on back, Hayden."

"When did you switch offices?"

"I didn't." Savannah grinned as she brushed a wayward strand of hair behind her ear.

Hayden entered the office and then stopped. "Leigh? What are you doing here?"

Her former paralegal sat in one of two leather chairs in front of a cherry desk and credenza, looking as bewildered as Hayden felt.

Savannah's grin widened. "We were getting to that, so your timing is perfect." She gestured to the open chair, and then moved behind the desk. "I have a proposition for you. A proposal to consider as you evaluate your options."

"Okay . . ."

"Set up your own practice." She raised her hands as Hayden's mouth opened. "Hear me out. You haven't been happy at the litigation mill, and this would allow you to take the cases that matter to you. You'll want to run with the Rodriguez case, which means you don't have time to hunt a location. I'm willing to front four months of Leigh's salary." She named a figure that was less than Leigh had made, but still more than being unemployed. "And I'll let you use offices here. You'll have to front your expenses and salary. It's the risk we all take when we go out on our own."

"But I don't have any clients other than Maricel."

"You run this one well, word will get out. You take court appointments while you wait. You've loved those cases and the judges will appoint you. I've already checked. It'll get you going."

Hayden looked from Savannah to Leigh, her mind racing with possibilities and fears. "What do you think, Leigh?"

"I can give you four months and see how this works. You need a good paralegal, and I find myself needing a job." There was a twinkle in her eyes. "It's gotta be more fun than Elliott & Johnson."

"*Fun* was not the word coming to me." Hayden blew out a breath. "I don't have the ability to pay rent or utilities or really anything."

Savannah waved her words away. "I'm not worried about that. I want you to have the space to make a good decision, not rush into the first job that walks your way."

Hayden blew out a laugh. "Isn't that what I'm doing if I say yes?"

Savannah leaned forward and shook her head. "You are taking a risk and giving yourself the gift of four months to make this work."

"Actually, I think you are."

"Then call me your fairy godmother, but you

need a place to run the Rodriguez case to make it a success. Campbell was right. This case could make your career." She leaned back and crossed her arms. "Seems awfully unfair that this opportunity should come to such a babe in arms, but"—she shrugged—"I want to help you succeed. You don't have to do law the way everyone else does. You're one big verdict and a bit of wisdom away from the impact you've wanted."

Hayden felt a burble of excitement stir inside her, warring with the voice of caution that screamed that the idea was crazy and fraught with danger. "I'll think about it."

"Do more than that. Pray about it. And until you know for sure, you're welcome to work out of this office. The computer isn't the latest model, but it works." She turned to Leigh. "I can only pay you if Hayden says yes, so you might work on those persuasive skills." She stood and waved her arms open. "Talk and let me know what y'all decide. You've got a government to get into settlement conversations, and that happens best with properly applied pressure."

Savannah swept from the room, and Leigh turned toward Hayden, her jaw hanging open. "Is she always like this?"

"A presence to be reckoned with? Yeah." Hayden shook her head, but it did nothing to slow her spinning thoughts. "So what do you want to do?"

"I need a job, even a temporary one, so I'm in if you are."

A slow warmth spread from Hayden's center. It really was now or never. "Then let's get down to work."

She had not expected Savannah to sweep onto the scene with a plan for her to hang out her own shingle—a plan that eased without eliminating the risks. With Leigh on board, even temporarily, she could restart without much of a hiccup. Hayden handed Leigh her flash drive and asked her to ensure the discovery requests were ready for a review when she got back. Then she headed to her town house.

Her phone rang on the way, and she sat down on a bench to answer it. "Andrew, is Emilie okay?"

"The doctors say she will be. She's showing signs of regaining consciousness."

They would know more when she started talking, but the doctors thought that other than deep bruises and broken ribs, a headache would be the worst of Emilie's long-term issues.

"I'm trying to work on the fair while I sit here, but I'm considering postponing it."

"You can't do that. Emilie will be furious if she wakes up and finds you cancelled it because of her."

"We shouldn't do it without her."

"She'll wake up and I'll get her there. All we have to do is implement her plan."

"All." Andrew snorted. "I might have thought I could do the day without her in the beginning, but this binder seriously has three pages of tasks left, and I'm coordinating Maricel's release from the hospital."

"I seem to remember Emilie saying you could turn on the Wesley charm and people would jump."

"Ouch, McCarthy. I thought you were in my corner."

"I am. You'd better get busy. I'll help tonight." She considered telling him Leigh and the other girls would help, but decided to wait until she could talk to them and explain the event and why it mattered. "We'll do this. We've got a week."

"A whole week." He blew out a breath. "You really think we can do this?"

"We'll do it for Em."

Chapter 45

SATURDAY, APRIL 15

Andrew slouched in the uncomfortable chair next to Emilie's bed. His cousin's usually perfect blond hair looked like a rat had taken up residence in it, and a deep bruise discolored her face, but she still appeared beautiful to him. The monitors beeped and clanged in their annoying way, but he was relieved there was something to assess.

"Come on, Em. I need you to wake up and tell us what happened."

The police had remained largely silent about her accident, telling him only that she'd gone off the road on Rock Creek Parkway. The road twisted and turned, but it didn't make sense that Emilie would be out there in the first place.

The last forty-eight hours had been long ones he didn't want to repeat. He rubbed his hands over his head, then his stubbled face. "I have to leave soon to make sure Maricel is okay. It's been crazy while you've been sleeping." A tiny cough caught his attention, and he looked up.

Her eyes locked on his. "Water."

"Yes." He hurried to push the nurse button. "I'd about get you anything you want, but we have to clear it with the nurse."

He breathed a prayer of thanks as he turned back to his cousin and grinned. Time to figure out what had happened and fix it.

An hour later Emilie was slowly telling an officer what had happened while Andrew waited in the hallway. He'd called Hayden and updated her. Other than a killer headache and a plea not to make her cough or laugh, Emilie would be okay, if very sore.

He left long enough to get Em her favorite

chocolate milkshake, and when he returned the officer was gone.

"Tell me what happened."

She gestured for the glass of water beside her bed, and he held it for her to take a sip.

"I got home to find a man destroying my room. I turned and ran for my car. But another car followed me, so I panicked and found myself across the river and then on the parkway." She swallowed as she rubbed her temple. "Then some hunter shot the car, and I lost control. At least that's what the officer said."

"No one stopped to help?"

"Not that I know of. But I must have blacked out."

Andrew's gut tightened at the thought of his cousin having to handle that all alone. "What were you calling me about when I was in Texas?"

She looked at him blankly. "I didn't call you."

"Repeatedly. Then you stopped leaving messages."

She screwed her face up as if thinking hard, then shook her head before putting a hand to her temple with a grimace. "I don't remember."

"Did it have something to do with your article?"

"Article?"

"The one that came out Friday." At her blank look, he continued. "It was good, Em, and focused on a young man who was murdered while detained in Texas."

"I don't know. I talked to Uncle Wesley and his staff about the murder. They were going to do something."

"Who did you talk to?"

"That catty woman." Emilie's face scrunched up. "I can't think."

"Okay." He let silence fall between them, knowing she meant Lilith.

Maybe thirty minutes later, Em stirred with a groan. "Where's Hayden?"

"She'll come as soon as she can. She's filing the Rodriguez case."

"That poor boy." Emilie eased toward him, and there was a look in her eye that warned him she was about to ask something he wouldn't like. "How's it going with Hayden?"

"I like her, but I'm not sure about us yet."

Emilie raised an eyebrow.

He laughed and put his hands up. "Fine. She's fascinating. Frustrating. Intriguing. Makes me wonder why I didn't notice her earlier."

"Want me to tell you what I told her?"

"Sure. What pearls of wisdom do you have?"

"You weren't any more ready for her than she was for you." Emilie reached for his hand with a slight wince, and he inched forward on his chair. "You had a few wild oats to sow."

She tightened her grip as he opened his mouth to protest.

"Not the ones the media would have everyone

believe, but you've been as skittish as a cat in a room full of rocking chairs about having a family of your own. Your cartooning feeds that side of you. The New Beginnings kids remind you that you can make a difference and break out of your family's mold." She loosened her grip. "Hayden does that too."

"When did you get so wise?"

"It's easy to see what others need." She looked away. "Not so easy to see what I need."

His eyes widened as he studied her. "You're ready for a relationship?"

"Don't look so surprised." She gestured toward her face. "It's not like I have to worry about it too soon, if I look as battered as I feel."

"It's not bad. You just need a little makeup to help hide that color show."

She wrinkled her nose at him and then yawned.

"Ready for a nap?"

"Maybe."

He leaned onto her bed. "Emilie, this was serious. You were almost killed."

"No." She shook her head and tried to smile. "You don't think a hunter mistook my car for a deer?"

"Rock Creek Parkway is not usually a shooting gallery at twilight."

"It is overpopulated." A shudder rippled her thin shoulders. "What if it's tied to one of my cases or an article?"

"The police will figure it out."

She nodded, but refused to look at him. He reached over and tipped her chin up so he could see her eyes.

"I won't let anything happen to you."

"Don't make promises you can't keep. Besides, I'm pretty good at looking after myself."

He hated how cynical she sounded. "Hayden and I won't let you be alone."

She rolled her eyes, but before she could say anything snarky his phone rang. He pulled it out and frowned. "It's Dad."

"You should never keep a senator waiting. Important advice my mom gave me." She shooed him away. "I'll take a nap." Her eyes were already closing as he stood and walked out of her room.

"Hey, Dad."

"Son. Are you with Emilie?"

"Yes sir."

"How's she doing?"

"Trying to convince the doctor she can go home, but it will be at least another night." He stepped out of the way of an orderly pushing a wheelchair. "What's up?"

"Your mother asked me to remind you about the fund-raiser. She hasn't heard about your date."

"I've got it covered."

"Exactly what I told her, but you know how she is. Determined to confirm every detail."

Andrew took the stairs rather than risk losing

his dad's call in the elevator. "Why'd you really call?"

"I've heard some disturbing rumors." The congressman let his words sit out there as if that would entice Andrew to break his silence. "The kind I want to immediately dismiss, but Lilith and Dan tell me it would be unwise."

Andrew took a stabilizing breath as he pushed out of the stairwell and into the hospital's sterile lobby. With its dark wood and tall windows, it should look clean and artsy, but the pharmaceutical, sterile smell ruined the visual effect. "Sir, there's going to be an article in the *Times* today."

"About?" The word lingered in the air between them.

"My editor is revealing my alter ego." Andrew stepped out into the sunshine and tipped his face to the rays. Maybe exposing this secret could warm him the same way. "I'm political cartoonist Roger Walters."

"The one who did that great caricature of me?" His dad chuckled. "Son, I've known you were Walters since college. If you wanted to keep your secret, I figured it was okay. I liked seeing how you thought about politics. In spite of all your protesting, when I saw the cartoons I knew you were thinking deeply about the issues."

Andrew tried to absorb his words as he walked across the parking lot. "You knew all along?"

"Sure. Your mom wasn't happy, but I didn't

care." There were a few beats of silence. "I wish you'd told me you were ready to come clean so I could help you set the stage."

"Dad, it wasn't my idea. Someone's been black-mailing me—threatening to destroy your campaign by revealing the information. We haven't found whoever it is, so Hayden suggested the best defense is a good offense. The article runs tomorrow."

"I don't like the idea that someone thought they could use it to hurt me. The FBI might be interested in that information."

"Maybe. I've got to survive that article and then the New Beginnings Fair."

"Your mother said to let you know we'll come for a while. We're trying to hold the day free from campaigning—at least an hour or so."

"Thanks." Andrew leaned against his Jeep. The knowledge that his father had known all along and let him keep his secret stirred something uncomfortable inside. "I'm sorry I kept it a secret, Dad."

"We all have our secret endeavors we keep close to our chests."

Andrew could almost see his dad's wry smile, the one the cameras loved.

"It's part of the human condition. I never saw the harm in it. Your perspective was usually insightful . . . though I don't think my nose is as big as you drew it."

"Caricature, Senator."

"Almost." They shared a laugh, and then hung up. Andrew stood taller than he had for weeks. Now to find Hayden and let her know the incredible turn his fears had taken.

APRIL 17

Rafael adjusted the headphones plugged into his phone. The device allowed even the simple listening devices he'd left in the man's home to pick up conversations, while he listened in the comfort of his car in a parking lot over the hill. The community was big enough, giving him plenty of places to hide without becoming noticeable to residents.

Miguel's brother had stayed hidden, and Rafael hadn't seen them at home since Miguel's mother was released from the hospital.

How he wanted to explain to Maricel that it had brought him no pleasure to hurt her. He wasn't a man who took delight in inflicting his power on those weaker, but he'd had specific instructions. She had insisted she didn't have what *el jefe* demanded. When he heard the police sirens he'd slipped out the back of the building while tires squealed to a stop in front. He'd been careful, but *el jefe* always knew . . . he had a network that rivaled a great country's.

All seeing.

All knowing.

Like a god to defy at one's own risk.

As he listened to the conversation about balloons and inflatables, he knew Jorge would be at the event they were describing. In that place, with the milling crowds and activity, he could pull Jorge aside and find out if he had the device. If the child did not know, then his search would return to the attorney.

She may have moved offices, but her new one would be easier to breach than the first. Changing desks would not prevent him from finding the device. Only then could he use his new identity to melt into the vastness of this country.

Chapter 46

Hayden stood in front of her mirror wishing Emilie were home to help her dress for the fund-raiser. After all that had happened in the last few days, this day with Andrew had more importance than merely helping him with an event. They'd talked on the phone since returning to Virginia, but missed each other while she filed the lawsuit and he worked on the fair while helping the doctors keep Emilie in the hospital.

Hayden's wardrobe consisted of black suits that worked for the courtroom, but not for a political fund-raiser. Emilie had several sheaths that were great for her roommate's willowy and athletic frame. Finally she decided on a navy sheath with a lace overlay. It wasn't courtroom approved, so she prayed it would be okay for the fund-raiser.

Andrew knocked and was about to knock again when the door swung open. Hayden stood there, wearing a dress that looked a lot like one Emilie had worn to a family wedding last spring, and his breath about died in his chest. It had to be Emilie's dress, but his cousin hadn't filled it out in all the right places and he had to work not to stare. Hayden looked amazing all the way down to her heels. She wobbled a moment, then her lips curved in a stiff smile.

Time to set her at ease. "Ready to steal the show?"

"Actually I was thinking about hiding by the back door."

His phone vibrated, and he snagged it from his sport coat pocket. Lilith again. He thumbed in a message, then deposited the phone back in his pocket. "Shall we?" He held out his elbow, and Hayden placed her arm in his.

"Thank you." She grimaced as she tripped down the stairs. "I'm out of practice."

"No problem. I've helped enough women to know most don't wear shoes like that on a regular basis." And those who did often had the knee problems to go with the crazy heels. He helped her into his Jeep, then headed the vehicle toward Great Falls. "Thanks for coming." Andrew glanced at her as the spring sunshine filtered over her. He could get used to having her around.

"Anything I need to know or make sure I don't do?"

"Nope." He spent the thirty-minute drive filling her in on the people he knew would be there. He hadn't received an advance list so he winged it, knowing some of the standards who would show up with a check and a wish.

Hayden stiffened as they turned into the long

driveway. She'd gotten quieter as they started passing the larger estate homes, but now that they joined the line of Jaguars, BMWs, and the occasional Porsche, she froze. "This is already worse than I expected."

Andrew tried to see the event through her eyes, eyes unjaded by years of events and scores of interactions with the attendees. Valets ran to meet the cars and park them on the side lawn. Not even the weather would think of ruining his mother's event, so only an occasional cloud marred the cyan sky.

Andrew pulled his gaze from the drive long enough to grab Hayden's hand and catch her attention. "Hey, remember, they're all just people —maybe they have a little more cash than some of us, but you belong here as much as they do."

She nodded, but he could feel the moisture on her palm as he squeezed her hand, then let go. Hayden stared out the windshield as she drew in a breath and blew it out very slowly. Then she pulled her shoulders back, lifted her chin ever so slightly, and stilled her hands. She nodded and turned to him. "I'm ready."

And she was. Just like that.

———

Two hours later, Hayden was ready to pitch the demon shoes over the cliff into the Potomac somewhere below. She also felt like a plastic smile had affixed to her face and her cheeks felt frozen like Tour Guide Barbie at the end of *Toy Story II.*

Andrew had stayed with her for a while, then his father and chief of staff pulled him aside. He'd apologized when he returned, only to be tugged aside again, this time by the beautiful Doreen Wesley, who seemed highly unsure of this woman her son had brought to the event. She'd spent half an hour taking Andrew around while Hayden nibbled crab cakes and hors d'oeuvres. A waiter had kept her supplied with sweet tea until she was sure she could buzz home from the sugar.

The event was flooded with lobbyists and special interest representatives who all wanted their moment of time with the almost-senator from the Commonwealth. Hayden wondered what it would be like to move in such circles, even run for office. But as the event wore on, she found that idea dying. It was the epitome of boring as she spoke with more strangers. Then she'd frozen as Jason Randolph approached, looking a bit overdressed in a tuxedo and slicked-back hair.

"Interesting to see you here, McCarthy." Randolph swirled his mixed drink as he studied her. "Isn't this event a bit rich for your taste?" The stiff aroma wafting from his words made it clear this wasn't his first drink.

She tipped her chin and met his gaze. "I enjoy events like this."

"Party crashing. I didn't think you were the

type. But there's a lot about you I didn't know."

"Like what?"

"Climbing to the top on the shoulders of someone better than you. What on earth did Gerard ever see in you? You weren't his first mistake, though it seems you were his last. He got everything he deserved."

The cold in his words froze her.

Andrew slid up behind her. "Everything all right?"

She forced a smile as the warmth of his hand found the small of her back, and she introduced the men. "Andrew, this is Jason Randolph, one of the partners I worked with at Elliott & Johnson." And the partner who seemed to have a finger in each element that had gone wrong at the firm: Angela's termination, Gerard's death, Hayden's forced leaving, and probably a dozen other things.

Randolph's smile looked reptilian as he stepped forward and shook Andrew's hand. "Your father and I share an interest in immigration reform. I'm a great admirer of the congressman and would hate for anything to inhibit his move to the Senate."

Andrew's face froze. "That's an odd thing to say." He took a step toward Randolph, but the older man's cocksure grin never budged.

"Not as odd as what you've been doing." Randolph smirked and then turned as Lilith strolled over wearing a gown with the elegant cut of Audrey Hepburn's from *Breakfast at Tiffany's*.

She even had a small tiara nestled in her upswept hair. "Andrew, your father wants you to join him on the dais as he thanks everyone for coming." She turned, and her eyes widened as she saw Randolph. "I'm so sorry. Am I interrupting something? You all look so serious."

Randolph's stance hardened as he looked at her. "Not at all, Lilith." He turned back to Hayden and Andrew. "A pleasure to see you both." The scowl on his face didn't match his words.

Hayden took a half step closer to Andrew and wondered how Lilith and Randolph knew each other.

As soon as he stepped onto the dais, Andrew noticed a man with swarthy features standing beneath a tree. In his midtwenties, the man looked as out of place in his jeans and polo as Jason Randolph had looked in his tux. What kept Andrew's attention was the way the man's gaze was fixed on Hayden.

As he watched the man watching Hayden, his father stepped next to him.

Perfectly turned out in a hand-tailored suit that cost more than many of Andrew's families had to survive on for a month, his father looked every part the patrician senator. Old Virginia family, wealth earned the old-fashioned way, and smart enough to attend an Ivy League school and top tier law school, the man had all the résumé lines.

"Try not to frown so much when you're up here, son," he murmured.

The way he said *son* made Andrew wonder if he occasionally forgot his only child's name. Then he scolded himself for the unkind thought. His dad cared, he was just unsure how to show it.

"Give the illusion you enjoy these events."

"Yes sir." Andrew tried to relax his arms and loosen his stance, but his mind buzzed with tension as he kept the man in his sights.

"Nice article, by the way. Looks like you didn't need my help to get the right tone."

"Thanks." Who was that guy, and how had he made it onto the property? His dad didn't hire much security for these events, but maybe that should change. Andrew made a mental note to raise the idea with Dan Washburn. One more detail for the overpaid, overstuffed chief of staff to manage.

His mother made her way through the crowd, the perfect image of a woman who attended the best private girls' schools in the late sixties. Makeup flawless, hair that wouldn't dare ruffle in the wind, dress in perfect taste. A true southern belle to the tips of her pointed shoes.

As Andrew's gaze slid back to Hayden, he noted she looked perfect as she chatted with an attorney from Old Town. Hayden had introduced the woman as Savannah Daniels, her friend and mentor. It looked like the two had much to discuss.

Senator Cole, an influential member of the Senate, addressed the crowd. Then his father rallied the troops. Midway through his speech, Andrew noticed the Polo Shirt Man pivot from his position under the tree and disappear into the mix of staff. Maybe that's what he was after all. One of the many hired by his mother for a behind-the-scenes job. But even if that explained the man's presence, Andrew didn't like the way he had honed in on Hayden.

As some other dignitary spoke, Andrew bit back a smile as his mother shifted her feet. The dais time was stretching long, even for a campaign event. Finally the speechmaking ended, and his father urged everyone to take advantage of the food and open bar.

Several people stopped Andrew as he tried to wend his way to Hayden.

The county chairwoman asked a question he'd heard numerous times, her white hair taking on a blue tinge in the light of the setting sun. "Ready to run for your father's seat?"

Andrew met her gaze as he weighed his words. He couldn't admit to her that public office was the last thing he wanted. "I'll leave his seat to the professionals."

"Maybe what we need is fewer professionals and a few more people who see people." Her eyes might hide behind red-framed glasses, but Andrew realized Mrs. Hopner saw straight through him. "Give it some thought, young man. DC could use more people who don't want to be here."

Her words rolled through his mind, colliding with ready protests and a few seconds of "maybe she's right." He glad-handed a few more of the congressman's supporters before he finally found Hayden headed his direction.

She looked slightly uncomfortable, and he knew he'd left her on her own too long. Though he had to say, she'd proven she was more than up to the challenge.

Hayden kept an eye on Lilith and Randolph as they left. She followed behind them, their coziness contradicting their earlier tense exchange. She stopped a few feet away from them and turned around, but not so far that she couldn't make out their conversation.

"Are you ready to move forward?" Lilith's words were harsh, even as she hung on Randolph's arm.

"I took care of her, didn't I?"

"Not quite the way the boss anticipated. He's willing to give you another try to find it."

"It's not at the office."

"Then get creative."

They wandered off and Hayden turned toward the dais as the program started. What were they looking for? And who had Randolph taken care of? Her? Angela? The speeches were long, leaving her wishing for an Abraham Lincoln statesman among them. Then it finally ended and Andrew moved toward her.

"Did a Hispanic-looking man bother you?"

Andrew's words, married with a concerned look on his face, pulled her up short. "Excuse me?"

His clear eyes met her gaze head on. "The whole time I was on the dais, a man was standing a few feet away, focused on you."

Maybe if she focused on anything but the man Andrew had seen, she wouldn't panic in front of his family. "I knew this dress was a bad idea."

Andrew laughed. "That dress was anything but a bad idea."

"Thank you." She tried not to smile but couldn't help it, there was such admiration in his eyes. Her heart sped up. There was something electrifying about this man. Something that felt dangerous, too, as though if she got too close she'd be singed.

"Andrew, I believe you have some duties to attend to." Lilith was coming their way, walking way too fast for stilettos. What was she thinking wearing those to an outdoor event? And how did she keep from sinking into the ground with each step?

The LD stopped in front of them and hooked her arm through Andrew's. "I need to speak with you privately. I heard something important you'll want to know." She gave Hayden a catty grin.

"You can say anything in front of Hayden." Andrew's smile warmed her from the inside even as Lilith tried to ease him away.

"Not this." There was a fire in her eyes that put Hayden on edge.

"Not gonna happen. Say it here or it'll wait. I've already left Hayden on her own too long."

"You interfered where you shouldn't have." She stepped away, then she turned back and locked eyes with Andrew. "You will regret this."

Chapter 47

MONDAY, APRIL 17

Monday morning Hayden reluctantly went to the office. After the fund-raiser she and Andrew had brought Emilie home, and while her friend insisted she was fine, Hayden knew better. The shadows that lingered in the depths of Emilie's eyes belied her words.

Now as Hayden sat in a borrowed chair in a borrowed office, she doodled on a legal pad, wondering what on earth she was supposed to do next.

She had one client. One client who hadn't paid.

Maybe she should hold the Elliott & Johnson

partners accountable for her summary firing. At Gerard's memorial service Saturday, it had felt . . . odd. Angela and Seth had sat with her in one of the middle rows, while the partners acted like they'd never seen her or Angela before. Seth kept Hayden between Angela and himself, tension radiating between them.

It was as if with Gerard's death Hayden's connections to the firm had been completely severed. She didn't know how to handle that, since the firm hadn't given her any type of commitment she could enforce. That came with the coveted partnership.

So she was appropriately somber as she sat in the pew and listened to the eulogies. Her gaze had roved over those there, wondering whether the police watched in case Gerard's death hadn't been an accident, but she didn't notice either Detective Grearson or Officer Tucker, and she didn't know who else to look for in the crowded sanctuary.

The eulogies had seemed heartfelt, but she couldn't buy Randolph's sincerity when he had so callously pushed her and the support staff out in the days after Gerard's death. Words about the firm being family didn't fit the reality she'd experienced.

Hayden pulled her thoughts from the memorial. She had to get clientele or Leigh would be as good as unemployed, while Hayden would have a list of debts to Savannah and the bank. She stood and headed to the door. "Leigh, have a minute?"

Her friend scurried into the office with her stenographer pad, colorful skirt swirling around her ankles. "What do you need?"

"Let's get some notices out to the local courts that I'm available for cases."

"Which counties?"

Hayden mentally reviewed her options. "I don't want to waste time in the car if I can avoid it, so let's stick with Fairfax, Arlington, and Alexandria, and see how that goes this month." She felt a little lightheaded at the thought of how long it would take to get paying clients. "What was Savannah thinking?"

"That you could do better than the discovery mill." Leigh set down her pad of paper and leaned into the desk. "You'll be fine, Hayden. Savannah and I believe in you. Just think: you can focus on the cases you care about."

"If only I knew what those were."

"Look at this as your chance to find out." Leigh stood. "I'll get these letters ready for your signature. The courts always need more willing attorneys."

Hayden nodded. "I've seen the e-mails. Guess we'll see how serious the need is."

Then she called Maricel. The woman sounded tired—but who wouldn't after several days of interrupted "rest" in a hospital. "I wanted to give you my updated contact information."

"*Gracias*." The woman took a breath. "What did you learn in Texas?"

"Nothing conclusive. However, several of the staff I talked to believe there was a cover-up. Maricel, I need to know if you want me to continue to be your attorney." Hayden tried not to think of the plane ticket and other expenses sitting on her credit card. "The complaint is filed and I'm ready, but are you committed to the case?" Better to learn now than after she'd invested more in the lawsuit.

"You are my attorney." The words were simple, clear, direct.

"Okay. I'll send the paperwork to continue." Tears threatened and Hayden tried to will them away. "Thank you."

"*De nada*." There was a rustling sound as Maricel shifted the phone. "Thank you for believing in Miguel. And thank you for your help with Jorge while I was sick."

"Do you have any idea who attacked you?" There was silence to the point Hayden wondered if she'd lost the call. "Maricel?"

"I don't know." She hesitated as if weighing her words carefully. "Jorge thought he knew the man, but I don't know how. I have guesses, but it makes no sense."

"Andrew said Jorge told him it was '*el jefe*'s man.' Who's that?"

"I couldn't tell the police. I can't tell you."

Was it a *can't* or a *won't?* There was a difference, but Hayden could hear the fatigue in her
client's voice. "Was it your husband?"

Only silence.

"I'd like to help. I'll swing by tomorrow and we
can talk."

After she hung up, Hayden stared at her desk.
For the Rodriguez case, all she had left to do
was send the discovery requests. She'd reviewed
the initial discovery plan, but she couldn't file
until after the initial case-planning conference,
and that could take weeks. It all depended on the
judge, and the file on her desk was amazingly slim.
Nothing had come back from the court yet, though
they should get something that week if the court
knew how to find her. Another task for Leigh.

She could call Caroline and see if the case had
been assigned to a judge that she could see
through her position at the court. That wouldn't
make the court move faster, but it would help
her plan her approach.

One phone call later, she had a name.

Judge Meredith Devers.

The name left a heaviness in her. The woman
was über smart, a Yale grad who had worked
her way to partner at a prestigious East Coast
firm only to leave for an appointment to the
Court of Federal Claims. She'd claimed she
could teach the law or impact it, and when it
was put like that, there was one choice.

Hayden hadn't worked with her at the court, but she'd watched and seen that she was a no-nonsense judge focused on running a tight ship and following the law.

That fact could give Hayden serious heartburn.

Her legal theory was not a straight by-the-book approach that allowed a judge to easily draw a connection from one case to the next, all fitting in a neat, connected line. Instead, she was asking a judge to interpret the next step—a logical step—but an extension of theories.

Would Judge Devers be open to novel arguments, or would she perch her reading glasses on the bridge of her nose and look over them at Hayden with an expression of scorn? She must tighten the argument and clearly lead the judge from current law to the new ground in a seamless fashion, removing any bumps from the road.

With a knock on the door, Leigh jolted Hayden from her thoughts. "You've got a lunch delivery."

Hayden looked at the clock on her computer with a frown. Surely it wasn't already time for lunch? "I didn't order anything."

Leigh waggled her eyebrows with a goofy grin. "You'll want this one."

She stepped back and Andrew moved into view, his khakis and polo casually perfect. "I brought sandwiches and soup. Thought I could buy a bit of your time." He set a Panera bag on the desk she still couldn't think of as hers.

"Um, great." She turned to Leigh. "Can you find some waters for us? I'm sure Savannah has them somewhere." She started opening drawers on the desk. "I think I saw napkins in one of these."

Andrew eased onto the edge of the chair in front of her. "Is it okay that I'm here?"

Hayden blew hair out of her eyes as she paused and looked at him with a slow smile. It felt really good to know he'd come. "Yes. I'm just feeling a little discombobulated, trying to figure out what to do. I never expected to be working here." She forced herself to close the drawer and relax. "A week ago, life felt different."

The clear blue eyes of DC's most eligible bachelor studied her, and she felt herself sinking into their depths. As she did, she decided she didn't want to come out. There was a peace and acceptance in his gaze that made her wonder what he saw in her and why he kept coming back. Finally his scrutiny made her shift in her chair like a kid sitting in the principal's office. "What?"

He shrugged with a completely disarming grin. "What if I've missed you?"

She laughed. "You haven't had time, with getting Maricel and Jorge settled and watching over Emilie."

"While we're listing my mighty feats, let's not forget the board meeting tomorrow." He pulled the bag over and took out sandwiches and two containers of soup. "I chose cream of broccoli and tomato, because who doesn't love them? One sandwich is Italian and the other is chicken. Pick your favorites, and I'll eat what's left."

Leigh bustled in with two bottles of water and a stack of napkins. "Here you go. Anything else you need before I slip out for a bite?"

"No, thanks." Hayden smiled at her assistant. "Enjoy the sunshine." She selected the tomato soup and chicken salad sandwich. "Thanks for these, but why are you really here?"

"I figured we both had to eat, and I wanted to catch you up on a couple things before we knock out the rest of the details for the fair. Thought that would keep us busy for an hour."

"An hour?" If there wasn't a twinkle in his eyes, she might seriously question his sanity. "Who says we can do a fraction of that in an hour? Or that I have the time?"

He opened his arms expansively as if taking in the full office. "I don't see an overflow of clients. Yet." He winked at her.

"Give me time."

"I'll give you a lifetime."

Electricity crackled between them as she took in his words.

She swallowed as he stood and came around the desk toward her. "Hayden, I've missed you."

"It's only been a day." But she knew what he meant. She'd missed seeing him too.

"You know what I mean." He stepped closer and then extended his hand.

She studied it, wondering what he wanted. Then slowly, deliberately, she decided it didn't matter. She would trust him and not analyze every thought and motive. He had proven himself a man who could be trusted, and her heart cried to know if there was more she could hope for.

Chapter 48

The ringing of the phone interrupted the dynamic hold Hayden's gaze had on Andrew. He felt odd standing near her, around the desk, but knew he wanted more. And he'd let her know as soon as he could get her attention. Given the way Hayden was frowning as she listened, whatever news she heard wasn't what she wanted. When she hung up a minute later, he'd moved back to his side of the desk and was calmly eating his soup. There'd be another time and place better suited to letting her know the direction his thoughts were heading where one Hayden McCarthy was concerned.

Hayden picked up her soup spoon and worked it through the creamy soup.

"Anything wrong?"

"Just the police from Texas. Someone definitely cut the brakes to the rental." She dropped her spoon back in the bowl. "He claimed nobody showed up in the surveillance footage. It had to have happened at the detention center though, because I had no problem getting there Thursday morning. It was only when we left that the car wouldn't respond."

"You weren't inside long."

"Exactly." She picked up a pen and rocked it along her fingers as she frowned at the desktop. "One of the guards told me that the cameras monitored the parking lot at all times. But what if someone disabled them so the murderer could get into the building unseen, and then they were never turned back on?"

"It's possible, but unlikely. Someone would have noticed."

"Maybe. Anyway, there's no way to prove it."

"That's what discovery is for."

"Yeah." Hayden turned the conversation to the fair, and while eating, they knocked out most of the prep that could be completed before the weekend.

"This was great." Andrew glanced over Emilie's careful notes again. "The remaining details are perfect for Emilie to work on when she's not resting."

"If you don't give them to her, she'll drive us both crazy."

He collected his trash into the bag. "One last quick thing."

Hayden brushed some crumbs off her desk and then looked at him with an open expression. "Yes?"

"I took your advice, and Dad and I talked before Saturday's article." He still couldn't believe his dad had let him keep his secret all those years. "He's known all along I was Roger Walters."

A big grin spread across Hayden's face, and in that moment Andrew wanted to lean across the desk and kiss those lips. "Really? That's incredible."

"It wasn't the way I expected the conversation to go. I was sure he'd be furious, but he even mentioned it at the fundraiser. I'm still questioning whether I heard him say he was proud of me." He glanced at his phone again. "The best part is no more messages or threats, though I still want to find the person behind them."

Hayden's grin slipped a bit as if she'd thought of something disturbing. "Have you considered it was someone who knows you who wanted to expose you?"

"Yeah, though I don't like it. No one I've thought about so far could have been involved." Maybe he'd never know for sure who lobbed the threats, but he'd keep looking.

Hayden wiped her hands down her pant legs, then grabbed the pad of paper on her desk. "Let's list everyone who knew. I bet your dad's staff knew, if he did."

"What?" Andrew settled back in the chair and crossed his feet at the ankles. "I hadn't thought of that." Though as he thought about the relationship Dad had with his key staff, the idea didn't seem so crazy.

"Maybe he was giving you the space to tell him when you were ready."

"Maybe."

Hayden glanced up at him. "I'm just glad he knows and you don't have to worry anymore."

"I'm glad it's behind me. The stress of the reveal was real."

Hayden's smile said more than words could. Was a promise buried in it? Then she turned back to the notepad. Andrew leaned closer for a look. Her list consisted of interlocking rings with data in each. He pointed to the list, grateful to move on from his alter identity. "Maybe the attack on Maricel is tied to your case."

"Maybe." She tapped her pen against another bubble. "Look at how the attack on Jorge's mom intersects potentially with the break-in at your apartment." Hayden filled in information on another ring.

Andrew leaned closer and frowned as he read. "Gerard?"

"His death might be tied to the case. He was the one who assigned me and kept the partners motivated to keep the case. The car in Texas is tied to the case."

"What about Emilie?"

"Maybe the attack was connected to the story she wrote on Miguel's murder." Hayden paused and looked up at him with a concerned expression. "Andrew, she learned more about the murder than I did. I'll have to prod her for details, because she kicked over a hornets' nest with her digging. She's so bulldogged when she's on the trail of a story."

Hayden's heart hiccoughed in her chest as she stared at the interconnecting circles. "It's all connected. The girls and I talked about it late Thursday night, and we were right."

"So what kicked this whole thing off?"

"Jorge must know. Do you think he'll talk to me?"

Andrew shook his head. "He'll barely talk to me. Whoever he saw at the burglary scared him to the core. I'll try again today or tomorrow at New Beginnings. Wish the guy had still been there when the police arrived. We'll probably never know who he is."

"Something followed Miguel here. Do you have any kind of information in a file about him? Some kind of paperwork on Jorge when he joined the New Beginnings program?"

"Sure. It's pretty basic, but I can forward it."

"I'm most curious about relatives and where he was from in Mexico. Rodriguez is a common name, but I believe there are ties to the cartel. *El jefe* means the boss, but I wonder if it also means his father."

Andrew frowned. "Why would his father terrorize Jorge that much?"

"I don't know, but he is paying for the lawsuit. What if he's the one who needs the information?"

"I suppose it's possible." Andrew tapped the paper. "And the government still won't confirm Miguel was murdered."

"Despite the photos I have showing his body. Somebody took those and sent them to his mother. What if the photos weren't to let her know he died, but to make sure she stayed quiet?"

"Or cooperated."

"Exactly." This line of thought felt right. If she could find that thread, she could trace it through the connecting circles of cascading events. As she looked at the events, she felt the certainty someone would do whatever was necessary. Someone like a drug kingpin. "Two people are already dead."

Andrew's mouth pressed into a grim line. "That number could grow. And our accident in Texas and Emilie's accident could have been fatalities."

"We were lucky." She'd known it, but to articulate it left the thought in stark relief, the words painful as they played to a logical conclusion. "If we get in this person's way, we could be next." She looked at Miguel's name and then Gerard's. "Miguel brought something with him, or sent it, and that's why my office and Gerard's were searched. This person didn't find what they wanted, so they searched my home."

"Whoever is searching is a soldier. The real person stayed behind the scenes, unless you're right and it's Daniel Rodriguez. But if it's him, why not stay in the safety of Mexico?"

"I don't know." Hayden felt a chill roll over her as if a monster had just breathed down her neck, leaving a trail of goose bumps and fear behind. "Rodriguez was the last client who saw Gerard. If he's the drug lord, it would make sense that he's directing everything."

"It does." Andrew's phone buzzed. "A reminder to get to Dad's swearing-in." Andrew shook his head. "He's really a US senator."

"Congratulations." Hayden crumpled up the sandwich wrapper and then pitched it in her trash can. "Thanks for lunch."

"No problem. I'll let you know if I get anything out of Jorge."

"Thanks." Hayden stood and walked Andrew to the reception area.

He gazed down at her, and the look in his eyes dragged her a step closer. He ran a finger down the profile of her cheek and she froze, wanting to lean in to the motion. "When this is all over, I'm taking you on a proper date, Hayden McCarthy."

"I . . ." She cleared her throat and started again. "I would like that very much."

"You pick the day, I'll pick the place. We'd better get this figured out, so we can talk about something other than accidents and injuries."

"Yes sir, Mr. Most Eligible Bachelor, sir."

Andrew tweaked her cheek. "Stay safe."

"You too." She watched him through the front window until she couldn't see him, then turned and followed the sound of her ringing phone to her office. "Yes?"

"Hayden McCarthy? This is Art Blanchard with the Department of Justice. You've got quite a legal theory."

"It's a strong one."

"Maybe. My boss has instructed me to find a time for us to get in court as quickly as possible. Let's not waste the court's time arguing. If you'll agree, we can ask the court for a preliminary hearing on a motion to dismiss for lack of jurisdiction in the next couple weeks."

"The court might see things our way. I think most people would agree there's a contract between the government and its detainees. That contract would certainly include the health and safety of the detainees, a duty the government breached."

The man snorted, his northeastern accent becoming stronger as he spoke. "Look. We can make this case drag on and die an extremely slow death, or we can agree to schedule the hearing and get this over with. You don't need discovery on jurisdiction. Either you have it or you don't."

His superior attitude was beginning to annoy Hayden, and she wanted to push back on each of his self-righteous points. Instead, she gritted her teeth and forced a calm into her words she wasn't feeling. "Let's get the judge on the phone and see what she says."

The court calendars were packed. There was no way this case was going anywhere any time soon, even if she loved the idea of fast-tracking it.

"Just a minute." After only a couple minutes of silence, his arrogant voice returned. "Ms. McCarthy, I have the judge's secretary on the phone. We'd like to schedule a preliminary hearing to address a motion to dismiss."

"When would you like to schedule this?" The woman's voice was familiar. Guess that meant the judge hadn't changed core staff in the years since Hayden's clerkship.

"As soon as possible," Blanchard replied. "We'd like the court's read on how this case will proceed."

"Ms. McCarthy?"

"That's fine." It would be nice to get an initial read, but an adverse decision would kill the case before she had the chance to do anything.

"Next Monday at nine. I can schedule it for an hour."

And just like that, Hayden had one week to formulate the argument that would keep the case alive or force the government to settle.

Chapter 49

The aroma of peppermint tea brought Hayden's head up from her desk where she was reviewing her legal arguments for Monday's hearing.

"All work and no play makes Hayden a very grouchy woman." Andrew's rich voice had her smiling in spite of herself. He held the venti cup in front of her. "I thought you might need this, since I haven't seen you in a few days. Emilie mentioned you're working a lot."

"Thank you." Hayden reached for the tall cup. "Monday I panicked I wouldn't have enough to keep me busy, and now I'm on the other side. So much is riding on this hearing I can hardly breathe."

"So skip Saturday's fair. I think between the board and interns we'll keep everything moving. A local church's college group will run the games, which helps." He sank into a chair.

She liked the way he looked there—like he belonged. The thought caught her breath and made her smile. Could this man really fit into her life? Could she fit into his? She studied his relaxed nonchalance, a persona he'd adopted that

410

hid a man with a sharp intelligence and keen wit. A man who cared deeply about those around him and would do anything to help them. A man she would trust with her life.

Something of her thoughts must have flickered across her face, because he straightened a bit and studied her. "What? Do I have cookie crumbs on my chin?"

She shook her head and tucked her thoughts back where she could examine them later. "No. And don't think you can get rid of me so easily. The opportunity to help Saturday has kept me motivated. Still setting up at ten?"

"What isn't finished tomorrow night will be at ten Saturday morning. Shouldn't take long." He took a sip of his coffee and then grinned at her. "You can't stay away."

When he looked at her like that with those come-hither eyes, she couldn't imagine why she'd want to.

"Jorge asked me yesterday if I'd found anything he left at my condo, but he didn't say what he'd left."

"You should ask what he meant."

"I will." Andrew pushed to his feet. "I'm off to check on Maricel and Jorge. I'll ask again when I see him. Maybe he'll tell me more."

"Please let me know if he does. Thanks for the tea." Hayden watched him walk out of her office, then reluctantly forced her attention back to hearing prep. If she didn't find the right hook, the judge could kill the case.

She simply had to invest the hours to find that one past case decision that would work best.

By Saturday morning Hayden was ready to be anywhere but her borrowed office. Only a few clouds hovered in an otherwise blue sky as she finished dressing in denim capris topped with a colorful paisley top. She added an extra T-shirt to her bag in case she got sweaty or spilled something.

Emilie eased into the room as she tossed in a pair of shoes. "Expecting to give shoes away?"

Hayden chuckled as she leaned into Emilie's tentative hug. It was so good to have her friend back. "Just trying to make sure I don't forget anything. You and Andrew have worked hard, and I want to help with anything you need."

An evil twinkle appeared in Emilie's eyes. "Did I mention your shift in the dunking tank?"

"Ha-ha." Hayden rolled her eyes as she picked up her bag. "It's not warm enough for one of those. Are you sure you should come?"

"Leave me behind, and I'll drive there myself."

"Not on your pain meds. The moment you get tired . . ."

It was Emilie's turn to roll her eyes. "I'm a big girl, Hayden. I can get to Andrew's if I need a break. Or maybe I'll let a hunky fireman take pity on me." Her grin returned. "That might be my best idea yet."

"Let's get the doughnuts for the volunteers and head over."

Soon Hayden was pulling into a parking slot near the community center. "We'll have to walk from here."

"I'll be fine."

As she watched Emilie climb from the car, she knew her friend was right. Emilie would be fine. Other than her ginger movement, an unknowing observer wouldn't look at her and think she'd been in a serious car accident a week earlier. But Hayden knew, and until the police caught whoever had hurt her, she wasn't sure she'd take a full breath.

Andrew was easy to spot, the center of a melee of volunteers. His voice carried over the group as he gave final instructions, then turned with a grin toward Hayden and Emilie.

"You arrived just in time. I've got a bag of balloons with your names on them."

Hayden grimaced as visions of passing out from a lack of oxygen filled her mind. "No thanks. You don't need the distraction of me keeling over."

"A few balloons won't do that to you."

Emilie put a hand on Andrew's arm. "This is Hayden. It absolutely will put her flat on her back." She shooed them off to work with the group setting up games.

413

Before the fair opened at noon, Andrew's clients began to arrive. The kids all ran up to him on arrival, as if they were answering the cry of the Pied Piper. Hayden watched him interact with them, giving each an affectionate tug on a ball cap or a side-armed hug. His love for them was evident.

When Maricel and Jorge arrived, Hayden hardly recognized her client. Her face was gaunt, as if she hadn't eaten all week, and her eyes had a haunted look. Hayden hurried to her.

"Maricel, I'm so glad you came. We have a chair where you can watch everything and be off your feet."

"Thank you." Her client's wan smile almost broke Hayden's heart. "I do not want to burden."

"You aren't." Hayden led her to the chair while chatting with Jorge about his week. The young man was reserved, saying only what he needed o be polite. Concern rose in Hayden as she looked back and forth between the two. "Jorge, are you ready for an American hot dog? Andrew is over by the grills and can give you food for you and your mom."

Jorge glanced at his mom as if to ask for her approval. This was not the same outgoing and exuberant boy she had met only weeks earlier. "Okay."

"We'll be right back, Maricel."

Her client waved a manicured hand as if shooing them away. "I will be here."

The crowd was building, with some children playing games or jumping in bounce houses while others munched cotton candy or deep-fried pickles. The area smelled like a county fair food aisle. To her surprise, Jorge ignored it all, his attention focused on the people swirling around them.

"Are you looking for someone, Jorge?"

He startled. "No. I am trying to see it all."

She put a hand on his shoulder and waited until he looked at her. "Jorge, you are safe here. You are in the United States, and we won't let anything happen to you."

"Miguel was too." His quiet words, spoken with a thrust-out chin, cut through her.

"You're right. We failed Miguel." She searched for the right words to convey that what happened to Miguel wouldn't happen to him. "Miguel took a path to get here that put him in danger. You didn't."

"*Yo sé.*" I know.

But as a man with his small son sitting on his shoulders jostled into Hayden, she got the distinct impression Jorge knew something he wouldn't volunteer. She glanced around the growing crowd. This wasn't the place to force conversation. The cacophony of voices and laughter would make it hard for anyone to overhear, but it would also be hard to keep Jorge's attention.

A woman breezed past, her hair pulled into a chic chignon. Lilith? What was Senator Wesley's legislative director doing here? It wasn't the type of high power event she favored.

Then Jorge stiffened. His gaze was locked on a man standing across the cordoned-off street, watching them from a vantage point that placed him in shadow, hiding his features. He turned to the side, and as Hayden squinted to get a better look she saw a tattoo crawling around his neck.

"Let's get back to your mom, Jorge." She turned on her heel and gripped the boy's elbow as she power walked back to his mom. But when they reached Maricel's chair, it was empty.

Chapter 50

SATURDAY, APRIL 22

A surge of satisfaction flooded Andrew as he moved around the fair. While the area only covered a couple blocks, it overflowed with families and smiles. The event was bringing people together. If this built unity and defrayed the sense of isolation many immigrating families had, it would be worthwhile.

He moved through the crowd, stopping to say

hi and a quick word to each person he passed. On occasion he introduced families, and could hear continued conversations behind when he moved to the next.

It was the coming together he'd prayed for.

He passed a bounce house and smiled at the shrill happiness erupting inside.

"Looks like you're a politician after all." Senator Wesley strode up, a big grin on his face. "Your mother wanted to see your shindig for herself. You've done well, son."

Andrew allowed the words to wash over him. "Thank you, sir."

"We can't stay too long, but I'm glad we could stop." His father did a slow one-eighty where he stood. "This is impressive. Did you organize it all?"

"Oh no." Andrew quickly recounted the various sources of help. "I'd say I managed the process, but that was Emilie's doing."

"How is she?"

"Hanging around the game booths. Stubborn gal won't leave the work to us."

"Then give her management. It always works for me."

Andrew's mom walked up to them, looking elegant in a navy pantsuit with a colorful scarf adorned with butterflies looped around her neck. "Nice job, Andrew."

"Thank you. I didn't expect you to come."

"Nonsense." His mother leaned in for an air kiss and smiled. "This is a worthy cause and a great photo op."

Andrew groaned. "Mom, that's not what this is for." Activity over by the tables where his board was serving the foil-wrapped hot dogs and bottles of water snagged Andrew's attention. "Excuse me."

As he neared the tables, Hayden hurried up to him, her face pale and strained. "Have you seen Jorge?"

Hayden fought to keep her voice low. The last thing she wanted was to create a scene and cause a panic. Jorge had been beside her one minute, and the next he was gone.

She frantically scanned the crowd as she waited for Andrew's answer.

His parents had followed him, and he turned to them. "Mom, Dad, I need to help Hayden."

"Sure." Senator Wesley seemed unabashed by her edge of panic. "If you see Lilith, tell her we'll be ready to leave in fifteen minutes."

Andrew nodded, then led Hayden to the side under a shade tree. "What do you mean 'where's Jorge'?"

Hayden didn't seem to hear him. "So that's why Lilith is here."

"You've seen her?"

"Yes, and she sticks out. She was looking for

418

someone . . . probably your parents." She forced her shoulders down from her ears, but couldn't get her body to relax. Something was terribly wrong.

Andrew, with his extra height, looked over the heads of the crowd. "I think I see Jorge." Then he frowned. "Why is he going with Lilith? Come on."

He took off at a quick clip, and Hayden hurried to keep pace.

Hayden stood on her tiptoes and bounced, trying to see where Lilith was taking Jorge. "Looks like they're headed toward the parking lot."

Just then a large Hispanic man stepped in front of her, cutting her off from Andrew, who didn't seem to notice. Hayden side-stepped around the man, intent on keeping Jorge in view, but then froze as she noticed the man's tattoo: a snake that twisted up his neck. This man looked like the one the kid on the bench in the courtyard at the juvenile detention center had described. Could he be the man from the Cherry Blossom Festival and the hospital, too? He was large, intimidating, with the right kind of tattoo. What was he doing here? She picked up her pace trying to think. She pulled her cell from her pocket and prepared to hit the emergency button. What could she tell the dispatcher? A man was following her in a crowd? It would take too long to explain why that mattered.

She hurried away, but when she glanced back the man walked toward her. Steady. Determined. With an edge of brutality. Hayden shivered and kept moving. She looked around for Andrew and saw he'd been stopped by someone new, so that left her to get Jorge.

Hayden dialed Andrew's number, and prayed he'd hear the tone as she continued searching for Jorge. He didn't pick up, so she ended the call.

She ran from the man. "Jorge." Hayden yelled as she ran, and Jorge's head turned as if he wanted to find her. "Wait for me, buddy."

The Hispanic man kept coming, his face frozen in an intent mask. She needed to get help now. She'd have to explain why she knew he was after Jorge and her later. She pushed the emergency button as she searched for the boy.

Hayden ducked into a family group walking the same direction as she scanned the area for Jorge and waited for the dispatcher to connect. The parking lot looked empty as she jogged into it, so she headed to the black SUV that looked similar to the one the congressman and his entourage had used in Texas. As she stepped forward, Lilith stepped out of the shadows between the vehicles. "Time to get in the vehicle, Miss Priss." A gun pointed from her grip.

Hayden frantically looked around as she held her hands up. Could the dispatcher hear anything if they'd finally picked up? "Where's Jorge?"

"In the back. Cooperate and you can join him."

"What do you want with a young immigrant boy?"

"Get in the car."

Lilith cocked the hammer on her gun and waved it toward the vehicle. "Drop your phone."

Hayden hesitated and then Lilith pointed the gun at the vehicle's back door. "I'll shoot." Her words were cold, and Hayden hurried to comply even as she knew dropping the phone ended her hopes of alerting the police.

Lilith waved toward the door. "Climb in. It's your choice: easy way or hard."

"Easy." At least for the moment, while she formulated a plan. Hayden obeyed, relieved to find Jorge on the floorboards. Then she saw a welt rising across his cheek and lips. "What did you do to him?"

"Nothing serious. Just what was necessary to gain his cooperation."

Hayden pulled the boy next to her on the seat and turned her full glare on Lilith, who was already pulling from the parking slot. "You'll pay for taking us."

"Not anything like the price I'll get when I get this kid's father what he wants."

Jorge clamped his lips together at her words, but a whimper escaped.

"His father isn't here."

"Au contraire. I'm meeting him at Theodore

Roosevelt Island at two thirty. I doubt he'll want you, but that's up to him. Maybe I'll get a reward for bringing both of you."

Hayden's mind was racing. How could she escape with Jorge?

She took a deep breath and said a prayer for guidance and peace. "Why are you doing this, Lilith?"

"A very powerful man told me to jump, and my only response could be 'how high.'" The words were matter-of-fact, brooking no argument.

"Why would a man like that be able to tell you what to do? You're an accomplished woman with a good career on Capitol Hill." Yet here she was, wielding a gun and kidnapping.

Lilith took a turn and plummeted down the hill from Fairlington toward Shirlington. In the distance Hayden could see the Pentagon and beyond that the DC landmarks. A city filled with power, yet Hayden was powerless to get help. Jorge shifted against the seat, his eyes wide. Hayden had to make sure he stayed calm. The car was plummeting too fast down the hill for her to try to get out, but that could change.

"You think you're better than me, but you're wrong. One secret, that's all I need."

"What do you mean?"

"Ask Andrew. One secret can make people do anything I want. So when someone asks me to do something and they'll pay me, I listen."

Jorge turned his panicked gaze on her, and Hayden reached out and squeezed his arm. *We'll be okay,* she mouthed, hoping she could honor that promise even as Lilith's words confused her. The woman acted like what she said made more sense than it actually did. Then it hit her. "You were the one threatening Andrew about the cartoons."

"How it stayed unknown is beyond me. Andrew always acts so superior. Not anymore."

Lilith jerked the wheel to swerve around a mini-van turning into an apartment complex, and Hayden slammed into Jorge. "Sorry." She turned her attention back to Lilith. "Nothing will happen because of that. People expect cartoonists to have opinions."

"They don't expect them to be related to a senator."

Jorge took a breath, and then another, followed by another in quick succession.

"Jorge, look at me." She couldn't risk him hyperventilating, not when she might need him to cooperate on an instant's notice. "Take a deep breath. Like this." She demonstrated and did it again until he mimicked her. "Good."

She glanced in the rearview mirror and caught Lilith's mocking stare. "If he doesn't have what his daddy wants, he might as well die here."

"His daddy?"

"Señor Rodriguez pays well when I do what

he asks. Tell the boy I'll let him go if he gives the item to me."

"*No lo tengo.*" His words were low and earnest.

Hayden scrambled back to her college Spanish. "You don't have it?"

He shook his head then glanced toward the front seat. "*No lo tengo.*"

Chapter 51

They had disappeared.

One moment Hayden stood beside him, dodging a large man, and then Andrew had been stopped by one of the college interns. When he turned back around, Hayden and Jorge were gone.

Okay. Take a minute. Assess the situation.

There were a lot of people. The fact that he couldn't immediately see two in the crowd didn't create a problem.

Andrew pulled out his cell phone and dialed Hayden's number before he slowly turned. His height should help him find Hayden in the crowd. Her colorful top would be easy to track, but the small fair area was filled with a kaleido-scope of moving pieces. It was impossible to track one person.

Hayden didn't answer her phone. In itself not worrisome. The crowd was loud with lots of laughter and yelling from excited kids. Then why did it feel like a gray streak of worry had overshadowed the afternoon?

"Son, have you seen Lilith? She's supposed to take us to the next event and isn't responding." His father shielded his eyes and mimicked the circle Andrew had completed earlier. "It's not like her to disappear."

"She's not the only one disappearing." Maybe everything was related, like Hayden thought. The question was how. Andrew took off toward the parking lot. He had to find Jorge and Hayden, because something warned him it was urgent.

———

What was Lilith talking about? What was the thing Jorge didn't have? Obviously Jorge knew exactly what she meant. Otherwise, he couldn't insist he didn't have it.

But what was *it*?

That was the missing piece of the equation. If Jorge didn't have whatever it was, then getting out of this by talking could be impossible. Her thoughts scrambled. Whoever broke into Jorge's apartment was looking for something, and since they hadn't found it, they now wanted Jorge.

"Is this about Miguel Rodriguez's father?"

The confused look Lilith gave her in the rear-view mirror made it clear the question didn't make sense to the woman driving this crazy train.

Lilith slowed and turned into Shirlington Village, then parked near the movie theater.

"Do you know how stressful it is to keep the senator organized and on task day after day? Do you know how little he pays me? When Señor Rodriguez asked for a little help and promised a big payday, I agreed. The senator's planning a presidential campaign, making the Senate race a dress rehearsal. When he asks for something, I get it for him. His passion for immigration reform was the perfect foil for me to learn more about specific immigrants. It worked every time."

Hayden frantically glanced around and tried the handle of the door, but the child safety locks must have been engaged.

"Why are we here?"

"Killing a minute until my help arrives."

A small domestic sedan pulled in, its color muddied by a coat of dirt. The man from the fair stepped from the car and then climbed into the SUV. He turned and looked at her and then Jorge, eyes full of intelligence yet empty. "*Vamos.*"

"Yeah, yeah, big guy." Lilith pulled back onto the road and soon headed up 395 toward the George Washington Parkway. She executed the turns and in less than fifteen minutes pulled into one of DC's hidden treasures. After this Hayden doubted she could ever see the peaceful island the same way.

Lilith parked in a small lot. A second, smaller black SUV drove up and stopped next to them. The door opened, and the man who had been the client Gerard was worried to see stepped out. He fastened his jacket button as he scanned the surroundings. He looked like a man who knew exactly what he was looking for, and as his gaze landed on her, Hayden realized he wasn't surprised to see her with Jorge. Had that been the plan all along?

"Son." The word lacked warmth.

"*Papá*." Jorge's voice sank as if coming from his toes.

Daniel Rodriguez turned to Lilith, and his face looked like it had been set in flint. "Where is the device?"

Lilith bobbed her head in a quick acknowledgment. "I don't think the kid has it."

"Where is it?" He raised a gun and pointed it squarely at Hayden, who refused to flinch even as Jorge tightened into an even smaller ball next to her on the seat.

Hayden held her hands up as confusion raced through her. "Where is what?"

"The information my son stole from me."

"Miguel? But what did he have?"

"Do not play dumb with me, woman. You are his attorney. You have his belongings. You must have found it."

Hayden's mind scrambled. The break-in at Elliott & Johnson had been after Miguel's backpack arrived. When whatever he wanted wasn't found, he must have applied pressure to Gerard.

If Gerard was as confused as she was, had that confusion led to his death?

"I don't have it."

"But you know what I want." His gun never moved, as if his arm had turned to steel. Then it swiveled to Jorge. "I will kill him if you do not give it to me."

Hayden's thoughts scrambled as she positioned herself between Jorge and the gun.

"Don't be a hero, Hayden. Just give him what he wants." Lilith stiffened her posture, but Hayden could see the fear in the woman's eyes. Fear that turned to terror as the man shifted and fired one bullet between her eyes. Lilith folded to the ground without a sound, and Hayden stared in horror as blood seeped into the ground around Lilith.

The sound had been muffled, too silent to draw attention, but she doubted he cared, if he killed a senator's staffer in such a public way.

Chapter 52

Andrew turned to his dad, the ticking of a clock incessant in his ears. "Does Lilith have her government phone?"

"Sure. She always does."

Andrew's mom leaned around him. "You know your father expects his staff to be available at all times. You never know when an emergency will arise."

"Let's get the find-the-phone app working. I have a really bad feeling about this."

"I have a bad feeling about your father missing his next event."

His father patted his mother's arm, then tucked it through his. "We still have plenty of time. Let's find Lilith, then worry about that."

Andrew watched as his father placed a phone call and waited several minutes that felt like they stretched into hours. He said a couple words, then looked up with a frown. "Her phone's at Theodore Roosevelt Island."

"That doesn't make sense." Andrew's mom frowned, a pucker developing between her carefully Botoxed eyebrows. "That's twenty minutes from here."

"Fifteen on a weekend with no big DC events." Andrew tugged his phone and pulled up the information for Detective Harlan. After a quick introduction, he got right to the point. "This could be off base, but my father's staffer has disappeared to Teddy Roosevelt Island and we're concerned. Hayden McCarthy has also disappeared, and I'm wondering if it's related to what happened to Emilie."

"I can send a car out there and have the National Park Police meet them." There was a pause and Andrew could hear scratching. "You were on my list for today. I've got a possible suspect for the attack on your cousin. I'd like you to come by and look at a photo."

"Could you text it to me?"

"I'd rather see your reaction."

Andrew let the pause lengthen, ready to hand the phone to his dad.

"Fine, I'll text it, but make sure you let me know if you recognize him."

A minute later his phone dinged, and Andrew opened the image. It was a rough sketch, but the tattoo twining up the man's neck convinced him this was the man Jorge had described.

The knot in his stomach tightened, and he turned to his dad. "Do you need a ride anywhere?"

"I'll get Dan out here. Where are you going?"

"Roosevelt Island." He looked around the crowd still enjoying the festival. "I'll get a board member to take over." He couldn't leave Hayden and Jorge to deal with whatever trap they had walked into.

Hayden felt the silent scream she couldn't release echoing in her ears.

Lilith's shell lay on the ground, the pool of red spreading beneath her head.

Jorge had dropped to the floorboards of the SUV, his arms clamped over his head, curled tight as a ball. Hayden looked around, but there was no place to run. Rodriguez turned back to her, but

430

she kept the tattooed man in her peripheral vision.

"Now you see I am deadly serious." Rodriguez's voice was arctic and detached. "Where is the device?"

"What is on it?"

"A list of my operatives inside the United States. For a country that prides itself on ethical behavior, it is easy to bribe officials to look the other way. A border patrol agent here. An ICE agent there. Even your lauded FBI. If the data is released it will cripple my empire. I will have it."

Hayden nodded, but she also understood that the moment she gave him the device she didn't have, she and Jorge would die. Maybe she could stall him.

"Do you mean a flash drive?" Maybe she could find one in her purse, though she had a stripped-down purse since she hadn't expected to need a Mary Poppins trick to pull the perfect item from her bag.

She prayed one was in her bag as she waited for his response. The big, silent guy never moved from his spot on the other side of the SUV. There was nowhere to go. No way to grab Jorge and disappear before they were both killed. There was no use yelling as no one else was around.

"Where is it?" His gun was pointed at her, and she couldn't think around the knowledge that he was willing to use it effectively.

She held up her hands. "I didn't know what you

meant." She gestured toward her purse. "I may have the one you mean. It was all I brought from my job at Elliott & Johnson." There was nothing on the flash drive that she could use if she were dead. And if it bought her time to stay alive, then she'd sacrifice the files, glad she'd downloaded the flash drive's contents to the computer in the new office. "Can I dig it out?"

He waved the gun her direction.

"Okay." She opened the bag. How long could she stretch out rummaging through its contents? It would have been easier with her bigger bag. Slowly she pulled out each item and then set it on the seat. "It's got to be in here." *Please, God.* Sweat slipped down the small of her back as her hands trembled. Where was it? "It's . . . it's not here."

He yanked her arm, ramming her into the door. "Do not play with me." Spittle flew onto her face and she tried to keep her back straight when she wanted to cower. "Where is it?" He placed the barrel of the gun on her forehead.

"Let me check the side pocket."

He eased back one foot. "Find. It."

Each word sounded like the pulling back of a hammer on a gun. Her hands trembled so that she fumbled the bag on the seat. "Jorge, I'm so sorry." Then her fingers closed on it. "Here." She yanked it out and then tossed it behind his SUV. She had to get him away from her.

He backhanded her with his gun across the face and she slumped against the vehicle as he nodded to the man on the other side of the SUV. "Get it."

The man recovered the small drive. "Got it." His accent was heavy, but he didn't step nearer to his boss.

A vehicle pulled into the parking lot, but Hayden didn't dare look at it, afraid that even one second of diverted attention would be the one he chose to kill her.

"Is there a problem, folks?"

"No problem, officer." Rodriguez spun and shot him.

In that same instance, the sidekick turned and fired two shots into his boss. Then he placed the gun on the ground, walked two steps away and sat on the ground, his hands on his head.

Another vehicle pulled into the parking lot, tires squealing. Hayden couldn't tear her eyes from the man on the ground, then she looked at the boss's body and kicked his gun away in case he managed to survive the two chest shots.

"Hayden!"

"Andrew?"

He ran toward her, leaving his car door open, engine running. He slowed as another police car pulled into the parking lot. "Detective Harlan, we're going to need some ambulances. There's one officer down and probably two dead or seriously injured." He turned to the officers piling from vehicles with their guns drawn. "I have Detective Harlan with the Alexandria City police on the phone. Would anyone like to verify that?"

An officer scuttled toward him, took the phone, asked a question, listened a moment, and then nodded. At the same time more officers hurried toward the man sitting on the ground.

Hayden sank to the edge of the SUV, all strength seeping from her body.

Chapter 53

SUNDAY, APRIL 23

Andrew stood in front of the town house, another bouquet of flowers in his hands.

Why Lilith had decided his cartooning needed to be public he might never know. But while he'd been so sure the revelation of his second career would affect his father's political future, that was nothing compared to the shocking revelations that were coming one after the other. The revelations about the LD's role in the murder and cover-up were startling in their brazenness.

Apparently the Rodriguez cartel had taken the information that she used drugs recreationally in college and kept it from her background search, earning her lifelong allegiance. Couple that with a woman who believed she wasn't paid what she was worth, and it gave them easy leverage. She'd taken Rodriguez's calls for five years, accepting the slow escalation until the cartel needed access to Miguel, and she'd used her position to lean on others. Director Snowden had been eager to make the murder disappear, and followed her instructions.

Right now, Andrew wanted to forget the last days and the terror he'd felt when he'd realized Hayden was in the line of fire and there was nothing he could do to get to her in time. When all he could do was pray that somehow the cavalry would arrive before she was dead. Even that hope had faltered when he'd seen the first responding officer on the ground beside his vehicle.

Then when it was over he had stayed next to Hayden and Jorge as Hayden answered question after question. Somehow she had held on and kept Jorge safe. Then he'd spent time with Jorge, giving him space to talk or forget.

Now he had another agenda. One he hoped Hayden approved of.

"Are you going to stand there all night staring at the door or come in?" Emilie stood there, the door somehow open, laughing at him.

"Getting ready to knock."

Emilie stepped back and made room for him to enter. "Those for me?" At his frown, she laughed again, the sound he'd loved since they were kids.

"Just teasing." She walked the few steps to the stairs. "Hayden, you've got company."

"I'm not up for any."

"Trust me, you are for this kind."

Andrew could track Hayden's progress across the second floor by the steps she took. "She okay?"

"She'll be fine. She's made of tough stuff."

He'd certainly seen evidence of that last night. But he'd also held her as she wept when the stress was over and Jorge had been delivered to his relieved mom. She'd stopped being strong for everyone and allowed him to be strong for her. In that moment, he knew with every muscle in his being that he loved her and wanted to protect her the rest of his life. Now as she came down the stairs, her eyes lighting when she saw him, he handed the flowers to Emilie and hurried to meet Hayden at the bottom of the stairs.

She paused on the last step, and he closed the space between them, took her face in his hands and scanned it over and over, wanting to assure himself she was okay. The welt that was forming across her cheek incensed him. "Did he hurt you anywhere else?"

"No." The word trembled in the air between them.

He gently rubbed a finger along the bruise, and then leaned in and kissed her.

"I love you, Hayden McCarthy."

"I'll just leave these on the counter." Emilie had the audacity to wink as she walked by. "Sounds like y'all have stuff to discuss."

Hayden stiffened, but then he kissed her again. He'd never willingly let go of her again.

Hayden wanted to cling to Andrew, the solidness and firmness of him. She'd recognized it the moment he'd arrived at Roosevelt Island, and drawn strength from him as she answered so many questions. When Detective Harlan had arrived, things had streamlined a bit. Today she'd wanted to pull the covers over her head and hide, but the revelations and questions kept coming. Now she fully expected a call from the Department of Justice. Frankly, if they didn't call her, she'd call them Monday. Between Lilith's involvement and Daniel Rodriguez's fingerprints dotting his son's death, her mind was spinning. It seemed that while a grieving mother simply wanted to know what happened, the father behind it all wanted to know exactly what the government knew. But Gerard hadn't cooperated, and Rodriguez had taken care of him.

But now, here, in this moment, she wanted to sink into the comfort that Andrew was here and he cared. Wait a minute.

"What did you say?"

"I love you, Hayden McCarthy, beautiful woman with the brain that never quite turns off."

His breath warmed her as he spoke, then he leaned in for another kiss, one that had her melting into his arms.

"Did you come by to tell me that?" She couldn't resist tugging him closer as he began to pull away.

He tipped his forehead until it touched hers. "Hayden, don't ever do something like yesterday again. My heart can't take it."

"I couldn't let her take Jorge." She shuddered at what could have happened. Then a thought hit her. "Did Jorge tell you about the flash drive?"

"Yep. Turns out it was at my condo all along."

"Wait a minute. I'm confused."

He shook his head and led her to the matching chairs. "Seems Miguel was smarter than anyone gave him credit for. He knew he couldn't come to the United States legally because of his father's cartel. There was plausible deniability for Jorge and his mom, but not for Miguel. So he took matters into his own hands and downloaded a list of federal and state law enforcement who were on his dad's payroll. Then he gave the flash drive to Jorge to bring north. When they reunited here, Miguel planned to take that information to the feds to negotiate for his citizenship."

Hayden sank against the chair's back. "Wow. What an elaborate plan."

"There's more. Jorge knew the device was important, but not what was on it. But when the big guy started showing up, he decided he had to do something with the flash drive to get it out of his place. But he wasn't sure who to trust. So one day when I had Zeus with the New Beginnings kids, he slid the device into a slit in Zeus's shock collar. I don't take it off Zeus even though I don't use it, so I didn't notice it."

"So while I was frantically digging through my purse looking for a decoy . . ."

"Zeus had it all along."

"Who has it now?"

"The appropriate agencies." Andrew grabbed the flowers from the counter where Emilie had placed them. "These are for you. Thank you for keeping yourself and Jorge alive."

"Thank you." Hayden buried her face in the bouquet of Gerbera daisies. "When Rodriguez shot Lilith, I thought it was all over."

"But you stalled long enough for help to arrive."

"I'm just glad you thought to track Lilith's work phone."

"One advantage of being a senator's son is that sometimes you can make things happen."

"Just never forget me while you're doing them."

He grabbed her hand and pulled her back into his arms. "Never."

And as she nestled against him, Hayden believed it was possible a woman like her could find a happily-ever-after. If only she could create one for Miguel's family.

Chapter 54

The Court of Federal Claims building loomed in front of Hayden as she stepped from the Metro and walked across Lafayette Square. The towering brick building had been Hayden's home away from home the year of her clerkship, but now its facade felt imposing and intimidating. She slowed her steps to match Maricel's slower pace. The woman's steps had dragged as they left the cool depths of the Metro and stepped into the sunlight. They lagged even more as they climbed the stairs to the building.

"It'll be fine." Hayden tried to assure her client of a truth she wasn't sure even she believed. The call from the Department of Justice had never arrived, so Hayden felt she entered the court for the hearing blind.

"This will not bring Miguel back."

"No, but maybe we can help ensure there aren't more Miguels."

The woman nodded but remained silent through the security scans and the elevator ride. Hayden led her to the third-floor courtroom, where she was surprised to find Emilie waiting in the back row. "What are you doing here?"

"Needed to see the end to this chapter." Her roommate was slowly recovering from the car accident, and hadn't fully returned to work. She'd muttered something about needing time to evaluate her options.

"Here's hoping it's a good ending or beginning."

"I'm voting for a happily-ever-after."

Hayden smiled as she led Maricel to the plaintiff's table, though she wasn't sure a happy ending was possible. Not this time.

Two suited men stood at the defendant's table and slowly approached Hayden. The older of the two stuck out his hand. "Ms. McCarthy, the woman of the hour."

"You are?"

"Johnson Talbott, with the DOJ."

Hayden shook his hand. "Have there been any developments over the weekend?"

"A woman who cuts to the chase. I like that." He gestured to the chairs. "Why don't you have a seat?"

Once they were settled, the younger attorney adjusted his glasses and then leaned forward. "The man who killed Rodriguez . . ."

"And saved Jorge Rodriguez and me."

"Yes, he has been talking. Seems that he's provided a lot of information about what the federal government did and did not know about Miguel Rodriguez's death. We've been given authority to proffer a settlement."

Hayden sat up and looked at Maricel. The woman looked like she wasn't paying any attention to them, but Hayden sensed she understood every word. "It will have to be a good one for my client to be interested. She's lost her son."

"Yes, we know." Talbott nodded, taking control of the discussion. "With this young man's testimony, we'll catch more members of the cartel."

"And with the flash drive of evidence Miguel and Jorge brought here . . ."

"We'll be able to prosecute some corrupt officers." He turned to Maricel. "Ma'am, you can rest assured the FBI and Department of Justice have already launched a joint investigation to ensure this information brings as many as possible to justice."

She nodded, but didn't speak.

"What safeguards will ICE put in place to make sure this doesn't happen in another juvenile detention facility?"

"There's already a full review of security policies in place. That started with Miguel's death. And Director Snowden is under investigation. If he participated in the cover-up as we believe, he will likely get jail time as well."

Hayden nodded. "What about the people in the facility who tried to expose the murder?"

"As long as they weren't involved, they will be immune from prosecution. Frankly, we need the facility open, which means we need them there, working with detainees."

"How will my client be compensated?"

The younger of the two attorneys took over again. "You know it's highly unlikely that this case would have made it past our motion to dismiss. However, the government acknowledges that the young man was murdered on our watch. We are willing to pay a settlement to Mrs. Rodriguez, in exchange for an agreement from her to never talk about this case or settlement with anyone." He named a number and sat back.

"I will need to discuss this with my client."

"Of course. We've got ten minutes until the judge arrives. We'll need an indication of your answer then."

Hayden nodded again, and watched until they'd left the room. Then she turned to Maricel. "Did you understand what they said?"

"Yes. The government will pay me for Miguel's death." Two tears rolled down the woman's cheeks.

Hayden reached out and took her hands. "I know it won't bring Miguel back."

"But the government will admit its fault."

"Yes, as long as you agree to keep the settlement confidential."

Maricel frowned. "What does that mean?"

"That you'll never speak of it. No one will ever know the government paid you."

"But it will be enough to take care of Jorge and me. And to pay you."

"Yes." The thought of having some money to start over with was a huge blessing, but she couldn't take it unless her client agreed, and that was a decision only Maricel could make. "There are many things we must agree on, but I don't think you'd get more at trial. And there's a risk we'd lose."

"This has never been about the money." More tears coursed down Maricel's cheeks.

"I know."

"I want the government to acknowledge to me it is sorry for allowing Miguel's death. If they will do that in a letter with the money, I will agree." She wiped one of her cheeks with the back of her hand. "I also want them to pay your regular hourly rate and fees. That must be separate."

"I can ask."

"Do. And if they agree, you may tell them we have an agreement."

The men were waiting to pounce the moment Hayden stepped out of the room. "She agrees, with a few conditions of her own that you should find reasonable."

Ten minutes later when they reentered the courtroom, they had the outlines of an agreement. The bailiff called, "All rise."

Judge Devers swept into the room and settled behind the bench. "Counsel. Am I to understand that we have a settlement?" She looked to the government's attorneys, then to Hayden.

Hayden rose to her feet. "Your Honor, if I may."

"Proceed."

"The Department of Justice presented my client with the outlines of a settlement agreement fifteen minutes ago. We've since fleshed out a bare bones agreement. However, I would ask this court to supervise the settlement."

"You want to make sure the settlement actually arrives."

"Yes, Your Honor. There are several things that could go wrong. And in the event they do, it is in my client's best interests to have this case pending."

The judge made some notes and then turned to look at the DOJ attorneys. "Gentlemen?"

Talbott eased to his feet. "Your Honor, we are willing to allow the case to pend. However, we would like to schedule a hearing for two weeks out to make sure the plaintiff has cooperated. At that time, we should have a settlement and be in position for the plaintiff to withdraw the case."

Judge Devers looked at Hayden. "Does that work for you, counsel?"

"Yes ma'am."

"All right. We'll schedule a follow-up hearing for two weeks from today. However, I fully expect at that time to receive a report from you that this matter has been settled and is simply awaiting court approval." When she received nods from the attorneys, she picked up her gavel and banged it down. "The order will go out this afternoon. See you in two weeks." She rose and left the room.

The moment she disappeared into the hallway that led to her chambers, the DOJ attorneys stood.

Talbott stopped next to Hayden. "We'll have the proposed settlement agreement to you by tomorrow." He reached out to shake Hayden's hand. "It's been a pleasure." Then he nodded to Maricel. "Ma'am."

After they left, Hayden sat in the chair, stunned at what had transpired. "I'd hoped we'd get to settlement quickly, but Maricel, this is unbelievable."

"Keep them accountable."

"I will."

As Emilie hurried toward them, she squealed. "That was amazing."

"I think it was God," Hayden said. As she looked back over the month, she could see that it was a series of interlocking events that led to the result that Miguel's family would receive justice. As she saw His hand in the events, she knew her doubts about His presence in her life were misplaced. God hadn't changed even if her father had. He was still trustworthy in all ways.

And with that justice, Hayden could sink into

the reality that this time she had been enough, but not on her own. It had happened with the help of friends and wisdom from God.

"I'm setting up a celebration dinner." Emilie typed away on her phone. "Maricel, can you and Jorge join us tonight?"

"Emilie . . ."

"Hayden, we are celebrating. While we can't bring Miguel back, you got the government to admit they're making a series of significant changes. That's something to celebrate."

And as she watched the slow smile dawn on her client's face, Hayden knew Emilie was right, and it felt so good.

Hayden walked out of the courtroom feeling light, yet wondering where that next game-changing case would come from. Somehow she knew it would come. It would just be a matter of time.

———

That evening Il Porto's private room filled with people who had helped Hayden. Somehow Emilie had known whom to invite. Dan and Ciara Turner chatted with Angela Thrasher over the salads the waitress had deposited. Hayden had been surprised to see Seth Jamison, looking a little overwhelmed as he sipped a Coke while Jaime and Caroline chattered at him from either side. Then she'd decided he did belong. Friendships were important, and he'd only followed instructions reluctantly. Maricel and Jorge sat next to Savannah Daniels, and Andrew was right where he should be . . . next to Hayden. By the way he had his arm draped possessively around the back of her chair, she thought the odds were looking good.

Savannah turned to Hayden. "So now that you have this big win, what's next?"

"I don't know."

Savannah nodded toward the other end of the table, where Leigh sat with her young daughter. "Leigh's getting calls from the courts."

"She is, and I'll accept many of those appointments. I need to decide what cases I want. And whether I want the risk of being on my own."

Savannah waved a fork in a gesture that took in the whole table. "I don't think you were alone on this one."

Hayden smiled at how true that statement was. "You're right." She leaned into Andrew's shoulder and relished the small squeeze he gave her. "Has anyone heard from Emilie?"

It wasn't like her friend to plan a party and not show up.

Jaime held up her phone. "She said she was on her way fifteen minutes ago."

"All right. Guess I'm glad she already had the salads and appetizers ordered." Hayden took a bite, and then Andrew leaned toward her.

"You worry too much."

She shook her head. It wasn't worry so much as awareness of her friends and their needs.

In a swirl of leopard trench coat, with a red dress peeking out beneath it, Emilie entered. "Sorry to be late."

She worked her way around the table greeting everyone, but her cheery smile couldn't hide her concern. As she plopped next to Hayden, she held up a hand. "We'll talk later," she muttered. Then she smiled in a dazzling way. "Thanks for coming, everyone. Any excuse to get together is good, but this one is special, because today Hayden moved beyond justice with Miguel Rodriguez's family. We also have a big decision to help Hayden with. She needs a name for her law firm."

"I don't have a law firm." Hayden felt heat travel up her cheeks.

"Oh, but you do." Emilie reached into the bag she'd carried in. "How about this?"

To whoops and hollers, she displayed a sign that read "Daniels, McCarthy & Associates."

Savannah clapped her hands. "Perfection down to the ampersand."

"But we don't have any associates, and you're just renting me space. I'm not a partner."

"You can be if you want." Savannah glanced around the table. "And there might be a few associates out there for us."

As the table went back to eating and celebrating, Hayden rested against Andrew again and realized she was content. Truly content. She'd used her legal skills in a way that mattered. And she had people in her life she loved. She sneaked a peek at Andrew and smiled.

Acknowledgments

All of my books come to life in a garden of friendship. This book was no different. In fact, because I was moving into a new genre, I was helped by a host of friends, writers, and editors. Many thanks to Michelle Lim, Colleen Coble, Rachel Hauck, and my daughter Abigail for helping me brainstorm the initial what-ifs into something that could fill a novel. Jaime Wright and Carol Moncado also provided key encouragement when I was convinced this idea wouldn't come together. Andrea Cox served as a first-reader, and her enthusiasm for this story was contagious! Thank you, friends! Anne Gentry helped me fill in election law details for the great Commonwealth of Virginia. Thank you!

With this book, I've had the joy of joining the HarperCollins Christian Fiction team. Amanda Bostic and I met at our first ACFW conference many moons ago. From that first conference, I knew I wanted to work with her . . . The experience and team has lived up to my dreams. Thank you to Amanda, Daisy, and the full team in Nashville for helping this dream come true. LB Norton was a delight to work with as we worked to make this manuscript sing. Thank you for your kindness as you helped me become a stronger writer and trim this fat and sassy manuscript down to size.

Karen Solem, my agent, has believed in me and my writing for years. Her message has always been to slow down and dig deeper. I listened and this book is the result. Thank you, Karen, for constantly pushing and prodding me.

My husband and kids are my biggest cheerleaders and fans. They endure a mom who's had too little sleep while writing on deadline, a wife who is occasionally distracted by the characters vying for attention in her mind, and help me brainstorm and research all manner of details.

To the Grove Girls and Writer's Alley, you gals make writing so fun. I love being in community with you and celebrating your successes and praying with you as you walk your journeys.

Hayden's story is mine in some ways. We attended the same law school, clerked for the same judge, and have a passion to seek justice in our world. Some days it is hard to find and see justice in a world that seems to tilt perilously out of control. My prayer is that as you read Hayden's story, you will be reminded that God is present as we live our lives for Him. He is in the details and He is in the big picture. He sees you and He cares.

Discussion Questions

1. Hayden brings her past into her present as she sees the world around her through the lens of her experiences. How do your past experiences color your current relationships?

2. Headlines and the Internet bring global issues to our phones, computers, and reality, which can lead to the very real challenge of compassion fatigue. It is exhausting to care about all the issues that exist around the world. How do you combat compassion fatigue?

3. Hayden endeavors to find justice for Miguel and his family by learning what actually happened to him in the detention facility. Do you believe justice was served? Is it even possible in a situation like this?

4. Immigration has been a real issue as I wrote this book. It's a multifaceted and many dimensioned issue with no easy answers. If you were working at a detention center, how would you view the children held there?

5. Andrew has what he considers a deep secret in his past and is committed to keeping it there. When it is revealed, he feels his world is threatened. The reality wasn't the extreme he'd imagined. Have you had similar experiences? What did you learn from them?

6. Hayden has a great group of gal pals who know her at a core level. But finding time to be with them and maintain the relationships is hard. Do you have a similar group in your life? If so, what steps do you take to maintain those relationships? If not, is that something you'd like to have?

7. Family relationships are complex and tend to color our views of the relationships we want in our lives. How did Andrew's color his view of Hayden initially? Was it a realistic lens?

About the Author

Cara Putman graduated high school at sixteen, college at twenty, and completed her law degree at twenty-seven. She has published more than twenty books, teaches college courses, practices law, and is a homeschooling mom. She lives with her husband and children in Indiana.

www.caraputman.com
Facebook: cara.putman
Twitter: @cara_putman

Center Point Large Print
600 Brooks Road / PO Box 1
Thorndike, ME 04986-0001 USA

(207) 568-3717

US & Canada:
1 800 929-9108
www.centerpointlargeprint.com